Souls

Book Five

USA Today Bestselling Author

Ednah Walters

NEIL HELLMAN LIBRARY
COLLEGE OF SAINT ROSE
ALBANY, NY

813.6
W 2353 s

COPYRIGHTS

Reproducing this book without permission
from the author or the publisher is an infringement
of its copyright. This book is a work of fiction. The names
characters, places, and incidents are products of the
author's imagination and are not to be construed as real.
Any resemblance to any actual events or persons, living or
dead, actual events, locale or organizations is entirely
coincidental

Copyright © 2014 Ednah Walters
All rights reserved.
ISBN-10: 0991251725
ISBN-13: 978-0991251728

Edited by Kelly Hashway
Cover Design by Cora Graphics. All Rights Reserved.
Front Matter Design and Formatting By Carolina Silva. All
Rights Reserved. No part of this book may be used or
reproduced in any manner whatsoever without permission,
except in the case of brief quotations embodied in critical articles
and reviews.

First Firetrail Publishing publication: Sep 2014
www.ednahwalters.com

FIRETRAIL PUBLISHING

EDNAH WALTERS

ALSO BY EDNAH WALTERS:

The Runes Series:
Runes (book 1)
Immortals (book 2)
Grimnirs (book 3)
Seeress (book 4)
Souls (book 5)
Witches (book 6)
Demons (Book 7)
Heroes (book 8)
Gods (book 9) June 14th 2016

The Guardian Legacy Series:
Awakened (prequel)
Betrayed (book one)
Hunted (book two)
Forgotten (book three)

WRITING AS E. B. WALTERS:

The Fitzgerald Family series
Slow Burn (book 1)
Mine Until Dawn (book 2)
Kiss Me Crazy (book 3)
Dangerous Love (book 4)
Forever Hers (book 5)
Surrender to Temptation (book 6)

The Infinitus Billionaires series
Impulse (book 1)
Indulge (book 2)
Intrigue (book 3) Coming 2016

SOULS

TABLE OF CONTENTS

DEDICATION

This book is dedicated to my fans.
Thank you for helping me make a living doing what I enjoy.
You guys rock!!!

ACKNOWLEDGMENTS

Many thanks to people who've supported me over the years: To my editor, Kelly Bradley Hashway, you amaze me always. Thanks for streamlining the book and weeding out the verbiage. To Cora of Cora Graphics, your covers are stunning. Thanks for your patience during the process. I know I can be hard to please sometimes. To my beta-readers and dear friends, Jeanette A. Conkling and Cheree Crump, you ladies don't miss a thing. Thanks for finding those pesky typos. To Carolina Silva, You make my life much easier. You listen, scold, and support. THANK YOU, Thank you for taking my finished product and formatting it so perfectly, for being my sounding board on everything, and being the best PA an author could have. Raquel Vega-Grieder, thanks for leading the pack! You are awesome. Special thanks to superfans who inspired me with the names—from Druids and Celtic to angels and demons. Emily Owens, you rock! I don't know where you found them, but I used quite a few. The same goes to Katrina Hill, Kayla M. Crow, Claire Monaghan, Christine Herrera ODell, Darcie Niewald, Kassidy Cockrell, Collie James, Jennifer Bryant Johnson, Laura Dirtrock, Renee Kate Booth, Rachel Souza, Katherine Wilburn, Amber Garcia, Nette Cooper, Michelle Ndiaye, Sarah Haybden Davey, Samantha Alyssa van Petersom, and Terri A. Williams. Thanks for all the names. I plan to use them in the upcoming books. If I left anyone's name, it's not intentional.

To my husband and my wonderful children, thank you for your unwavering love and support. Love you, guys.

TRADEMARK LIST:

Google
Mercedes
Elantra
Sentra
Harley
Twizzlers
Supernatural
Grey's Anatomy
Warner Bros
CWTV
ABC.COM
Youtube
Apple Inc.
Cheetos
M&M
Skittles
Coca Cola Company
Dean and Sam Winchester
The Great Gatsby
MTKO
Bon Jovi
NPR
The Matrix
Marvel
The Fifa World Cup
Raggedy Ann
DC Comics

GLOSSARY:

Aesir: A tribe of Norse gods
Asgard: Home of the Aesir gods
Odin: The father and ruler of all gods and men.
He is an Aesir god. Half of the dead
soldiers/warriors/athletes
go to live in his hall Valhalla.
Vanir: Another tribe of Norse gods
Vanaheim: Home of the Vanir gods
Freya: The poetry-loving goddess of love and fertility.
She is a Vanir goddess. The other half of the dead
warriors/soldiers/athletes go to her hall in Falkvang
Frigg: Odin's wife, the patron of marriage and
motherhood
Norns: deities who control destinies of men and gods
Völva: A powerful seeress
Völur: A group of seeresses
Immortals: Humans who stop aging and self-heal
because of the magical runes etched on their skin
Valkyries: Immortals who collect fallen
warriors/soldiers/fighters/athletes
and take them to Valhalla and Falkvang
Bifrost: The rainbow bridge that connects Asgard to
Earth
Ragnarok: The end of the world war between the gods
and the evil giants
Artavus: Magical knife or dagger used to etch runes
Artavo: Plural of artavus
Stillo: A type of artavus
Grimnirs: Reapers for Hel
Hel: The Goddess Hel in charge of the dead

Hel: Home of Goddess Hel, dead criminals, those dead from illness and old age
Nastraad/Corpse Strand: The island in Hel for criminals
Garm: The hound that guards the gates of Hel

CHAPTER 1. THE VISITORS

Cool air drifted across the room and fanned my face. Anticipation coursed through my core, and my heart trembled. I no longer freaked out whenever a chill swept the air. It used to be a warning that a soul was nearby. A reason to panic, close my eyes, and hope they'd go away. I'd even been admitted to a psyche ward because I'd thought the souls were ghosts out to get me. Ghosts. Boy, was I ever naïve. But that was then.

Now I welcomed the cool breeze. A flutter coiled in my stomach, and I was sure a stupid grin curled my lips. I was about to get a visit from the man I was desperately and completely in love with.

Echo.

Hel's number one soul reaper.

My boyfriend.

I still pinched myself whenever I was with him to confirm I wasn't dreaming. After pining for a guy I'd known since junior high—like, forever—it was nice to have someone who was mine. And Echo was mine in every way possible. Body, heart, and soul. He adored me and didn't care who knew it.

Whenever he walked into a room, a cold draft followed him like the tail of a comet. Not that he was dead and cold. No, Echo was fire and passion. Unpredictable yet steadfast. The cold clung to his clothes from Hel, the coldest place in all the realms, the place where he escorted souls of the dead. As his chosen mate, I always welcomed him home with open arms and warmed him. Willingly and without complaint.

"Come to bed," I whispered without opening my eyes.

A second passed, then two. He didn't lift the covers or touch my face as he often did in the dark as though drawn to my warmth.

My eyes flew open. It was dark. An inky blackness that said something wasn't right. There were no glowing runes criss-crossing a face so breathtaking I could stare at it for hours. Or wolfish golden eyes so mesmerizing words couldn't begin to describe them.

Okay, so it was not Echo turning my bedroom into an ice cave. No need to panic. It was probably a soul needing my help.

I peered into the darkness, heart pounding despite my silent pep talk, but I couldn't see anything. The souls often looked real, like humans. Except for the iciness. I touched the lamp, and light flooded my room.

"You can come out now," I whispered, trying not to scare it. New souls were like newborn babies. Helpless. Confused. Scared. Incapable of expression, except through gestures. Loud noises from my room could wake up my parents, too. Their bedroom was down the hall. Usually, I kept things quiet in my room or used my computer to cover up any sounds. My parents couldn't know about my supernatural activities or they'd freak out again.

"I'm waiting. I promise I won't bite."

Actually, I could, but that naughtiness was reserved for Echo. I giggled at my thoughts and immediately regretted it. This was no time for fantasies. I turned my head and looked around the room, expecting the soul to show himself or herself.

Nothing happened.

Times like this, I wondered if I was doing too much. Helping souls find closure before Echo escorted them to Hel's Hall wasn't exactly easy. They had to possess me first, which was like being dunked in ice-cold slime, breathing and swallowing some of it. Totally disgusting and bloodcurdling. So no, I didn't just wonder. I questioned my sanity. I needed sleep and rest, and helping some soul in the middle of the night was not my idea of either.

I glanced at the clock on my bedside chest. It was eleven-twenty and Friday night to boot, too early for bed unless you were me. I should be making out with my superhot boyfriend, but Echo was out reaping. Instead, I had lessons first thing tomorrow morning with a Valkyrie and a date with senior citizens in the afternoon.

"Listen, I don't know how you got in here, but I promise I'm not mad," I said. "So be nice and show yourself."

No one walked through the walls. Souls might look solid, but they were made of pure energy. Or rather they sucked the energy around them to create an image, which explained the coldness whenever they appeared.

Anger slowly replaced my patience. Time for tough love.

"Okay, I'm going to say this once. Helping you guys is a choice and I usually don't mind, except when I deal with psychos, sociopaths, and pervs. So if you want to play games, get lost or deal with Echo."

I turned off the lights and pulled the covers to my chin, but I didn't dare close my eyes. When I was in the psyche ward, I'd wake up to find souls staring expectantly at me. Totally freaked me out.

Of course, I hadn't known at the time that I was a beacon, glowing from afar, begging them to find me. The glow came from runes scribbled on my body by an Immortal psycho-bitch, but that was another story.

My eyes wide, I studied my room for unusual movements, wishing Echo was here. Souls never bothered me when he was around. The runes he'd etched around the house stopped them from coming to our farm, which made me worry. What kind of soul could walk right past soul-repellant protective runes? Even as the question crossed my mind, the cold chill swept through my room again.

Bastard! I reached out and turned on the bedside lamp.

"Get out, jerk!" Something moved in the corner of the room, and I whipped around, my heart pounding. There was no one there, yet I felt a powerful presence.

Panic surged. Refusing to drown in it, I inched sideways and reached under the bed for a weapon. Before Echo, I'd disperse souls with an iron fire rod, something I'd seen Sam and Dean Winchester do in the hit TV series Supernatural. It actually worked. Now, I let souls take over my body, listened to their thoughts, and helped them find closure. Yeah, I know. I was certifiably insane. But what was a girl to do when her boyfriend was part of the supernatural world? I wasn't a stand-by-the-sideline kind of girl.

Gripping the knotted end of the rod with two hands, I slipped from the bed, walked slowly to the bathroom like some ninja warrioress holding a katana, and I ventured inside the closet. Both were off my bedroom and favorite hiding places before Echo came into my life. I poked between dresses, skirts, and folded sweaters.

There was no one there. I opened the door and peered down the hallway. Empty. Refusing to lose it, I locked my bedroom door so my parents wouldn't walk in on me hurling curses like a sailor while attacking something they couldn't see. Another trip to the psyche ward was not in my immediate plans.

To bring the noise level to zero, I headed straight to my wall mirror and let the image of Echo's home fill my head. At the same time, I engaged the portal runes on my body until I glowed brighter than a strobe light. I loved that I could do this now. Loved the rush, too. The lessons I'd been taking from Valkyrie Lavania were paying off big time. I had healing runes, portal runes, and even strength and speed runes. Then there were the other runes. Nameless. Black. Yet Souls saw them glow. Totally weird.

The mirror responded and dissolved into a portal.

Echo's place was in total darkness, but that didn't bother me. I knew the room, and I always felt safe there. When I was a child, I'd crawl into my parents' bed when I had nightmares. Now, I ran to Echo. Even when he wasn't here, his essence was strong enough to scare souls away.

Closing the portal, I crawled under his covers, the poker clenched in my hand. His musky scent clung to the sheets and pillows. I inhaled and let it sooth my jumpy nerves. Sleep, unfortunately, eluded me, and my eyes stayed locked on the portal.

I was still new to the supernatural world. I called it the Runic World because etching runes on skin with magical blades gave people superhuman abilities and immortality. I became an Immortal after the same psycho who'd etched soul-magnet runes on me severed my spine and Valkyrie Lavania healed me with powerful healing runes.

But my tango with the supernatural started with my BFF, Raine Cooper, and the Valkyrie she loved. Their story was complicated, but their love and devotion to each other was beautiful. Now, I knew that Norse pantheon wasn't a myth. The gods and goddesses, giants, dwarves, and elves were real. Valkyries and Grimnirs roamed the world collecting souls. Valkyries took fighters and athletic people to Valhalla and Falkvang to train for Ragnarok—the war between the gods and the evil giants, the mother of all battles that would end our world. Grimnirs like Echo collected souls of criminals and those who died of old age and illnesses, and took them to Hel, the realm of the dead. Norns, deities in charge of destiny, moved around weaving destinies and screwing with people's lives. And Immortals roamed the world, fighting with humans for worthy causes and supporting Valkyries.

Then there were special Immortals like Raine and me. Raine was a powerful Seeress, a living, breathing Norn in the making. She hated it, but sometimes you can't escape your destiny. She would signal the start of Ragnarok. Then there was me. No one knew exactly what I was, only that lost souls could find me in their darkest hour.

My eyelids grew heavy. The next second, I sat up, my eyes widening as the portal opened. Echo. I'd left the lights on in my bedroom for him, knowing if he didn't find me, he'd look for me here.

My heart pounded. My room and the door leading to the hallway were now visible, and I could see a shadow in my room.

"Over here," I called out.

Instead of Echo, something dark drifted through the portal. Shaped like a person, the core was so dark it appeared to suck in light. Images of black holes flashed in my head. Thanks to my association with Echo, I'd developed a morbid fascination with the cosmos. Anything to visualize the realm my boyfriend disappeared to several times a day. He hated talking about Hel's Hall.

The edges of this moving black hole were blurry. I couldn't see his features or clothes, but it was definitely coming toward me.

Panicking, I jumped off the bed, tripped on the covers, and pitched forward onto the floor, the rod slipping from my hand. I cursed, grabbed the poker, and scrambled to my feet. The dark thing, person, or whatever floated around the large bedroom and completely ignored me.

My heart pounding so hard I thought it was going to burst, I gripped the poker and widened my stance like a baseball batter.

I had a mean swing, courtesy of my father. Being homeschooled on a farm meant my P.E. classes involved climbing trees or playing whatever games my parents enjoyed. Dad was a serious baseball fan. In fact, he had a favorite team in almost all sports. That was one thing he and Raine's father had in common.

A quick glance at the portal and a weird thought flashed in my head. I could make it open into Raine's room. Her house was full of supernatural people. They could protect me.

Nah, Raine had just finished dealing with a horde of angry Immortals led by her boyfriend's father and needed a break from supernatural mayhem. This was my problem. I had to deal with it.

"Who are you, and what do you want?" I asked, trying to sound brave but failing miserably. My voice came out breathless and squeaky.

It stopped moving. I stepped back when it changed directions and moved closer. A cold front followed him, making me wish I wasn't wearing silk cami shorts and top. Where was a thick winter robe when you needed one?

I shivered and waved the poker menacingly. "Stop or taste the iron."

The Shadow vibrated, and a sound rumbled from its core. *Was that a chuckle?*

"You think that was funny?" I asked, continuing to brandish the poker like it was Excalibur. "Wait until this baby slices you into a gazillion energy pockets. It takes months, years even, to come back together," I lied.

The Shadow stopped and drifted back toward the portal.

"That's right," I said, becoming cocky. "Run. I don't know what kind of soul you are or care about what you want. Leave. Now." It stopped moving and did that vibrating thing again. It sounded whiny and pitiful this time. "What? You don't want to leave?"

It pointed at the portal, and for the first time, I saw fingers. The edges were undefined like the rest of it. At least it wasn't threatening to possess me.

"What about my room?"

He floated toward my room and gestured that I follow him.

I stopped near the portal, scared of following him. "Are you asking me to come back in there?"

The Shadow nodded. At least I thought it did. The dark mass that was his head moved up and down.

"Why?"

More vibration and humming.

"Come on. You can do better than that."

The Shadow gestured frantically, pointing at something inside my room.

"Okay, I get it. Sheesh. I'm coming, but don't try anything funny. I'm still holding this baby." I shook the rod.

This time, I recognized the chuckle. I left the portal open in case Echo returned. Just because the Shadow hadn't tried to possess me didn't mean it was friendly. Inside my room, I realized he'd been pointing at my laptop.

"What do you want me to do with that?"

He kept pointing.

"What kind of soul are you? Why don't you have features?" It made a growling noise, which I assumed meant he was getting frustrated. "Yeah, you and me both, pal. I should be asleep, you know, yet here I am playing Gestures with you. Okay, I get it. You want me to open it. Move aside and give me space."

The Shadow floated away and stayed by the wall. Keeping my gaze on it from the corner of my eye and pointing my poker its way just in case, I opened my laptop, pressed the power button, and backed away.

"What are you going to do?"

The Shadow slithered inside my laptop through a USB port, like a genie getting sucked into a lamp. I moved closer warily. A weird squiggle appeared on the blue screen, then another and another... They looked like the ones on Echo's rings and chains.

The writing stopped, and the Shadow slithered out through the same USB port and moved back to the wall.

"I don't read Druidic," I said. "But Echo does." I grabbed my cell phone and took a picture of the screen. "I'll show this to him and he can figure out what you want, okay?"

A groan came from the mass, and I jumped back. "Hey, enough with that. I'm willing to help you, so don't get pissed at me. Is this message for Echo?"

He nodded, then appeared to change his mind and gave an emphatic shake of his head.

"Can't make up your mind, can you?"

He folded his arms and tapped his foot. Bet he was glaring at me. I smothered a giggle. When his hands landed on his hips, I knew he was definitely pissed by my attitude.

"Okay, no Echo. But how am I going to read Druidic?"

A shrug.

"Yeah, big help you are. How about I go to sleep now and you come back tomorrow, and together, we'll figure out what you want? In English," I added.

It seemed to shrink, shoulders drooping.

"Listen, Master of Different Body Languages and Sounds. I don't know whether you can see my world, but it's nighttime. It's almost midnight, and I have to get up early tomorrow for lessons. I promise to help you, so go home or wherever you came from, and come find me tomorrow," I said.

I was surprised when it nodded and drifted through the wall. Laughing with relief, I crawled back into my bed. This time, I wasn't worried. I even put away my energy-dispersing poker. Still, sleep eluded me.

I debated whether to turn on my computer and research shadowy figures in Norse pantheon and the meaning of the Druidic letters the thing had written, but I didn't want to touch my lap top yet. Who knew what it had left behind? Dark energy or gooey ectoplasm stuff, another thing I'd picked up from the Winchester boys.

I did the next best thing. I picked up my smart phone and got busy.

***

I was still awake when Echo swaggered through the portal wearing nothing but his leather pants and runes on his face and chest. My heart melted. He was such a beautiful man. Eyes like a wolf's. Chiseled cheekbones. Sensual, totally kissable lips. Skin so smooth… except for the scars criss-crossing his back. But I didn't mind them. They were his badge of honor.

"Not asleep, *Cora mia*?" he whispered, stroking my face. His fingers were freezing, but I didn't care. I loved it when he called me *his* Cora.

I covered his hand with mine and engaged the few runes I had. We generated heat faster with them, and he needed to be warmed. "I was waiting for you. We need to talk."

"Later." With smooth and graceful movements he shed his pants. He didn't believe in sleeping with a stitch on. Not that I was complaining.

He slid beside me, and a shudder rocked his body when our skin met. The pulsing sensations we generated whenever we touched were nothing new, but the effect on him never failed to amaze me. Sometimes he sucked in a breath and closed his eyes with a bemused expression on his face. Other times he looked like he was in pain.

I melted in his arms and welcomed him with a kiss, savoring the taste of him. The combination of his hot tongue and cool lips was stimulating. But he was in one of his moods, super intense and hell-bent on driving me insane, which meant he'd had a rough night or something was wrong. It couldn't be because of me since I hadn't been possessed by some selfish soul. Whenever that happened, the Hulk in him emerged.

He lifted my leg around his waist and rolled so I was on top. His hands journeyed down my back, leaving heated skin behind, while his mouth trailed along my neck. My breathing grew shallow. Then it became raspy.

His masculine mouth seared my flesh, his tongue sending flames through my body. He knew me. Knew what pleased me and what drove me crazy. Our lips met again and again, my hands stroking parts of his body I could reach, his muscles spasming underneath my palms.

His skin was no longer icy. He was burning hot. He rolled me over again and pinned me to the bed with his leg. Glowing eyes met mine questioningly.

Was it time to turn off the heat and cuddle, or move to the next level? Funny, he always let me decide, even when he needed me like tonight. He might not have said it, but I felt it in his taut muscles and the fire in his eyes. Something bad had happened tonight.

The Shadow could wait. I wound my arms around his neck and nodded.

Echo sat up then stood with me in one fluid motion. We had an unspoken rule never to let things go too far under my roof. It was wrong and disrespectful to my parents.

The portal responded to his runes, and he ate the short distance between my cute little bedroom and his mammoth one. He dropped me right in the middle of the bed and smirked when I glared at him. But it was hard to stay mad at a man who looked like an avenging angel, runes flashing and eyes smoldering. He was all my fantasies rolled into one delicious, hot body.

"We need to set a date and get a place of our own, *Cora mia*," Echo said, deft fingers tugging at the strings holding my cami top together. "I'm tired of sneaking around and using portals. I want to come home to you. I want to make love to you while you wear nothing but my ring. I want to watch the sun's rays kiss your skin first thing in the morning and make love to you in front of a fireplace in the evening."

Holy crap, he was in a bad way. Whatever had happened must have scared the crap out of him for him to be discussing marriage. I was eighteen and of age, and he'd already given me a Druidic promise ring, which I loved to death, but I had a year of high school left. I also planned to attend college, so marriage hadn't really crossed my mind. I'd never thought beyond the present—loving him and making him happy.

I shed my top, and he sucked in a breath, conversation forgotten. The awe in his eyes would never get old.

"There are no words to describe you, *Cora mia*." He ran a finger from my chin to my chest and stayed there. Heat followed his finger, and my senses hummed. "The things you do to me."

I teased back, stroking him. He sucked in a breath as though I'd scalded him. We reached for each other, his touch electrifying, his sensuous mouth scorching. He nipped my shoulder, sending heat down my spine.

"Think about it," he whispered along my neck. It sounded like a plea. Something had definitely happened tonight to explain his intensity. "No more sneaking around," he added. "No more worrying about your parents finding out you're gone. No more vacationing with others."

That again? Raine had invited me for a three-day weekend getaway in Florida after the fiasco with the Immortals, and Echo had joined us. He hadn't liked sharing me with the others. He said he was selfish when it came to me. I liked to think he was just possessive, a flaw that would lessen with time when he realized my love for him was constant and unwavering.

His runes glowed and dimmed, throwing shadows on his chiseled cheekbones and sensuous lips. I stroked his chin, spreading my fingers through his brown locks as we kissed. He ran a hand down my side and around my waist, and then pulled me closer, our bodies fitting perfectly together. We were perfect together, flaws and all.

"I'll talk to my parents," I whispered. "Now, can we do less talking and more fun stuff?"

He did just that, his tongue sliding between my lips to caress mine. He moved lower, making me squirm and moan as my senses responded.

For the next hour, he was the center of my universe. His intoxicating scent became the air I breathed. His sighs the music in my ears. His touch the reason for my existence. With our runes blazing, every touch and nip was magnified and mind-numbing.

He pushed me to the limit, until my world exploded, only to start over again. Yet he was there with me every step of the way. He made it easy for me to let go without fear of looking or feeling silly.

Just when I thought we were done, he took it to another level, his touch infinitely gentle as he took his time, pushing me until I begged. And that said a lot because I wasn't the begging type. He was unstoppable, driven as though to reclaim his soul, which he swore was in my keeping, or his sanity, which he claimed he'd lost centuries ago.

In the final stretch, tremors shot through him and a shimmer of tears added an eerie glow to his eyes. He didn't try to hide them from me. He never did. We clung to each other, both of us shaking.

It was awhile later before I lifted my head and peered at his face. His eyes were closed, canopies of lashes on his high cheekbones. He was at peace now. His demons allayed.

Funny how unique and different he was. While other guys I knew would punch holes through a wall when frustrated, Echo needed his anchor—me. Sometimes he just wrapped himself around me as though creating a barrier between me and the world. This usually followed a session with a difficult soul where he thought he'd lost me.

Other times, he needed a deeper connection to rejuvenate his soul, as he called it, and went primal. Some might find that barbaric or unrefined, but I loved his rawness. It was who he was. Temperamental. Passionate. Deeply scarred, but he was mine. My one and only true love.

"What happened?" I asked, gently stroking his back.

CHAPTER 2. DARK SOULS

Echo didn't bother to ask me how I knew. I read him well.

"I reaped some evil souls tonight. The meanest bastards I've ever dealt with."

Something shifted in my stomach. "What kind of souls?"

"Dark souls, but I triumphed like always," he bragged. Childish, but cute. "And delivered their worthless cores to Hel's torture chambers." He sighed. "I hate dealing with dark souls. Hunting them down might have been a challenge centuries ago, but now they're just a pain in my ass."

Yikes. Could the Shadow I'd dealt with be a dark soul? If so, Echo was so not going to like what I was about to tell him. "Are they that bad?"

"Every reaper's nightmare, especially when they're in a group, which is rare. I met four of them tonight. Why in Hel's Mist would dark souls join forces? Rounding them up wasn't the problem. Escorting them to Corpse Strand was a freaking nightmare."

"But I thought there were guards to do that," I whispered, mortified. Corpse Strand was the island where the damned souls were confined and tortured for eternity. The river to its shores was filled with venom.

"Not tonight," Echo said. "The goddess was in a foul mood and insisted I do the delivery. It didn't matter that there was a gale and the venomous water kept sloshing against the boat and spraying us. Their screams mixed with the hellhound's howls might amuse her, but it's bloodcurdling." He shuddered.

My chest hurt, visualizing what he'd gone through. I hugged him tighter.

"Tell me more," I whispered.

He shook his head. "No. The less you know, the less you'll worry."

Impossible man. Didn't he realize that not knowing only scared me more? He rarely talked about Hel. In fact, he often changed the subject whenever I asked about how he got there and what happened to the souls, which only made me worry more. What I'd read online about Hel's Hall was sketchy and often inaccurate. I knew about Goddess Hel and her massive home for the dead, the river around it, the hellhound guarding its entrance, and the giant escorting the damned souls. The rest was shrouded in mystery.

Online sources claimed that anyone who went there could never leave, yet Grimnirs moved back and forth freely, and Eirik, my former crush, had gone there and come back. But then again, Eirik was Goddess Hel's son, a god in his own right. The goddess, on the other hand, sounded like a nutcase. Online literature was right about that.

What if she decided to keep Echo, her favorite reaper, indefinitely? I wouldn't know how to get to him. He'd alienated his fellow reapers eons ago. In fact, I'd never met a Grimnir that wasn't an a-hole.

"What is it, doll-face?" Echo asked.

"Nothing," I whispered, burrowing my face in his chest. It was almost two in the morning, and I didn't feel like talking anymore, especially about dark souls after what he'd gone through tonight.

He chuckled. "I can tell when you're worried. Did I scare you with talk about Corpse Strand?"

"No," I lied. "I know about the hellhound guarding Hel's realm, the river, and the guard on the boat. It's kind of like Greek mythology. The Greeks call the hound Cerberus while you call it...?"

"Garm. It doesn't have three heads. It has four red eyes, and it howls nonstop. So, was it talk about marriage?"

Getting information from him was like getting a root canal. One day...

"No. That's kind of exciting." I tucked my face under his chin, wrapped my arm around his chest, and closed my eyes, but my thoughts kept going back to the Shadow—uh, dark soul.

"But if you'd rather wait, I'll understand," Echo said, stroking my neck, his breath fanning the hair on my temple. "Then I'll do my best to change your mind. It might take several weeks or months, but I can be relentless and very creative."

I giggled. "Then I'll wait."

He grinned. I could tell by the way his lips moved against my forehead. "You want me to change your mind?"

"Why not? Relentless and creative sounds like something I might enjoy," I said.

He leaned back and peered at me. Runes lit up his face, and a cocky smile curved his lips. "If you knew the naughty things I have planned for you, you'd not be teasing me," he warned. "We can start now."

Where the heck did he get his energy? "Can I finish high school first? Maybe get a degree in psychology, too?" I added.

He rolled his eyes and sighed. "Okay, but on one condition. I help you study."

I scoffed at the idea. "That's a scary thought."

"Your professors and the students won't even know I'm there. I'd be the invisible ghost smacking the guys staring at you."

I loved the idea, but a girl had to show some pride. "No haunting my college, Echo. Besides, you hate school."

He smirked. "Ah, but you are the reason for my existence now, doll-face, which means putting your needs first."

"And whining about it," I said and traced a line across his chest, still undecided whether to tell him about tonight's encounter with the dark soul or not. His muscles leaped and responded to my touch.

"I don't whine. I complain forcefully." The smile left his face. "You're beginning to scare me. What's bothering you?"

I could never keep a secret from him when he spoke like he could single-handedly rip apart anyone or anything that hurt me and enjoy every second of it.

"I had a strange visitor tonight," I said.

Echo stiffened. "Define strange?"

"A soul. I think."

He sat up. "What do you mean *you think*?"

"It wasn't like the other souls. This one was black. You know, dark. I think he was a dark soul."

He peered at me with narrowed eyes. "What? Did he attack you? Try to possess you? Did you feel lightheaded and weak?"

"No." I shook my head. "It was like the other souls. Shy. Maybe colder."

"Tell me exactly what happened."

"At first I thought it was you when I felt the cold draft, but it wasn't. Stay here. I'll show you something."

I dragged the blanket, wrapped it around me, and hurried to my room for my cell phone, but he was right behind me. He picked up his pants from where he'd dropped them and yanked them on.

"He entered my laptop and wrote this." I touched the pictures icon and showed him the writings.

Echo went pale.

"What is it? What does it mean?"

"Devyn. The conniving, traitorous bastard," Echo spat. He gripped my arms, and his eyes bored into mine. "Don't ever communicate with him or another dark soul, Cora. They suck energy from everything in their path."

I frowned. "He was kind of nice."

"Nice?" he snapped, his voice rising.

I glanced toward my bedroom door. "Keep your voice down."

"You have no idea what you are dealing with."

"Then tell me."

"Mortals possessed by dark souls go crazy." He sighed, took my arm, and led me back to his room. "Sweetheart, I know you love helping lost souls, but this is one breed you don't want to mess with."

"Condescending much." I yanked my arm from his grip. "I told you before, I decide who to help, not you."

His eyebrows flattened, eyes narrowing. "You never decide. You help everyone. Murderers. Psychopaths. Perverts. How many times have I told you to ignore some psycho and you went ahead and helped him anyway, only to have me step in and haul him out of you? You think *their* effect on you is bad? Dark souls are worse."

Wow, he really was worried about this or he wouldn't remind me of those bad moments. Whenever a possession went on for too long, they'd drain my energy and I'd fall asleep right afterwards.

I wrapped my arms around Echo's waist and hugged him tight. "You are my hero. I don't know what I'd do without you."

"Nice try, but kissing up doesn't suit you." He carefully peeled me from his body and put some distance between us. The green in his eyes was overtaking the gold. Not a good thing. "You cannot help dark souls, Cora. They're nothing but trouble. They lull you into a false sense of security then stab you in the back. Fuckin' slime balls." He stepped back and went into hyper-speed, and within seconds, he had his shirt back on. He yanked his socks on.

"Where are you going?"

"To find the bastard and haul his icy ass to Hel. I should have done it centuries ago."

"No, you can't." He reached for a boot. "Echo, stop."

He didn't. He laced up, his movements jerky.

"Please," I begged.

The unease in my voice had him slowing down. I gripped his hands and stopped him from starting on the second boot. I stroked his hand and finally got his full attention.

"Talk to me. Who is Devyn? Why do you call him a traitor?"

Echo scowled. "I don't want to talk, Cora. I gotta go. The Valkyries will want to know about this."

"It's two in the morning. Torin and the others are asleep."

"I don't care. Devyn's sudden appearance has everything to do with Torin's father and the deluded Immortals we fought last week. They sent him to you."

"Who?"

His eyes glowed. "Recently departed Immortals. This was a deliberate attempt to get your attention. That was their first mistake."

I wanted to remind him that lost souls came to me all the time, but I doubted he'd listen. Devyn hadn't seemed hateful.

"You think they learned about me from what I did for Torin's mother?"

"Maybe. I've escorted every soul you've helped straight to Hel's Hall. They don't talk to anyone."

I'd let Torin's mother possess me, so she could talk to him. That had been weird. It had taken me twenty-four hours to fully recover. "You think Torin told someone I helped his mother?"

"No. St. James is never careless or stupid." He scowled, and then a weird expression crossed his face. I couldn't explain it, but I'd hate to meet him in a dark alley when he looked like that. "Devyn crossed the line coming here," he said softly.

He just switched from red-hot anger to cold and vengeful. Somehow, I had to stop him before he went all *Lokhi* on some poor Grimnirs and created more vengeful dark souls. "Talk to me first, Echo."

His expression said he was conflicted. Echo tended to charge in first and ask questions later. But when it came to me and my safety, all bets were off.

"What can you possibly do right now?" I pushed. "It's dark out there."

"Grimnirs work twenty-four-seven. Someone sent Devyn, and I plan to find the shithead responsible, too."

That temper of his would be his destruction. If he left pissed, he'd only kill someone and alienate more of his fellow Grimnirs, or worse, get himself killed. The thought sent a fresh dose of panic through me.

"Can't it wait until morning?"

"No." He tried to wiggle his hands free from my grip, but I didn't let up.

Anger replaced logic. "Listen here, Mr. Tough-Grimnir. I need you here now, so you're going to sit down and talk to me, or I swear…"

He stopped and cocked his eyebrows, a slow smile lifting the corners of his lips. "Or what?"

"Or I will hurt you in ways you couldn't possibly imagine. The more I worry about you, the more I'll make you suffer when you come back. Have you stopped to think that the people you claim are responsible might just be innocent? What if their target is really you? You storm in and they have a reason to hurt you."

"Grimnirs, not people." His grin broadened. "You're worried about me?"

"Really? You're going to ask me that?" I stood, nudged his arms aside, and sat on his lap. Sighing, I stroked his hair and kissed his temple. "Of course I worry about you, you impossible reaper. You are the slayer of my dragons."

He scoffed at the idea. "You do a damn good job on your own while I'm gone. I'm just your eye-candy."

"Now that we are in total agreement, start talking so we can go back to bed. I like to fall asleep in your arms and wake to find you watching me. Totally creepy, but I forgive you. Know why? Because I'm crazy about you." He grinned, and I knew I had him. He wasn't going anywhere. "What are dark souls, and why are they dark? And who is Devyn?"

Echo's eyes narrowed as he studied me. Crap, he was going to blow me off. He could be so unpredictable sometimes. Then he grinned, wrapped his arms around me, and flopped back on the bed, taking me with him. For a moment, he stared at the ceiling. I waited. I'd won, so no pushing. His expression said he was rearranging his thoughts. It seemed like forever before he spoke.

"Dark souls are from evil Immortals, Valkyries, and Grimnirs," he said. "You know, the ones the Norns decide are bad for humanity."

"Evil Norns?"

"Good Norns. Not that it makes a difference. Good or evil, they're all manipulative hags. They don't do the actual killing. No, good Norns are a lot more subtle than that. While their evil sisters direct accidents, plagues, and so called natural disasters, they alter destinies by creating situations that result in the deaths of the Immortals."

"Like the battle with Torin's father and his followers?"
Echo nodded.

So Raine was right about the Norns deliberately letting Torin's father kill Seeresses. They could have taken him out anytime, yet they'd chosen to look the other way. Raine never said how many Immortals died that night. Only that Torin's father still lived.

"When Immortals, Valkyries, and Grimnirs go bad, they know what's waiting for them on Hel's special island."

I shifted so I could look at his face. "Go bad? How?"

"Valkyries and Grimnirs get tired of reaping and go underground. Immortals can choose not to help Mortals and set themselves up as their ruler. It's happened too many times to count. Every civilization has had their share of Immortal dictators and warlords. They die and run like the cowards they are, roaming the world and growing bitter and vengeful. They suck everything that's good wherever they go. Air. Energy. The essence of anything they touch. When they enter a room, most Mortals can't cope. They faint. The dark souls reduce their vessels to blubbering idiots after a possession. Being possessed by a dark soul is worse than anything you've ever experienced."

Okay. That was brutal. I couldn't imagine anything worse than the psychopaths I'd helped. I waited for Echo to continue. He shifted uneasily, his arms tightening around me. Somehow, I knew his next words were going to be personal.

Echo might be tough and cocky on the outside, but inside, he carried a lot of pain. That I could never completely know every detail of his past or take away the pain he'd endured made my heart ache.

"Dev and I were close once," he said, his voice low, "until the day he betrayed me and I killed him."

Killed? Yikes. From his grim voice, he'd hated doing it, which said a lot. Echo had never regretted his past decisions or actions. They were justified and I agreed with him one hundred percent, but something about Devyn was different. He'd even shortened Devyn's name, a giant red flag.

"Dev had some nerve showing his face. I don't care what he wants. I don't want him near you."

He cared. The pain in his voice whenever he said "Dev" screamed it. His jaw was taut with tension, his sensuous lips pinched tight, but what surprised me were his eyes. They'd darkened, and for once, the green had outrun the gold. I'd never seen them like that before.

"What did Dev do?" I asked softly, stroking his hair.

Echo's eyebrows flattened. "Dev?"

"You called him Dev, so I assumed it was his nickname or something."

He frowned. I bet he hadn't realized that he'd shortened Devyn's name. He was also not ready to talk. He could be so easy to read sometimes.

I slipped my hand down his back and stroked his scars, remembering his stories about how he'd gotten them and what he'd done to the Roman soldiers responsible. I'd also seen him yank out hearts of Grimnirs who'd threatened me. Echo could be vengeful and not lose sleep over it. I had no idea what he'd do to Devyn's soul, but I was sure it wasn't going to be pretty.

"How do you make a dark soul wish they'd never betrayed someone you love?"

Echo chuckled. "Why? Are you planning on avenging me?"

"No one hurts or betrays mine without dealing with me. And you," I tilted my head, so I could look into his eyes, "are mine. Mine to love and protect. Your enemies are my enemies. Your friends—"

"I don't have or need any, except you. You are enough for me. My alpha and omega." He wrapped his hand around my nape and pressed our foreheads together. "When you say things like that, it reminds me how lucky I am to have your love. How honored I am to have the right to touch and love you." He kissed me. It was gentle, a mere whisper, yet more powerful than all the passionate kisses we'd shared earlier. "I must have done something right to be rewarded by you."

I rested my cheek on his chest and listen to his heart. The heart he insisted was damaged, yet it was capable of giving so much. Despite his claim that I was his only friend, he'd fought alongside Torin, Raine, and Andris when they'd needed him, and they'd previously fought with him when Grimnirs had come after me. That was friendship. Being there for each other. Watching each other's back. Now there was Dev, his former buddy. I wondered how he fit in the whole friendship spectrum.

Dev's soul had approached me for a reason, and I planned to find out why. I hadn't felt the air get sucked out of the room like Echo had described, just the chill that usually accompanied souls. If he needed help, that was my department, but if he wanted to hurt Echo, he'd have to go through me first. Literally.

"Tell me about him," I said.

"Who?"

I chuckled and propped my chin so I could see his face again. "You know who. How did Dev betray you?"

CHAPTER 3. DEV

The silence stretched until I was convinced Echo wasn't going to answer. His eyebrows were a straight line, his eyes narrowed as though his thoughts bugged him.

"Dev, Rhys, and I grew up together," he said slowly.

"Who's Rhys?"

"A Grimnir. We attended lessons, practiced archery and magic together. We had a crush on the same girl. She kissed me first." His lips curved into a nostalgic smile that made me hate her. "But she gave Rhys a ribbon when we jousted a few days later."

Bitch. "How old were you?"

"Seven."

I laughed. I'd been imagining the worst.

Echo bumped me with his shoulder. "It wasn't funny. She was the first girl to break our hearts, yet we were still fighting over her ten years later."

Echo was in love with some Druidess at seventeen? I hated her again.

"When the Valkyries came, they chose Rhys and me, not Dev. He ended up with the girl."

Could all this be about a girl? If it was, I was going to smack him into next century. He wasn't supposed to get pissed over anyone except me. "Go on."

"When I decided to help my people and make them Immortal, the first person I changed was Dev."

"And the girl?" I asked, keeping my voice light when I wanted to ask if she was a Grimnir, a Valkyrie, or an Immortal.

"Teléia was killed by the Romans."

Okay, no more bitchy thoughts about the Druidess. Knowing how the Roman soldiers had hunted down Echo's people, the poor woman's death couldn't have been pretty.

"Dev helped find our people and escort them to safety, but then he decided to become an informant for the

Romans." Echo sounded like he'd swallowed a rotten egg. "We lost so many of our people because of that bastard."

I winced at the fury burning in his eyes. Thousands of years later and he was still pissed. "How did you find out?"

"Some of our people saw him visit a soldier at a nearby prison. I didn't believe them. I just assumed they were jealous. Dev was a handsome bastard and a ferocious fighter, and women adored him. He became even cockier as an Immortal. Made so many daring rescues our people considered him a hero, the piece of shit. But when our people were ambushed by the same garrison several times, I knew we had a traitor."

Knowing Echo, he'd beat the crap out of Dev first and ask questions later. "Did he tell you why he did it?"

"He didn't give me a chance to ask. He bragged about how he'd do it again and there was nothing I could do to stop him because he was Immortal. He forgot Immortals had hearts and heads like everyone else. He lost both."

Okay, so he'd stopped him in the only way he knew how. Yanking his heart out and snapping his head. Probably not in that order. "It sounds like he wanted you to kill him."

Echo shrugged. "He was a disgrace to the Druids and got what he deserved. No one betrays our kind. No one. You do, you die. End of story."

Why, then, did I feel like there was more to the story? "Do dark souls talk?"

"No. They possess, take, and use. Then they move on. I'm surprised he didn't take you over."

Yeah, there was that and the chuckles, and the fact that he'd left when I'd told him to. Hardly the behavior of someone evil.

"Maybe he liked me."

"He would, the conniving ingrate. Dead or alive, no woman is safe from him." He sounded jealous, which was silly.

I kissed his chin. "I know that new souls can't talk, but they understand gestures, which is weird. If they can communicate by simple gestures like Neanderthals, dark souls should be up on the soul evolution chain. Maybe use sounds or words."

"Never met or heard of one that could." He pinched the bridge of his nose and frowned. "If you'd seen Torin's mother's soul before Raine brought her to the mansion, you'd have seen she'd faded to nothing. Souls that don't feed on energies fade. They become invisible and stay that way unless they're taught by a dark soul how to possess Mortals. The ones I met tonight graduated at the top of the class. They're busy living vicariously through their victims. They don't feel the need to learn to be self-reliant."

Maybe Dev was learning to be self-reliant. "Dev made sounds. You know, to show he was amused or frustrated."

Echo growled.

"Yeah, just like that," I teased and received a glare. "Do dark souls start out dark?"

"No." He shook his head, his expression serious. "They start out looking like any regular soul, but when they begin to fade, they start possessing things around them, stealing their essence. Instead of going back to their human form, they slowly become shapeless forms of stolen energies. Dark energy." He cupped my cheek and dropped a light kiss on my forehead. "Aren't you sleepy?"

"A little." I sighed. "Are we done talking about Dev?"

"No, we're done with dark energies. Stay away from Dev."

No point arguing with him. "We should go to bed."

His grip tightened. "What are you doing tomorrow?"

"I have runic lessons with Lavania in the morning and my volunteer thing at nursing home in the afternoon."

He frowned. "Want to have dinner with me tomorrow night?"

"Really?"

He chuckled. "Am I such a sucky boyfriend?"

"No, you're the best." When he was around, which wasn't often. What was the point of having eye-candy without showing him off? We hadn't had a date except once with Torin and Raine. We needed more time alone. Prom was next Friday, and I wanted him by my side.

"I'll make it up to you," he vowed. "I can pick you up from the hospital or home."

"Home. Are you going to court me?"

"Court you? Isn't that doing things backwards? I've already tasted every inch—"

I covered his mouth, my face burning. "I'm talking about romance. Flowers and candlelight dinners. Staring into my eyes while the waitresses watch me with envy."

He pulled down my hand, eyes twinkling. "Our entire life will be an endless courtship, doll-face. I plan to give you the world, but if you want me to start now, I will."

"Well, not now."

"Good, because I really need to go." I didn't try to stop him this time. Knowing him, he wouldn't sleep if he was worried about someone hurting me.

Hugging a pillow, I watched him get dressed, his movements graceful. It never failed to amaze me how beautiful he was and how unaware of it he acted. He was humble about his looks because of a few stupid scars. He didn't get that they made him hotter in my eyes.

Echo glanced at me and smirked. "I know what you're doing."

"What?"

"Mentally taking off everything I put on," he said, the golden glow in his eyes intensifying.

I was. It was uncanny how well he read me. "So?"

He smirked. "So, I love being your boy toy." He closed the space between us. This time, the kiss was deeper, branding. "I'll fortify the farm with protective runes before I leave. I don't know how Dev made it past my runes, but then again, he was always so clever, the devious prick."

He stepped back, adjusted the hood of his duster, and pulled a scythe from the inner pocket. It was small, the size of a dagger, but the instant he engaged his runes, the blade and handle grew until it arched and towered above him. He sliced the air and a portal appeared. He studied me one last time as though engraving the image of me in his head. Then he was gone. The portal closed behind him.

I padded across the room, through the portal to my room, and crawled under the blanket. I was falling asleep before I realized I'd left my pjs at his place.

**

I'd barely fallen asleep when Mom knocked on my door. I grabbed the nearest thing to cover my nude body and it turned out to be Echo's expensive sheet. I rolled it up and hid it under my pillows, then dragged my comforter around me.

"Hey, sleepyhead," she said when I unlocked the door and squinted at her through a narrow opening.

"What time is it?"

"Almost ten." She pushed the door and I had no choice but to let her in. "I'm just here for your laundry. Aren't you working at Moonbeam Terrace this morning?"

"This afternoon," I mumbled and followed her. "I have lessons with Raine this morning."

"Lessons?"

Did I just say that out loud? Argh, I sucked at lying. Hated it. "She's helping me with math. You know how good she is at math, and I suck at it."

"Suck is such an ugly word, Cora," Mom scolded, throwing me a censuring look. "You and Raine are good at different things. That's all." She grabbed the wash hamper from the bathroom, then went behind the door and got used towels from the pegs.

I rearranged the pillows so she wouldn't notice the grey sheet. "She's kind of a math genius." I was laying it on thick. Like I said, I sucked at lying.

Mom dismissed my words with a wave, propped the hamper on her hip, and studied me. "And you are an amazing writer. I stopped by your vlog and noticed you have quite a following now. Over half a million. I love reading your pieces."

I made a face. "Really?"

"Of course. They're insightful and thought-provoking."

"Oh. Thanks." That was the sweetest thing she'd ever said about my vlogging. She'd hated my first vlog because it was mainly about boys and why they were hot. Gah, was I ever shallow. Now I focused on helping grieving families.

"You do know there's a rule against parents stalking their kids on social networks," I teased.

Mom laughed. "You have no idea how often I want to tell your subscribers I'm your mother. I'm so proud of you."

"No." I sat up. "Don't joke about that. Not the proud part, but the part where you tell my followers that my mother watches my videos and comments on them. You'll ruin everything."

Her eyebrows shot up. "How?"

"You just will."

She sighed. "At least tell me it's okay if I tell my friends about it."

"As long as they don't mention they know me personally."

Mom frowned. "I don't understand. I thought you wanted to share your thoughts with people."

"I do, but once my teen subscribers realize some of the comments are from you and your friends, they'll stop following me."

Mom's bewildered expression said she still didn't get it. She was so generations back. Cassette players and records. Hunchback TVs and huge mobile phones.

"Mom, most teens don't want to hang around the same social websites as their parents. It's nothing personal. They want to express themselves without worrying about censures and Mommy scowls, so please, no comments about me being your daughter."

She no longer frowned. "That explains the colorful language I noticed some of them use. Very distasteful." She gripped the basket and started for the door. "Oh, do you want a pie to take to your friends at the nursing home?"

"Definitely. Mrs. J and the gang would never forgive me if I didn't." Lauren, Mrs. J's daughter, dumped her at Moonbeam Terrace Assisted Living Home and had never returned to visit. Worse, she was only an hour away in Portland. I'd never do that to my parents, no matter how annoying they got in their old age. Just before Mom closed the door, I remembered my conversation with Echo. "Mom?"

She poked her head back into my room, her eyebrows up.

"How old were you when you got married?" The brows went way, way up. One would think I just told her I was about to have an alien baby.

She re-entered my room. "Thirty-two. Why?"

"Nothing. I was just wondering." My cell phone dinged, but I ignored it. It was probably a text from Lavania about my lessons. For a woman born millennia before the industrial revolution, she had mastered the use of a cell phone fast.

Mom closed the door, her eyes wary. "Honey, you're not pregnant, are you?"

"Mom! No-oo, of course not." Echo and I used protection. "I'm going to college, and babies are not part of my plan."

The relief on Mom's face was comical. "Good. I know you're eighteen now, but…"

My phone dinged again. Lavania to the rescue. I grabbed it and checked the LCD screen. It wasn't her. "I need to answer this, Mom. It's from Raine." And yes, I was eighteen, an adult, which meant she couldn't legally stop me from marrying Echo, but I wanted them on board. The secrets I kept from them were enough. Too much. I needed their blessing on this.

She nodded, then left my room frowning. I sighed with relief. Telling them I wanted to get married wasn't going to be easy. It didn't matter that Echo had come to our house several times or that Mom thought he was a good influence on me and Dad loved discussing history with him. I was their only child, and they wanted the best for me. Echo had to prove to them he was. I glanced at my phone.

"Lessons canceled. Lavania left this morning. Going to the site. Want to come?" Raine had texted.

Frowning, I stood. *The site* was the section of forest where Echo and the Valkyries had fought Torin's father and his Immortal followers. I'd barely known that Norse gods were real and already I was filled with curiosity about Asgard. I couldn't imagine protecting humanity on behalf of the gods for centuries and never being thanked or asked to visit the gods' realm. So in a way, I understood the Immortals' warped reasoning. They might have gone about it the wrong way, but there should be a way to thank Immortals for their devotion to the gods and the Mortals. A yearly pilgrimage to Asgard or something.

"Going with Torin?" I texted back.

"No. Just me. He and the others are rpn. Mom too."

Rpn meant reaping. "I thought the place was off limits."

"It's been a week. I'm worried. Don't trust the Norns."

I frowned. Raine had the kindest heart and she felt things deeper than most girls I knew, but sometimes I feared for her. She was so reckless. She and Eirik had taken me under their wing in middle school when they'd found me crying after P.E. I'd just started at their school after being homeschooled and had been miserable and totally ill-equipped to cope at a public school. She inspired loyalty in people, and there was nothing I wouldn't do for her. It wasn't because she was a powerful Seeress or the announcer of Ragnarok. Even Eirik, my first crush and grandson of Odin, had proven over and over again that he'd sacrifice the wrath of the gods for her. Raine was loyal and courageous and annoyingly stubborn. Chances were she was going to the battleground against everyone's will.

"Wait for me," I texted back.

She sent back a smiley emoji with heart eyes. I showered, changed, returned Echo's sheet, retrieved my pjs, and then headed downstairs. Mom stuck her head out of the laundry room when I stepped off the stairs.

"Leaving already?" she asked.

"Unless you need help with something," I said.

She dismissed my words with a wave. "I'm fine. Don't forget to eat something."

"Hi, Daddy." Dad was at his writing alcove off the living room. I kissed his cheek and got a pat on my hand. He was editing a hard copy of his latest story. Interestingly, it was about aliens invading a small rural town. He was inspired after Echo chased some Grimnirs across a neighbor's vineyard and left behind flattened vines. Speculations had followed. Alien invasion. Local hooligans. Kids playing a prank. Rival farmer. Of course, Dad didn't know Echo had been involved.

"How's the story?" I asked.

He grinned. "Coming along nicely. They're from a planet several light years from earth and didn't just crash land on earth. They're after something." He tapped the papers. "That's what I need to figure out."

If only he knew. "I'm going to the nursing home after I'm done at Raine's, Mom," I called out, heading to the kitchen.

"Then don't forget Mrs. J's pie," Mom said, leaving the laundry room. "I also packaged two for Raine's family."

She'd already put them in boxes. Mom supplied local stores with pies made from our farm's organic produce. Of all her pies, the apple ones were the most popular. I hated anything with apple in it. We made our own apple cider for pity's sake.

I grabbed the boxes, a pear, my keys, and cell phone, and headed outside. Sometimes I wished my parents knew everything about Echo. I'd use the portal instead of driving to and from Raine's house. I sent her a text that I was on my way.

Flipping through radio frequencies, I found ninety-four-point-five, the station that played pop music, and sang along. I was close to Raine's home when a sudden blast of cold air filled my car and Echo appeared in the back seat.

Now that I knew about portals and how to access them, I realized he took too many chances teleporting into a moving car.

"You really shouldn't do that when I'm driving," I warned him, hiking up the warm air. "You could get hurt."

"You are my beacon, doll-face, not the car." He dropped a kiss on my nape, his lips cold. "Where are you going?"

"Raine's. Do you want me to pull over?" Every time he came from Hel's Hall, he needed to be warmed. Sometimes I wondered how he'd survived without me.

"I can wait. Why are you visiting the young Norn?"

He had a nasty habit of not using people's names. It was so impersonal. Must be his way of keeping distance between him and others. He still called Torin and Andris Valkyries.

"Her name is Raine, Echo," I corrected him, my eyes volleying between his reflection in the rearview mirror and the road ahead. "And she's my best friend."

He rolled his eyes, rubbing my nape and stealing my heat. "Why Raine's?"

"She's decided to visit the forest."

Echo groaned. "And she chose the moment St. James is gone."

"I don't think she planned it. She's worried the Norns didn't fix the trees."

"Probably her witch side itching to come out. That's how it is with elemental witches. Once they connect with their source of power, it pulls them." He forked his fingers through my hair and then pressed the strands to his face and inhaled. He had a heightened sense of smell because he could tell every scent on my body. Shampoo. Conditioner. Body wash. Cream. "Hmm, nice," he murmured.

I reached up and stroked his hair as I entered Raine's cul-de-sac. His hair was cold, the tips still frozen. I brought the car to a stop outside Raine's house. Every time I came to her house, I was reminded that her father was terminally ill. She was dealing with so much crap, yet she'd managed to stay upbeat. I didn't know how she did it.

"Come here," I said to Echo after moving the pies out of the way.

Echo moved to the front seat, pulled me onto his lap, and buried his face in the crook of my neck, his arms looping around my waist. He was still freezing.

I rubbed his back and let him warm his hands under my shirt. I'd bet old Mrs. Rutledge, Raine's neighbor from across the cul-de-sac, was cataloguing our every movement for her gossipy friends.

"So, it's just you and the Norn, uh, Raine going to the forest?"

"Yes. Do you want to come?"

"I *am* coming," he said in a voice that dared me to contradict him.

"Are you worried about Dev finding me?"

"Nope. He'll be taken care of." His voice changed when he said it.

"How?"

"Grimnir Bounty Hunters." The look that crossed his face said he hadn't meant to say that. "I'm coming with you guys in case the Norns appear. I don't want them focusing their attention on you. So far they've left you alone, and I prefer it that way."

I'd never met a Norn—Maliina didn't count—but from what Raine said, I shouldn't wish it. They were manipulative. Powerful. Raine was more powerful though. I had a feeling they feared her.

"You're warm enough. Come on. Time to go inside."

"Not yet." His caresses became intimate. I closed my eyes, helpless to control my responses or resist him. Not that I wanted to.

"When we have kids, I'll have to remind them that this and this," he point at various parts of my body, "are mine. They can borrow them, but I claimed them first."

Echo and children? The idea was mind-boggling.

He stopped messing with me, peered at Raine's house, and frowned. "I'll wait here."

I gathered my wits and shook my head. "No. You're coming inside with me."

"Her parents are home and the Immortal nurse—"

I kissed him, shutting him up. He always acted like people would reject him just because his Grimnir Druid brothers and sisters did. What he did—insisting they help turn their people Immortal and earning eternal servitude to goddess Hel—he'd done for the love of his people. He wore a loopy grin when I stopped kissing him.

"Do it again," he teased.

"I'd love to, but Raine's waiting. Come on. *You* have pies to carry."

I scooted to my seat and opened my door. He was still in his seat when I walked around the car. He didn't put up a fight when I opened the door, took his hand, and pulled him out of the car. I opened the back door and pointed at the boxes of apple pie.

He grabbed the boxes and grinned. "I love it when you're bossy. Major turn-on."

"Keep walking, Mr. One-track-mind."

Raine answered the door when we rang the bell. She didn't mask her surprise when she saw Echo. We hugged. Then she gave Echo a "Hey."

He smirked as though he enjoyed seeing her flustered. "Don't I get a hug?"

She rolled her eyes. "You're carrying pies."

I plucked them from his arm and nudged him toward her. They'd better work on being friends without all this awkwardness. She hugged him. This time, he was the one who couldn't mask his surprise.

Raine swept her hair away from her face, her cheeks pink. It amazed me how she could look incredibly sexy without much effort. Her brown hair had a tousled look as though she'd just gotten out of bed. I'd have to work on my hair for hours to pull off that look.

"Come inside," she said, stepping back.

I glanced around. Her mother was back on Valkyrie duty and was gone, but her father's nurse was always around. "Where's Femi?"

"With Dad." She glanced at Echo. "Are you coming with us?"

"Cora insisted," he said.

I laughed and elbowed him. He was such a liar. Good thing Raine appeared relieved by his response. "I'll put these in the fridge. Two are for your family, and one is for Mrs. J at the nursing home."

"Someone ought to track down her daughter and force her to visit. It's been what? Three months since you started there and she's never visited?"

"The nurses said it's been over six months. Maybe there's something *you* can do?" I glanced at Echo.

He smirked. "Sure, hun. I can scare Mrs. J's daughter to death, then take her soul to Corpse Strand for being ungrateful."

Raine laughed. "Good one."

I shook my head. "Don't encourage him."

Raine led the way to the mirror portal in the living room. It responded to her and opened to a forest. Cool. She could do surface to air portals now. My attempts were pitiful. I could only do portal-to-portal. We followed her.

"You sure this is the place?" Echo asked, kicking a rock.

Raine shook her head. "I've spent the last couple of hours searching different sections of the forest, but I couldn't see—" She moaned and clutched her stomach.

"What is it?" I asked, rushing to her side. She doubled over again, her face scrunched in pain. "Raine—"

"The trees are dying," she whispered, her breathing shallow.

I glanced around and frowned. What was she talking about? There was not a single dead tree anywhere. It was spring and sunlight bathed the green foliage, casting shadows all around us. I turned to ask her what she meant, but she was already staggering down a path, her runes engaged.

I glanced at Echo. "Do you know what she means?"

"She has elemental magic. Her powers are connected to the earth. If the trees are dying, she'd feel it. Come on." He took my hand as we followed Raine, who was way ahead.

It was nice to have him around, but I didn't want to be selfish. "Shouldn't you be reaping?"

"I'm playing hooky."

"By chasing my friend through an Oregon forest? Is there something you're not telling me?"

"Like what?"

"I don't know. You went to search for Dev and didn't find him. Earlier you mentioned Grimnir Bounty Hunters."

He scooped me up. I smothered a scream and wrapped my arms around his neck. He continued walking without breaking stride, his runes flashing.

"Put me down," I protested.

"When we catch up with her. She's engaged her runes, and you still don't have enough speed ones. What exactly has that Valkyrie been teaching you?"

"Lavania is…" My voice trailed off when we entered a clearing and I saw Raine looking around with her hand covering her mouth. All around us were fallen trees, their leaves withering. Most had been uprooted, a few cracked near the base or split as though someone had hacked them with a giant axe.

I wiggled out of Echo's arms and went to Raine's side. The look in her eyes was hard to watch. Could she really feel the dying trees?

"I hate them, Cora," she whispered, fighting tears. "They could have fixed this, but they chose not to."

I gripped her arm and tried not to cringe at the devastation. It was huge, yet I hadn't heard anything on the news about it. But then again, the area was far off the trail. Most people probably had missed it.

"Can you contact them to fix this?" I asked.

Raine shook her head. "I'm fixing it. It's my fault."

"How do you figure that?"

"It just is." She freed her arms and reached down to touch a tree trunk. Then she knelt near an exposed root and stroked it, her touch gentle. A sob escaped her.

"Raine?" I squatted beside her, but her eyes had changed color. They were glowing golden. I'd only seen them like that once when she'd gotten a vision. Was she getting one now?

Then she did something strange. She pushed her fingers into the soil. Maybe the strength runes on her face and arms made the act seem so effortless. Or maybe she was really one with the earth. Her eyes closed, tears rolling down her cheeks and dropping on the ground.

"Come," Echo whispered, taking my arm.

"She needs me." I tried to jerk my arm away. His grip tightened.

"Not now. She needs to heal them, and you'll only get hurt."

"Get hurt? What are you talking about?"

"You'll see. Come on." He led me to edge of the nearest standing trees, leaned against the trunk, and wrapped his arms around my waist.

Raine was muttering something under her breath, tears still streaming down her face. I wasn't sure what to think. I stopped being skeptical about supernatural abilities the day I learned soul reapers were real. But what could she do?

"What is she chanting?" I whispered.

"Probably apologizing for having ignored them. Her kind doesn't usually chant."

My eyes widened as the fallen trees around Raine slowly moved as though being pushed and pulled by invisible fingers. Their roots sank into the earth. One tree near Raine would have hit her, but it shifted ever so slightly and missed her on its way up. Once upright, the leaves appeared to lose their limpness as though water filled them. More trees rose, the effect spreading from where Raine knelt as though she was the epicenter, and the magic flowed from her fingers.

"Wow," I whispered, awed.

"A Norn's work is never done."

"You call her that again and you won't like the consequences," a familiar voice said calmly from behind us, and we turned to find Torin leaning against a tree, arms crossed, his eyes on Raine. He didn't seem angry, just resigned.

"Still in denial, Valkyrie?" Echo teased him.

Something flashed in Torin's eyes. "Screw you, Grimnir."

Echo chuckled. "Sorry, don't swing that way."

"Thanks." I wasn't sure whether he was still talking to Echo or me, until his eyes connected with mine. "Somehow I knew she wouldn't resist coming out to check on the forest. I'm happy she didn't come alone."

Raine said he could sense when she needed him. He'd probably felt her pain and come running. Echo claimed he knew when I needed him, too, and had proven it over and over again when difficult souls hijacked my body. Each time he smirked smugly. I hugged his arm as we watched Raine practice her elemental magic.

The forest healed. No tree, bush, or vine was left on the ground. Even the ones with broken branches and cracked trunks were whole again. Leaves no longer looked starved for food and water, buds bloomed and even petals on the ground were back on the branches. It was hard to believe my best friend could do something this, I don't know, amazing. Made what I did with the souls and their loved ones seem so unimpressive.

Raine stood and looked toward us, her eyes still glowing. She laughed and turned around with her arms stretched. Hugged a tree. Smelled a flower. Kissed a leaf. A few seconds ago, she'd been performing something only a goddess would do. Now she was acting like a child at a candy store.

"You have a tree hugger for a best female friend," Echo murmured.

Literally. I grinned.

Torin chuckled and walked past us. I didn't hear the exchange between him and Raine, but her laughter rang out. I could swear the trees swayed and whistled back.

"She's a healer," I said.

"A Norn," Echo corrected. "Unless she finds a way to use her powers to her advantage and beat the older Norns at their game, she will leave him to join them."

"Don't say that. He'd be devastated."

Echo shrugged. "He'll get over it."

I glanced at him. "You, my love, have no idea what you are talking about. If you knew how he feels about…"

Jealousy flared in his eyes. "And how do you know about his feelings for her?"

"He told me," I teased him, but it only made him scowl harder. "When his mother used my body to communicate with him, you impossible reaper."

The jealousy melted away. He grinned. "Want to have lunch with me?"

"Will you tell me about GBHs?"

He frowned. "What's that?"

"Grimnir Bounty Hunters."

"Nope." No explanation or excuses.

I studied his expression and saw through his tough exterior. He was mad at himself for not finding Dev. Echo was a hands-on kind of guy who hated depending on others. That he had to use these bounty hunters to find Dev must have been eating at him, and I wasn't going to rub it in. He'd tell me everything when he was ready.

I glanced at my watch. I had several hours to kill before heading to the nursing home. "Okay, let's do lunch, my reaper. Can we ask them to join us?"

"No."

"Echo—"

"I want you to myself, and I know the perfect place to go. First, we have to stop by a sandwich store."

"We're having a picnic? I know the perfect spot not far from here."

He looked around and shuddered. "No. I hate outdoors. Especially forests."

I didn't ask him to explain because I already knew. His people had hidden in the forest while being hunted down by Roman soldiers. I wanted to replace every terrible memory he had. It might take centuries, maybe even millennia, but I wasn't giving up.

I reached up, wound my arms around his neck, and kissed him, pouring all my love, hopes, and dreams into the kiss. He welcomed me as usual, not holding back, taking charge of my senses and owning them. Every shaky breath, every nip, every groan claimed me.

Laughter penetrated the sensual haze surrounding me, and I ripped my mouth from Echo's.

"You guys need the forest to yourselves?" Raine teased.

"Yes," I said, my arms tightening around Echo's waist.

He shuddered. "No. We're right behind you."

I sighed. Some ghosts were harder to run from. The forest could wait, but I wasn't giving up. I would find a way to make those ugly memories go away.

CHAPTER 4. GRIMNIRS

"Let's hang out, guys," Raine said, her eyes volleying between me and Echo. Was it my imagination or did she seem more energetic than earlier? It was as though healing the forest had sparked something inside her. Torin couldn't seem to rip his eyes away from her.

"What she means is we need to talk, so grab a seat while *I* make lunch. You forgot to say please, Freckles."

"Like this?" Raine walked to him and kissed him. Not an innocent peck. More like an I-want-to-devour-you, tongue-dueling invasion of the senses. I felt the heat from across the room.

Torin staggered backwards when she finished. "Hel's Mist, Freckles," he muttered then turned and stumbled toward the kitchen.

Raine grinned and glanced at us. "I needed that."

"What happened to you?"

"Using my powers unleashes this thing inside of me, and I just want to—" She blinked as though realizing what she'd said, and color rushed to her cheeks. "Kissing him makes my world right again. Um, come on."

She led the way to the kitchen. Echo and I followed slowly. Raine had just acted out of the norm, totally blindsiding me. Did magic affect her that much? There were certain things she didn't discuss with me, but this was one I needed details about. Everyone knew my reaction to possession. Heck, they kept Twizzlers in every house just for that. I often craved them once I was done with souls. She obviously craved Torin.

Femi, Mr. Cooper's nurse, cut us off, her eyes on Echo's face. "Ah, here's my hero and his lovely girlfriend."

Echo stiffened, and my antennas buzzed.

"Hero?" I asked.

"We fought side by side, that's all," Echo said quickly.

"He's being modest," Femi corrected. The combination of blue eyes and golden-brown skin gave the Egyptian an exotic look. She only reached up to Echo's chin and had to tilt her head back to stare into his face. "You saved my life more than once."

"It was nothing."

Femi chuckled. "I'll have you know, my dear, that my life means everything to me. If you ever need a favor, find me."

"That won't—"

"Ever happen, I know," she finished and laughed. "What could I, a mere Immortal, possibly do to help Hel's favorite son? Men." She shook her head, and we exchanged a smile. Female bonding moment ensued. "Come find me if you need anything, doll."

I nodded. "I will."

She patted my arm and continued toward the den where Raine's father now slept. Echo and I joined the others. He was uncomfortable with praise. How silly.

"You're my hero," I whispered, hugging his arm.

"That cape I wear with pride."

In the kitchen, Torin was busy arranging condiments on the counter. Echo had been itching to leave when we were in the forest, but now he seemed, I don't know, content to stay. Worse, I saw the look he and Torin exchanged. It had serious ominous undertones.

"What's going on?" I asked.

Torin paused in the process of opening the fridge door. "Echo told us evil souls were around. The Earl lost about six Immortals, and their souls disappeared before the fight ended. They might be gunning for us."

"We just want to make sure we're on the same page on what to do if they bother you," Raine said, going to stand by Torin. She rubbed his back. She couldn't seem to keep her hands off him.

I glanced at Echo. He looked preoccupied. "You didn't tell them about Dev?"

"He is none of their business," Echo whispered back. "He's mine."

"Ours," I corrected.

Lunch turned out to be fun and long. Echo even relaxed and teased Torin about his miniature sandwiches, which were amazing. Then conversation became serious.

"I think you should go on a helping-souls freeze until we round up all the souls of the Earl's Immortals," Torin suggested. Echo nodded with more enthusiasm than I liked. Raine didn't jump on their bandwagon. Possibly because she knew me. I never ran from anything.

I shook my head. "What if I knew the people before they died? I've helped quite a few from the local hospitals and nursing homes, and I'm not going to stop just because of a few angry souls."

"Cora," Torin and Echo said at the same time, but Raine raised her hands and stopped them.

"Don't gang up on her," she said. "I agree with her. She can't stop helping others out of fear." Both men groaned. She just ignored them. "We have to come up with another way to protect her."

"Thanks for the support," I said, and we high-fived.

Torin looked ready to argue. He glared at Echo. "You need to reason with your woman."

My jaw dropped.

Echo laughed. "How about you focus on yours. I don't see her agreeing with you. One kiss and you turn into a doormat."

Torin glanced at Raine. "Really?"

"We don't kiss," she said, leaning into him. "We affirm. With a touch, a look, or a smile." She kissed him again. Or maybe it was the other way around because when he lifted his head, she wore a dazed expression.

Okay, whatever she was on, I wanted some of it. I tried to jump from Echo's lap and drag her upstairs for a girly chat, but Echo's arms tightened. He'd pulled me onto his lap during lunch.

"Where were we?" Torin asked. "Oh yeah. You said you had everything covered when Cora's not at school."

"Yep." Echo rubbed his cheek against my arm. "They won't bother her, or if they do, I'll know."

Torin frowned. "What if you're at the bottom floor in Hel?"

"I'll know, Valkyrie," Echo vowed.

Their gazes locked. Then Torin nodded as though some super macho message had just passed between them.

"Alright, the others will cover the school. If you see any soul you don't recognize, find Raine, Blaine, or Ingrid. Yeah, I'm bringing them in the loop," he added when Echo scowled. "Andris and I are gone most of the day. We only have one class this semester, and even that's for show. Do you carry your artavus to school, Cora?"

"Yes. I've used it to threaten a few difficult souls."

"Make good on your threat next time," Torin said. "Immortals' souls are not like Mortals'. They're sneaky and will not leave your body until they're good and ready. By then it'll be too late."

"Not if I have anything to do with it." Echo's voice was chilling.

"Your scythe won't work on them the way it does on regular souls, Echo," Torin snapped. "Once they're inside her, there's not much you can do unless you slice her open."

I shivered while Echo snarled. "Is that supposed to be funny?"

Torin shook his head. His expression was calm. "No, it's not. She's one of us and we'll do whatever it takes to protect her, but I want you to be realistic."

Echo told him what he could do with his realism in three different languages—English, Druid, and sign. If they were plotting to scare me, they'd succeeded.

Raine elbowed Torin. "You didn't have to be so graphic."

"We're dealing with dark souls, Raine. Graphic is all I have."

"If a possession happens, I can take care of it. My staff is a lot more powerful than a scythe or an artavus."

"Staff?" I asked.

She glanced at Torin, who didn't look too thrilled with the change of topic. "The dagger the Norns gave me is not what it seems."

I sat up. "Really? What is it? Can we see it?"

Another glance at Torin then Raine nodded. He wore a weird expression as he watched her walk away. Once she disappeared through the portal, he sighed, glanced at us, and scowled. I noticed why. Echo was studying him with a half-smile.

"Something funny, Grimnir?" Torin asked.

"They gave her a *staff*, Valkyrie. Who's not being realistic now?"

Torin leaned back and pushed his fingers through his hair, but the locks fell back on his forehead. "Evil hags."

"Ahh, they're the good ones. Sometimes you can't fight the inevitable."

Torin cocked his eyebrow. "Wanna bet?"

"How many rules are you willing to break?" Echo shot back.

Torin's eyes drifted to me before reconnecting with Echo's. Then he smirked. "Every last one of them."

His British accent tended to be more noticeable when he was angry. He hated what Raine was becoming.

"What do you think, doll-face? Should he break rules to stop Raine from joining the Norns?"

"Absolutely. As long as Raine is in on it," I said. "You go behind her back and she'll never forgive you." I tilted my head, and my eyes met Echo's. "You help him and you'll be sorry, too."

"You couldn't hurt me, doll-face," Echo said.

Torin laughed softly, but I ignored him, choosing to focus on Echo.

"Could too. And I don't mean what you two do, pounding on each other. That's just stupid."

Echo kissed my arm. "But it's also a fun way of releasing steam."

I cocked my brow. "There are more fun ways of de-stressing."

He glanced at Torin, and the two of them exchanged grins. Heat rushed to my cheeks. Seriously? "I didn't mean the two of you should, uh, you know."

"Define *you know*," Torin said, blue eyes twinkling.

"Yes, *Cora mia*," Echo piped in. "What exactly is *you know*?"

The stinker. He was supposed to be on my side. I elbowed him and jumped off his lap. "You two," I pointed at them, "have filthy minds, worse than old man Reeds." My watch said it was a quarter to two. "I'm going to find Raine. Then I'm heading to the nursing home before my shift starts."

"Who in Hel's Mist is Reeds?" Torin asked as I walked away.

"One of her charges at the nursing home. He has a crush on her and is always complimenting her. I'm thinking about putting the old fart out of his misery and personally escorting his soul to the island."

I stopped by the portal and looked over my shoulder at them. They were laughing, having a bro-moment. I almost felt bad I had to intrude. "You touch one of my boys and I'll make you sorry, Grimnir."

He grinned as though relishing the thought. He knew the way I'd make him sorry and, in his perversion, actually enjoyed it. I shook my head and turned to face the portal. It led to Raine's room. I couldn't see her, but I heard her.

"Stay," she said. "And if you're really nice, I'll take you downstairs."

Curious, I walked into her room. She was by the window seat. "Who are you talking to?"

She glanced over her shoulder at me and made a face. "A cat."

"You have a cat? Since when?" A black cat with gorgeous green eyes curled up on the window seat and watched Raine as though listening to her words.

"Since last night. She refused to leave my room and now I'm stuck with her."

"Oh, she's cute." I reached out to pet her, but she hissed and I snatched my hand back. "Is she feral?"

"No, just weird. She hates everyone, except me."

"Even Torin?"

"Yep. He calls her Evil Claws while Femi insists I name her Bastet or Isis." Raine rolled her eyes. "Anyway, I got the dagger."

I dragged my attention from the cat, who I swore was listening to us. Her eyes volleyed between Raine and me, and seemed to become less adoring whenever she looked my way. Didn't witches have cats as companions? What was that word? Familiars!

"Is she your familiar?" I asked.

Raine rolled her eyes. "She's an *unwanted* guest. I'd tell you how I got her, but that's a story for another time. Let me show you how the dagger transforms."

***

Moonbeam Terrace Assisted Living's parking lot was packed. It was a typical Saturday. Visitors walking in and out. Couples plotting how long they'd stay or trying to come up with an excuse for a quick exit before leaving their cars. Adults scolding their children to stop whining or reminding them Grandpa was paying for their music lessons. I'd heard it all. People didn't like being around sick, dying, or elderly people. I worked mainly with residents whose families dumped them at the facility and rarely visited.

We found a place to park, and I turned to study Echo. He'd gone silent and broody after Raine showed us the dagger. Like his scythe, when she engaged her runes while gripping the handle, it elongated into a staff, except her blade coiled into a round end the size of a baseball, and cradled in its core was a blue crystal. I'd seen enough witch movies to know that witches channeled their power through a crystal.

I reached out and stroked Echo's cheek. "What is it?"

"I'll always know when you need me, but just in case I'm detained, find Raine. Wherever you are, you can create a portal to her."

He really was worried about this. He might act cocky in front of Torin, but with me, he always kept it real.

"I will, and I promise to stay away from dark souls." Silence followed. I wasn't sure whether he believed me or not. I indicated the entrance of the building with a nod. "I have to go."

"I know." He stroked my cheek, brushed his lips across mine, and smiled. "You remember what I taught you about air portals?"

It was a work-in-progress. "Yes," I fibbed so he wouldn't have to worry. "I. Will. Be. Fine."

"You better be or I swear..." His eyes glowed for a second. Then his hands left my face and dropped to his side. "I'll see you tonight."

His movements fast, he etched runes in the air in front of us, and in seconds, the windshield, the dashboard, and the steering wheel disappeared and a portal took their place. All I had to do was stand and I'd be in it. This was why I sucked at creating air portals. You had to be really, really fast. I didn't recognize his destination, but it looked like an empty room. When the portal closed, I grabbed the pie box from the back seat and headed toward the entrance of the nursing home.

Mrs. Sallie Jepson was the resident I spent time with every Thursday and Saturday, and sometimes Tuesdays. She had some weird neurological disease that left her bedridden. She was one of the many residents who were wheelchair bound, but one of the few who was still mentally sharp. She had a mouth on her and rarely got visitors.

Squeals of children's laughter and adult voices reached me from the common room. I peeked inside, but didn't see Mrs. J. She must still be in her room. All this activity would only bring her down. Her daughter was one woman I would love to strangle. No matter how bad things were between them, she shouldn't just ignore her mother.

Some of the residents were staying inside with their families or used the back porch for their activities. Others were on the many benches scattered in the back lawn of the wooded compound. Mr. Reeds, the resident player, and the mysterious Captain Gerald were playing chess. The captain usually kept to himself. He was one of those whose family never visited.

Instead of heading to Mrs. Jepson's room, I swung by their table. "Be careful, Captain G. He cheats."

Reeds laughed, his heavy jowls moving, gray eyes twinkling. His son and daughters with their children never missed a visit, so I knew they'd be here. He had five children, and they took turns.

"Ah, more pie," Mr. Reeds said. "Do I get more than a slice this time, or will that beady-eyed witch put a spell on me? No, don't answer that. From the light flashing in your eyes, you're about to blister my ears. She's not a witch. She's an angel disguised as the devil."

That was a good one and I almost smiled. He always said outlandish things about his fellow residents, and none flattering, but he'd never gone after Mrs. J. Even the Captain's mouth twitched.

"You're impossible, Mr. Reeds. Good afternoon, Captain G."

The captain grunted and moved his piece. It was his howdy grunt.

"That means he's just fine, not that it's any of your business. I never knew anyone who could say so much without opening his mouth. It makes our conversations very interesting. Do you want to play, Cora?" Reeds asked, studying the board. He was a terrible player, but an interesting companion. "Or would you rather play strip poker in my room," he added, winking. The captain grunted again. That was his disapproving grunt. No wonder I'd deciphered Dev's sounds.

I leaned down and whispered to Mr. Reeds, "You can't handle me, old man. You will lose, and then my boyfriend will bury you in an unmarked grave for trying to seduce me."

He laughed hard, slapping his thigh. "If I were young, I'd give your man a run for his money."

I laughed. "You'd lose. I'll see you two later." I weaved my way through the room and headed toward Mrs. J's room. I turned a corner and my feet faltered.

A couple stood outside her room, runes all over their faces. The black dusters, gloves, woolen scarves around their necks, and heavy boots screamed Grimnirs. Other than Echo, the only Grimnirs I'd ever seen were those who'd tried to capture me and use me as bait. I swallowed, debating whether to find the nearest exit and head to Raine's or pretend I couldn't see them. The runes said they were invisible.

Then another thought flashed through my head. They could be here for Mrs. J, which meant the spunky lady was dead and her soul had either run or refused to leave with the Grimnirs.

I forget about running away and instead raced toward them, my heart pounding. The girl looked up, saw me, and nudged the guy.

"Are you here for her?" I asked, managing to infuse anger and fear in that one question.

A nurse peered out of a room, saw me, and snapped, "No shouting or running in the hallways, Cora."

I slowed down. "Is Mrs. J okay?"

"Last time I checked," the nurse said. "We just moved her to her chair. She's waiting for you."

"Thanks. I thought… Never mind." I continued down the hallway. The Goth-meets-hipster pushed against the wall and moved forward to intercept me, but I didn't slow down. If they were poaching on Echo's turf, they'd better think again. He reaped all souls around here.

I'd thought Echo looked like my worst nightmare when we first met, but this guy took it a step further. Problem was the long black hair, tats that were definitely not runes, Gothic black studs, and chains were over the top. At least he didn't go for heavy makeup, which would have distracted from his violet eyes. Still, Echo had looked more intimidating with less and beat him hands down on a hotness scale.

The girl was surprisingly clean-cut with an angular face and cat-like eyes. In fact, she could be Olivia Wilde's Doppelganger, except her hair was black and streaked with fuchsia highlights.

A quick glance over my shoulder confirmed that Mallory, or was it Melody, was wheeling a resident toward the hall and couldn't see me.

"What do you want?" I asked, focusing on the two soul reapers. "I hope you're not here for my friend."

"Are you Echo's girl?" the girl asked.

Suspicion slithered in, and I narrowed my eyes. "Why?"

"Are you or are you not his girl?" she asked rudely.

"Nara," the guy warned.

"This is not the time to be nice, Rhys," she snapped.

"Rhys?" I asked, remembering Echo's childhood buddies. "You're Echo's friend?"

He blinked, clearly surprised, then his face hardened. "That was a long time ago."

"No one can be friends with that psycho for long," Nara butted in.

Now she was pissing me off. "Call him psycho one more time... Just once. I dare you."

Fear flickered in her eyes, and I knew it wasn't because of me. Echo.

"I didn't think you would. Excuse me." I tried to pass them, but she grabbed my arm.

"We need to talk," Nara said.

I yanked my arm from her grip. "Don't ever grab me like that, Grimnir. Not if you want your head to stay attached to your neck. You want to talk, try saying please." I glanced up and down the hallway, but no one was there. More of this and someone might see me and presume I was talking to myself. "Now go away." I walked past them.

"Is it true Dev came to see you?" Rhys asked. He sounded hopeful.

I glanced back and our eyes met. Now him I can deal with. Plus he had that tortured look down to a science. After hearing Echo's story and the fiasco with Torin's father, I knew most Valkyries and Grimnirs carried a lot of baggage.

"Yes."

"Liar!" Nara snapped. "Dev is nothing but black smoke of nothing. Do you get a thrill out of Echo going on the rampage for you?"

I was really beginning to dislike this Grimnir, but her partner's pained expression had me reaching for my cell phone. It was obvious he didn't share her attitude. I found the screen shot and showed it to him.

"I don't read or write Druidic. Dev wrote this on my computer."

Rhys' hand shot out, but he stopped before touching my cell, his eyes wide as though he recognized the handwriting.

Nara peered at the screen and a spasm crossed her face. I could swear it was pain.

"I'm not a liar, Rhys. And if Echo gave you grief over this, I'll talk to him. Dev came to me for a reason, and I mean to find out why." The two reapers didn't say anything, but I had their attention. "What does it say?"

"He needs your help," Rhys said.

"But don't tell lover boy," Nara added, smirking.

I focused on Rhys. "If you're interested in what I learn, I'll let you know. But first, *she*," I jabbed my cell at Nara, "needs to lose the attitude."

Rhys' mouth twitched as though he was suppressing a smile. Nara glowered. I turned, pushed the door open, and disappeared inside.

Mrs. J was by the window staring outside, probably hoping her daughter was here for once. She looked so frail and alone. I pushed the annoying reapers from my thoughts and plastered a smile on my face.

"Good afternoon, Mrs. J," I said in my most chipper voice, while placing the pie on the table.

"Took you long enough to come inside," she griped. "I heard your voice outside my door hours ago."

Grinning, I walked around her wheelchair so I could see her face. "I missed you too, Mrs. J. Do you want to go outside?"

"If I wanted to go outside I would have told the nurse."

She was in one of her moods. "How about a slice of pie?"

She glanced at the boxed treat. "Brought more leftovers, did you?"

"More like first-outers." I opened the box and removed a plastic plate and fork from where I'd stashed them. "Meaning it was the first batch to come out of the oven. I took two of them to my friend's house. Remember Raine? I told you how her dad has cancer and her mother had to go away for a while, leaving her with her father and a nurse."

"Weak woman. I despise weak people," Mrs. J grumbled. "Your friend is better off without such a mother."

Was that a hint at the problem between her and her daughter? I waved the plastic knife at her. "Hey. We don't write off family just because they fall short of our expectations."

Instead of a smile, she sunk lower in her seat. "What would you do if you were your friend?"

"I'd be disappointed, maybe angry, but then I'd forgive her and move on." Not that Raine needed to forgive her mother. Svana Cooper had gone to meet the Valkyrie Council so she could get back her Valkyrie status. I wondered if she would reap her husband's soul when he died.

Mrs. J shook her head. "To be so young and naive. What do you know about living with regrets and the power of forgiveness?" She moved a trembling hand and grabbed the controls on the arm of her chair. Slowly, she wheeled herself to the table. It might take her forever to move around, but she liked her independence and I respected that. "Okay, I'll have some pie, Ms. Jemison, and you can continue reading where we left off."

Mrs. J loved historical romances. I placed her plate on the table, got her a drink, and reached for the book. We'd stopped where the rake, Lord of Something, was about to ravish the spinster sister of his fiancé. Even though there were other volunteers who came during the week, she only allowed me to read to her. I'd tried to introduce her to audio books, but she was old school.

She ate two slices of the pie as I read. Then we left the room. Rhys and Nara were still outside. Still cloaked. I glared at them and mouthed, "Go away."

They didn't bother to respond, but followed us down the hallway. I ignored them. Mrs. J liked to control her wheelchair when indoors. Except for corners, she was pretty good. Voices came from other rooms we passed. Captain G's room was quiet, the door open. He sat by the window reading a book, long, grey dreadlocks hiding his face. Poor guy.

"Do you ever talk to the captain, Mrs. J?"

"That cantankerous old fool? No."

"He's new and needs a friend," I said.

"I don't have time for friendship. This is a place for the dying, not relationships. You check in, and you check out in a body bag. Let's go to the river. Maybe I'll fall in and drown when you're not looking."

Mrs. J was a piece of work, but then again, it couldn't be easy to stay positive in her situation. Dumped here by her uncaring child. Her health worsening. Personally, I thought she was dying of heartbreak.

I switched the controls on her wheelchair to manual and took over steering. The first people I saw when we left the building were the Grimnirs. What was their problem? They followed us down the ramp, past families picnicking, until we reached the path along the river. When we found the perfect place under a tree and went back to reading, they sat on large rocks down the path from us.

For the next hour, I completely ignored them. At least, they didn't follow us inside the building. I gave Mrs. J another slice of pie before I left.

I always felt sad whenever it was time to leave her. She was so lonely and bitter, and although I knew she looked forward to my visits, a visit from her family would mean much more.

"I'll see you next weekend."

She gripped my hand. "Bring this boy you say you plan to marry to see me sometime."

I stared at her suspiciously. "Uh, why?"

"No need to look at me like that. I want to see if he's worthless like most young people I see walking around with headphones and pants so low their underwear are visible because they can't afford a decent belt."

I laughed. "They can afford belts, Mrs. J. That's just a craze."

"I know that. You think I'm senile? Why are you reluctant to bring this boy to see me?"

"Because you might steal him from me. I don't trust you."

She pursed her lips. "Likes older women, does he?"

"Or some of your meanness might rub off on him. I like him just the way he is."

She harrumphed. "A sweet boy, is he? No woman wants a doormat."

Doormat and *sweet* weren't words I'd use to describe Echo, and he didn't like older women. "Okay, Mrs. J. You win. I'll bring Echo to meet you if you do something for me first."

She blinked, her lined face creasing into a frown. "You're blackmailing me? A helpless old woman?"

"Helpless? Ha! You put the fear of God in everyone every time you open your mouth. I'm never sure what barbs you're going to lob at me. You," I pointed at her, "are one scary lady."

She grinned, her dentures rattling. "What do you want me to do?"

"Reach out to Captain G and I'll bring Echo."

Her wrinkly face scrunched up in folds as she frowned. "No."

"Then no deal," I said.

"You're an impudent girl."

I laughed. "And you are a cantankerous fool. See you next week."

"Don't bother coming back."

"Fine. I won't." Mrs. J might act like she didn't need anyone, but she did. I was coming back.

I was still laughing when I reached the captain's room, saw that the door was open, and knocked. He grunted a response, which meant come in. I heard it every week. Didn't stop me from leaving him a piece of pie.

"I brought you some pie, Captain G." Another grunt, a pleased one. I placed it on his table with a plastic fork. "See you next week."

I turned to continue down the hall when a sudden chill crawled up my spine. Even before I turned to look, I knew Dev's soul was nearby. The chill accompanying him was different from Echo's or a regular soul's. It was sharper.

I turned and saw Dev's dark soul hover a few feet away. Somehow I thought I'd see through him during the day. He was still dark, his edges blurry. This end of the hallway tended to be busy because it was close to the entrance. Everyone was either rubbing their arms or tugging the lapels of their robes, jackets, and sweaters as they walked past us.

Two nurses walked right through him and visibly shuddered. "Why is it so cold in here?" one asked me.

Would they think I was crazy if I told them a ghost was in the building? Probably. Most people didn't believe in ghosts—humans' name for souls.

"I'll see if someone adjusted the thermostat," the second nurse said and hurried away. The other one smiled vaguely in my direction and disappeared inside a room.

I signaled Dev and nodded toward the staff bathroom a few yards away. I hurried forward and disappeared inside. Just in case he was planning possession, I pulled out my cell phone and dialed Raine. She answered in two rings.

"If you don't hear from me in five minutes, find me," I said.

"Cora, what's going on?"

I heard the concern in her voice, and Dev chose that moment to drift through the wall and join me. "I'm dealing with an unusual soul. Make it two minutes."

I hung up and gripped my cell phone. My other hand slipped inside the pocket of my vest and closed around my artavus. Despite what I'd told the two soul reapers earlier, I wasn't sure I wanted to help this soul.

"What do you want, Dev?"

CHAPTER 5. A MELTDOWN

He angled his head, and a chuckle shot from him. He pointed at me then at his chest. I knew that gesture only too well. It meant he wanted my help. There was no way was I letting him inside me.

"I know you want my help, but I don't think I can give it."

A sound rumbled from his chest, and I took a step back, my grip tightening on my runic blade. Had a minute passed since I'd spoken with Raine? I readied my phone for a redial. As though he sensed my fear, he took a step back and pointed tentatively at my hand.

"What? My cell phone?"

He nodded.

"What about it?"

He pointed at his chest then my phone. I scowled. "You want to use my phone."

Another nod.

"Uh, you are an energy with no physical form, Dev." He made a gesture, and I realized what he meant. "Ahh, you want to enter it like you did my laptop."

He tapped his head and nodded.

"Yeah, I'm a genius. Okay, I'll let you haunt my cell, but first, I have to make a quick call." I redialed Raine's number. "It's about you, so try not to take offense." Raine picked up after one ring.

"You okay?" she asked, not sounding too worried. She was a Seeress, so maybe she'd seen my future and knew I'd be okay.

"For now. The soul needs my help, so he won't do anything stupid."

Dev spread his arms as though to say, "What could I possibly do to you?"

"He knows Echo would haul his ass to Corpse Strand if he hurts me," I added.

"Echo's not there?" she asked.

"I can handle souls without his help, you know."

"But just in case, I'm coming—"

"No! Don't, Raine." She was such a worrywart, but this was my business, and I wanted to do it without her help or Echo's. "You'll only scare him away. Besides, I'm sure Echo is waiting for me outside in the car and will charge in here if I'm not out soon." *Got that Dev?* I glanced at the soul to make sure he did. He grunted.

"Be careful, Cora," Raine said. "After you called, I touched the bracelet you left here last week and saw something I don't like."

My stomach dropped. There were perks to having a Seeress for a best friend, and then there were the non-perks. If such a word existed. I didn't want to know about my future unless… "Am I going to go crazy from a possession, or just get decapitated and die?"

Raine laughed. "Ew. Nothing that dire, but be careful. There are a couple of not-so-happy Grimnirs who might be paying you a visit soon."

"Met them already. They're friends of Echo's, and I'm using the term friends loosely here." I gave the faceless Dev a toothy grin. "Okay, gotta go. Talk to you in a bit." I cut the connection and placed the cell by the sink. Dev slithered into my phone through the headphone opening.

My eyes didn't leave the LCD screen. I wasn't sure whether to open the notepad to see what he'd written when the speakers buzzed and a voice said, "Can you hear me, Cora?"

I jumped. He'd hijacked my cell phone's personal assistant and navigator. His voice was deep with a strong accent. I wondered if Echo had spoken with the same accent. Maybe once upon a time.

"Cora?" he asked again. "Am I saying your name correctly?"

I was actually talking to a soul. Ha, how cool was that! "Yeah. I mean, yes you are."

"Good. How did you know my name is Dev? You found a decoder for my language?"

I liked his accent. It was close to Irish, my father's people. "No. Echo told me."

Dev let out a string of words that didn't need translation.

I tried not to cringe. He was loud, and I wasn't sure whether I should tell him to chill. Most phone assistants spoke in a monotone. "I hope you're not cursing me out there, pal."

"Of course not," he said sarcastically. "You just had to tell him after I told you not to."

"You grunted something, Dev. I'm not a grunt expert. Besides, I don't keep secrets from Echo. Why didn't you just enter my laptop or phone and talk to me before, instead of skulking around and writing mysterious notes I can't read? It's obvious you can speak English."

"Doesn't mean I can write it."

"Why didn't you want him to know you're around anyway?"

"Because he'd come after me before we got a chance to talk, and he did. I was specific. I wrote that I need your help. *Yours*, not his. And not tell him. But what do you do? You tell him."

I made a face. "Well, you are here. He's not."

"Doesn't mean he's not searching and plotting my demise," he retorted.

Humility was obviously not sewn into his DNA. I leaned against the counter so I was closer to the phone. "News flash, pal. You've already met your demise."

"News flash, Immortal. There are far worse things than death. Did he tell you how I died?"

I really loved his accent. "Yes."

Silence followed.

"Dev?"

"You still want to help me?"

I rolled my eyes. "Just because he's angry with you doesn't mean I have to be, too. I don't follow him blindly. As for helping you, I haven't decided yet." Echo had to be on board, and it was going to take some serious kissing and begging to convince him.

A chuckle floated from the phone. "I think my friend finally found a worthy mate."

"Happy to know I passed the test. What do you really want, Dev?"

"Help me talk to Echo. I need, um, what's the word? Closure."

So did Echo, but his reaction to Dev's name said he'd never seek it. "Uh, I don't think I can."

"Why not? It's your job to find closure for souls, right?"

"No, it's not. I choose to help souls from the goodness of my heart."

"Echo is one lucky man. He didn't just land a pretty face; you're kindhearted too."

"Kissing up won't win you brownie points." I cocked my eyebrows. He had no face. "How do you know I'm pretty?"

He chuckled. "Most Mortals and objects are blurry, but you glow. Unlike Valkyries and Grimnirs, the runes on your skin act like a beacon whether you engage them or not. I'd have to be blind not to notice you. Also, only a pretty woman can talk to Rhys the way you did. One look into his violet eyes and most women tend to turn into blabbering idiots. By the way, I like the dress. Suits you. Loved last night's lingerie better, though."

Heat crawled up my face. "If, and that's a big if, I decide to help you, we will start with a few ground rules. At the top of the list is you never ever come into my bedroom. Second, the rest of the house is off limits, too. My parents don't know what I do, so I can't talk to you while they're around. You're also ice cold. Dad has an active imagination without you fueling it. You don't pay me a visit at night period. Doesn't matter whether I'm at Echo's or at a friend's, movies, or whatever. You want to talk, we do it during the day. I like that you can crawl inside electronics."

"Commandeer electronics, sweetheart," he corrected. "Not the same thing. It took a lot of work to master that move."

Vain, just like Echo. "So what do you want to tell Echo? Ask for his forgiveness? Explain why you betrayed him? He's still pretty pissed."

Dev groaned. "A couple of millennia and he's still holding a grudge. He's so petty and hot-headed."

"And right to be angry," I finished, the need to defend my man making me lean toward my phone. "You were his best friend and you betrayed him. People died. Your people. Echo sacrificed his position as a Valkyrie for them, and you pulled a shitty move on him. How did you expect him to react?"

Silence followed. I was sure Dev was going to slither out of my cell phone and do something I wouldn't like, but all he asked was, "Are you done?"

His voice dripped with ice. Good thing I wasn't easily intimidated. "No. If you are here to hurt Echo, I will disperse you."

He sighed and backed down. "You know there are two sides to a story."

"Are you saying the version Echo told me is wrong?"

"No, but there's more, and he needs to hear it."

"Why can't you just appear to him and tell him?"

"He doesn't use electronics and he carries a stick, a very large stick with a sharp iron tip and deadly runes that do strange things to souls."

"It's called a scythe," I said.

Dev chuckled.

Smart-ass. He knew what it was. "Get to the point, Dev. Remember you're trying to show me you're worth helping."

"Ouch. I need a mediator. I try to talk to him once every few centuries, and each time, he threatens to take me to some torture island in Hel's realm before he can listen to anything I have to say. And if you know him as well as you claim, you know he'd do it and not lose sleep over it."

"Sleep over it," I said at the same time.

Dev laughed. "I tried using Nara, but he got pissed when he found out and broke things off with her."

My stomach shifted. I'd gone into selective listening at "he broke things off with her." "Nara was Echo's girlfriend?"

I didn't realize I'd spoken aloud until Dev said, "Oh. You didn't know?"

No, I didn't. But then again, we rarely talked about his past conquests. I never wanted to know. Nara was a

Druidess. Older than me. I'd bragged to Mrs. J that Echo wasn't into older women. Obviously, I was wrong.

A commotion in the hallway drew my eyes to the closed door. I expected a nurse to burst in on me and Dev.

"I have to go. Can you get out of my phone now?"

"I'm sorry," he said.

"For what?" I asked absentmindedly, my attention on whatever was happening out there. Someone shouted something, and running feet followed.

"I shouldn't have mentioned Nara," Dev continued. "I thought you knew her and Rhys when I heard you talking to them earlier. On the other hand, I only caught the tail end of your conversation, so—"

Thuds and shouting came from the front entrance, and a bad feeling washed over me. Chaos usually meant Valkyries and Grimnirs.

"What was that?" Dev asked.

"I don't know, but I have to go."

"When will I know if you've decided to help me?"

"After I talk to Echo. Now get out of my phone," I snapped.

"Okay. No need to be snippy." He slithered out of my cell phone. I grabbed it, hurried to the door, and yanked it open.

Two security guys almost knocked me over as they rushed past. Then I heard, "How can her car be in the parking lot if she's left the building? She's in here somewhere."

Echo!

I broke into a run even though I knew the rules about not running in the hallway.

"Mortal, get your hands off me," Echo snarled.

Crap! He was going to bring the roof down.

"CORA! Where are you?"

The fear in his voice pelted my senses like a gust of hailstones. I careened around the corner, almost bumping into Joan, the head of entertainment. I burst into the foyer, which was streaming with the staff. I pushed past them, my eyes locked on the four men dragging Echo toward the entrance. That he let them grab and move him was a testament to his self-control.

"Echo," I called out. "Here."

His head whipped around, his usually golden eyes a stormy wildness I'd never seen before. He shook the four men holding him like they were ragdolls, sending them flying. Then he closed the gap between us. I flew into his arms, wrapping my arms around his neck and my legs around his mid-section. He was shaking.

"I'm okay, baby," I whispered. "I'm okay."

"I couldn't feel you." He buried his face in my nape, his arms almost cracking my ribs. I engaged my runes just in case. "I couldn't feel you," he added again.

"That's because I was safe." Stroking his hair, I absorbed the tremors shooting through him. "I'm here now. Nothing bad happened."

He turned and carried me out of the building, his strides long, tremors still shooting through him. I could feel eyes following us. I didn't know how I'd explain him to the nursing home staff or if they'd understand, yet I had to try if I wanted to continue helping out there.

Echo propped me against the body of my car and leaned back to study my face. He looked like Hel swallowed him and spat him out.

"I'm sorry I worried you," I whispered.

Instead of answering me, he forked his fingers through my hair, gripped my head to hold it in place, and crushed my lips with his. The unfiltered fear I'd seen in his eyes translated into something dark and stormy. I wasn't ready for the total invasion of my senses.

He ravished my mouth like a man starved. The adrenaline coursing through his veins made him ruthless in the way he molded me to his will until I couldn't think of anything else but his mouth, his tongue, his hard body pressing against my softness.

We strained against each other. Soon the need to reassure him and ease his fear mushroomed into something more primal. Runes blazing, senses exploding, I wanted to rip the clothes off him.

When he yanked his lips from mine, we were both panting. His gleaming golden eyes bored into mine, telling me what he still couldn't put into words. He'd thought he'd lost me, and he needed to reconnect with me, to confirm I was really here and allay his demons.

Still cradling me, he opened the car door and sat with me on his lap, arms tight around my waist. I buried my face in the crook of his neck. We didn't speak until our heartbeats settled to a normal rhythm. I stroked his nape and kissed anywhere I could reach on his face.

"Look at me," I said.

He did, his eyes still haunted.

"I stopped to talk to a soul, and I thought it would only take a few minutes. I didn't know I'd taken long."

He kissed my nose, still not speaking. Echo was a talker, so for him to clam up said a lot.

"Open a portal and take me home," I whispered.

He nodded then nudged me to my feet. In the next second, he engaged his speed and invisibility runes, and pulled an artavus from inside his duster. He was gone before I could ask what he planned to do. Probably to etch forgetful runes on the people who'd witnessed his brief meltdown.

Less a minute later, he was back. He slid behind the wheel, but didn't start the engine. Instead, he gripped the steering wheel and stared straight ahead. I reached out and rubbed his back. Splayed my fingers through his hair and massaged his scalp, imagining how he would react if something bad ever happened to me. He'd probably lose his mind.

"I need you in my life, *Cora mia*," he said.

"I know."

"If someone took you from me…" He let out a shaky breath as though the thought was too painful to voice.

I gripped the back of his head and tilted it so he could look into my eyes. "No one will ever do that, Echo. Never. Remember our vow. I'm yours and you are mine. Alive or dead."

His eyes blazed. "Engage your invisibility runes," he added in a voice gone husky.

He reached under his duster and removed his portal artavus. His movements fast, he created a portal like he'd done earlier. This time it led to his bedroom.

He took my hand. We stood and entered the room. He faced me, hands fisted on his sides, his eyes raw with emotions I couldn't begin to understand, his entire posture defenseless.

"I need you," he whispered.

"I know."

He swallowed. "Will you love me?"

My heart squeezed in my chest. "Always."

He went into hyper-speed, duster, shirt, pants, and shoes flying from the whirlpool that was Echo. When he finished, he stood before me.

I stared, my mouth dry. He never failed to take my breath away.

He walked to where I still stood in the middle of the room, cupped my face, and lowered his head. The kiss started sweet and soft, but shot up to sizzling hot in seconds. He took off my clothes faster than he'd taken off his. My head spun as he scooped me and lay me gently on the bed.

He paused and studied me with an unreadable expression.

"What is it?" I asked.

He ran a finger down my chest, leaving a heated trail, past the swell of my stomach, and found me. "I can't lose you."

"You won't." I ran a hand along his chest, past his taught sculptured abs, and found him. He sucked in a breath. I squeezed and a shuddered rocked his body. "You're mine."

"You unman me, *Cora mia.*" He joined me, legs intertwining with mine, skin speaking to skin. "The feel of you. Like warm silk." He took my hand from my favorite play toy and trapped it with the other above my head. Then he ran the tips of his fingers down my arm, stroking my face and my shoulders, while his legs moved up and down mine.

"The taste of you," he whispered against my lips then kissed me, focusing first on my upper lip, then the lower one, which he trapped with his teeth. My entire body trembled at the sharp nip. Then he proceeded to take away the sting, his hand scuttling down to my chest to play and torment. He moved lower and his lips replaced his fingers. I writhed and bucked, as he strummed me like a fine-tuned guitar.

"The essence of you," he whispered against my skin when he moved even lower and my skin quivered in response.

His enthusiasm and utter joy in driving me a little crazy with his mouth and lips triggered so many responses I cried out his name more than once, but it wasn't enough. It was never enough until we were one.

He crawled up my body, kissed me long and hard, then ordered, "Look at me."

I did through a haze.

Eyes locked, he carefully joined us, taking my breath away. It was always the same. Getting used to the feelings that simple act churned inside me was going to take a long time.

Taking his time, he rocked, watching my every expression. I felt vulnerable, like everything about me was there for him to see. He knew what to do to make me tremble with anticipation, gasp with pleasure, and cry out in frustration.

Rolling us over so I was on top, he whispered, "Love me, *Cora mia*. Make me yours."

I did, starting slowly, watching the play of emotions on his face. Picking up tempo as runes exploded on his skin and starting that crazy reaction where I couldn't tell where his feelings ended and mine began. He pulled me down for a gut-wrenching kiss as the heavens burst open and stars exploded around us, my name a victorious yell from his lips.

Still wrapped in each other's arms, bodies glistening with sweat, we rolled to our sides and floated slowly back to earth.

"I'm an ass," he whispered.

I wasn't arguing with him on that, but at the moment, I didn't see the relevance. He'd just rocked my world. Again. "What did you do this time? Other than cut the circulation on my poor leg?"

He rolled on his back, taking me with him. Blood rushed in the leg he'd trapped under his, and it tingled as sensations returned.

"I use your body instead of dealing with whatever crap my screwed-up head can't deal with."

I stroked his back and smiled. Nothing grounded him like connecting with me. When he got scared or pissed, he craved contact in any form to calm down. I was beginning to anticipate his moods. I knew when he wanted me to love him. Knew when he needed to wrap himself around my body and absorb my essence as he called it. I never knew the power of skin-to-skin contact until I fell for this man. It was insane, but it was Echo.

"You don't hear me complain," I said.

"You should if you'd like. I'd feel like the lowest worm, but I'd bounce back. I'm tough like that."

My heart squeezed. I'd never do that to him. I lifted my head and studied him in the dark, the blazing runes providing enough light. It might be around six in Kayville, but it was nine in Florida.

"I'll always want you, silly. No matter how messed up your head is, I'll always be here for you."

He stroked my lower lip. "I know I don't always say this, *Cora mia*, but I don't deserve you."

I hated it when he put himself down. Too often I'd play along and tell him in excruciating detail why he was right. Not tonight. He'd had enough of a scare. "Why?"

"You're loving, sweet, and selfless, everything I'm not." He ran his fingers down my back then up again. I trembled, but I doubted he noticed. "My greatest fear is one day you'll take a really good look at me and decide you could do better."

I was done. First he tells me I should fight him when he needed me, or used me as he put it, and now I could do better? I sat up and touched the lamp on top of the bedside chest. I wanted to kick him from here to next century.

"Explain exactly what you mean so I can go out there and find someone opposite you."

Surprise flickered in his eyes. He sat, his expression serious. "I'm mean and ruthless. I like to win and will do whatever it takes to do it. I don't forgive a slight and get a great deal of pleasure from punishing those who've hurt me or those I love. I, uh, I…"

So far he hadn't said anything I didn't already know. Know and not particularly care about, except for the last part. I planned to teach him the power of forgiveness if it was the last thing I did. Could take centuries. Didn't care. He was perfect, damn it. He must see that.

"Yes?" I urged, my stance softening.

"I don't know how to love." His brow crunched up, his eyes darkening. "I don't think I can the way you deserve to be loved. I said I wanted to court you, starting with dinner. Yet here we are instead of sitting at some restaurant."

Dinner was overrated. "Echo—"

"Love is sharing, yet I don't want to share you with anyone." He growled, his eyes brightening in intensity. "Not with the dying people in that stupid Mortal nursing home or gawking idiots in restaurants. I hate sharing. Don't know how. Love is putting your needs above mine." He shrugged. "I'm a selfish bastard. Maybe I've been alone for too long. But…" He sighed and I waited even though it was killing me. I wanted to tell him I didn't mind his way of doing things, but I knew he wouldn't believe me. "But I'm willing to learn and become a better man for you. So if I promise to do something, don't let me distract you with this." He indicated the bed.

I didn't know if I could ever tell him no. I loved the way he shared himself even though he didn't see it. And yes, he could be selfish, but he always put my needs first. Always. Even when he yanked clothes off us like a demented fool, his touch was always gentle.

"Cora?" he asked and peered at me.

"Okay. We'll learn together because I don't know how to share either. I'm an only child. Spoiled. Never learned to share. And let's be honest, I distract you too, so we're even." I gave him a toothy grin.

He glared. "Don't compare yourself with me, *Cora mia*. You are perfect the way you are. I'm trying to tell you I plan to change. I promise."

I sighed. Hel's Mist. Time to play along. "And I promise to be patient as you learn to love me."

"Good." He swung his legs to the side of the bed and stood. "We're going to dinner. Then I have a surprise for you afterwards." He pulled on his pants. "I'll pick you up in an hour."

I didn't feel like going to dinner, but if it made him feel good, who was I to argue. I wasn't good with the few speed runes I had, so he was done before me. He watched me finish with a wicked gleam in his eyes.

"We could always skip dinner," he said, helping me button the front of my dress.

Was he testing me? I narrowed my eyes, wanting so badly to call his bluff. "Nah. I'm hungry."

"We could order takeout."

I smacked his arm. "Cut it out. You're not distracting me. I want to be courted."

He grinned with approval. Clueless man. Oh well, he was going to find out soon enough he couldn't control me. He picked up his duster from the floor, pulled out an artavus, and created an air portal to my car. I planted a kiss on his lips and walked through it.

"One hour," he warned before the portal closed.

CHAPTER 6. FINALLY A DATE

Halfway home, Dev appeared in the seat next to me. I didn't even blink. "Use the radio."

He chuckled and slithered through the CD slot. "Where did you two disappear to?"

"None of your beeswax," I retorted.

He chuckled. "Same ol' same ol' Echo. Acting first and asking questions later."

I wasn't sure whether he meant the incident at the nursing home, so I tried to contain my annoyance. "If you don't cut out that mocking tone, mister, I'm so not going to help you."

"I'm starting to think you can't, gorgeous. Echo hasn't changed. He'll ditch you the way he did Nara."

I smiled. "You don't know anything, Smokey."

"Was that a smile I heard in your voice?"

"Yes. And I plan to prove you wrong. I will help you." It meant helping Echo too, which was more important.

"As long as you don't call me, Smokey."

"Too bad. It suits you."

"It's insulting. Okay, I'll play. Surprise me. Show me Echo has changed."

"Just remember my rule—no coming to my home."

"I heard you the first time." He slithered out of the radio.

For the rest of the drive, I tried to think of a way to bring up Dev with Echo. I'd have to be subtle, starting with the importance of forgiveness, and take it from there.

"I'm home," I called out, but my parents weren't in the kitchen. The scent of pot roast hung in the air. Mom was probably in the barn collecting eggs from the chicken coup. Dad could be anywhere since he wasn't in his writing cave.

I left the house and headed toward the barn. I heard their voices before I entered. "I don't know, honey," Mom said. "Rushing into something that big can be disastrous, but at the same time, she's eighteen now, an adult."

"She's a child," Dad said, not sounding absentminded like he often did. "She will listen to us."

Okay, I was obviously the subject of discussion. "Hey, Mom. Dad."

They turned toward the barn entrance, both looking guilty.

"Hey, hun," Mom said.

"Pumpkin," Dad said at the same time. "Did you just get home?"

I nodded, my cheeks warming. "Mrs. J was in one of her moods today."

Mom sighed. "Her daughter is still not visiting her?"

"No. I tried to make her become more involved with the other residents, but…" I shrugged. "You need help with that, Dad?"

He was too happy to give me the basket of eggs, but he didn't leave. I wondered which one of them would bring up whatever they'd been discussing. What big thing was I rushing into?

"How's Echo?" Dad asked.

I hid a smile. Dad for the win. "Good. He's picking me up for dinner in," I glanced at my watch, "less than an hour."

"Why didn't you say so this morning? I've already made dinner," Mom piped in.

Mom hated serving leftovers, but this morning my head had been elsewhere. "Sorry, I forgot."

"He can join us for dinner. Right, dear?" She glanced at Dad for support.

Dad's eyes volleyed between me and Mom. He shrugged. "Why not? The more the merrier."

"I'll ask him, but he wants to show me something tonight, a surprise."

My parents exchanged a glance, and Mom said, "Okay, but we'd like to have him over for dinner. Maybe next weekend?"

"Sure, Mom." I turned to leave.

"Not so fast," she added, and my stomach dropped. She exchanged another glance with Dad, and I braced myself. I wasn't going to like this. Silent communication between them usually meant bad news.

"I'll be at the house," Dad said and escaped.

Definitely bad news. The big mistake I was about to make. Of course, she had to be the one to talk to me. She'd given me the pep talk about boys and sex just before I started middle school. Then there was the botched up talk about pills and other forms of contraception. I had stared at her with wide eyes, my face hot. That was two years ago when I'd turned sixteen.

We left the barn together. Mom looped her arm around my right one, forcing me to cradle the basket of eggs in my left.

She picked up my hand and studied the ring. "This is such a beautiful ring."

Echo had given me a promise ring a couple of months ago. It had Druidic writings and had been in his family, like, forever. It had belonged to his great grandmother and been passed down to the eldest daughter. With his sisters dead, Echo had inherited it.

"Thanks. Echo said he'd replace it, but I really love it."

"Me too." She patted my hand. "Do you think you're ready for contraceptives now?"

Heat rushed to my face. When I'd turned sixteen, she had told me to tell her when I was about to be sexually active, so she could put me on the pill. My mother was practical. Sometimes too practical.

"Mom," I protested weakly.

Mom stopped walking, and I did too. "You're eighteen now, Cora. A woman. If you and Echo are ready to hook up, I want you to be prepared."

My jaw dropped. That was just wrong. "Hook up?"

Mom chuckled. "I can be hip. I was a teacher, and I read comments on your vlog."

I closed my eyes, totally beyond mortified. If I said I didn't want the darn pills and ended up pregnant, I'd look like a moron. If I said I did, she'd know that Echo and I were *hooking up*.

"Mom…" Then I thought about Echo and his wish to be a better man for me even though he didn't need to be. "Yes, I'll go see your doctor. Just promise me one thing."

"Anything."

"Don't ever use the expression 'hook up,'" I said. She laughed and I joined her.

***

An hour later, Dad was talking to Echo when I came downstairs. They stopped talking when I appeared, both of them got to their feet and turned toward me. The two most important men in my life. Together. I had a girly moment and got a little emotional.

Echo had changed into jeans, a gray shirt, and a navy blazer. I loved him in jeans. He looked hot. His eyes flashed with heat even though I wore jeggings, boots, and a flirty red top.

"Sorry, I took so long." I walked to his side.

"It's okay." Echo intertwined our hands and turned to face Dad. "Thank you, sir. I'll definitely take what you said into consideration."

"That's all I ask, son." Dad shook his hand.

Son? I almost giggled. I kissed Dad on the cheek and waved to Mom. I was dying to find out what they'd talked about. Echo was driving the rental SUV he often used whenever we went out. He waited until I was in the passenger seat, closed the door, rounded the hood, and slid behind the steering wheel.

"So, what were you and Dad discussing?" I asked.

"Where's my kiss?"

I rolled my eyes. "You're hedging."

"Not when it comes to kisses." He turned and cocked an eyebrow, runes flaring on and off. I leaned in and kissed him, making it brief. Then I sat back in my seat.

"Tease," he murmured.

"About you and Dad?"

"He wanted to know when I'll finish college. I told him next year, which makes me about twenty-one." He gunned the engine, grinning. "What exactly am I studying at Walkersville?"

"Um, I don't know. Business? What did you say when he asked?"

"I managed to redirect the conversation to his work."

Close call. Then I saw Echo's smug smile. I bumped him with my shoulder. "We agreed. No runing my family."

He chuckled. "Totally forgot. Old habit. We still haven't come up with plausible background information for me."

I sighed and stared ahead, my mind racing. The first night I'd brought Echo home for dinner, Dad had only asked Echo what he did. A transfer student from back east to Walkersville University had seemed like a perfect answer. Major? Echo had directed the conversation to history, Dad's favorite subject, and the night had gone smoothly. Echo needed a Google-proof fake background.

I peered out the window. We were on the wide road splitting two of the largest vineyards in the county. A few souls wandered out of the rows of vines and stared after us. Echo didn't even acknowledge them. It seemed so long ago I had to worry about Grimnirs attacking me on this very road. Echo had leveled some of the vines and trees while fighting a couple of Grimnirs who'd come after me. Now there was Rhys and Nara.

Her pretty face flashed in my head, and I pushed down the green monster.

"What backgrounds did you use before we started dating? I mean, you did date Mortals before."

"Ones who cared more about what we did behind closed doors, or in public places, and the expensive trinkets I bought them."

Public places? How like him. And how come he'd never tried it with me? Now I was jealous of faceless women who were probably long dead. Or maybe not. "Any of them alive?"

"A few here and there. Why?"

So I could check them out. On the other hand, I'd met Nara and she was hot. "They must be really old, right?"

Echo brought the car to a halt at the stop sign and glanced at me. "You never have to worry about my exes. I runed those who asked too many questions, so they don't remember me. The rest are long dead."

The bitch Nara was very much alive. I really needed to let my obsession with her go, but darn it. She'd said terrible things about Echo and I couldn't bring her up without Echo knowing about our meeting.

"How about the Immortal, Valkyrie, and Grimnir girlfriends?"

Echo completely ignored the car that pulled up behind us, and he took my hand. "Listen, *Cora mia*. You want me to tell you I never hooked up with my kind? I can't. I did. Will my exes cross our paths? Possibly. Would they want a repeat of history?" The owner of the car behind us backed up, honked, and gave us the finger as he shot by.

Echo's eyes narrowed on the car.

"Don't," I warned.

"A blown out tire should teach him to respect other motorists."

"You stopped at a stop sign, Echo, and didn't move. You started it."

"Then I'll end it." He started the car and stepped on the gas. In seconds, he'd caught up with the poor guy.

"Echo, leave him alone. You're just trying to avoid the question."

He slowed down. "What question?"

"Would you hook up with your exes?"

He chuckled. "Nope. They hate my guts."

"Why? Did you cheat on them?"

"No." He shook his head. "I never cheat. I always make a clean break. It's not my fault they bored me after a few months." He indicated and made a right turn onto Main Street. "I've been told no woman was sane enough to put up with my bullshit. I could be the last man on earth and they wouldn't touch me with a beanpole. I would die alone and miserable." He rolled his eyes. "Some were just plain cruel. One hoped I'd catch some rune-resistant disease and die, just so they could reap my soul and tether it to a brothel. Another hoped my jewels would shrivel and fall off," he added, wincing.

I was laughing hard by the time he finished, whatever jealousy I'd felt gone.

He grinned as he pulled up outside La Nonne, an Italian restaurant I'd driven past yet never visited. He switched off the engine, took my hand again, brought it to his lips, and kissed my knuckles. "You are stuck with me. No woman wants me except you, doll-face."

"Good. And if you ever thought of walking out on me, I wouldn't insult you or threaten to hurt your jewels."

"Thank you." He came around to my door, and opened it. He gripped my waist, lifted me down, and brought my body flush with his. "I know you love me too much to try to hurt me."

So full of himself. I gave him a toothy grin, before delivering my salvo. "Oh, I wouldn't *try*. I'd personally chop them off then keep you around for the rest of our lives. We'll see how fast you become un-bored."

Echo was still laughing when we started toward the restaurant. Most restaurants were on Main Street, which had enough parking up front and around the back. The more secluded La Nonne was on a side street and the main parking was across the street. Souls appeared from the shadows.

"Get lost," Echo snarled.

"Be nice." I waved to one woman. "I'll help you later," I mouthed to another.

"No, she won't. Tonight is her night off, so leave her alone."

He tried for the rest of the walk, but I could feel his mounting frustration. I was getting used to souls popping up whenever I was out and about. Usually, they ran from him.

Inside, the hostess led us to a table, handed us the menus, and promised to send a server. Her eyes lingered on Echo as she poured water into two glasses, but he was completely oblivious, his focus on me.

"This is nice." I glanced around. Linen tablecloths. Fresh flowers. Romantic lighting. I liked it. I didn't care what I ate. I was on a date with Echo. Then something occurred to me. He was a stranger around my town and wouldn't know local, fancy restaurants like this. "How did you find it?"

"I know friends who know places and swear by their food and services."

Torin. He was the food expert around here. The server was annoyingly bubbly, but the breadsticks were warm and garlicky, and we got extra olive oil dip. She must have forgotten she'd brought us some, or she needed a second look at Echo.

We were munching when he excused himself. I watched him disappear outside. I had been aware of the souls peering at us through the glass window. By the time Echo came back, they were all gone.

"Were you nice to them?"

"Very." He touched my cheek. "I didn't reap them."

That didn't mean he hadn't threatened them. When he looked over my shoulder and groaned, I turned, expecting to see more souls. Instead Blaine Chapman nodded at us. Blaine was an Immortal and friend of our local Valkyries. On his arm was Jennifer Sorenson.

Jen was the co-captain of the cheer squad. She and Blaine's ex-girlfriend could never stand each other. Possibly because she'd been eyeing Blaine, like, forever. Jen slithered from guy to guy without caring about their girlfriends.

"My favorite Immortal," Echo mumbled. He was such a liar. He couldn't stand Blaine.

"And my least favorite cheerleader."

Echo's eyebrow rose. "Why? You're prettier than she is."

My jaw dropped. "You think I can't stand her because of her looks? I'm not that vain. She steals other people's boyfriends." I glanced at Jen. She'd found us and her eyes were eating up Echo. Vamp. "I'm prettier than she is?"

"Don't ever doubt it." He leaned across the table and planted a slow one on my lips. "Why do you think we're drawing attention?"

Probably because of him. I turned my head to check out the other customers, but he turned my chin and kissed me again.

"Do you two want to find a room?" Blaine asked, and my cheeks warmed.

"Very original, Chapman," Echo said.

"Always nice to chat with you, Echo. Short and sweet." More like short and tense. Blaine winked at me. "Hey, gorgeous."

Once upon a time, I'd thought he was the hottest guy in school. Raine and I had even drooled over his hot bod when he was the QB. With his topaz eyes and wavy brown hair, he was still one of the hottest guys around. He just didn't do anything for me now.

"Hey, handsome," I said. "Fancy meeting you here."

"The food and the setting are a big draw."

Echo made a derisive sound between a chuckle and a snort. "More like spying for St. James. Tell him I'm a choirboy tonight." He glanced around. "A few oglers are pushing their luck, but they're safe."

"The night is still young," Blaine said.

Echo's eyes flashed. "Go away, Chapman."

"I'm Jennifer Sorenson but everyone calls me Jen," she said, leaning down, invading Echo's space and blocking us out. She must have gotten tired of being ignored, and Blaine hadn't introduced her, which was unlike him. He was the quintessential gentlemen and even dressed the part. Very preppy. "I think I've seen you around the school, Echo," Jen added.

Echo shuddered. "I'm way past high school, sweetheart, but I stop by now and then for someone I can't resist." He slid his hand across the table and took mine, threading our fingers.

Jen gave him a tiny smile and stood. Serious disappointment and envy filled her eyes when she glanced at me. "Cora."

"Jen." She must have ditched Drake again. "I heard you'll be cheering for the Beavers."

"I haven't decided yet. So, Echo, are you in college?"

"Yes. If you two don't mind, I'd like to devote the rest of the evening to my lovely companion here. Chapman, let's talk later."

A look I couldn't explain passed between them, and Blaine nodded. He took Jen's arm and escorted her to their table.

Echo had a way of making everyone around him pale in comparison, so ignoring the other customers and focusing on him was easy. He might act possessive and admit he didn't like sharing me, but he wouldn't punch men who ogled me. Except when he shot death glares at the two college guys at the adjacent table, dinner passed smoothly. I fed him some of my chicken fettuccine, and he gave me his meatballs, then laughed when I licked my lips. The few times I looked up, I caught Jen's envious eyes on us.

"We'll pass," Echo said to dessert when the waitress came to clear our table.

Now that was a surprise. Echo had a serious sweet tooth. My poison was junk food. "Don't mind me."

"I have plans for dessert." He pulled out his wallet and placed enough money on the table to cover the bill and a very generous tip.

I was intrigued, but he didn't give me time to ask. We left the restaurant, strolled down the sidewalk, and crossed the street. The night was pretty cool, and I wasn't surprised when Echo removed his coat, draped it over my shoulders, and pulled me close as we headed to his car.

"My parents want you to come to dinner next weekend," I said.

He groaned.

"Hey." I elbowed him. "Drop the attitude."

"He's going to grill me again."

"Then you need a cover story," I said, turning to face him.

"I have one."

"Really? Since when?"

He chuckled at my incredulous tone and skimmed my temple with his lips. "Since an hour ago." He unlocked the door of the SUV, opened it, and made sure I was seated before he went to his seat. "I'm majoring in economics and minoring in history. I plan to go to business school, preferably at whatever college you'll be attending next fall. And oh, the reason I changed schools is because of Blaine's family."

"I don't understand."

"Immortals offer us and Valkyries support. He'll back up whatever story I tell any Mortal, including your family. Remember, I already told them my parents died when I was a child. If they want details, I was raised by a distant aunt who's dead now. My parents put my money in a trust fund controlled by Blaine's father, which will explain the surprise I promised you."

He had everything covered, but would Blaine really support his story? Echo almost snapped the poor guy's neck because he'd thought Blaine had hurt me.

Then what he'd said registered. "What surprise?"

He chuckled and gunned the engine. "If I tell, it won't be a surprise."

CHAPTER 7. BEST BREAKFAST

At first, I thought we were going to Raine's, but we passed the turnoff and headed east. Then I was sure our destination was the mansion, where the Valkyries lived, but he took a left turn and kept going. A few more turns and he pulled up outside a nice house on the southeast part of town. The house was at a dead end and had a cute wooden fence separating it from the neighbor's. Lights were on, but I didn't see movement behind the curtains.

"Whose place is this?" I asked when he opened the passenger door and offered me his hand.

"Let's find out." He pulled out a key and placed it in my hand.

The patio lights came on when we stepped onto the porch. Six white pillars and a low-lying metal rail wrapped around the porch, and a heavy-duty mat welcomed us.

I unlocked the door, an idea taking root in my head. I glanced at Echo, but all he did was indicate that I go ahead with a smug smirk. The living room was unfurnished but spacious. New paneling. Spotless, plush carpet. It had the smell of a newly remodeled home, and the room temperature was on the cold side. I spied an electric fireplace, but it wasn't on. I wasn't complaining though. Echo's coat was keeping me warm.

Echo grabbed my hand. "Come on. I'll show you around."

There were two self-contained bedrooms. The master suite had a huge bathroom. An arch connected the dining area to the kitchen. The backyard was enclosed and had a flat backyard and wooden swing set. Echo didn't say anything until I turned and faced him.

"What do you think?" he asked.

"I like it. Is it ours?"

He smiled, wrapped his arms around my waist, and pulled me close. "Not yet, but I'm working on it. There are two more we should check out before deciding."

He'd said *we*. Internal Squeal! I wrapped my arms around his neck. "What if I decide to attend a college in Portland or California?"

"You can stay in the dorms if you want, but I'll get a house in town in case you want to visit me." He wiggled his brows. "The whole point here, doll-face, is to have a place we can hang out without stepping on some roommate's toes or worrying about your parents. But that doesn't mean you shouldn't enjoy the rest of high school or have a wonderful experience in college."

"Really? You do know that the college experience is really a four-year paid vacation filled with frat parties, keg parties, girls' nights out, puking your guts out, and hookups, don't you?"

He paled. "I'm trying here, sweetheart. Don't rub it in."

I reached up and kissed him. Even in heels, he topped me by several inches. When he lifted me clear off the ground, I wrapped my legs around him. The kiss grew intense fast.

"I was just kidding," I whispered when we stopped.

"No, doll-face. I've been reading about what goes on in colleges and trying hard to pretend it doesn't matter, but this is a rite of passage. So yes," he caressed my cheek, "attend frat parties, flirt with some idiot Mortal, go to concerts, and have sit-ins and rallies. I'll wait." He planted a kiss on my forehead. "There's absolutely nothing I wouldn't do for you. I'll even hold your hair back while you puke your guts out."

Silly guy. Like I'd attend parties without him. I planned to drag him to every party, concert, and lecture, give him a taste of campus life. Create memories to replace the bad ones from his past. "We'll see."

"There's nothing to see. I'll willingly share you no matter how hard and painful, or how much I want to snap some pimply-faced coed's neck." His lips met mine in one possessive kiss that belied his words. He lifted his head and whispered against my lips, "You want dessert?"

"I thought this was my dessert."

He chuckled. "I love the way your naughty mind works, but I was talking about a different dessert."

He surprised me when he headed to the kitchen, set me on the counter, went to the fridge, and pulled out a plastic bag. I had expected him to create a portal and go to his place, but this was nice.

I hopped down and followed him to the living room, where he proceeded to turn on the electric fireplace heater. I peered inside the plastic bag and grinned. Two tubs of ice cream—rum raisin and cookie dough—my favorite frozen yogurt, luscious lemon, and plastic spoons.

We settled in front of the fireplace, lying on our stomachs side-by-side. We ate in silence. I nudged him with my shoulder. "Did you really mean it? You know, about doing anything for me?"

He hummed as he savored a scoop of rum-raisin ice cream. "Anything."

"Help me with Dev."

"Anything but that." He went back to his ice cream as though the subject was closed.

"Come on, Echo. I've decided to help him, but his issues—"

"Are none of my business. You said you'd stay away from dark souls."

I groaned. He just had to bring up that. "Other dark souls. Listen—"

"Not when it comes to that jackass." He stared me down with wolfish eyes. "I admire what you do for souls, and I know I can't convince you to ignore him. I've also learned that once you make up your mind, there's no stopping you. You are stubborn and opinionated, yet sensitive and kind. I love all those qualities in you, but I also don't forget or forgive those who've betrayed me. Dev is at the top of that list, so screw his issues."

My jaw dropped. I sat, and for a brief moment words escaped me. Finally, I found my tongue. "How can you be so rigid and—?"

"Honest?" He cocked his eyebrows, leaning on one elbow and tilting his body, so he could look at me. "Quite easily. He means nothing to me. You want to help him, go ahead. I'm not going to stop you."

"But—"

"If he hurts you or makes you shed a tear, I will put all my powers and resources into tormenting his worthless soul, and I'll enjoy every second of it."

I closed my eyes and blew out a breath. "If you interrupt me again, Echo, I swear I'm going to bitch slap you into next century."

He chuckled, noticed I was serious, and muttered, "Sorry. I didn't mean to be rude."

"Oh, you did, you... you impossible man." I jumped to my feet. "You're so stuck in your ways you'll never change."

He rolled on his back, propped up his body with his elbows and watched me pace. "You're just pissed I'm not a bleeding heart like you."

I gave him the finger.

He grinned. "Crass, *Cora mia*. Really beneath you."

It was, but I didn't care. "You're so petty, vindictive, and vengeful."

"And proud of it."

I stopped by his side, glaring at him as though to force him to do my bidding. "You're never going to change. You said you're willing to do it for me then turn around and act like a douche. What's the difference?"

"I'm willing to change for you, not him."

Why couldn't he see it was the same thing? "I'm going home."

I turned to leave, but he caught my ankle and yanked. I screamed as I lost my balance, but he was there to break my fall. His arms wound tightly around me. When I struggled to free myself, he trapped my legs with his.

"Let me go, you Neanderthal," I screamed.

"I can't." He buried his face in my neck and whispered, "I wouldn't know what to do if you left me, *Cora mia*."

I stopped struggling. Just like that, he sucked the fight out of me. "I didn't mean it that way. I'm mad at you and disappointed, but that's just now."

He lifted his head and studied me. His expression grew pensive. "How long are you going to stay angry with me?"

"What kind of question is that?"

"I just want to know, so I can mentally prepare myself."

"I don't know." I wiggled and tried to get out of his arms again, but he tightened his grip. "A week."

He paled.

"Two days," I relented.

"Can I at least get a kiss?"

"No."

"Can I hold you while you sleep?"

"When you're mad at someone, Echo, you don't want to hear or see them. Kind of like the way you feel toward Dev."

Echo winced. He let go of me and stared at the ceiling. "Fine. I can be on my own for two days. Done it for centuries and survived." He glanced at me from the corner of his eyes to see my reaction, but I wasn't backing down, even though I felt like an ass-hat. Both he and Dev needed closure. Echo was just too stubborn to see it.

I got to my feet and watched him pick up our leftover ice cream. Part of me wanted to go to him, wrap my arms around him, and admit I wasn't really angry. Another wanted to yell at him.

He put everything back in the plastic bag and led the way to the car. He didn't press his hand on the small of my back or take my hand as he often did, making me feel so alone.

"It's his fault, the snake," he mumbled as we took off.

I knew he meant Dev, so I said nothing.

His grip tightened on the steering wheel. "Even dead, he manages to screw with my life."

I rolled my eyes. He could be such a drama queen. Once again, I was tempted to reach out and reassure him, but giving in to him might become a habit. Echo, I'd learned, loved getting his way too much.

He sulked until we were halfway home, then pulled a one-eighty. "You know what we could be doing now instead of driving you home while imagining the next forty-eight hours?"

I sighed, refusing to take the bait. I stared out the window at the passing scenery. A few more souls popped up here and there.

"Making out," he said. "I could be kissing you right now. Want to know where?" He didn't wait for my answer as he warmed up to the subject. "Your neck at your favorite spot. I'd start at the sensitive area behind your ear and work my way to your shoulder while you encourage me with sighs and slight tremors that usually drive me out of my mind. But I won't stop and feast on your lips. Not yet. The sounds you make are like a shot of pure endorphin. I'd savor your silken skin, move across your neck to the pulse beating furiously at the base of your neck, and feel your heartbeat under my lips. Then I'd move to the other side of your neck..."

My breath quickened as I got sucked into his word play. He didn't play fair and telling him to shut up would only egg him on, so I sat there, counted souls we passed, and tried to tell my heart to behave.

Seven... eight... nine...

"Want to know where my hands would be all that time? Since you always grip my head to hold it in place, I'd worship your warm, soft skin, run the tips of my fingers up and down your arm, before caressing down your side."

He distracted me at thirteen, the jerk.

"Nothing turns me on like the curves and dips of your body, the responses you give so freely and unselfishly. When you moan and whisper my name, buckle and writhe as you seek closer contact, beg me for more."

I was sweating, crossing and uncrossing my legs. Part of me wished he would stop. The siren in me welcomed the images his words evoked.

"Want to know where your hands would go next?"

I almost said yes and pressed my lips tight.

"I know you do. All over me like always. You have no idea what your hands do to my senses, *Cora mia*. This time, I wouldn't let you mess with my insanity. I'd do something I've never done before."

He stopped and all I could think about was *what?* He deliberately tortured me with his silence as he narrowed the distance to my home. I was close to giving in and begging him to continue when he chuckled.

"Do you remember the silk ties you bought me before I came to your parents' house for the first time?" Again he didn't wait for my response. "I've been planning to put them to good use. Maybe take both of your hands and tie them above your head, giving me freedom to love you in ways you couldn't possibly fathom. I could…"

He entered the road leading to my farm, and I wanted to cry. Beg him to stop the car and tell me more. Forget he was deliberately tormenting me and jump him.

"Look, home sweet home," he murmured, and I could tell he was smiling. The despicable man. I sat there not moving when he stopped the car.

"You're a jackass," I whispered in a voice I didn't recognize.

He laughed, jumped down, and came around the car to open my door. He stepped back and bowed. Ignoring him, I got down and marched to my door, aware of his smug presence. I turned and faced him, not sure what to do.

He leaned in, and my lips tingled with anticipation. He was going to kiss me. Thank the gods. Our noses touched. I stopped breathing.

"Goodnight, doll-face," he whispered. "Have hot, hot dreams about me." Then he stepped back, smirking, and waved.

My jaw dropped as he turned and sauntered back to the SUV, whistling and twirling his car key. Arrogant bastard. Still, I couldn't help admiring the way his jeans hugged his narrow hips. It didn't matter what the man wore, he rocked it.

"Hey," I called out.

He turned and cocked an eyebrow. I beckoned him with a finger. The triumphant smile on his lips said he thought I'd caved. When he reached the first step leading to the porch, I shrugged off his dinner jacket.

"Tonight, I'm going to be thinking of you when I…" I touched my lips and sighed. I handed him his jacket with a tiny smile. "Thank you. Nice dreams."

He was the one staring after me when I turned and entered the house. My parents had gone to bed, so I didn't have to explain my smug smile.

***

Where was Echo?

I'd been sure he'd ignore me and then hound me until I stopped being angry with him. He didn't sneak into my room on Saturday night, and he wasn't there when I woke up the next day.

I glared at the ceiling, wondering when he'd appear. Hoping he'd appear. Talk about being whipped. Twelve hours and I missed him like crazy.

I kicked off the covers and sat up. I caught my reflection in the mirror and sighed. I needed a trim. Since it was a Sunday, maybe just a home treatment.

I headed downstairs to make breakfast for my parents. My parents slept in on Sundays, leaving me in charge of the kitchen. I was no Martha Stewart or Mom, who was an amazing cook, but she'd taught me well. Between whining and daydreaming about boy bands, I had picked up a thing or two.

The scent of bacon and pancakes reached me as soon as I hit the stairs. I frowned and checked at my watch. Eight. Mom must have gotten up early. Dad's cooking was a cross between dog food and pond water, so he couldn't be the one turning our kitchen into food heaven.

I angled my head and started downstairs. Usually, Mom would be humming or watching morning news as she cooked. She must have heard something she didn't like. She was weird like that. Annoying news often meant turning off the TV as though the very act made the incident go away.

"Hey, sleepy head," a familiar voice said when I reached the bottom of the stairs, and my jaw slammed down.

Echo was in my kitchen. Cooking. A cup of coffee in his hand.

"What are you...?"

A pile of steaming strawberry pancakes sat in the middle of the kitchen table, which was set for three. My stomach growled. They looked so good. Another plate had a pile of crispy bacon that had my mouth watering. Eggs were on the pan on top of the stove. The setting was straight out of some food magazine.

"Are you crazy?" I whispered, keeping my voice low, trying to sound disapproving and failing miserably. "My parents will be downstairs any second."

"Is that a way to greet someone offering you this feast?" he asked. "Besides," he spread his arms, "they can't see me."

Of course, they couldn't. Runes blazed on his skin. Like last night, he was dressed in normal clothes—jeans and a T-shirt. He didn't play fair. He knew I loved it when he went all boy-next-door. No one could wear jeans like Echo.

"Why?" I asked, trying to focus on our conversation and not the hot vibes he was sending my way.

He sipped his coffee and cocked an eyebrow. "Why can't they see me?"

My eyes narrowed menacingly when all I wanted to do was slide into his arms. Gah, I was a fool for this man.

As though he read me, he chuckled and sauntered toward me. "You're angry with me, and I'd rather you weren't."

"So, this is an apology?"

He flashed a smile. "Is it working?"

That sexy smile was irresistible, and he knew it. A quick glance in the garbage and I spied the telltale boxes from his favorite Miami restaurant. They make the most amazing fresh fruit pancakes ever.

"What if my parents had walked in here while you were transferring your treats?"

"Have you seen me move? Faster than The Flash," he bragged. "You still angry with me?"

"Will you agree to meet with Dev?"

"No."

"Then I'm still disappointed in you."

"Angry to disappointment is progress." He reached out to touch my cheek, but I stepped back. His hand dropped to his side, a scowl settling on his face. "I guess no touching. At least we're talking. You ignored me during our drive home yesterday."

"Echo—"

"You know, there's something breathtaking about you first thing in the morning."

Was he serious? I reached up to touch my messy hair.

He grinned. "Hair mussed, eyes heavy-lidded, lips soft, and body relaxed from sleep. You look vulnerable and sweet, yet utterly sexy. I want to pick you up and tuck you somewhere safe where no one can hurt you, but at the same time, I want to kiss you senseless. Get lost in your warmth."

My mind went foggy. I wanted to run into his arms and forget about our fight and Dev.

"You get me, doll-face," he added, reaching out to twirl a lock of my hair. "Be mad at me all you want, but I'll keep coming back and showing you how much I love you until you forgive…" he looked toward the stairs, "me."

Dad's voice reached us first, then Mom's laughter. They were coming downstairs. Panicking, I debated whether to ask Echo to leave or stay. I opened my mouth, and "I love you too" came out.

He smiled. "I know. Want me to leave?"

I swear he was a mind reader. Now that he'd voiced my thoughts, it sounded selfish on my part, especially after what he'd done. "Um, the boxes."

He stared at the garbage can, then glanced at me with an expectant expression. Mom and Dad were at the top of the stairs. Grrr, what to do?

"Am I staying or leaving, doll-face?" Echo sounded serious, like he'd go if I asked him to, but his expression said he wanted to stay. I wanted him to stay, but first, a few ground rules.

"Will you behave?"

He chuckled.

"I'm serious, Echo."

He pressed a hand against his chest, golden eyes gleaming. "What could I possibly do while cloaked?"

A lot. Most Sundays, he liked to watch me make my parents breakfast, wolfing down some food while I cooked. But he usually left before they came downstairs. "You can stay *if* you promise to behave."

"Anything for you, doll-face. Oh, you may want to head to the stove and pretend to be serving the eggs."

He followed me to the stove and stood close, our bodies almost touching. He leaned in and smelled my hair. My unwashed hair. I cringed.

"I want to kiss you," he whispered.

I knew it! Behaving was not coded in his DNA. I turned to tell him to behave or else, but the look in his eyes stopped me.

"I miss your scent," he whispered. "Holding you while you sleep. Waking up next to you. I miss your warmth," he added, wolfish eyes gleaming. "And the way you open your eyes slowly in the morning, then quickly squeeze them tight as though to will the morning away."

I couldn't drag my eyes away from him, but I knew exactly where my parents were based on their voices. Halfway down the stairs. Bet I would see their legs if I turned and looked, but I couldn't look away from Echo.

"But most of all," Echo continued, "I miss the way you burrow into my chest and breathe softly against my skin while you sleep, reminding me how lucky I am."

I was a puddle of goo.

"Something smells good," Dad said at the foot of the stairs, and I glanced toward him, wishing I could send them back upstairs, offer to serve them breakfast in bed. But Mom was staring at the set table with an appreciative grin.

"Oh, honey, this looks amazing," she said.

"It's all in the presentation, future mother-in-law," Echo said, bowing.

I fought a smile. "The eggs are ready, too."

"The things I do for you, *Cora mia*. Taking credit for my work. Forcing Chef Lavre to prepare this meal after he'd finished serving breakfast."

"Thank you," I said, sweeping the eggs onto a serving bowl.

"No, we should be thanking you, sweetheart," Dad said, erroneously assuming I'd thanked them. He'd moved closer and was pouring coffee into mugs. He pressed a kiss to my temple. "The food looks good, and we brought our appetites."

A giggle escaped Mom, and my face heated. My parents weren't usually overtly affectionate, but I could always tell when they'd made love. They'd have lost-in-their-own-world moments, which were both endearing and disturbing. Moms weren't supposed to giggle, and Dads should only wear certain expressions when their children weren't around. He handed Mom her drink, kissed her, taking his time, and sat. She giggled again.

Echo studied them with a gleam in his eyes. "I think your mom got some—"

"Shut up," I said through clenched teeth, my face flaming.

"What did you say, dear?" Mom asked, serving the pancakes.

"Syrup," I improvised. "Do you want maple or strawberry?"

"Nice come back," Echo said.

"Maple is good. We might be out of strawberry." Then she looked at Dad, and they both smiled. I wasn't sure what that smile was, but if it had anything to do with last night, I was swearing off strawberry syrup.

"I think your parents are into something kinky," Echo chimed in, dodging my footsteps. "I wonder what *we* could do with—"

I stomped on his foot.

"Ouch! What was that for?"

"Go away," I mouthed and carried the eggs and syrup to the table. I pulled out a chair and sat, aware that he came to stand behind my chair. My parents gushed over the food while Echo continued to push my boundaries. His elbows on my chair, he stroked my shoulders and responded to every comment they made as though he was part of the conversation. He twirled a lock of my hair. Telling him to stop would be pointless, so I let him.

"This is great coffee, pumpkin," Dad said, sipping his coffee. "I couldn't have made it any better."

"Score," Echo said.

"Where did you get fresh strawberries?" Mom asked. "I used the last batch when I made shortcake a few days ago."

"Oops," Echo said.

I was so going to make him pay for this. With all the big secrets I kept from my parents, I didn't want to add another. "Echo bought some last night."

"What a thoughtful young man," Mom said, and Dad nodded.

Echo chuckled. "They adore me, and I've barely started impressing them."

I leaned back, pretended to scratch my nose, and mouthed, "Go away."

"Come to the pantry with me," Echo whispered.

I ignored him and continued to eat. The pancakes were amazing, and the bacon crispy.

"Want to know why?" he whispered, pressing a kiss on my shoulder and reminding me I was still wearing a tank top and pajama pants. He skimmed my arm with his knuckles, sending a delicious shiver through me. "I want you to kiss me before I leave."

"Are you cold, hun?" Mom asked and reached out to rub my arms, almost touching Echo.

I moved back. "No, I'm okay."

"When is Echo coming to dinner?" Dad asked.

"Tonight," Echo said, but I couldn't help teasing him.

"I don't know. I'll know when he comes back in two days. Between finals and his work, he barely has time for anything else." His hands left my shoulder.

I waited for him to do something else. When he didn't, I looked over my shoulder and frowned. He was gone.

Breakfast lost its appeal.

I spent the rest of the morning looking over my shoulder while helping Mom with laundry, hoping to find him. It took me twice as long to finish my chores because I kept expecting him to appear.

Restless, I popped into Raine's room, but she wasn't there. The black cat I'd met yesterday was curled up on the window seat. She lifted her head and stared at me suspiciously.

"Still here?"

Her answer was a disdainful look.

"Yeah, right back at you," I said.

She stood and stretched, then curled back again on the seat, her eyes on me.

"What? Think I want to steal something? Tell your mistress I stopped by."

"I don't think she speaks yet," Femi said from behind me, and I whipped around. She was framed in the mirror portal entrance. Behind her was the living room. "Hey, doll. I heard sounds up here and thought Raine was back."

"Hey, Femi," I said, trying not to look guilty. I was so used to popping in and out of Raine's room I'd never thought how someone else would perceive it. "Just stopped by to see if she was home."

"She left with Torin. Have you checked the mansion?"

The mansion was home to the rest of the Valkyries and Immortals in our little town. "Heading there now." An awkward silence followed. "Oh, uh, how's Mr. Cooper doing?"

Femi grinned. "Better now that Svana is home. He even went for a walk today."

"Wow. That's amazing."

"Love has a way of making us do the impossible."

Raine's father had terminal cancer and, for months, had been bedridden while her mother faced the Valkyrie Council in Asgard. My resolve to help Dev and Echo increased. Yes, love could make us do the impossible.

CHAPTER 8. UNEXPECTED ATTACK

I cranked up the radio as I left for school on Monday. I was halfway there when a cold draft filled the inside of my car. My first thought was Echo, but then Dev appeared in my rear window. Major disappointment coursed through me. He was the last person I wanted to see or talk to now.

"Sorry, can't talk now," I mumbled.

Dev did his gurgling chuckle sound, but my decoder of soul language was off.

He didn't ask before slithering through the CD slot of my car. Static replaced MTKO, who was singing their latest hit song. Then the announcer said, "This is ninety-four-point-five, Kayville's number one pop radio station. Talk to me, doll-face."

For a second, I was too shocked to speak. Then I realized it was Dev. He sounded like the announcer, American accent and all. "Don't call me that."

"Uh-oh, you're in a bad mood. You talked to Echo and he stormed off."

"No, he didn't."

"Of course he did. He wouldn't be Echo if he didn't get angry and melodramatic. He didn't throw you out, did he? I saw the two of you having dinner Saturday night."

My jaw dropped. "Oh, now you're stalking me?"

He ignored my question and shot back, "What did he say?"

"He'll think about it," I fibbed, feeling terrible.

Dev sighed. "You're a terrible liar. At least you tried. I'll try again in a century or two." He sounded so sad and defeated I felt worse.

"Tell me something I can use to persuade him. I know I can convince him if he knows why you want to talk to him."

"I love your attitude, Cora, but I know Echo. Once he makes up his mind, there's no changing it. How about some music?"

"No, music. Talk to me. You said things weren't what they seem. What did you mean? Were you framed?"

The radio crackled, and Bon Jovi's *It's My Life* filled the car. Dev sung along.

Un-freaking-believable. Too bad he sounded good for a dead man.

I reached out and switched off the radio. "Listen, Dev. I want to help you. No, I *need* to help you. Not because I'm on some stupid mission to help every soul with a sob story." Gah, I was a total wimp and a pushover when it came to sob stories. I even helped criminals. Petty criminals, psychopaths, perverts. Their crimes weren't written on their foreheads or anything helpful like that. "Echo regrets what happened between you two."

"Did he say that?" Dev sounded hopeful.

"Uh, no, but I know Echo. He's never regretted the things he's done. Not turning your Druid brothers and sisters into Immortals, making sure he's on Hel duty for eternity just so he could punish the Romans who persecuted your people. He does what needs to be done and moves on. But when he talks about you, I can tell it bothers him. He needs to know why, Dev."

Silence followed.

"Why did you do it?" I asked.

Nothing. I waited. Bon Jovi was back on. I wasn't sure whether that meant Dev wouldn't talk to me. After a few seconds, I gave up. Soon I was humming along. The group was before my time, but I grew up hearing their songs because Mom had a crush on the lead singer or something.

I pulled up into the parking lot across from the school. Students hurried to the school building while others steamed the windows of their cars. Two girls walked by discussing school prom and reminding me of something I'd pushed aside after the battle with the Immortals. Junior prom was this Friday and the senior one was several weeks away. I planned to attend both. With Echo. Hopefully, we'd be talking by then.

I still hadn't picked up my dresses from Angie's Boutique. Because of my D-size cups, dresses off the rack never worked for me, unless I was going for spandex. I hated spandex.

I stared out the windshield as I waited for Dev to say something or slither out of the radio. Nothing happened. I wondered what he'd say or do if I gave him an ultimatum. Talk and get lost. Echo's face when he'd talked about Dev flashed in my head. No, I was doing this for Echo, too.

I glared at the dials, wishing I had the mental powers to bend them to my will. Seriously, Druids were the most stubborn and annoying men on earth.

I should talk to Raine about this. She was so level-headed she might just have the solution I needed. Plus, she'd understand about going the extra mile for someone you loved.

Torin's bike was missing from its usual place at the curb, which meant they hadn't arrived yet. He and Raine usually arrived about the same time as Andris, and Andris' SUV just pulled up beside Blaine's sports car. Blaine had given Jen a ride to school? Were they an item now? He could do so much better.

Ingrid saw me and waved. I like her. She was unlike her evil older sister Maliina who'd runed me and turned me into a soul magnet. In retrospect, I guess I owed Maliina. If she hadn't turned me and mimicked me, I would never have met Echo. Ingrid and Blaine were Immortal like me, though they were hundreds of years old.

A soul of an older man walked aimlessly around the parking lot and glanced toward me. Andris ignored him. Ingrid and Blaine probably didn't see him. They didn't need to. Immortals dealt with the living, not souls. Blaine had even told me he used runes so he wouldn't see souls.

"Dev?"

No response, just the NPR people talking about the Spring Fund Drive. "Listen. I want to help you, but I can't if you won't talk to me or try to at least meet me halfway."

More chances to win an NPR mug instead of the voice I wanted to hear. Annoyed by his silence, I switched off the engine and reached for my backpack. The moment I stepped out of the car, I spied Andris sauntering toward me.

He blew me a kiss. Androgynously beautiful, sarcastic, and a hoot and a half, Andris was a Valkyrie like Torin. When I wasn't with Echo, he was my second favorite guy to hang out with.

I was about to close the door when I noticed my cell phone in the front passenger seat. I reached for it, glared at my radio, and closed the car door.

"I appreciate what you're doing, Cora," Dev said, speaking from my cell phone and blindsiding me. I almost dropped my phone. He sounded like a male version of Siri. "Whether you succeed or not, it's been a pleasure meeting you."

"When did you...? Seriously, stop moving around without warning me. It's creeping me out."

"Okay, here goes. Tell Echo I did it because of Teléia."

Teléia? The woman Echo, Dev, and Rhys had a crush on? "What do you mean?"

"He'll understand once you tell him."

"Tell me more."

"No. There're people who don't want the truth known, so the less you know the better."

"That's a copout, Dev. I can protect myself."

"Not against Grimnirs. You barely became an Immortal."

"I have Echo," I bragged.

"Do you really want him going against the other Grimnirs to protect you? Again? The last ones he and your Valkyrie friends killed are not happy."

"Cora?" a student said from behind me, and I whipped around.

Jeff Lancaster, the super geek from my English class held out his hand. My keys dangled from his finger. "You dropped these."

"Oh." I took the keys. "Thanks, Jeff."

"Hi, Jeff," Dev said.

Jeff stared at my phone then me. "Um, hi?"

"Don't mind him," I said. "Shut up, Dev."

"I miss talking to people. You have no idea how lonely it gets inside electronics."

"Dev—" I glanced at Jeff and groaned. His eyes were locked on my phone like it was the freaking Holy Grail.

"You've upgraded Siri?" Jeff asked in a whisper.

I opened my mouth to say no, and inspiration hit. "Nah, this is a new app for androids. More interactive than anything out there."

"I haven't heard anything about it." He spoke slowly and inched closer. "Can I try it?"

"No." I put the phone in the pocket of my jacket. "I'm an apps tester." He gave me a suspicious look. I wasn't geeky enough to be a software tester, but he didn't have the guts to call me out. "So, this is FMEO."

He grinned. Using the acronym for "for my eyes only" just gave me some cred.

"Is this guy bothering you, Cora?" Andris asked, coming to stand behind Jeff. The poor guy froze, his expression shifting from curious to uneasy. One, Andris towered over him. Two, being associated with our popular and beloved QB, Torin, had some serious perks. Since everyone assumed Andris was Torin's cousin, they put up with his rudeness and tried not to piss him off.

"Nah. Jeff and I are buds. We were discussing homework, so bye-bye." Hopefully, Andris would get the clue and keep walking. As a Valkyrie, he could see things Mortals couldn't. Like a soul slithering from a cell.

"You heard her, Jeff. Shoo. Go away," Andris said rudely, deliberately misunderstanding me. "She's way, way out of your league, and she has a boyfriend who will break every little bone in your body if he catches you staring at her boobs again."

Jeff turned beet red, his eyes volleying between me and Andris. "I wasn't staring. I swear. She has this cool phone with, uh, with a new app—"

"Don't care. Run along," Andris said and wiggled his fingers dismissively.

Jeff took off as though the devil was on his tail. Maybe he had been staring at my chest, maybe he hadn't. Still...

"Why are you such an ass all the time, Andris? Or are all Valkyries douches?" I spoke aloud so Dev wouldn't come out while Andris was around.

"Mortals bore me and being nice to them serves no purpose." He glanced around. "Where's our resident grim reaper?"

"He should be here any minute, so go away."

"Can't." Andris leaned against my car and crossed his arms. "He told Torin dark souls were in town, and I want the deets. Have they been bothering you?"

"No. Just go."

He smirked. "Me thinks you want to get rid of me, blondie. Hiding something?"

For a self-absorbed guy, he saw way too much. "Fine. Come on. Let's go." The first bell was about to ring anyway. I started toward the crosswalk.

"I thought you were waiting for Echo."

"Not with you around." I glanced back, but he hadn't moved. "What?"

"Don't you feel it?"

"Feel what?"

"A presence," he said, glancing around.

My stomach dropped. Valkyries and Grimnirs could sense a soul faster than Immortals. The sound of Torin's Harley reached us. Great! The two of them would ferret out Dev and start asking questions I wasn't ready to answer.

"It's a... Aah."

I followed the direction of his gaze and groaned. Nara and Rhys stood under the trees lining the north end of the parking lot. With runes inking their skin, we were the only ones who could see them.

"Grimnirs," Andris said.

"Friends of Echo's," I corrected. "They probably want to talk. Just a sec." I started across the parking lot. He followed. "Privacy, Andris."

"Not happening. They don't look friendly."

"Ever met a friendly Grimnir other than Echo?"

A snicker escaped him. "Echo is friendly? Since when?"

I death rayed him with my eyes.

"Okay, tiger girlfriend. Go, but I'm going to hang around just in case. Tell them to stay cloaked. We try to blend in around here, and their Matrix-inspired garbs are not exactly high-school uniform."

"And your two-thousand-dollar cashmere sweater is?" I asked, glancing over my shoulder at him.

"This body is too fine for knockoffs." He smirked and tapped at his watch. "Hurry up or I'll leave."

"Please do." I turned, pulled out my cell phone, and whispered, "Dev, Nara and Rhys—"

"Are here," Dev finished. "I heard. Don't trust them."

I slipped the phone into my pocket, glanced back to make sure Andris was keeping his distance, and approached the dynamic duo. Andris was busy talking to some girl, probably another conquest.

***

"Where's Dev?" Nara asked.

I lifted my cell phone and pretended to talk into it. "Good morning to you too, Nara. Hi, Rhys." He gave a brief nod. No smile. Still, I directed the question to him. "What's going on?"

"Have you seen—?"

"We were tracking Dev and lost him near your farm," Nara cut off Rhys. "Are you hiding him in your house? Because we'll have no problem ransacking the place until we find him."

My jaw dropped, anger building fast. "You go anywhere near my family and I'll—"

"Do what?" she snapped.

"Make you sorry," I shot back.

She laughed. "How? By sending Echo after me? Please, like that's supposed to scare me. He's not been the same since he met you. Before you, no one would think twice about crossing him. Now? He's weak and pathetic. An idiot in love."

No one called Echo weak. My grip tightened on the strap of my backpack, the urge to swing it at her washing over me.

It didn't matter that she wouldn't feel it or my backpack might end up being the casualty.

"You know what, Nara? I don't feel like listening to your voice, so zip it. And FYI, I'd watch who you call weak or pathetic. Echo is still the best Grimnir around here." I ignored her again and focused on Rhys. I angled my phone in case anyone was watching. "What do you want with Dev?"

Rhys' hand shot out and gripped Nara's arm when she opened her mouth, effectively silencing her.

"A lot of our people lost family members because of Dev," he said, "and they haven't forgotten or forgiven him. Every time he's sighted, the word spreads fast. Others are coming, Cora, and they won't be nice."

He made it sound like a horde of angels of death were about to descend upon us. "So, you're here to, uh, warn me?"

"Yes," Rhys said.

"No," Nara said at the same time. "We are here for Dev. We take him, and you go back to your little love nest or whatever you and Echo have going on here."

Oh, that must kill her. I ignored her. "Why can't you guys just leave the poor guy alone? He's dead."

"Most of the people he betrayed ended up in Hel's Hall," Rhys said. "They're pissed, and they've been waiting a long time for him. They want him on Corpse Strand, but *we*," he nodded at Nara, who made a face, "plan to protect him."

I wasn't buying their benevolence. "Sorry, guys. Souls come to me for help, and until I help them, they're under my protection. Mine and Echo's. You can have Dev after I'm done with him."

I turned to leave and waved to Andris, who was now charming a different girl though his eyes kept drifting to me. He waved me over, studying the Grimnirs with narrowed eyes. The second he looked away, everything happened fast.

A hand closed around my neck and yanked me backwards against a hard body, knocking the air out of my lungs. My backpack slipped from my shoulder and landed on my foot.

"Listen to me, you stupid girl," Nara snarled in my ear, squeezing my neck.

"Nara, stop it," Rhys yelled at the same time.

I engaged my runes to stop the pain and clawed at her hand with little effect. She was stronger, and she'd also engaged her runes. If the students hurrying past thought my posture was weird, they didn't show it. My sight grew blurry, and my ears started to ring.

"Damn it, Nara," Rhys said. The pressure around my neck eased, and I knew he was breaking his cousin's chokehold. "Think about what you're doing."

"I will not put up with her meddling just because she happens to be Echo's latest playthi—"

Blurs appeared in my periphery and they were gone, the force of the attack yanking me off my feet. Before I landed on the ground, someone grabbed me around the waist and stopped me from falling on my ass. A familiar face came into focus.

"Raine?"

"You okay?" she asked, looking furious.

I nodded. A few feet away Torin had Rhys slammed against a tree, his feet dangling off the ground. From his flexed muscles, he was barely containing himself. The Grimnir didn't look scared, but he wasn't fighting back either, which said a lot about him. They both had their runes engaged and fully cloaked. The few students walking past only saw Raine and me. Raine and I often hugged or walked arm-in-arm, so seeing us together was nothing new.

"Get off me, Valkyrie," Nara screamed and tried to dislodge Andris who was straddling her and pinning her hands to her sides. Andris might act like he was above getting down and dirty, but he stepped up and delivered in his cocky style.

"Come on, sweetheart," he crooned. "You know having me on top is the closest you'll ever get to Asgard, so enjoy the moment. Cora, sorry I was late to the party."

Nara hurled insults at him, twisting and bucking.

"Nara!" Rhys snapped, and she stopped. He looked down at Torin, eyes narrowing. "I don't want to fight you, Valkyrie, so let me—"

"Shut up," Torin cut him off. "Cora. Come here."

I'd never heard Torin use a voice like that. It was the obey-or-else voice. I obeyed. Or else Rhys' neck might go bye-bye.

"Did they hurt you?" His voice softened.

"No." I glanced at Nara who'd stopped struggling and was glaring at me. I could tattle on her, but it wouldn't serve any purpose. I was already worried about what Echo would do to them when he found out about this.

Torin studied me as though he knew I'd lied. Then he nodded and focused on Rhys. "When I let you go, Grimnir, disappear. If I catch you anywhere near her, you will not like it. Cora is under our protection. You mess with her, you mess with us."

"But she has a soul that belongs to us," Nara protested. Andris still had her trapped.

"He is under my protection." Everyone turned to stare at me as though I was a nutcase. Been there. Done that. Hated it. "I promised to help him," I added defiantly.

"Dev betrayed our people," Nara interjected.

"We don't care," Torin snapped. "If Cora gave him a promise, she'll keep it." He let go of Rhys and did something I'd noticed the football players do after roughing up someone. He adjusted Rhys' collar and brushed invisible lint from his duster. "Now be a good Grimnir and get out of town."

Rhys bristled. Obviously, he didn't like Torin's condescending voice. When he spoke, his voice was scathing. "Others will come for him."

Torin shrugged. "We'll deal with them, too." He glanced at Andris and gave him a nod. Andris jumped up and offered Nara a hand.

If a look could kill, he'd be barbecued. She ignored him, got up, and said through gritted teeth, "We'll meet again, Valkyrie."

"I'm free Wednesday nights," Andris said, opening his arms. "Don't bring anything but your lovely self."

Her hands fisted, and her eyes promised all sorts of bodily harm to Andris. She gave him a scathing once over, turned, and followed Rhys through the portal he'd created.

Left alone, I assumed we'd head to class. The parking lot was empty except for a few late students hurrying to the building and slow-walking slackers who didn't seem to care that they were late. Raine and the others continued to stare at me as though waiting for an explanation.

I pointed at the school. "Guys, the bell already rang."

"School can wait," Torin said. His commanding voice was starting to make me want to rebel. "You're protecting a soul? Why?"

I rolled my eyes. "He came to me for help and I promised to give it to him."

"Is he one of the old people at the nursing home?" he asked.

Logical conclusion, although I didn't know he knew I helped there. I shook my head, not sure whether to tell them about Dev. Valkyries escorted souls of healthy, sporty people to Asgard. Dark souls shouldn't interest them.

"Why do the Grimnirs want him?" he pushed.

"Is he someone Goddess Hel wants?" Andris shot at me.

"Does Echo know about him?" Raine added.

"Okay, stop with the Qs." I grabbed my backpack from the ground and gripped it tight. "We shouldn't be discussing this now. One of you will have to rune my English teacher, or it's Saturday makeup class for me." They still wore that look that said we weren't going anywhere until I came clean. "Fine. His name is Dev. He was once one of them. A Druid. Echo turned him into an Immortal during his rescue mission. Then Dev betrayed them, or they think he betrayed them, and they're still pissed. Even Echo won't talk to him."

The three exchanged glances. I hated it when people did that. It meant they knew something or were on the same page, while I lurked in the dark.

"Was he one of the Immortals we fought last week?" Torin asked.

"No. Echo killed him thousands of years ago. He's, uh, a dark soul."

This time, I knew exactly what they were thinking. I was a nutcase. "I know what you're going to say," I said with a touch of attitude.

118

"No, you don't," Torin said, his voice gentle.

"Yes, I do. I can see disapproval on your faces. I know what I'm doing and why, so just respect that." Torin's eyes narrowed, but he didn't say anything. Andris appeared amused by the whole situation.

Raine looked worried and I was sure she'd tell me in excruciating detail why I shouldn't be messing with a dark soul. "Is he the one you were with on Saturday when you called me?"

I nodded. "I was careful. I only agreed to help him once I realized he wasn't after me. And please, don't tell Echo. He cannot know about this morning with those two. I mean it, Andris," I added when he opened his mouth. "He's already alienated enough Grimnirs without making things worse."

"But you *will* tell him," Torin said as we started toward the school.

"Yes."

"When?"

Pushy much? I sighed. "When I'm ready, Torin."

"What were you doing when she got attacked?" Torin asked, his blue eyes flashing as he focused on Andris. "You were supposed to keep an eye on her the second she left her car."

"I did," Andris shot back. "Besides, I was to protect her against *dark souls*, not idiotic Grimnirs. She was done with them and was walking toward me, and that's when it happened." He glanced at me, expression remorseful. "Sorry about that, blondie."

"No need to be sorry." I shot Torin a glance. "It's not his fault. I told him they were Echo's friends and I wanted to talk to them alone. I didn't know Nara would lose it when I refused to tell her where Dev is hiding."

Silence followed, then Andris slid beside me. "Since he's not tethered to you, where are you hiding him?"

"What does he look like?" Raine asked from my other side.

I managed to evade their questions, but I knew I was only delaying the inevitable. One more gang-up on me and I'd cave in.

CHAPTER 9. MY POOR CAR

Raine escorted me to class and runed my English teacher, Mrs. Bosnick, so I couldn't talk to Dev.

After first period, I was so ready for some serious soul ass-kicking. I hurried to my locker, dropped off my backpack, grabbed the books I needed for the rest of the morning, and practically ran to the nearest restroom. A girl was checking her reflection in the mirror.

"Out!" I snapped.

She blinked and opened her mouth, but something in my eyes stopped her. She harrumphed and left. I locked the door and pulled out my cell phone.

"Are you still there, Dev?"

"I'm here. Thanks for letting me lay low and not telling the Valkyries where I was."

"You'll have to meet them sometime. They're my friends. Why didn't you tell me the other Grimnirs were after you?" I asked, not masking my annoyance. "That bitch Nara tried to strangle me, and when Echo hears about it, and he will... He'll go all Hulk on everyone."

"Okay. Enough with the yelling. I'm dead, not deaf."

"If you want me to help you, mister, cut out the smart-alecky remarks."

He sighed. "The others have been after me for centuries, so I do what I can to lay low and avoid them."

The conversation with Echo about dark shadows flashed in my head. "Like what?"

"I hide in electronics, but they can force me out of them. Their scythes are too powerful for Mortal gadgets."

Someone tried to open the bathroom, but I pretended not to notice. "Ever possess Mortals?"

"Yeah. Everyone does."

"Doesn't mean you have to do it," I said. A banging ensued on the door. "Go away," I yelled.

"In my defense, it was like being alive again. I could feel, eat, and make love again." He sighed. "By the time I realized what it was doing to me, it was too late. The darkness had crept in. But I stopped and use animals now."

Thoughts of rabid dogs and psycho cats flashed through my head. "What happens to the humans you possess?"

"It depends on whether they're willing to work with me or not. Unfortunately, Mortals don't trust what they don't see. We could let them share the experience, but since they're not interested, we take over completely. When we do, they have blackouts."

This was way, way out of my league. "It doesn't sound like a good thing to do."

"No, it's not. You stay too long, they go crazy. No one cares about wild animals or the dead."

I stared at my phone as his words sank in. "The dead? Holy crap! You're talking about zombies."

He chuckled. "Yep. Uh, don't you have to go to your next class?"

I looked at my watch. Dang. The info he was giving me was more interesting, and the banging on the door was beginning to piss me off.

"Can we talk later? I want to hear more."

"Great. I miss talking. Most Mortals lose it when I try to make contact."

Yeah, I could just imagine how people would react to a talking animal. "Then lucky you I'm a willing listener. You can contact me any time after I leave my home."

"Oh, come on. Why can't I come to your bedroom and hang out? I could watch you do your hair."

Was he there on Sunday when I'd treated my hair? "We have to set boundaries, and you know mine. I don't want you listening to my phone calls or reading my texts."

"What? Do you receive dirty texts from Echo? Naked selfies?"

"Out!"

He slithered out of my phone, bowed, and disappeared through the wall. Shaking my head, I opened the bathroom to find the girl I'd kicked out with a couple of her friends waiting outside the door. They glared.

"Why didn't you knock?" I asked.

"We did," one of them said.

"Weird, I didn't hear knocking, just someone making a ruckus in the hallway," I said and grinned as I walked away. Their eyes shot death rays at my back.

***

For the rest of the morning, I kept going over the things Dev had told me. I didn't want to feel sorry for him, yet I couldn't help myself. How did Teléia fit into his betrayal?

I was by the lockers putting my books away when Raine joined me. She was minus Torin. She looked sad or tired.

"Please, tell me you're eating lunch here," she said.

"Why?" I'd been planning on going to Echo's.

"I don't feel like going home for lunch." Pain flashed in her eyes. Her father's prolonged illness was seriously screwing with her. Torin tended to distract her, but when he wasn't around, the pain and despair in her eyes intensified.

I linked our arms and led her toward the cafeteria. "Where's Torin?"

"As of this morning, he and Andris are working part time in Carson."

Someone was about to die. "Who's Carson?"

"A training camp for soccer players or some sport."

"And your mom?"

"Keeping an eye on a college team in Washington," Raine said, making a face. "She even has a partner. I'm still not used to the whole my-mother-is-a-reaper thing. Anyway, Lavania is coming back tomorrow."

"Great! I need to work on my speed runes. Oh, don't tell her about Dev." She gave me a blank look. "The soul I'm helping. I have a feeling she won't approve."

Raine rolled her eyes. "For starters, I wouldn't after the speech and look you gave us. Second, she's the coolest person I know and might surprise you. And third, don't you mean the *dark soul?*" she asked in a whisper.

"Shut up." I pushed her with my shoulder.

"Dev, the dark soul. Sounds like a title of a romance novel." She pushed me back. "When you decide to do something, you go all the way."

"No lectures, please. Happy souls, sad souls, regular souls, or dark souls, I'm an equal opportunity Soul Whisperer." The girl I'd kicked out of the bathroom walked past us with her two friends and turned to glare.

"What was that about?" Raine asked, frowning.

"They needed the bathroom when I was conferring with Dev. Like there's only one bathroom in the freaking school." She stopped smiling. "I know. I know. I should be careful when it comes to what we are. You will not believe what he told me."

I was still dazzling Raine with my knowledge of all things souls when we turned the corner and I groaned. Drew and his jock friends were by the entrance of the cafeteria. Because Maliina, the Immortal-turn-evil-Norn, had seduced then ditched him before Andris dispatched her to Hel, Drew treated me like I had crawled from a sewer. It was not my fault Maliina had chosen to mimic me while I was in the psych ward and screwed with his head.

Raine slowed down when I did. "Ignore him," she said.

"I can't. Part of me feels sorry for him. He must have really been into her, and seeing me just reminds him of what they had. Can't you erase his memories or something? Make him forget their affair."

Raine grimaced. "I'm not ready to do something that grand."

She was right. She might have Norn abilities, but she was still learning. "I just hate the way he stares at me like I'm lower than a worm."

"Actually, when you're not looking, he wears a different kind of look."

"Yeah, like he knows intimate stuff about me." Echo who'd slept with Maliina had also thought he knew personal things about my body down to scars in intimate places. "Maybe I should just talk to him and apologize."

"No. You don't want to do that. Just stay away from him. Come on. Paste on a smile and no eye contact."

Raine did the talking when we reached the guys. I pretended to listen and avoided looking at Drew. I rarely ate at the cafeteria, so our paths didn't cross often.

Inside the cafeteria, Kicker and Sondra waved at us from a table. They were both on the swim team and I considered them friends now. Sort of. They didn't know about the new me or what I could do. Naya used to be part of their group, but she hooked up with one of Drew's buddies and ditched us for the jocks' table. Funny, I was the one who'd taken them to Drew's party. Drew, I noticed, didn't come in to eat. Or maybe he was part of the first lunch.

Lunch was chicken nuggets with mashed potatoes and watery gravy. It was usually either thick and lumpy or watery depending on whether you were first or last in line.

"I'm so ready for the prom," Kicker said, twirling a lock of her hair, a nasty habit she'd recently picked up. She shot me a beseeching look. "You're still planning on doing our hair and makeup, right?"

"Depends. Will you drive out to the farm?" I asked, hoping they'd decide the distance wasn't worth it. The prom was Friday night, and we had a half-day because of Teachers' Work Day. I had been looking forward to the prom, but now all I could think about was helping Dev and Echo.

"Umm…" Kicker and Sondra exchanged a glance then looked at Raine, probably hoping she would suggest her house as a temporary salon. She didn't. Instead, she chewed on a chicken nugget and smiled without commenting. With the stuff going on at her house, the last thing she needed was nosy girls. And Kicker was the mistress of gossip.

"Yes. We don't mind," Kicker said.

"Then come to my house right after school," I said. "I can do you guys first. Have you gotten your outfits?"

"Last week," Kicker said.

"Mom is making mine," Sondra said. "She can recreate any gown down to the finest details. I found exactly what I wanted and she's almost done."

"Your mom is a seamstress?" I asked, leaning forward.

Confusion flashed in Sondra's gray eyes. "Yeah. I thought you knew."

"No, I didn't. I must meet her."

She glanced at Kicker, who shrugged.

"I always adjust gowns I buy to fit these." I pointed at my chest. "Or I look like a hooker or the president of the PTA." Raine laughed, and I glanced at her. "We all can't just walk into a store and pick up a size two and rock it."

Raine rolled her eyes. "I'm a size four, not two. When are they posting junior prom court?"

The teachers usually nominated six couples for the prom king and queen, and the couples formed prom court. For junior prom, they posted the list the day before the prom. For senior prom, it was posted a week early.

"You shouldn't even worry about it, Raine," Kicker said. "You and Torin are the most popular couple, so you'll be nominated to the court and maybe even win. The only problem is you," she pointed at me, "will be nominated, too. Everyone reads your blog, so you're a shoo-in. The question is who will we," she pointed Sondra and herself, "vote for?"

"Cora," Raine said and pushed her food around her plate. "I don't want to be nominated."

"Too bad," I said. "You might even be a princess in the senior court because of Torin." I didn't mind being a queen, but I doubted I'd have chance if I went against Raine.

The conversation shifted to books and their movies. The good, the bad, and the epic failures. Of course, they blamed the producers, not their favorite authors for okaying the actors. Sondra and Kicker only read paranormal and fantasy. Raine read anything that caught her interest. It was hard for me to get lost in anything but contemporary books. One was recently made into a movie, a real tearjerker. Luckily, it was a bestseller and we all watched the movie. We dissected every scene.

Echo didn't swagger into the room, despite my hopes, and he wasn't waiting by my car after school. Blaine was. He watched me with an unreadable expression.

"Why the long face?" I asked.

"Who did you piss off?"

"Why would you...?" My voice trailed off when I saw my tires. The front two were flat. I dropped my backpack and walked around Blaine to check the back ones. They were flat, too. "The petty, vindictive Hel's minions!"

"The ones from this morning?" Blaine asked.

I whipped around. "You saw us?"

"I was in the foyer. I had to etch forgetful runes on a few people. Torin and the others forgot they draw attention and perceptive people notice when they disappear. So you need me to fix your tires? I know runes that can fix them."

"Oh. That's nice." Nara's smug face flashed in my head. "No. Let them do the fixing." By the time I was finished with them, they'd never mess with me again. I reached down and grabbed my backpack. "Can you give me a ride?"

"Me?" He glanced around as though searching for someone. "Are you sure?"

"The last time I heard, you had my back. Immortals united and all."

"Where's Echo?"

I shrugged. "Out and about."

"You do know there's no way those two Grimnirs poked holes in your tires. One punch should have made the point."

"And they would have reduced my car to junkyard scrap," I said.

"Your car is already a junkyard scrap."

I slapped his arm. "We can't all drive expensive foreign toys, you car snob."

He laughed. "I'm just saying. I'm surprised Echo hasn't offered to replace it."

"Because he knows I wouldn't accept it."

"Why not?"

"I'm not a charity case, Blaine Chapman. Besides, I love my Sentra. She and I have seen many actions together."

"Like?"

"None of your business. Can we get lattes?"

"Sure." When he reached the light, he turned left. He glanced at me and smirked. "So when you say action..."

He was flirting with me. A year ago, I would have been flattered and flustered by the attention. Now that I had Echo. No other guy mattered.

"If you must know, I had many firsts in this car. My first drive-in movie. First kiss. First…" My voice trailed off, memories of many firsts with Echo flashing through my head. I sighed.

"What?" Blaine asked, pulling into the parking lot of The Hub.

"Nothing." A soul wandered into The Hub. "Do you see the soul?" I whispered to Blaine.

"No, but I know one is nearby. Do you need to help it?"

"It's a he. And the answer is no. I don't do the asking. If they need help, they come to me." We got our lattes and took off.

Blaine drove like a maniac. Lucky for him, cops rarely lurked around the roads leading to the large vineyards near my farm. He didn't slow down until he reached my place.

A familiar car was in front of my house. I grinned. Echo.

"Looks like you have visitors," Blaine said.

"Echo." I jumped out of the car, eager to find him. "You coming in?" I asked.

Blaine glanced toward my house and shook his head. "No, thanks. You sure you don't want me to fix your car and drop it off?"

"No. The Grimnirs—"

"Didn't do it, Cora," Blaine said. "Slashing tires is a Mortal thing. Someone at school did it."

Who? Only one person at school hated me enough to want to hurt me. Drew. The problem was I couldn't see him vandalizing my tires.

"Maybe. Thanks for the ride. See you tomorrow." He sped off while I headed for our front porch.

CHAPTER 10. MOM AND ME TIME

No one was in the kitchen. "Mom? Dad?"

No response. I angled my head. No sound. I grabbed a pear from a bowl and left the house. Shading my eyes, I looked toward the fruit trees then the barn.

Could Echo be out there with my dad?

I bit into the pear as I started toward the barn. The barn was empty. Where were they? I headed back to the house. Then a thought occurred to me. What if he'd told my parents who he was and had whisked them away through a portal? Mom would freak out, but Dad would want to see how everything worked.

I shook my head and ditched the thought. Echo would never tell them who he was. Norns had a rule everyone lived by. Humans were not supposed to know they existed, and that rule extended to Valkyries and Grimnirs. The consequences of breaking that rule were severe.

Back in the house, I grabbed my backpack and started for the stairs. Mom appeared at the top of the stairs.

"Hey, hun. I thought I heard a car, but when I looked outside I didn't see your car."

"Blaine dropped me off."

She frowned. "What happened to your car?"

"Flat tires. Someone deliberately slashed them."

She shifted into mother-bear mode, eyes flashing. "I'm calling your school first thing in the morning."

"No, Mom—"

"The school is responsible for whatever happens in school. They should have better security and a surveillance system."

I took the last few steps that brought me to her side. I grabbed her arm. "It's okay, Mom. I know the people responsible."

"Good. I'll need their names before I talk to the principal tomorrow."

"Mom, no. I'll take care of this." She didn't look convinced. "Please. It was a misunderstanding, and they promised to fix them all."

"The school should at least know. This is a form of bullying. Who are they, and why did they pick on you?"

I shouldn't have mentioned the slashed tires. "Mom, I've got this." She wasn't budging. "If things get worse, I promise to let you know. Right now, let me handle it."

"Only if you promise to report it."

Yeah, like that was going to happen. "Promise."

She pressed a kiss on my temple. "I guess I keep forgetting how grownup you are. You don't need me to fight your battles anymore or kiss your boo-boos."

"Boo-boos, Mom?" She laughed. "Where's Echo? His SUV is outside, but I can't find him anywhere."

"That's because he and your father took the truck. They said not to hold up dinner."

"They went to dinner without us?"

Mom chuckled. "No, they're at the Blue Bird."

Blue Bird was a sports bar where Dad and Raine's father would hangout on Saturday afternoons to watch sports and drink beer. Professional basketball was in session, and NHF draft was around the corner. Dad liked to watch them live with his buddies.

"Why?"

Mom took my arm and led me to my room. "I think they wanted to talk without us listening and interrupting." She gave me a pointed look.

"I never interrupt."

"You're very protective of him, which is perfectly fine."

He was protective of me, too. "Do you need help with dinner?"

"No. I thought we'd run into town and get some Chinese food."

My eyes widened. Mom was not big on eating out or takeout. "Really?"

She nodded. "I don't feel like cooking tonight, and it's just the two of us."

"Can we drive by Blue Bird?" I asked.

She laughed. "No. We're definitely not spying on your father and Echo."

Oh, we were so spying on them. I grinned and walked back to hug her. "You're the best."

"We're still not going. I'll call Chang's." I started to walk away, but she added, "Oh, before I forget. I made an appointment with Dr. Steiner. She expects you tomorrow at four."

My face warmed. Dr. Steiner was her doctor, an obstetrician and gynecologist. I've always seen Dr. May, a pediatrician. "Mom, I don't really need contraceptives."

"You don't just see her for that. You can talk to her about anything. You're a woman now, and I believe a woman should know certain things about her body, so she can take charge of her health."

I rolled my eyes. "I know my body, and we did have the talk."

"I know, honey. But an OB/GYN can answer questions I can't. Just go see her, okay?"

"So, you won't be there?"

"No. At eighteen, you earn the right to see the doctor without me hovering."

"I never minded. Do you remember when I had a high fever a couple of years ago but Dr. May was out of town, so we went to the clinic? You ripped that young doctor a new one when he insisted I didn't need more tests."

She laughed. "Nothing is stronger than a mother's intuition."

We didn't leave the house for another two hours. Chang's was crowded and even the takeout had a line.

"Can we stop by Blue Bird?" I whispered to Mom.

She shook her head. I waited until we'd picked up our takeout and she was backing out of the parking lot. "Mom..."

"No."

Whining ensued. "I swear I'll be in and out. I just want to make sure he's okay."

She signaled and entered Main Street. Blue Bird was several blocks ahead of us. "You don't think he can handle himself around your dad?"

"No. I mean, yes, he can, but it's not only him and Dad. Dad is probably in there with his poker buddies. They are a bunch of mean old men."

"Your father is not old. He's in his prime."

"You know what I mean, Mom. Jake's Dad made it clear he considers me his future daughter-in-law. He's going to dissect Echo or worse, go on and on about his perfect, Navy Seal son and me. Echo won't like it."

Mom chuckled. "You're like a mother bear with her cub."

"He needs someone to watch out for him. He's been alone for too long."

The smile left Mom's face. "It couldn't have been easy losing both parents at such a young age. He told us how he was raised by an aunt who died when he was starting high school and how Blaine's father became his legal guardian."

"But it's not the same," I murmured.

"No, it's not." Mom stopped at the traffic light and glanced at me. "You really love him."

"With all my heart. He's perfect." A tiny smile that showed her skepticism drifted across her lips. "I'm serious, Mom. He's loving, generous, and protective." I grinned. "He's the one."

"Okay," she said laughing, "I believe you, but you still can't go checking on him in a bar. First of all, beer and sports brings out the worst in men, so if you walk in there, Echo won't be the only one breaking noses. Don't let your father's geekiness fool you. Second, Echo will think you don't believe he can take care of himself. Men have delicate egos, sweetheart. And we, women, must learn when to stroke it." The light turned green and she stepped on the gas. "I'll pull up outside the bar. You text him and ask him to come outside. Make this about you, not him."

Echo didn't own a phone. I'd pushed and begged, but he'd insisted he didn't need Mortal machines to know when I needed him. Super big ego.

"Echo hates modern technology and rarely carries a phone."

Mom glanced at me. "Really? How unusual. What if he wants to talk to you?"

"We make a new date every time we end one."

"He's old school. I like that." She left Main Street and headed west toward Blue Bird. "Okay, I'll go in and check on your father. I can't have him drinking if he plans to drive."

"So, why is it okay for you to go inside and not me?"

She parked and shifted to smile at me. "Because, your father and I have been together for so long we're secure in our love. Catcalls from other men will only make him proud." She fluffed her hair. "How do I look?"

At fifty-nine, Mom still had it. Her hair might have grayed, but it was still full and luxurious. She had amazing cheekbones I wish I'd inherited, and she still had curves in just the right places. If I ever aged, I wanted to look just like her.

"You look beautiful, Mom."

She chuckled and planted a kiss on my cheek. "Thank you, sweetie."

I watched her leave the car and disappear behind the blue door. Above the door was a sign with a blue bird. A few couples left their cars and disappeared inside the bar.

I drummed my fingers on the steering wheel, my eyes not leaving the door. Waiting sucked. Every time the door swung open, I expected Echo to come out.

I was slowly losing my patience when the door opened and Mom stepped out. I frowned. She looked up and down the street as though searching for something.

"Where is he?" I called out.

"He's gone. He left a few minutes ago with the Chapman boy." Mom started toward the car. "He's the designated driver, so he'll be back. You'll see him when he brings your father home."

***

The first thing I noticed when we got home was my car. The guys must have driven it here, which meant Echo knew someone had vandalized it. Knowing him, he'd want to know who, then hunt down the person responsible before asking why.

"Your car is home," Mom said, not masking her surprise.

"Echo and Blaine must have fixed the tires and brought it home," I said.

"Oh. How thoughtful. We'll reimburse them for the tire, and you must still report what happened to the school."

"I will." As soon as I entered the house, I texted Blaine. "Thanks a bunch for NOT listening to me."

Seconds later, my phone bleeped and a smiley emoji with "U r welcome" appeared on my screen.

Didn't he get that I was being sarcastic?

"Derp!" I texted back.

"What do you want to watch?" Mom asked.

I looked up from my phone and stared at her blankly.

"Put your phone away, dear, and let's pig out in front of the TV. You choose something." She headed toward the kitchen. "I won't even care if it's one of those teenybopper movies you like."

I pushed the phone into the back pocket of my pants. "I'm so offended you think I watch such movies." I had at least a dozen of them on my list on Netflix.

"You could at least pretend you don't know what I'm talking about," she teased, serving us. Mom would never eat out of Chinese cardboard boxes or use plastic utensils that came with the food. But she removed the spoon and fork from their plastic containers and placed them in a drawer.

"I'm checking the TV guide to see what's on Lifetime. Nothing like a good chick flick movie and Chinese food on a Monday night."

Mom ignored the dig and smiled. We rarely had these girls-only nights or ate in front of the TV. While I flipped through the guide, she poured us orange juice, placed our dinner on a tray, and joined me.

I ended up choosing a movie about a woman who'd lost her child in a plane crash, but believed her son was still alive. At first, I rolled my eyes. Mom might complain about teenyboppers, which had a wealthy boy falling for a poor but spunky girl, but most Lifetime movies were about women losing something and finding the strength to pick up their lives and move on. They were just as formulaic.

I even spaced out and sneaked a look on my phone to make sure I didn't miss a text from Blaine. But then the movie got interesting when everyone started to deny the woman's son ever existed. Halfway through, I was so invested in the story a phone call or text would have been a distraction. Memories erased left and right, people being sucked into the sky. It all seemed possible if one knew about Norns and their meddling. When the movie ended, I was on the edge of my seat.

"Wow," I said.

Mom chuckled. "That's one of my favorites. There's nothing in this world like a woman's love and intuition when it comes to her child."

Just like the way Norns erased Torin's memories, yet he ended up falling in love with Raine again. Sci-fi movies like this made me realize how close people were to the truth about what went on under their very noses.

I stood and took Mom's plate. "Do you want more juice?"

"No, thanks, hun. I'll have some water and watch the news until your dad gets home." She turned and watched me walk into the kitchen. We had a floor plan that was open from the alcove, or Dad's writing cave, past the living room to the kitchen. "Are you heading upstairs?"

"Yeah. I have homework, then bed."

"I'll call when Echo and your father come home."

I would see them the minute they pulled up. So I waited. Finished my homework and reading, showered, and changed into my pajamas. Then I realized what I was doing. I had become one of those annoying girls who ceased to function because her boyfriend was out bromancing.

I texted Raine, but when the portal didn't open and she didn't return my text, I crawled into bed.

***

I woke up crabby. Echo had come and gone. I must have fallen asleep, and he wasn't around when I woke up or went downstairs. So much for hounding me until I forgave him.

The drive to school was uneventful. I pulled up just as Sondra and Kicker stepped out of Kicker's older brother's truck. I waved. By the time I got out, they were talking to Naya. Naya kept throwing glances my way. Then the three girls walked toward me.

"Hey, guys." They exchanged a glance that said they wanted something. Please, not another person wanting her hair fixed for prom. "What?"

"You need to talk to Drew," Naya said.

Drew was the last person I wanted to talk about. He was still my number one suspect in the tire-slashing caper. "Why? He hates me."

"He's hurt, and from the way he goes on, hate is the last thing on his mind," Naya explained.

Damn Maliina for sleeping with him. "What am I supposed to tell him? I thought we had something but I've moved on. Why can't he see that?"

"You're dating a guy in college, who's never around," Kicker jumped in.

I pointed at her. "Hey, hey, you stay out of this. You're my friend, and friends stick together like glue. Echo is around plenty, thank you very much. I see him during lunch and most evenings." Except for the last two days. "Look, I'm totally into Echo, so tell Drew to move on already."

"I think he needs to hear it from you," Naya said, making a face.

Not going to happen. Then an idea popped into my head. "I'll be at the prom on Friday with Echo. If that doesn't convince him, I don't know what will."

A car stopped beside us and a window rolled down to reveal a familiar face—the girl I'd locked out of the bathroom yesterday. "Hey, blondie. How's your car? Have a nice drive home yesterday?"

I stared at her with round eyes. "What?"

"The car. You know, that box with wheels under it," she added as though talking to an idiot. Her friend in the passenger seat laughed. "I hope you drove it home okay yesterday."

Realization hit me hard. These three idiots were the ones who'd poked holes in my tires. All because I'd locked the stupid bathroom door? "You! You slashed my—"

"Oh, she finally gets it," the first one who'd spoken said.

"Dumb blonde," her friend said.

"Next time, don't act like you own the damn school." They drove off laughing while my thought process slowed down to nothing. Rage washed over me.

"What happened?" Kicker asked.

"They called me dumb. Those two wannabe rung crawlers think they can take me down?" Their car was disappearing around the row of cars. I started after it, but Kicker grabbed my arm.

"You can't fight them," she protested.

"I don't plan to fight." I yanked my arm from her grip. "I'm going to let them know they can't mess with me." I brushed past them, but the next second a firmer grip locked around my wrist. "Darn it, Kicker." I tried to break free, but it tightened. One look over my shoulder and I realized why. "Blaine, let go."

"Your friend is right," Blaine said.

"They slashed my tires. They're not getting away with it."

"Go," he ordered the three girls, and they scurried away without protesting. "You come with me."

He led me back to my car and nudged me into the front passenger seat. He slid behind the wheel. Through the windshield, I could see Kicker, Sondra, and Naya cross the street. They glanced toward us.

"Engage your invisibility and speed runes," Blaine instructed.

"My speed runes are iffy."

"Then go with invisibility."

"Why?"

"You want payback, don't you?"

I engaged my runes. "What do you have in mind?"

"Do you have your artavus?"

I pulled one from inside my boots.

"I'm going to come around the car and open your door, so people don't see it open and close by itself. You go off and slash one of their tires."

"All of them," I countered.

"One, Cora."

"They slashed four of mine."

"And Echo and I fixed them at no charge. Tires are expensive, and they don't have an Immortal guarding them against holes and cuts. One tire and that's it." He glanced over his shoulder. "They haven't found a parking spot yet. Do it now, so they won't suspect you."

"I want them to know I did it," I retorted.

His right eyebrow shot up. "And what will that accomplish? Feuding with members of the women's basketball team?" He glanced over his shoulder. "They're parking." He jumped out of the car, came around, and opened the door. "One tire. No need to be petty."

"Oh, you suck," I said and took off. The girl driver was just stepping out. *This is for you, bitch.* I plunged the narrow blade into the tire. The sound of air releasing from her tire was so loud she heard it.

"Oh no," she exclaimed and leaned down for a better look. "I don't know how to change flats."

Her friend, the one who'd called me a *dumb blonde*, joined her. "My cousin can fix it during lunch. Do you have a spare?"

"I think so." She kicked the flat tire and walked to the back.

Let's see how you deal with two flat tires. I glanced toward my car to see if Blaine could see me then went after the second tire. I whistled a happy tune back to my car and got rid of the runes. Blaine studied my face, which I was sure screamed guilty.

"What?" I asked with attitude.

"How many tires?"

"Two." I grabbed my backpack and got out of the car. "You can't get mad at me. She called me a dumb blonde."

Blaine's eyebrow shot up when he joined me. "Since you're not, what they think shouldn't matter."

"I know that, but blonde jokes hurt, especially when you happen to suck at math and have a chip on your shoulder."

Blaine laughed. Then he tilted his head and studied me, a bemused smile on his lips.

I bristled. "What?"

"You're funny. I never knew that before." A thoughtful expression settled on his face. "I can definitely see why Echo is crazy about you. You're brutally honest, you're crazy as hell, and you're pretty hot in your own way."

I pursed my lips, my eyes narrowing. "Uh, thanks for the backhanded compliments, but you'd better not start crushing on me. First, I have enough on my plate dealing with Drew and his obsession with Maliina. Second, Echo will kill you if he catches you looking at me. Third, I don't particularly like you."

He laughed as though he didn't believe me. "Everyone loves me."

Most girls did, but that was before Torin took over as the quarterback. "Not me. You don't know how to listen. I told you not to touch my car and let the people responsible fix the tires, but no-ooo. You just had to be the hero."

He scoffed at the idea. "I didn't fix your car. Just drove it to your house when Echo was done."

"You shouldn't have told him."

"If you haven't noticed, it is impossible to stop him once your name is mentioned. I mentioned giving you a ride home and he wanted to know why."

We crossed the street and joined the students entering the building. Something else occurred to me, and I stopped. "Did you tell him about the incident with the Grimnirs?"

"No, but if he asks me, I'll have to tell him the truth."

I sighed. "Like I told the others, I'll tell him when I'm ready. His meddling might interfere with my investigation." The smile died on my lips when we entered the building and the first people I saw were Drew and his friends. I groaned and tried to ignore him and the way his eyes followed us.

"Drew is seriously lusting after you," Blaine teased.

"Shut up," I said.

"You want me to talk to him?"

"Would you? Please?"

"Anything for a fellow Immortal." He took off while I headed toward the lockers. The basketball players arrived at their lockers across from mine and hardly paid attention to me. They were busy bitching about their flat tires.

I grinned.

***

I didn't see Raine until lunchtime. Once again, she was alone. Something was different about her; I just couldn't put my finger on it. "Please tell me you don't have to go home or meet Torin for lunch," I said.

"I don't."

"Good. You're coming with." I slipped my arm around hers. "We're going to Echo's for lunch."

"Oh. Won't I be in the way?" She eased her arm from mine to put her books away. "From my understanding, lunchtime make-outs tend to get pretty heavy."

Warmth crept up my face. "No, they don't." Yes, they did, and I missed them. "Come on." We headed to the same bathroom I'd used yesterday, but there was a line.

"We need a portal," I said. "You can create one from inside the car, right? I've seen Echo do it."

A perplexed expression flitted across Raine's face. "Why aren't we using the bathrooms? Mirrors make the best portals."

"I know, but after locking those basketball players from the bathroom, they slashed my tires."

Raine stopped. "What basketball players? Why didn't you tell me?"

"I did." Had she forgotten already? "At first, I thought the Grimnirs did it, then Drew... Poor Drew. This morning, I found out that the basketball players did it. Remember the three girls from yesterday?"

Raine looked up and down the hallway. "Let's pay them back."

I grinned. This was why she was my best friend. We thought alike. "Already did. I cloaked myself this morning and gave them two flat tires."

"Two? Why not all four?" she asked as we continued toward the front of the school.

"Thank you. Someone who finally gets it. Blaine wanted me to do only one and made a big deal about it. But they also called me a dumb blonde, which rankled, so I went for two."

"Want to finish the job?"

I laughed. "No, I owe it to Blaine to reign in my bitchy side. He's really a great guy, and I kind of like him on my side. You know, Immortals united and watching each other's back."

Students milled in the entrance halls. Some of the second lunch group, like us, hurried out of the building while the first lunchers sauntered back. We exited the building and headed toward the parking lot.

"Since when did you become so bloodthirsty, Raine Cooper?" I asked. "What happened to the girl who'd carry spiders outside instead of squashing them?"

"The Norns happened. You gotta give as good as you get or people will crush you."

I didn't know what to say. She'd been through a lot because of the Norns, so I kind of understood her attitude. I'd just never heard her voice her opinion with such anger or include people in her frustration with the Norns. Or maybe it was a slip of the tongue.

Inside the car, runes appeared on her skin, making her alabaster skin shimmer. She etched the right runes on the window and door of her car, her hand moving so fast it blurred.

"Whoa, you're fast," I whispered.

"Not as fast as Torin. He makes everything seem so effortless." The entire door of the car became grainy then shimmery like the surface of water. It peeled back to show Echo's living room.

Raine swung her legs and entered the room. Knowing we'd probably find Echo chomping on a bowl of soup with his feet propped up, I hesitated. Then I berated myself for being chicken. I wanted to see him. He was avoiding me, and it was time it stopped.

CHAPTER 11. FIRST ATTACK

The house was quiet. Too quiet. A bag from Echo's favorite restaurant was on the counter. I peeked inside. Soup. The containers were warm.

I put Mom's lunch on the counter and headed to the bedroom. His bed was neatly made. He hadn't slept here last night. He never made his bed, and his cleaners came on Mondays and Thursdays. I picked up a pillow and buried my face in it. His scent brought back memories.

How is it possible to miss someone this much?

"Hey," Raine called from the doorway, and I looked up. "You okay?"

"Echo and I fought." She blinked. "I know, shocking." I led the way back to the kitchen and pulled the soup containers from the bag. "I don't know if I should really call it a fight. He refused to help me with Dev and I, uh, got pissed." I handed her a bowl. She knew where the utensils were and got a spoon. "I told him I didn't want to see him for forty-eight hours."

Her eyebrows shot up. "And he listened?"

"Not really." I rolled my eyes. "On Sunday morning, he stopped by with breakfast, which was so sweet because unlike your guy, Echo's completely inept in the kitchen. I kind of reminded him he wasn't supposed to come near me for two days. I didn't think he'd take me seriously, the annoying reaper." I sighed. "I miss him."

Raine rubbed my arm. "Once he finds out about what happened yesterday with the Grimnirs, he'll be here breathing fire and threatening to decapitate someone."

I laughed. "He's not going to find out because Rhys, the walking ad for tats, used to be the third member of their trio and they don't talk, and you guys are…" I zipped my lips.

"You're forgetting the girl."

I sighed and put Mom's pot roast and potatoes in the fridge. "Nara is a pain. Everything about her bugs me." I fished the cell phone from my pocket. "Dev said she and Echo dated."

Raine's eyes widened. "Oh. I don't know what I'd do if Torin's ex appeared. Probably put a hex on her."

I laughed. "You wouldn't. You know he loves only you and you'd ignore her the same way I've been ignoring Nara. The problem with her is she keeps saying things that make me want to punch her in the nose."

"She's jealous, that's all. You have the power."

True. If only Echo would come home. I brought the phone to my lips. "Hey, Dev. You there?"

Raine's eyes flashed with amusement. "You talk to him on the phone?"

"He likes to commandeer my electronics to communicate. He's not back. Come on, let's eat."

We started on our soups, and I remembered something. Raine's behavior had been off, but between my issues with Echo and Dev, we hadn't really talked.

"How are things with you?"

She shrugged.

"Not you, too. I have had enough of reading body language, so talk. Watching you do magic is amazing. Does it affect you?"

"Oh yeah. The rush is off the charts. Scary."

"And?"

"That's it."

She was lying. "There's a lot more going on with you, Raine. Spill it."

"I need to marry Torin."

I choked on my soup. She grinned as she thumped my back. "Really?" I said when I could speak.

"Really. I need him in so many ways it scares me, but," a faraway look entered her eyes, "marrying him is at the top of my list. It's the only way we can survive all this mayhem." She nodded. "We need each other."

I was sure my eyes were like saucers. "Does he know how you feel?"

Before she could answer, a gush of frigid air swept the kitchen and Echo entered the room, filling it with his vibrant presence. I got up, raced past Raine, and jumped into his arms.

Unprepared for my reaction, he stumbled backward and chuckled, the sexy sound rumbling through me. He wrapped his arms around me until we were tightly pressed against each other.

"I missed you, too," he said, laughing.

I hugged him tight, everything that had been wrong with my world becoming right. He was frozen, from his toes to the tips of his hair. I slid my fingers through his hair. I'd missed him. His scent. His arms. The feel of his body against mine. Even his cold skin after a trip to Hel's was as normal as breathing.

I shivered, but didn't move away. Echo needed my warmth, so I did what came naturally. I warmed him. He lifted me clear off the floor and moved backward, until he leaned against the kitchen counter, his face burrowing in the space between my neck and shoulder. We stayed like that for a while.

"Are you okay?" he asked, his breath warm on my skin. This time, my shiver was not due to cold.

"Hmmm-mmm," I mumbled, turned my head, and squeezed him tight. My eyes met Raine's. She indicated the deck, where the afternoon Miami sun blazed, and I nodded. I waited until she disappeared outside.

"How could you disappear on me like that?" I asked, pinching his arm.

"Ouch! There are more fun ways to abuse my body."

My face warmed. I tried to create more space between us, but he wasn't ready to let me go yet. I managed to lean back and took a proper look at him. He looked like he hadn't slept in days or shaved. I stroked his chin.

"You don't look too hot."

"I haven't slept since Sunday."

"Why not? What happened?"

He shrugged. "Everything here reminded me of you, so I reaped nonstop."

I squeezed him tight. "That was a dumb thing to do."

"I've done worse. Tell me what happened yesterday morning?"

I blinked. "What?"

"Two people attacked you. Who were they?"

Andris and Torin were so dead. I bought time, crossed my arms, which wasn't easy since his arms were firm around my waist, and thought about a plausible explanation. "Who told you I was attacked?"

His eyebrows shot up. "Does it matter?"

Note to self: never share a secret with any supernatural being in a three-mile radius.

"Who were they? Dark souls?"

Souls, of course. Why hadn't I thought of that?

"No, regular souls. Poor things. I tried to explain to them that I couldn't help them, but they didn't want to hear it." I warmed up to the subject. "In fact, I almost got a tardy slip because of them. If Raine hadn't come to my rescue and runed my teacher, I'd be spending Saturday making up the class. And FYI, they didn't really attack me. They became aggressive, but I had the situation under control."

Echo's eyes narrowed, and I knew he wasn't buying my hard sale. "Can you recognize them when you see them again?"

"No, Echo. You're not going on a soul hunt just because I got careless." I eased out of his arms. "Do you want lunch?"

"Yes, but I'll warm it." He shrugged off his duster and gloves, dumped them on the table, and went to the fridge. "You sit down and give me descriptions."

I sighed. "There's nothing more to say."

He removed all the boxes, lined them up inside the microwave, and punched in buttons. "Now you see why I think you should take a break from helping souls. They're a bunch of self-serving shmucks."

"Don't you mean Dev?"

"He tops the list."

"Tell me about him," I said, leaning forward.

Echo glanced over my shoulder and scowled. "What's there to say? He made a mistake and I fixed it."

"No, I want to hear about your childhood. You two were best friends before all the mess with the Romans. Was he nice, sweet, or funny?"

Echo scoffed at my words. "Nice? Try reckless. Irresponsible. A real pain in my ass. He did things without thinking and then smirked when we got in trouble bailing him out. We'd come up with ideas, but before we could iron them out, he'd attempt them. The idiot."

From his voice, he'd enjoyed it. "And Rhys?"

"Rhys shot down every idea we came up with, which would drive Dev crazy. Nara had to keep peace between him and Dev." He removed the boxes from the microwave, placed in a tray, and got two sets of chopsticks from one of the bags. "Without her, they would have killed each other."

"Nara?" I asked.

"The only girl in our group—Rhys' cousin. At first, we barely tolerated her. But when she proved she could out jump, outrun, and even outthink us, she became my second in command."

I'd bet. Not only had he dated Nara, she'd been one of the boys. They'd shared special moments. He regaled me with stories about their escapades, but all I could think about was Nara.

Raine came in from outside and pointed at her watch.

"Hey, Raine," Echo said. "I didn't know you were there." He gave her a hug. While they talked, I threw my leftovers away. Lunchtime was over too soon. I wondered if I could skip school and just stay here with Echo. He'd probably love the idea.

"Let's agree on one thing, doll-face," Echo said, pulling me into his arms before we left. "We fight, we make up. No spending nights apart angry. It messes with my head, which affects my job." He peered at me and ran his knuckles down my cheek. "I probably set a record for the most reaping in the last thirty-six hours, and I wasn't nice to the souls. I don't want to be that person."

I nodded. The kiss that followed was too brief, but I didn't mind because I knew I'd see him later. I planned to fix this mess between him and Dev before we left for the prom on Friday night.

"We're still going to the prom on Friday, right?" I asked.

He smirked. "Try to stop me. See you after school. Raine, tell St. James we'll talk soon."

The portal Raine created opened into a bathroom. We could see a couple of girls in front of the mirror. Good thing humans couldn't see portals. We timed our entry when one left and the other entered a stall. I turned and waved to Echo.

"I forgot to thank you for breakfast," I said. "Mom now thinks I'm a gifted cook and whoever I marry will be one lucky man."

He smirked, thumbs hooked in the front pockets of his leather pants. "Good thing I'm only interested in your *other* talents."

The portal closed while I sputtered and fought a blush. Raine opened her mouth to comment, and I shook my head. "Not a word."

***

Echo was waiting for me after school, arms crossed, his back to my car. He made an effort to blend in and had once again traded his leather pants and sailor shirts for jeans and a T-shirt. But he still stood out and students stared as they walked past him. As usual, I doubted he noticed. His eyes followed me and Raine from the entrance of the school.

Raine grinned when she saw him. "Talents, huh?" she whispered. "Do tell."

My face flamed. "Shut up."

Laughing, she waved and headed toward her car while I joined Echo.

"See what I have to put up with because of you?" I said.

He straightened. "What did I do?"

"Other talents? And you said that in front of Raine," I scolded him.

"You mean you two don't gossip about us and compare notes?"

"Ew, no. That's reserved for book, TV, and movie boyfriends."

His hands came to rest on my hips. He pulled me closer until my body was flush with his. "Are you telling me you've never compared our kisses?" He lowered his head. "I'm a better kisser than St. James."

"I'll let you know after he and I kiss."

His eyes gleamed. "Then I'd have to rearrange his pretty face," he said against my mouth. "Then punish you for being a bad girl." He nipped my lower lip.

I was helpless against the shudder that rocked my body.

"Go ahead, then you'd have to deal with me and Raine." I went on my toes and planted one on his lips, taking my time. His hand left my waist and wrapped around my nape. Things were getting out of hand fast. I leaned back, breaking the contact. "I gotta go. I have a doctor's appointment."

He stiffened, eyebrows slamming down. "What's wrong? You're not sick, are you? You can't…"

I pressed my fingers on his lips and grinned. "No, I'm fine, but Mom insists I see her doctor for a checkup. I can't very well tell her I'm an Immortal."

He visibly relaxed and pulled me in for a hug as though holding me tight would reassure him I was okay. I rested my cheek on his chest and let him chase away his demons.

"When do you have to be there?" he asked.

"Four."

"Can I come?"

"Uh, no." I leaned back to see his face. "This is a gynecologist visit, Echo. We're going to talk about female issues, and you can't be there."

"Why not? I'll be invisible, and I know enough about female anatomy not to be shocked."

There was no way I was discussing birth control in his presence. "No, you're not going, and that's final. Don't give me that lost puppy look," I added. "It won't work."

"You're a cruel woman."

"I'll see you afterwards. The visit should be over in forty-five minutes."

"I haven't seen you since Sunday."

I sighed. "Fine. You can sit with me in the waiting room, then stay there while I see the doctor." He grinned triumphantly. Gah, I was so easy. "Come on. I'm dying for a macchiato." I opened the back door and threw my backpack on the back seat.

"We have time to check out the next house. I need to close the deal by Friday."

"Why the big hurry?"

"It's prom night. I'm hoping to get lucky." He laughed when my jaw dropped. He was being impossible. Worse, he hadn't lowered his voice and a few girls walking by giggled. I shot him a death glare, but he just smirked and glanced around the parking lot, eyes narrowing. "About your tires and those responsible..."

"Took care of them this morning. Come on."

He studied me from across the roof of my car. "You need a new car."

"There's nothing wrong with this one, Echo." I got behind the wheel and waited for him to settle into the passenger seat. How I've missed having him in my car. He took up too much space and often pushed the passenger chair back to accommodate his long legs.

"It makes weird noises when you drive," he said.

Blaine had been talking to him. "I'll get one when I can afford it. And don't even think of offering to buy me one."

"Why not? I can afford it."

"I can't accept such an expensive gift from you, Echo."

He lifted my hand to his lips and kissed the Druid ring he'd given me. He didn't have to explain what he was saying. The ring was priceless, yet I'd accepted it.

"Dad's pride would be hurt if you did, so let's not discuss it."

He didn't bring it up again. When I pulled up outside The Hub, my car made a weird noise as I shifted gears to park.

"Not a word," I warned.

Surprisingly, he didn't say anything. As we started for the building, he fell in step beside me and wrapped his pinkie around mine. Just before we entered The Hub, a tingle in the back of my neck had me glancing over my shoulder. There were no souls in sight, but I had a weird feeling we were being watched. Nothing seemed out of place around the parking lot and the line of stores. It was probably Dev. I didn't want to bring him up yet.

I untangled our pinkies and wrapped my arms around Echo's.

We got our drinks and scones. Echo even got a bag of cotton candy. A soul walked past, glanced at me, smiled, and disappeared through a bookshelf. Could she be the one I'd felt outside? I'd seen her before. Since she'd never come to me for help, I left her alone.

The feeling of being watched returned when we left the store. Echo insisted on driving, and I let him. Arguing with him was pointless. Plus, I wanted to get away from whatever was giving me the chills.

Maybe Echo wanted to see how the car felt, or maybe his "You don't know where we're going" was the reason, but he drove too fast.

"There's a speed limit on these roads, you know," I reminded him when we pulled up outside the house.

"I didn't notice." He smirked when I swatted his butt and pulled me to his side. We stood in front of the house and studied it.

It was even cuter than the first one and was inside a new subdivision with tennis courts and a pool. Neighbors studied us from their lawns and front porches. Echo hated it before we went inside. But I felt that weird feeling again and looked around, waving at a few people walking by and staring at us as we left.

"No privacy," Echo said.

"And it's near the forest," I added, knowing how much he hated wooded areas.

He crossed it off the list and promised to show me one last one after my appointment. I let him drive me to the doctor's.

"May I borrow your car?" he asked when he pulled up outside the doctor's.

I eyed him suspiciously. He'd made a big deal about visiting the doctor with me and now he wanted my car. Could he be any more transparent? "Why?"

"I'm going phone shopping and this way I can appear normal when I pull up."

I laughed. He'd never cared whether he appeared normal or not. "That's the lamest excuse ever. If it makes you feel better, yes, you can take my car to have it checked."

"Who said anything about having your car checked?"

"I can read you, Echo. And please, don't listen to Blaine. He is a car snob." I gave him a quick kiss. "Go, but take good care of it. And don't go changing anything without checking with me first."

"I'd never do that," he protested, but I saw through him.

"Yes, you would. Love you. Gotta run."

***

The gynecologists' offices were in a sprawling house that looked more like a home than an office building. The waiting area had leather sofas around tables with magazines like a furniture store. Women in various stages of pregnancy were seated with their husbands or alone around the room. I felt out of place. Worse, when I made eye contact, eyes shifted to my stomach as though to check how far along I was.

The women behind the counter were nice. Unfortunately, the room was quiet, except for the muted sounds of preschooler kids in the playroom to my right, so I felt like our conversation carried. By the time we finished, I was sure everyone knew this was my first visit and my mother had made the appointment for me.

I took the paperwork and found a chair as far away from anyone as possible and faced the window. They'd also given me some kind of a square beacon that flashed red. If the light turned green, it was my turn to go inside, which meant no one would be calling out my name.

I did the paperwork. It was all smooth sailing at first. I even called Mom when the questions were about family health history.

"I'm so proud of you, honey," she said.

I frowned. "Why?"

"You're taking charge of your health. If you want to talk later, I'll be here."

"Thanks, Mom." But I wasn't smiling a few minutes later when I got to the part asking if I was sexually active and if I had multiple partners. So intrusive.

My face red, I looked around, but no one was paying me attention. I was tense by the time I finished, wishing I didn't have to do this alone, yet I couldn't see myself asking Mom to come with me. Maybe Raine, but I was sure the doctors didn't encourage friends to accompany you. I was happy Echo wasn't with me.

Waiting for the green light became hard, and I actually sighed with relief when it flashed.

Better get it over with.

The nurse who took my blood pressure was nice, but Dr. Steiner was even nicer. We went over some questions: my periods, how far apart they were and how long they lasted, and of course, when I last had one. I just started this morning.

My face warmed when she asked, "Are you currently sexually active?"

I blanked out for a moment. My online research said they didn't ask such questions. "Yes."

I braced myself for judgmental comments and more personal questions, but all she talked about were different types of contraceptives, how they worked, and the ones she thought were suitable for someone my age.

I was more than happy to leave with my prescription and the sample of the vaginal ring she'd given me. Echo wasn't in the lobby, but I refused to wait for him there with eyes on me.

As soon as I stepped outside the building, I felt the presence again. This time, it was stronger. I searched the parking lot, expecting to see Rhys or Nara.

A cool draft swept my skin. I searched for souls.

"Dev?" I called out.

Silence. That was strange. He usually had no problem showing himself. Maybe it wasn't Dev. I couldn't continue talking to myself without attracting attention.

"Listen, whoever you are. Show yourself or get lost," I snapped.

A dark, shapeless mass floated toward me. With it came air so frigid it hurt my lungs to breathe. I wrapped my arms around me, but it was blasting me with evil energy, or sucking heat and air from around me. Flower and plants along the entrance shriveled and turned black.

I started to shake. My mouth went dry. I tried to take a step back, but I couldn't move. Panic wrapped like steel around my chest and brain.

"Who a... you?" I managed to gasp.

It charged at me and I opened my mouth to scream, but terror stole my voice. I braced myself for the possession, but a familiar dark figure appeared and cut it off.

Dev.

They tumbled in the air until I couldn't tell which mass was Dev and which one was the evil one. They barreled toward me like a giant swirling mass of my worst nightmare. I tried to step out of their way, but I wasn't fast enough.

The iciness hit me first when they plunged into me, followed by a feeling I'd never experienced before. Like my insides had turned into jelly filled with shards of glass. I was being ripped apart from the inside. My breath had turned into ice in my lungs. Nausea rose to my throat, and black dots appeared in my vision.

I wasn't sure whether they were inside me or not. I couldn't hear their thoughts. I just had the weird feeling that I was no longer in charge of my body. I tried to fight back, breathe, move, but I kept sinking. It was as though the dark energies had ripped out a part of me and filled it with something vile.

I staggered backward, and my elbows connected with the wall. My skin stung, but the pain was like an afterthought. I realized why. Blood circulation was returning to the surface of my skin.

They hadn't possessed me. They'd passed through.

I became aware of my surroundings. My little gift bag from the doctor was on the ground. I knew I should pick it up, but I couldn't move. My body shook so badly the only thing holding me up was the wall.

The door to the building opened, and a couple stepped out.

"Are you okay?" the wife asked, her voice reaching me as though from afar.

I nodded. At least I think I did. My breath was still a heavy fog in my lungs, and my vision was still screwy.

"Honey, get help from inside," the woman told her husband and moved toward me. A door slammed shut. In the next second, Echo was beside me.

"What is it? What happened?" he asked, gathering me into his arms.

I let go of the wall and sunk to his side.

CHAPTER 12. THE LIGHT IN MY DARKNESS

Echo scooped me up, and I buried my face in his neck.

"What happened?" I heard him ask, his voice sounding harsh. I clung to him. He was my anchor now, my buffer against the cruel, ugly, and painful world.

"We found her clinging to the wall when we left the doctor's office," the man said. "Should I get the doctor?"

"No. I got her." Echo started down the ramp.

"This is hers," the woman called out, and I knew she'd just handed Echo my ring.

Inside the car, he cradled me close as though to absorb my pain and cold. He had this down to a science because every time I had a bad encounter with a soul, he was there to help me, infuse me with his energy. This time was worse. I couldn't even engage my runes. I had to depend on his. He started the car and ramped up the hot air.

He didn't say anything. If he could wrap his entire body around me, he would have. He tried and warmth returned to my limbs. My insides still felt like I had just stepped off a spinning ride at an amusement park. I loved riding roller coasters, but hated spinners with a passion.

When I sat up, my stomach heaved. Echo studied me with bleak eyes. I hated seeing that look in his eyes. He reached inside the glove compartment and removed the bag of Twizzlers. I'd tried M&Ms, Skittles, even ice cream, but none seemed to work like Twizzlers after a possession. I shook my head. I didn't think I could hold anything down.

"A dark soul?" he asked in a voice that said he wanted to kick someone's ass.

I nodded. I was sure if I spoke, I might throw up.

He cursed softly under his breath. "Dev?"

I shook my head.

I swore relief flashed in his eyes before he lowered his lashes and hid them from me. That gave me hope. Maybe, just maybe, he'd listen to what Dev had to say. I burrowed in his neck, not ready to leave the comfort of his arms. He stroked my back and tried to absorb the occasional shudders that rocked my body.

"Every time I leave your side, some weird shit happens," he whispered in an unsteady voice. "I don't think I can take any more of these scary situations without going insane."

I didn't know how to respond to that. Telling him I'd be okay would be lame because we both knew I wouldn't be. He'd rescued me often enough from possessions gone bad, and dealing with dark souls was a whole new level of badness. The only thing I could do to reassure him was hug him tight.

"Tell me what happened," he said again later, his voice steadier.

"A dark soul came after me and Dev stopped it."

Echo stiffened. "So he was here."

I leaned back to look into his eyes and hoped he saw the truth in mine. "He saved me, Echo. I felt a presence outside The Hub and even the house, but it was too faint. At first I thought it was Dev spying on us."

"He's been spying on us?"

I sighed. His mistrust of Dev defied logic. "No, he hasn't. All he wants is a chance to talk to you and explain things, and so he checks on me periodically to see if you're ready. I told him you're not. He was going to leave and try a few centuries down the line, but I convinced him to stay around because I know that deep inside, you need to talk to him."

"No, I don't."

"It's a good thing I did or he wouldn't have saved me," I continued as though Echo hadn't interrupted me again. "The dark soul must have followed us and waited until I was alone." I shuddered, my stomach still churning.

"Damn dark souls," Echo mumbled. "I'm taking you home where you'll be safe. Then I'm going to find Dev."

"You're not going to disperse him, are you?"

For a second a look crossed his eyes that said he'd love nothing else, but he sighed again. "I haven't decided yet."

"Would it matter that he did it because of Teléia," I whispered.

He leaned back and cocked his eyebrows. "What?"

"He said he did it because of her." Echo didn't respond, and when I glanced at him, he wore a preoccupied expression. "Do you know what that means?"

He shook his head. "Teléia disappeared when we were under attack. We searched for her, but she wasn't among the dead or the living."

"Was she an Immortal?"

"No. She didn't want to be one. She was close to her parents and her brothers. When they were taken and presumed dead, she wanted to die, too. She begged me not to turn her, and I honored her wish. She…" His voice trailed off. "Teléia was like a delicate flower. Sensitive and fragile. She could not have survived the Romans. They would have used her, so she chose death. By the time Dev betrayed us…" He went quiet, and I could feel his pain. "Teléia had been dead for almost a year."

I squeezed his hand, trying to absorb his pain.

"So, I don't understand what Dev meant. Before the Romans started rounding us up, he begged her to reconsider the immortality thing, but she refused. He found her a hiding place, or a place he thought she'd be safe among non-Druid members of our society. She refused to go. Dev was insanely in love with her and would have done anything for her, but she didn't feel the same way. It's tragic when love is one-sided like that," he added quietly. "It makes me appreciate what we have more."

I stroked his face, and I wondered how Dev's betrayal was connected with Teléia. Could he have blamed his people for her death? Was that why he'd betrayed them?

"I'm so sorry," I whispered.

He lifted his head and frowned. "For what?"

"Making you relive the past, bringing up painful memories. All I want to do is take away your pain and replace all those memories with happy ones, yet I keep—"

"Shh." He kissed me, and for a moment, the queasiness went away. "You take away my pain, and we're creating new memories. Good or bad, as long as you're in them, I'm happy. I have to find Dev and get some answers about tonight."

"And the past?" I asked.

"We'll see. All this could have been staged, you know. Bringing up Teléia, then having a friend pretend to attack you, so he could rescue you."

Seriously? We were having a heart-to-heart conversation about something that affected him deeply and he thought he was being played? I wanted to knock some sense into his thick head.

Then realization hit me. He'd done something similar before. He'd played me the first time we met. I leaned back to look at him, and my stomach rebelled. Gah, when would this queasiness go away?

"Isn't that more your M.O.?" I asked.

Echo smirked. "Yep, and he graduated at the top of the class when I taught him and the others."

Yeah, well, isn't that just freakin' great? "I give up. I'm not reasoning with you anymore. Help him. Don't help him. You decide. You are annoyingly stubborn, arrogant, unreasonable, and impossible. If I wasn't insanely in love with you, I'd dump your ass."

He laughed. "And I'd create situations so you'd always need me to rescue you and make you feel safe, and you'd take me back." He stood up with me.

"I can walk, Echo," I said.

"Is the nausea gone?"

I started to nod, but the look in his eyes warned me not to lie. My insides still heaved like I'd swallowed a giant slug. "No."

"It takes a while for the feeling to go away. How about your lungs?"

"I can breathe okay now."

"Good." He carried me to the passenger seat, buckled me up, and closed the door.

We drove in silence. Instead of taking me to the last house, he headed straight home. I studied his profile, thinking about what we'd talked about. I loved this man with all his flaws. He drove me insane with his crazy ways of doing things, but I never wanted him to change.

We were almost home when I said, "Never change for me, Echo. Always be true to yourself. Your honesty is what I love most about you."

He chuckled and reached for my hand. "I thought it was my body."

I smiled. "I love that, too. It's okay if you want to change for *you*. If you do it for me, you'll end up resenting me and possibly even leaving. Because if you can't be yourself with me, you'll be yourself with someone else. When you're pissed and want to rant and rave, then rant and rave. I won't love you any less. If you want to yell at me, do it, because I'll yell right back."

He chuckled. "You don't yell."

"Really? Then you're missing out on an opportunity to find out my lung capacity and how fast you can duck, because I throw things."

He was laughing hard by the time we pulled up outside my house. "So what you're saying is when I hold back, you hold back?"

"Yes. I could easily hurt you, too. I have a mouth on me and a strong throwing arm." Of course, I'd never hurt him that way. He'd known enough pain to last any Immortal a lifetime.

"You could never hurt me," he threw my words back at me, jumped out of the car, and made it to the passenger seat just as I opened the door. He squatted, his eyes not leaving mine. "Want to know why?"

The sexy grin did it. I stopped arguing and fed my curiosity. "Why?"

"I'm the beast, mean and ugly, and you're the only one who makes these things seem insignificant. With a kiss and a touch, you make the meanness and ugliness go away. With your love, you calm the beast inside me. So yell at me all you want when you're pissed. Throw things at my head. Maybe I'll yell back or throw you over my shoulder, cuff you to my bed, and make love to you in ways you couldn't possibly fathom, but you could never, *ever* hurt me. You are the light in my darkness. The hope chasing away my despair. You are the keeper of my soul."

Just like that, the fight went out of me. I was an idiot, thinking about simple things like words you hurl when you're angry and physical pain, which he could withstand without blinking, while he was thinking bigger and deeper. My eyes teared.

He gulped when he saw them. "What did I do now?"

"Nothing. Everything." I threw my arms around his neck, almost making him lose his balance. "You're perfect."

He laughed. "See what I mean? You only see perfection where there's imper—"

"Oh shut up, Echo. Just shut it and let me hold you."

Not caring that my parents were probably watching us, he knelt right there on my driveway, let his head rest on my lap, and wrapped his arms around my waist. I stroked his hair. I was going to love this man fiercely until he saw himself through my eyes and through our children's eyes.

"I'm going to fill our home with children," I whispered.

He lifted his head and frowned. "No. No children. Not for a couple of centuries. Just you and me." He grabbed the bag with my Nuvaring. "I'll even put this in for you."

Face hot, I snatched the bag from his hand. "We'll revisit this topic again."

"Sure, next millennium." He stood and scooped me up. "Or two."

"Put me down. My parents will freak out."

"I'm sure they've been watching us since we pulled up. And as far as they're concerned, I've earned the right to carry you like this. Besides, it's going to take you hours to be yourself."

"Then how am I going to explain what happened? I utter the word souls and they'll send me straight to the crazy house."

"They wouldn't dare. I'd fight them. Reveal my true self to them before I let that happen." He walked to the front porch, effortlessly taking up the steps. Instead of entering the house, he sat with me on the porch swing. He rocked gently.

"What do you mean you've earn the right?" I asked.

"Your dad and I talked the other night. I passed with flying colors."

"You discussed me at a bar with his annoying cronies?"

Echo chuckled. "They all had a question or two, especially the old geezer whose perfect son is supposedly waiting for you to finish high school before he can pop the question. How come you've never mentioned *Captain America*? Where exactly is he stationed?"

"Uh, Echo. Stop the swing." I got off his lap and the contents of my stomach threatened to spew out. I raced to the door and burst into the house. Luckily, Mom wasn't in the kitchen. Unluckily, the scent of freshly-baked pie was in the air. My stomach rolled. Dad was in his writing cave and mumbled something that sounded like "you're home" without looking up.

I slapped my hand over my mouth and raced to the downstairs bathroom. Echo was right behind me and held back my hair. He even wiped my face down with a wet towel when I was done.

"Is she okay?" Dad asked from the doorway.

"I'm okay," I said quickly, not wishing to explain. I rinsed my mouth, but it wasn't enough. I needed to brush my teeth and use a mouth wash several times. The nausea didn't go away despite the fact that I'd thrown up. It was as though the dark energy was still trapped inside me.

"I'll take her upstairs, sir," Echo said and swept me into his arms. I couldn't protest with Dad watching me with worried eyes.

"It's probably something I ate," I reassured him. "You didn't have to carry me," I added in a whisper so only Echo could hear.

"I love carrying you, doll-face. If I could, I'd put you in the inner pocket of my coat and take you with me everywhere."

My face warmed when I noticed Dad staring at us from the foot of the stairs. Had he heard Echo? Probably. As soon as we reached my room, I wiggled out of Echo's arms and rushed to the bathroom to barf again.

"Is a possession by a dark soul always this bad or is it just me?" I asked, allowing him to help me to my feet.

"I'm hoping this was because I brought up *Captain America*," he teased, probably trying to change the subject. I threw him a disgusted look.

"I'm serious, Echo," I said, squeezing toothpaste on the thistles of my toothbrush. "I need to know what I'm getting myself into. Is it always this bad?"

"It's worse if they possess you."

I frowned. "Then I have to find a way to either deal with the effect or stay away from them."

"I vote for number two," Echo quipped. He leaned against the doorframe and watched me brush my teeth.

"Isn't that taking the coward's way out?"

"No. It's self-preservation. No one will blame you if you choose not to deal with them or souls altogether."

I'd blame myself. Frowning, I finished with my teeth, stared at my reflection, and cringed. I looked like crap.

"You have absolutely nothing to worry about with Captain America. Jason is a great guy, but he never had a shot. Besides, my heart belongs to you." I walked to where Echo stood, kissed his cheek, slipped past him, and headed straight to bed.

He followed, lifted his new phone, and snapped a picture of me.

"What was that for?" I asked, adjusting the pillows beneath my head.

"A memento."

I tried to glare at him, but failed. I closed my eyes. "You can't be serious. I feel and look like hell."

"You could never look like her. Half her face is a shriveled corpse." I opened my eyes when I felt the soft fabric of a throw blanket covering me. It was the same one I often used on him when he dozed off on my chair or on top of my bed.

"Thank you."

"You look cute," he said, grinning, "but utterly beaten down. I'll text you the picture every time you want to help a dark soul. What's your phone number?"

I was too tired to argue with him. Seconds after I gave him my number, my phone dinged.

"Now you have my number. I'm off to find your dark soul, and hopefully, he'll lead me to your attacker."

"Dev is not my dark soul. He's your best friend."

"That waits to be seen. Text me whenever, but don't bother when I'm in Hel. I hear the connection sucks."

Now he was trying to be funny. "Find Dev and let's close his case." I liked that. Every soul I helped now would be a case. I snuggled under the cover and closed my eyes.

"Do you need help with this?" Echo asked and once again, I opened my eyes. I saw what he was studying. It was the box the doctor had given me. He must have carried it from the car. Heat flooded my face.

"Go away, Echo," I said.

"Don't throw away the instructions. I want to read them, too."

"No, you don't." I pulled the covers over my head.

He pulled the covers down, planted a kiss on my lips, and smirked. "There's nothing about you that doesn't interest me, doll-face. See you tonight."

A thought occurred to me, but he was already gone. He'd used the portal. How the heck was I going to explain his disappearance to my parents? Maybe they wouldn't notice. I reached the bottom drawer on my chest and pulled out a bag of Twizzlers.

Mom knocked nearly an hour later and poked her head into my room. She frowned, and I wasn't sure whether it was the fact that I was alone or the Twizzlers.

"Your father said Echo was still up here."

Time to fake ignorance. "He must have slipped out while I was asleep. Blaine probably picked him up."

"I must have missed them while I was in the barn, and your dad is fast drafting a new story," she said and smiled. When Dad was in his fast drafting mode, he became very absentminded. "How are you doing?"

"Better. Must be the mystery meat at school," I said. I'd already thought up all excuses and that was the one she wouldn't question.

"Oh." She still looked worried, until her eyes fell on the box Echo had left on my nightstand. What had she thought? I had morning sickness? The doctor has explained I could only use the ring when I had my periods. "How did the visit with the doctor go?"

"Very well considering the crazy questions she asked."

She chuckled. "Count yourself lucky. In my day, they did pelvic exams and pap smear tests. The metal contraption used was enough to scare a young woman from wanting contraceptives. I'll let you rest."

"Thanks, Mom."

"Do put that away, sweetheart," she said, staring at the Twizzlers. "All those artificial colorings and additives are not going to do your stomach any good."

***

I was finishing my bedtime ritual when a cool breeze swept my room. Since I'd left the lights on, I didn't have to worry that it was anyone else. I poked my head out of the bathroom to see Echo entering my room.

He was still dressed for reaping, which said he wasn't staying. "How did it go?"

"He's gone underground again." He leaned against the doorway and watched me finish with my teeth. This was becoming a habit. "Finding a dark soul when it doesn't want to be found is a real pain, but I'll find it. No one attacks you and gets away with it."

Somehow, I knew the evil dark soul would be a priority with him, not Dev. I walked to where he stood, reached up, and stroked his cheek. He looked like crap.

"You haven't slept in days, Echo, and you look it. You need to rest."

"I will once I get the soul who tried to hurt you."

Arguing with him was hopeless. There were other ways to make him stay. "Do you want something to eat from downstairs? Mom baked your favorite Dutch apple pie, and we have whipped cream. Homemade." I didn't wait for an answer. I knew I had him. "Be back in a few."

The light under the door meant Mom was upstairs. She was probably reading. Dad was still writing and didn't look up. He really didn't notice anything when in the zone. I opened the fridge and removed a pie.

"How are you feeling?" he asked, making me jump. Maybe he wasn't as absentminded as we'd like to think.

Our eyes met. "Better."

"We missed you at dinner."

"I was out and doubted I could hold down anything." And now I was cutting a giant slice of pie. "I'm starving now."

"Your mother left you a plate. It's somewhere in the fridge."

I made a face. "I just want some pie, Dad. My mouth still tastes funny."

He nodded, and I sighed with relief. "Cut me a slice of that too, sweetheart."

I carried his piece of pie to his desk first and dropped a kiss on his temple. "Night, Daddy."

"Goodnight, sweetheart." I added extra whipped cream on Echo's and almost made it to the stairs when Dad added, "I still can't believe I missed Echo earlier."

Okay, he definitely had us fooled. Nothing escaped him. Echo would have to rune him and make him forget. "I was asleep when he left. So unless he disappeared into thin air, I'm sure he came through here."

"You two came in your car, and I don't recall hearing a car pick him up."

This could get crazy fast. "Blaine probably picked him up, Dad. You know how that car of his moves. The engine hardly makes a sound. I've decided I'd love to have a car like his when I graduate," I added, hoping to distract him. "Sleek and beautiful. The engine purrs instead of roaring."

Dad chuckled. "Foreign cars are expensive, and your mother would not like it. You know how big she is on buying American."

"Dad, I drive a Sentra," I reminded him.

"That was bought used. It doesn't count."

"Does too. Goodnight, Daddy." I escaped upstairs and found Echo pacing.

He was wired. I could always tell. Worries about my father became secondary. I put the pie on my dresser, pulled off Echo's gloves one at a time, and threw them on my bed. I pushed him on the chair and straddled his lap. A sensual smile curled his lips as he reached down to stroke my thighs. My pajamas left a lot of skin exposed.

"Behave," I warned, cutting through the pie.

"Mensies?" he asked.

I paused in the process of feeding him. "How can you tell?"

He smirked. "I just know. And FYI, I don't mind," he said.

"You're disgusting." I put the piece in his mouth before he could say anything else.

He grinned as he chewed and wiggled his brows. "It makes things even more intense."

Now I was curious. He was always promising me something kinky, piquing my interest. And he always delivered. I shoved more pie into his mouth, so he wouldn't distract me. When he finished the pie, I put the hair brush in his hand, stood, and faced forward.

"I know what you're doing," he said.

"I know. I love the way you brush my hair." I closed my eyes as he ran the brush through my hair.

"I'm still leaving, doll-face," he whispered.

He was the master of the obvious. "I know that, too. Stay with me a little longer." I got up and crawled under my covers. I knew he'd follow. He stayed on top of the covers, boots and all, slipped an arm under my head, and pulled me closer. I interlocked our fingers and closed my eyes. I couldn't sleep.

"Echo—"

"Shh. Go to sleep. We'll talk in the morning."

He fell asleep first and didn't wake up even when I pulled off his boots, loosened his vest and shirt, and covered him. He looked so peaceful asleep. So vulnerable.

I turned to switch off the light when I felt it—the dark soul that had attacked me. It wasn't close enough to make my skin crawl, but I felt it. My first reaction was to wake up

Echo. Together, we could take care of the soul, once and for all. But how could I? He was exhausted.

I reached under my bed for the poker. All souls, regular or dark, could be dispersed. The rod in my hand, I shifted and smothered a scream. Dev stood on the other side of the bed.

"What are you doing here? Echo came looking for you and couldn't find you." Echo stirred, and I instinctively placed my hand on his cheek to calm him down.

Dev touched his lips as though warning me to be quiet. Then he pointed outside.

"I know it's out there. I can feel it. Get inside my phone and talk to Echo," I said with clenched teeth, frustration and fear colliding deep in my core.

Dev shook his head and floated toward the window. I really needed to keep that window closed or any soul could just float into my room whenever they wanted, despite the runes around my house.

"Damn it, Dev. Come back here."

He didn't look back. Echo stirred again, and I was tempted to wake him up. He could follow Dev and all this would be over. Even as the thought crossed my mind, I knew it couldn't be that simple. Not when dealing with the supernatural. On the other hand, Dev had warned me to be quiet. It was almost as though he hadn't wanted Echo to meet the dark soul, which meant he knew it.

I gripped the iron poker and waited. I fell asleep still waiting for Dev to come back.

CHAPTER 13. MEDIUM RUNES

Echo was gone the next morning when I woke up.

"Thanks for letting me sleep," his text read. "See why I adore you?"

If only he knew everything. I texted him and got ready for school.

"Are you sure you should go to school today?" Mom asked while I ate breakfast like a starved convict.

I nodded. "After school, I'm going to Angie's to pick up my prom dresses." She and Dad exchanged a glance. "I'm fine. Really. If they serve mystery meat again—"

"I'll file a complaint against the school," Mom snapped in her scary mother bear voice that said she wasn't kidding.

Yikes. "Complaints only work if more than one student is affected, Mom. I won't eat it."

"You got that right," she said. "I'm making you lunch."

I couldn't complain, just sat there while she packed slices of rump roast and baked baby potatoes from last night. I gave her a kiss and hug, and an exuberant thank you before leaving the house.

There were new runes on my car. He must have added them before leaving. I threw my backpack in the back and slipped behind the wheel.

Mom came out of the house and waved. What now? I lowered my window, hoping this wasn't about school lunches or Echo.

"Are you going to the nursing home today?" she asked.

"Tomorrow. Why?"

"I have extra pies if you want to take one to your charges at the nursing home and one more for Raine's family."

"I'll drop them off tomorrow. I gotta go, Mom."

"Love you," she said and disappeared back inside the house.

"Love you, too," I said and backed out. Just before I could shift gears, a gray mass appeared at the corner of my eye and I froze, yesterday's incident flooding my psyche. It moved to the front of my car and sanity returned. It was Dev.

I really needed to get my act together. I shouldn't fear souls, normal or dark. I blew out air, tried to calm my racing heart, and waved him inside. He shook his head.

I had no time for this crap. "You have some explaining to do, so get in before you really, really piss me off."

He imitated death by decapitation.

"You're already dead, Dev," I reminded him.

He pointed at the runes. They were glowing. Weird.

I frowned. "What about the runes?"

He pointed at his chest and imitated an explosion. Oh, that was what they were for? To protect me against dark souls? I grabbed my phone and stuck it out the window.

"Get in."

He slithered inside my phone. I threw it on the tray between the front two seats and stepped on the gas. "Start talking."

"What do you want to know?" he asked.

"Who attacked me? And don't say you don't know because I know you do."

"You did it," he said and laughed. "You convinced him. I should have thanked you last night, but I had to get rid of another dark soul."

"Another one? Are you sure? It felt the same as the other one."

"All souls feel the same," he said. "I remember that from my years as an Immortal."

"No, they don't. Dark souls give out a different vibe."

"Oh. Do I give the vibe?"

"Not really. Maybe it's because you haven't tried to possess me. And FYI, you made the thing with Echo happen. You protected me when the soul attacked, and that's what convinced him you might not be a bad guy."

He chuckled. "You don't see it. If it weren't for you—"

"Thank me later, Dev, after you and your boy reconcile. You're sure the soul from last night is not the same one that attacked me?"

"I'm sure, but word is out about you. Every dark soul out there wants the Immortal with medium runes."

I stepped on the brakes so hard my body jerked forward. "Medium what?"

"Your runes, the same runes every lost soul tries to etch on the Mortals they possess, but fail to because they don't have the right artavus. Have you ever seen Mortals try to cut themselves?"

My time at Providence Mental Institute flashed in my head, and I shivered. "Yes."

"Mortal doctors believe they're mentally ill and cutting is their way of dealing with the pain. That may be true for some, but for others, the souls do it or make them do it. Some are regular souls, who've picked up the nasty habit from dark souls. The others are dark souls."

What he was saying actually made sense.

"But you, doll-face, already have these runes etched on you. Because of them, you can be possessed without the side effects Mortals feel."

A car honked behind me, and I realized I'd stopped too long at the stop sign. I hit the gas. "That's not true. Most possessions drain my energy. There are days when I sleep for hours after a possession-a-thon. And yesterday, I almost slipped into a catatonic state. I don't think I can survive a dark soul possession, Dev."

Silence followed. "Are you sure?"

"Yes," I snapped. "It took me hours to be myself again after you two passed through me." I stopped at the light on Main Street. "How do I stop them from coming after me?"

"Lose the runes. Disappear."

"Very funny. I'm not going anywhere, and I can't lose the runes. No one knows what they are or what they do, except that they attract souls. This is the first time I've heard them called *medium* runes."

"Only souls who've been around know about them. They're passed down from lost soul to lost soul."

Somehow Maliina had known about them and etched them on me. Why? I pulled up into the parking lot outside my school. "Find Echo, Dev."

"There's your answer," Dev said. "Echo can be your bodyguard twenty-four-seven. Every time a dark soul appears, he can reap it."

If only that were possible. I sighed. "Echo, like the other reapers, has a job to do, and it's not protecting me twenty-four-seven. I'll find a way." I needed a giant iron rod to disperse souls. "Go, Dev. Find your friend."

"Outside your car, please. I don't want to be blown into tiny pieces. Echo used the same runes on his scythe this time. He must be pissed. Bye," Dev added as soon as I stepped out of the car. Then he slithered out of my phone.

I didn't even look his way, my mind racing. What if Echo etched the runes on his scythe on me? I'd be safe from dark souls. On the other hand, I'd also be toxic to other souls, which meant not helping them anymore.

I hurried toward the school building. Would my life become less complicated if I stopped helping souls? Yes. Would I be happier? Possibly not. I couldn't see myself going back to being the old Cora, blogging about hot guys. Plus, I hated the idea of being an Immortal with a hot reaper for a boyfriend and nothing else. It might sound crazy, but I liked working with Echo. We were a team. I had to find a way around this.

Just before I entered the building, the sound of Torin's motorcycle reached me and I turned. Andris, Ingrid, and Blaine were right behind me.

"Why the long face, Soul Whisperer?" Andris asked, dropping an arm around my shoulder.

"Good morning to you too, Valkyrie," I said. "I thought you guys were at a stakeout somewhere in California."

"That's Torin's M.O. He gets chummy with his Mortals. I go along to keep an eye on him for Raine. Those Cali girls are hot and tanned all over. They sunbathe in the nude," he added in a whisper.

I doubted Raine sent him to keep Torin in check. Those two were crazy about each other. "In other words, you've been spending time on a nudist beach instead of working."

"And I have a no tan lines to prove it. Want to see?"

"Some other time." I looked over his shoulder, but Raine and Torin were taking their time. In fact, they were kissing. I noticed they did that more than before. They were also starting to dress alike. Raine wore a leather jacket. Designer. I recognized the brand. And fingerless gloves.

"Okay, something is definitely wrong," Andris said. "She didn't rise to the bait."

"Maybe if you were less obnoxious, she'd tell us," Ingrid said, and my focus shifted to her. Her sister had marked me with medium runes. Maybe she knew something about them.

"She's right, Andris. Try being less obnoxious. Come on, Ingrid." I wrapped my arm around hers and pulled her toward the school entrance. "You really should reel him in."

Ingrid chuckled. "Why? I don't want him."

I loved her Norwegian accent. Even after centuries as an Immortal and living all over the world, she still hadn't lost it. She was a cheerleader, popular, and the combination of pale blonde hair and light-blue eyes made her look like a model. Andris would be lucky to have her as a girlfriend. Or not. He'd mess up the relationship.

"Are you sure?" I teased.

Ingrid rolled her eyes. "Andris has a few more centuries of womanizing before he can be with one woman. I refuse to join his harem."

"I like your attitude."

"Thank you." She waved to some of her cheerleader friends.

We entered the hallway leading to the lockers. "Can I ask you something?"

"Sure."

"Don't get mad. I know how much you hate talking about Maliina, but I have to know something." When I was desperate for information, Ingrid was the one who'd told me that her sister had runed me. "Do you know anything about the runes she etched on me?"

She stopped walking, and her expression almost made me tell her to forget it. She looked like she was in pain. We were also in the middle of the hallway and students had to walk around her. I pulled her away from traffic.

"I know this doesn't make sense, but—"

"No, she never told me anything," she said abruptly, her accent becoming stronger. "I was her annoying younger sister. She either ignored me or used me. But..." A frown creased her eyebrows. "Just before she runed you, she said something that didn't make sense at the time."

"What?"

"There was the usual rhetoric about making Raine pay for trying to steal Andris." She rolled her eyes. "Then she said that you might become useful. I guess she'd known at the time she'd mimic you."

Or that she'd possess my body. I sighed. "Thanks."

We walked toward our lockers in silence.

"That's not the answer you wanted to hear, is it?" Ingrid asked.

I gave her a tiny smile, not sure whether to confide in her or not. She and I took private lessons from Lavania, but her knowledge of runes was just as limited as mine.

"I wondered why my runes attract..." I glanced around and lowered my voice, "souls. What's special about them?"

She shrugged. "Ask Lavania. She knows everything, and she's back early. We're going home for lunch. She insisted."

***

"Oh, I missed you, girls," Lavania said, giving us girls hugs. Blaine watched from the sideline. "I have so much to tell you. Come here, Blaine."

"Nice to have you back, Lavania," he said, but he didn't move an inch.

Lavania chuckled, walked to where he stood, and gave him a hug anyway. "As long as you live in this house, you put up with my idiosyncrasies. Where are my boys?"

"StubHub Center," Blaine said, extricating himself from her arms.

"Oh no, not one of the teams," Lavania said. "They're so young."

StubHub Center in Carson, California was the National Training Center for the U.S. Soccer Federation. There was no telling which team was about to have an accident because they held camps and competitions for all U.S. Soccer programs. Torin and Andris could be waiting for fourteen year olds or men in their twenties.

Lavania drew my attention with, "I have soup and meat-filled pastries from a recipe I got from Goddess Freya's personal chef. He insisted it was healthy and filling. So sit and enjoy." She waited as we each got a bowl of the steamy soup. Then she passed out the pastries. They were golden and flaky on the outside, but moist and meaty on the inside. She sat next to Raine and asked, "How are you holding up, dear?"

"Fine," she said. "These are really good."

"Thank you. I stopped by to see your father. I didn't know he'd slipped into a coma."

I hadn't known either. Femi had said he was getting better.

"He's not been lucid since yesterday," Raine said with a shrug, but I saw the spasm of pain that crossed her face. It hadn't been easy for her watching her father battle brain cancer.

Conversation focused on Raine's father, turning lunch into a sober affair. Lavania finally changed the subject to Asgard.

I knew the major gods and goddesses. Some names she mentioned were new to me, but she made them come alive. In fact, she made the place sound magical. I could see why Immortals would love to get a chance to see Asgard. Since I would never visit, I didn't want to become bitter like other Immortals. In fact, the thought of being an Immortal without a purpose scared the beegeebees out of me. I had to find a way to deal with the dark souls.

I didn't get a chance to talk privately with Lavania or Raine about my medium runes during lunch. But I wasn't stressing about that. Raine and I were going shopping after school, and Lavania wasn't going anywhere.

Raine, Blaine, and Ingrid were waiting for me by the car after school.

"We'll follow you guys," Blaine said.

Confused, my eyes volleyed between him, Raine, and Ingrid. "Follow us to where?"

"To the dress shop," he said.

A nasty suspicion entered my head. "Blaine, Angie sells only women's clothes. And you don't shop locally, Ingrid. In fact, you don't wear anything that's not designer label."

Ingrid shrugged. "I'd like to see what the local boutiques offers. And I do wear off the rack stuff. Nurse's and soldiers' uniforms are never designers."

I narrowed my eyes. "You've been a nurse before?"

"A spy. A teacher. An office manager." She exchanged a grin with Blaine. "We Immortals are good at reinventing ourselves. From high schools and co-eds to nursing wounded soldiers in the battlefield."

"Oh. I just assumed... I, uh, never mind. I need alone time with my girl here, so you two can't come with us." I was being rude, but I didn't care.

Ingrid dismissed my words with a wave of her hand. "Don't worry. We'll leave you two alone. I just want to see what this Angie's Boutique offers."

Raine was trying hard not to laugh.

"Are they babysitting me?" I asked.

She shrugged.

"Echo stopped by the mansion this morning," Blaine explained.

"Was that why Torin and Andris were at school this morning? Because I thought they switched to online classes or just runed teachers and skipped school all together."

"They have Brigg's class in the morning," Raine said and took my arm. "You are one of us, Cora. Get used to it. If you're threatened, we're all threatened. If you need back-up, we provide it. If someone hurts you, we hurt them back."

Why didn't her words make me feel better? I waited until we were inside my car and headed toward Main Street before saying, "What if I stopped helping souls?"

Silence followed. A quick glance at Raine caught her staring at me with wide eyes. "You're kidding, right?" she asked, enunciating her words.

"Yes… no…" I sighed. "I don't know. It's the dark souls' fault. They scare the crap out of me."

"What happened between Monday when you were defending Dev and today?"

"A dark soul attacked me," I said.

"I know, but Echo said it will never happen again."

I rolled my eyes. "And how will my all-powerful and all-knowing boyfriend guarantee that? He can't be with me all the time." I pulled up outside Angie's. Blaine drove past us, looking for a parking spot. We stayed in the car and waited for them.

"You have us too, Cora," Raine reminded me. She reached out and rubbed my arm. "You love helping souls find closure. Don't let the dark souls stop you from doing that. Just like I won't let the Norns stop me from doing what's right."

She made it sound so easy. I wanted to be in control like her, not always looking over my shoulder. "The runes on my body are called medium runes. Ever heard of them?"

She shook her head. "Although that makes sense. Mediums communicate with the dead and that's what you do."

"Dark souls, or lost souls as Dev calls them, etch them on the people they possess. Or try to."

"What?"

I explained what Dev had told me about possessions and psyche ward patients cutting themselves. "The runes protect and stop those possessed from going crazy, except I don't feel protected. I wasn't even possessed, and my body felt like it was being sliced from the inside." I blew out a breath. "Maliina deliberately etched those medium runes on me. And now the dark souls know about me."

"That evil bitch," Raine said.

"I asked Ingrid if she knew anything about them, but she doesn't. She said something weird though. The night Maliina runed me, she said I'd become useful. Why would she say that? Did she know she'd mimic me? Possess me? Are you guys sure she's really in Hel?"

"Whoa, slow down," Raine said, gripping my shoulder. "Let's not jump to conclusions. The Grimnirs took her after that battle at the mansion. Have you talked to Echo?"

"No. I only found out about this during my drive to school."

"There you go. Talk to Echo before you start worrying. He, Torin, Andris, and these guys," she indicated Blaine and Ingrid, who were walking toward us, "have been around and know a lot. I've come to realize that when I have a problem or an idea, my first stop is Torin. At times Mom or Lavania. When they're not around, I go to Blaine or Ingrid. They're a wealth of info. Talk to Echo."

She was right. Maybe I was blowing things out of proportion. We got out of the car just as Blaine and Ingrid reached us. Together we entered the boutique. The salesgirl looked up from her phone and was about to dismiss us when she saw Blaine. She turned on a megawatt smile.

"If you need any help, just let me know," she said, her eyes not leaving him.

I grinned. Once upon a time, that would have been me. I could see Angie through the glass window working on an outfit. As usual, she had a tape around her neck and her dyed red hair was pinned up and away from her face. She was a gifted seamstress.

"We're here to see Angie," I said.

The salesgirl dragged her eyes from Blaine, put her cell phone down, and went to get Angie. In seconds, the redhead entered the room with three dresses draped over her arm.

"Cora, I've been waiting for you," Angie said. The hug she gave me was a bit awkward. She only reached my chin. She turned and saw Raine. "Are you also looking for a prom dress, Raine? I hope so because I found the perfect outfit for you."

Raine bit her lip. "Uh, Angie. I'm not buying anything today."

"Why not? You're not going to the prom? Isn't your boyfriend the handsome quarterback?"

Raine's cheeks grew pink. "My mother already made my outfit, Angie, or I would have been here weeks ago."

Nice save. Angie would be hurt if she knew Raine had bought her outfit online. I took the dresses and waved Blaine and Ingrid over.

"We've brought you some new customers, Angie. Ingrid and Blaine are looking for something special, too." A speculative gleam entered Angie's eyes as she studied Blaine. "For his girlfriend, Jen."

Blaine scowled. "Jen is not my girlfriend."

"Could've fooled me," I teased him.

Angie beamed. She'd probably catalogued Ingrid's designer clothes and accessories and concluded she had a potential wealthy client.

"You're terrible," Raine said.

"Just helping the local economy."

"Spoken like a local farmer's daughter."

"Mom's starting to have a terrible effect on me." I grabbed Raine's wrist and pulled her into the changing room. Now, we could talk uninterrupted. I stripped while she got comfortable on the concrete slab slash bench.

"So you're thinking Maliina never made it to Hel and is trying to use you as a suit?" she asked.

"An Immortal suit, *Dean*." Dean Winchester from the hit TV show *Supernatural* always called the human vessels demons used "suits." I stepped into the first outfit and pulled it up. "But how did she know she'd one day need to borrow my body?"

"The same way I knew about the seeresses dying. Maliina was a powerful witch and an evil Norn-in-training to boot. She could have seen something. Dark souls are not exactly on our side or on humanity's side. They do terrible things. That's gorgeous."

"Really?" I studied my reflection, turned, and checked my back. "You don't think it's a bit too short?"

"No. It's perfect for the prom theme."

"All That Jazz" was the junior prom theme. The dusty-rose, knee-length drop waist dress with fringes was so nineteen-twenties. I loved it. It came with a hair accessory—a hair band with feathers—and satin gloves. I adjusted the hairband and studied my reflection again.

"Red lipstick and a fake cigarette folder, and you're a full-blown flapper girl," Raine said.

"I love the twenties." I shimmied out of the outfit and tried the second one.

"I like the first one better," she said.

"Me too." The third one was a contemporary also perfect for the senior theme—Midnight in Paris. "I'll take this one and the first one."

Scuffles and shouting came from inside the store. Raine pulled her artavus from inside her boot before I could blink. She engaged her invisibility runes and so did I. By the time I pulled out my artavus from the inside pocket of my jacket, she'd etched runes on the door and created a portal. We could see inside the store.

Angie was back in her little office while her salesgirl was behind the desk, her focus on her phone. Blaine and Ingrid were missing.

CHAPTER 14. DINNER WITH THE GANG

"Outside," Raine said, and I followed the direction of her gaze.

Blaine and Ingrid were with Rhys, who was glaring at Blaine as though he wanted to pound his face.

"What in Hel's Mist is going on out there?" Raine mumbled.

I didn't bother to change. I grabbed the clothes I'd worn to school, and the first dress I'd tried on and placed them in front of the salesgirl. "I'll take that one and the one I'm wearing. Tell Angie this," I touched the one I wasn't buying, "is just not me."

She stared at me with round eyes. "But you're wearing that—"

"I'm buying it, too. Okay? Just wrap those ones up." I placed my debit card on the counter, waved to Angie through the window, and indicated the dress I was wearing and the first one I'd tried on. She nodded. "I'll be back to sign the receipt."

"You can't leave the store—"

"I said I'd be back," I snapped and followed Raine outside. Rhys and Blaine turned, and their jaws dropped.

"What? Haven't you ever seen a girl try on a prom dress before? What are you doing here, Rhys?"

"Call off your Immortal watch dog so we can talk," Rhys said.

"Watch who you're calling a dog, Grimnir," Blaine snapped. "And we're not going anywhere."

I sighed. "Blaine—"

"Don't waste your breath, Cora. We're not going anywhere, not after what his partner did to you."

Men! "What is it, Rhys?"

"First, Nara sends her apologies for what happened on Monday." His eyes strayed to my cleavage, which was exposed by the sexy dress. "She would have come herself, but she had to reap."

"Then I'll accept her apology when she says it to my face. What else? And please, my face is up here, not on my chest."

Blaine laughed. Rhys glanced at Ingrid and pink tinged his cheeks. "I apologize. Um, I'm looking for Echo."

I crossed my arms. "He's not here."

A lopsided smile curled Rhys' lips, and dimples flashed on his cheeks. "I can see that. Could you tell him he and I need to talk?"

"Why?"

Annoyance crossed his face. and for one brief moment, I was sure he'd said something rude. Instead, he glanced at Ingrid again and said, "The dark souls are restless, and quite a number of them are headed this way."

My stomach dropped. "How do you know?"

"We reaped a few not far from here. Dark souls are loners by nature and territorial. We saw a group of them. If they're coming here because of you, Echo is going to need help dealing with them."

I studied him, not sure whether he was up to something or not. Like Dev, Echo hadn't spoken to him in years. "Are you offering to help us?"

"Yes. It's time to bury the past."

How convenient. "So this has nothing to do with Dev and the fact that you guys want him?"

"No, but chances are the dark souls followed him here. Dev tended to act without thinking and I'm sure that hasn't changed."

I frowned, not liking that one little bit. "Okay, I'll talk to Echo. How will he contact you?"

"He knows where we hang out." He frowned. "I hope you don't hold my cousin's rash behavior against her. She was distraught over Dev's sudden appearance."

Somehow I didn't see Nara getting distraught or making mistakes. "We'll see."

He nodded at me and Blaine, bowed slightly toward Raine, which meant he knew who she was, and he turned toward Ingrid. "It was nice meeting you, uh…?"

"Goodbye, Grimnir," Blaine said.

Ingrid backhanded Blaine's chest. "Stop being rude. It's Ingrid Dahl. Nice to meet you too, Rhys," she said, sounding so formal.

Those adorable dimples flashed again as Rhys turned to leave. He looked back, his eyes going to Ingrid, before he disappeared into an alley.

I released a breath and glanced at the others. Ingrid wore a look I'd never seen on her. Rhys had definitely caught her interest.

Raine gave me a look that said, "Here we go again." I wasn't sure whether she meant another romance with a Grimnir or another horde of supernatural beings gunning for us.

"Looks like trouble is headed our way," Blaine said, not sounding worried.

I was worried. No, I was petrified. It was the situation with the Immortals attacking our town all over again, except this time we didn't have a bunch of witches on our side. It was just us. Somehow I had to convince Echo to meet with Rhys and rally up support among the Grimnirs. I pulled out my phone and texted Echo. Hopefully, he wasn't in Hel.

"I gotta grab my clothes." I disappeared inside, changed, and paid for my purchases. Outside, I could see the others conferring. Then Blaine and Ingrid took off.

"Don't drop me off at my place," Raine said. "Let's stop at the mansion and talk to Lavania. I'd rather she hears what's going on from you than me, or someone else."

I didn't argue even though all I wanted to do was go home and wait for Echo. My phone didn't ding either, so no text from him. I wasn't sure what was worse, texting him and not getting a response, or not texting at all.

"Did you see how the Grimnir, uh, Rhys couldn't take his eyes off Ingrid?" Raine asked, and I shot her an annoyed look. "Yeah, I know, we have enough to worry about without thinking about romance. But peaceful moments are meant to be enjoyed. Worrying about what might happen will only paralyze us. Torin often says we don't let our enemies dictate how we behave. Let them come and think we're not prepared, until they attack and realize we are way ahead of the game."

I reached out and gripped her hand. "Thank you. I needed to hear that. Oh crap. I can't believe I forgot to ask Rhys about Maliina."

"I'm sure Echo would know if she's on Torture Island or not," Raine quipped.

"I don't know. Remember, he never left my side after the battle, and when I recovered, he left with Eirik. The other Grimnirs were envious of his reaping record and hated him. She could have escaped them and they wouldn't have bothered to tell him."

"Did you feel anything that could connect the dark soul that attacked you to her?"

"You mean other than the pure evil spewing from her core? No."

***

At the mansion, we found Lavania in the library. She had a sixth sense or something because she knew right away something wasn't right. She listened without interrupting. When Torin and Andris arrived, she asked them to join us and quickly explained what I had told her. She didn't miss a thing. Not the fears and doubts starting to consume me, or the dilemma I was having about helping dark souls.

"You poor child," she said, giving me a hug.

The urge to cry washed over me. I couldn't discuss the supernatural crap I went through with my mother, so Lavania and Raine's mother were often my confidants. When she rubbed my back, it reminded me of Mom. I wanted to bawl.

"Listen to me," she added firmly. "We've faced worse enemies and sent them running. So I don't want you worrying about these dark souls or doubting your gifts. Okay?"

The urge to cry ebbed. "It doesn't feel like a gift right now," I griped.

She chuckled. "I know. Once this crisis is over, everything will go back to normal."

I doubted that. Besides, her idea of normal was not my normal.

"Now," she added, her eyes narrowing. "I can't begin to understand why you've decided to help a dark soul, but I'm going to respect your decision. I only hope that if you need to talk, you know I'm here for you."

I fought tears again.

"Come now. None of that. Let's talk about medium runes. I don't think I've ever heard of them before, but I'm not surprised they exist. Most Mediums are witches, who use trance magic, not runes, in order to communicate with the dead. Have you guys heard of them?" She glanced at the others, but Torin, Andris, and Blaine shook their heads. Ingrid wore a preoccupied expression as though something bothered her.

"Now I understand why you asked me about Maliina," Ingrid said. "If she's the soul that attacked you—"

"No, she's not," Andris said quickly. "The Grimnirs took her straight to Hel's little torture chamber on Agony Island after I killed her. I saw them enter a portal with her."

"What if she escaped and is here now?" Ingrid shot back, her voice rising.

"Then we'll deal with her again," Andris said. "Anyone coming after you or Cora must go through us first." Sometimes he acted like he might have stronger feelings for Ingrid, and other times, he was a complete jerk to her. He was so unpredictable.

"Andris is right," Lavania said, rubbing Ingrid's arm. "But soon we won't need the boys to protect us. You'll be protecting yourselves." She smiled, her glance touching me, Ingrid, and Raine. "It's time for my great news now that you're all here. I got the go-ahead to start a new school, a special school to train Immortals and future Valkyries. We should be up and running by fall."

"I didn't think they'd go for it," Raine said.

"Why shouldn't they? As soon as they learned the idea came from you, they were happy to oblige. I'm still searching for the perfect location and once I find it, I expect you three to be in my senior class."

Since there was no way in Hel's Mist my parents would allow me to spend my senior year at some weird boarding school, I tuned them out, my thoughts shifting to Echo. I checked my phone again.

No text.

What was the point of having a phone when he couldn't take a moment to text me back? Unless he couldn't. My stomach clenched at the thought.

I made eye contact with Raine and indicated the door with a slant of my head. We excused ourselves. Torin cocked a questioning brow, but Raine didn't explain.

"I need to check if Echo is at his place and then head home."

"Let me tell the others." She walked away before I could protest. I sent Echo another text. A minute later, Raine came out with Torin. Andris, Blaine, and Ingrid followed.

"What's going on?" I asked.

"We're coming with you," Raine said. "You don't think we're going to let you out of our sight now, do you?"

It was sweet of them, but I just wanted to see Echo. "So if I said no?"

"We'd ignore you," Andris said and led the way through the portal to Echo's place in Miami. The house was in total darkness. It was eight p.m. We did a walk-through, but Echo wasn't there. I started to worry. I sent him two texts, first apologizing for my previous one and then begging him to come home.

"Did your mom bake pies today, Cora?" Andris asked, rubbing his stomach.

"Yeah, I could go for a slice now and a glass of her apple cider," Blaine chimed in.

I shook my head. They weren't exactly subtle. "If you want to continue playing Secret Service, just say so."

"We want to make sure you're safely at home, and we do love your mom's pies," Torin added.

It was hard to argue with Torin when he wore that look that said he was beginning to worry. An absent Echo when I needed him was a bad sign. We headed back to the mansion, piled up in cars, and drove to my place.

I kept glancing at my cell phone so much Raine offered to drive.

**

It wasn't often the whole crew gathered at my place, but Mom didn't seem fazed when we pulled up. The mansion was the meeting place of choice whenever we had a crisis.

Instead of going inside, they decided to sit on the porch after saying hi to my parents. Torin took the swing and pulled Raine onto his lap. She snuggled against his chest. Ingrid sat beside them while Blaine plopped on a wicker chair and Andris leaned against the porch rail. Once I dropped my dresses upstairs, I helped Mom serve homemade apple cider and slices of pie.

"Dinner will be ready in an hour, so don't take off," Mom warned us.

I followed her inside the house. "Mom, you don't have to feed them."

She chuckled and exchanged a glance with Dad. "What a terrible thing to say. Your friends are always invited here. Dinner will be ready in an hour. Now, shoo. Let me know if they need more cider."

For half an hour, I half-listened to my friends talk about soccer and US players. The Fifa World Cup was starting in June. I had no interest in soccer or what teams were likely to qualify. Blaine and Torin were typical jocks, but Ingrid surprised me by how much she knew about soccer.

I stared into space and stressed about everything—Echo, dark souls, Dev, Rhys and Nara, and Maliina—my worst nightmare. If she was back...

A hand landed on my shoulder. I jumped. Andris had come to sit beside me on the steps and I hadn't even noticed. The way the others stared at me said they must have tried to get my attention, too.

"May I use your bathroom?" Andris asked.

"Sure. There's one downstairs. I'll show you."

We entered the house, and Mom looked up. I was surprised to see Dad with her in the kitchen. From the looks of things, he was helping her.

"Just showing Andris the restroom," I said.

Andris caught my hand before I could turn and go back outside. "I should be out in five minutes. Ten minutes tops."

"Ew, too much information. Take your time."

He smirked, glanced over my shoulder at my parents, and said, "Keep your parents away from the bathroom, or you'll have some s'plaining to do." He disappeared inside the bathroom.

He was so weird sometimes. I turned around, and my eyes collided with my parents. "Need help with anything, Mom?"

"Maybe in ten-fifteen minutes. Is everything okay?" she asked.

"Yeah."

Mom wiped her hands on a dish towel, her eyes not leaving me. "You know I can tell when you're not okay. Did something happen at school?"

"No." If she hugged me now, I was so going to start bawling like a five year old.

"Are your prom dresses okay? I saw the dress bags, but with your friends around, I haven't really seen them."

"They're beautiful. I gotta go outside, Mom." I hurried out of the house before the tears started. Raine had kicked Torin from the porch swing. In fact, Torin and Blaine were talking by the orchard. She pulled me down between her and Ingrid.

"If anyone can find Echo, it's him," Raine said reassuringly. "Andris has connections in places that would shock you."

"Or make you blush," Ingrid added.

His behavior made sense now. I grimaced. "When he said he'd be out in five to ten minutes, I thought he was just being Andris."

"Nah, we thought Echo was taking too long, and he offered to go look for him."

"I wanted to go with him if he was going to visit a certain club frequented by Grimnirs," Ingrid added and sighed.

"You have it bad," Raine teased her.

"Rhys is gorgeous, but I've met gorgeous men before. I felt something with him, and I just want to explore it without Andris watching. He gets overly protective."

"So how many guys have you dated since you became Immortal?" Raine asked.

Ingrid laughed, drawing the attention of Torin and Blaine. "I'm not going to tell," she said.

"Why not?" Raine asked.

"Because you might think I'm just as bad as Andris."

Raine's jaw dropped. "No way."

"You don't live for a couple of centuries without leaving behind a string of broken hearts." She had our attention. "Or getting your heart broken. There was this soldier I met in France during World War Two…"

Ingrid just went from interesting to super cool in the blink of an eye. She was funny, outrageous, and naughty. I completely forgot about stressing, until Dad came outside and said Mom needed help. Then he went to join Blaine and Torin. Raine and Ingrid followed me inside.

"We girls can use the table and the men can take the stools or sit in the living room," Mom explained. Our table only seated four, which was perfect for my small family, not entertaining.

"How long is that boy going to be in the bathroom?" Mom asked.

I glanced at my watch. Andris had been gone for over ten minutes. What if something had happened to Echo? Rhys could have been lying about wanting to help us. Echo could have walked into a trap. I wish I hadn't texted him about Rhys's offer. Then there were dark souls. I was sure he didn't stand a chance against a horde of them.

"Cora?" Mom asked, snapping me back to the present.

I said the first thing that popped into my head. "Mystery meat."

Mom straightened and harrumphed. "That's two too many."

The principal was going to get a phone call tomorrow. She disappeared in the basement, where we had the pantry.

"Two what?" Raine asked when I joined them at the other end of the counter.

"Two people with stomach problems after eating mystery meat at school." Raine and Ingrid wore questioning look. "It's the only explanation I could think of when she asked about Andris' disappearance in the bathroom and me barfing yesterday after encountering you-know-what."

They laughed.

"It's not funny. Mr. Johnson is going to get a phone call tomorrow, and I'll be called to the office to explain. You two have it good. You don't have to make up stories for your weird behavior."

"I don't have weird behavior," Ingrid protested.

"Having dates with three guys at three different restaurants at the same time is super freaky," Raine said.

"I had to know which one was the better kisser," Ingrid quipped. "Which reminds me. I can do accents and change the pitch of my voice. If I make a few phone calls complaining about mystery meat, maybe the principal won't call you to the office."

"Perfect." I hugged her.

"Look who's finally here," Mom called out from behind us and I turned, expecting Andris to be out of the bathroom. Instead, she was staring outside at Echo's Escalade.

I was out the door and racing toward the SUV before Echo parked. This time, he was prepared. Probably saw me coming. I leaped into his arms and he caught me, turning around.

"You're here," I whispered.

"As opposed to being where?"

"Out there where terrible things are happening. Dark souls are headed this way. When you didn't answer my text, I thought I'd lost you."

He stopped and leaned back against the SUV, one arm around my waist, the other cradling the back of my head. "I have you to come home to, *Cora mia.* I'd never do anything to get hurt or lose my way."

I leaned back and smacked his chest. "Then why didn't you answer my texts?"

He fished his cell from his back pocket and frowned. "I'm supposed to respond?"

I pushed his chest, getting angry. "Of course you were. What's the point of…?" I realized he was teasing. "Very funny." I tried to wiggle out of his arm again, but his grip tightened.

"I'm sorry I missed the others. I'll read all of them and respond. Right now, I need my kiss. Then you can explain why the entire Valkyrie nation is at your home."

I reached up and planted a brief kiss on his lips, but he didn't let me get away with it.

"You cannot cheat on a kiss, not after that welcome home hug," he whispered against my lips, cupped my face, and kissed me properly. I forgot that my parents and my friends were probably watching us.

He leaned back. "Better?"

"Yes." I was so lame. "No. You still have to tell me what happened. But right now, dinner awaits." I grabbed his hand and pulled him toward the house. Everyone was inside.

Right before I opened the door, he stole another kiss. My cheeks were hot when I entered the house and I was sure my eyes sparkled. Mom shook her head, but I knew what she was thinking—I'd been pining for Echo earlier and that was why I'd looked miserable. If only she knew.

"Get some food and head over there, son," she said, pointing at where the men were seated in the living room. Andris was back. "Have you met her other friends?" Mom added.

Echo glanced over at Torin and the others, and for a second I was sure he'd pretend he didn't know them. I elbowed him.

"Briefly, ma'am," Echo said.

Someone coughed, and I was sure they'd choked on their drink or food.

"Ah, then this is an opportunity to get to know them better," Mom said and shooed him away.

The conversation at the men's table was going to be interesting.

"Briefly," I whispered as I scooped spaghetti. We were the last ones to serve ourselves. Mom had made garlic bread sticks to go with the pasta and meat sauce.

"It would have been hard to explain how I know them, don't you think? Besides, I want the Valkyries to squirm as they try to answer questions about their pasts."

"Be nice, Echo," I warned him.

His answer was to shove a stick of garlic bread into my mouth and smirk. Mom was at our table, so we couldn't discuss Echo and his antics. The conversation around our table revolved around food from different cultures, with Mom wanting to know more about Ingrid, who was perfectly happy talking about her Celtic roots. The only time she faltered was when Mom asked her about her family.

"My parents died when I was young, so my sister and I stayed with Aunt Lavania and her adopted sons, Torin and Andris."

"I haven't met Lavania yet, but Cora told me she was your aunt, Raine."

"Actually, she's Eirik's aunt," Raine corrected.

"Sorry, I got them confused," I added. This dinner might end up being a disaster. We should all sit down and come up with the perfect fake story for everyone.

"So, you're related to Eirik?" she asked Ingrid.

"No, Mrs. Jemison. Lavania took us in, but she didn't officially adopt us," Raine explained.

"And is your sister here with you?"

"No. She passed away recently."

Mom reached out and gripped her hand. "I'm so sorry for your loss, dear."

"Don't be, Mrs. Jemison. I know it's terrible to see death as a good thing, but for Maliina it was. She was very ill and in so much pain."

My admiration for Ingrid went up a notch. She had perfected her background. She kept Mom entertained throughout dinner. Then she and Raine helped me clear the table despite Mom's protests. The guys helped, too. They brought their plates to the sink.

Andris, as usual, didn't bother to get up. He was busy talking to Dad about the science fiction genre. I doubted there was a sci-fi book he hadn't read. Going by Dad's expression, he was impressed.

"Interesting friends you have there," Dad said after they left.

"Let me guess, Andris is going to get an ARC of your next book," I said.

He nodded. "Now I understand why he co-runs my blog. The boy has a mind like a sponge. He knows every character in my books and everything they did. He's even read sci-fi books I haven't read."

I kissed his cheek. "Goodnight, Daddy. I'm happy you finally met your number one fan."

"Number two," Mom corrected, coming to stand by my side. "Goodnight, honey. Your friends should visit more often."

"They will." Now that they had cleared the biggest hurdle—their backgrounds. "'Night, Mommy."

I raced upstairs, knowing Echo would be coming later. I entered the bedroom and froze. Dev was in the middle of my room, jabbing his disembodied fists at some poor soul.

Not just some soul.

Raine's father.

CHAPTER 15. POSSESSION

"HEY!"

The two souls looked at me, relief flickering on Mr. Cooper's face. Tears rushed to my eyes. I knew he'd been sick for months and had slipped into a coma. Still, it was a shock to see his soul. It was too soon for him to die.

"Leave him alone," I yelled at Dev. I locked my door, pulled out my cell phone, and extended it toward Dev. "Get inside." My eyes didn't leave Mr. Cooper as Dev slithered into my phone.

"I tried to scare the old dude, but he wouldn't leave," Dev said. "I thought you were supposed to have runes around the house to stop souls from getting inside."

"And somehow *you* got inside after I told you my house was off limits," I reminded him.

"I used Echo's place and came through the portal. He came through the window. You shouldn't leave your windows open. Get rid of him because we need to talk."

"Not now. And FYI, he's not an old dude." A quick glance at Raine's father told me he was no longer scared. Just unhappy and maybe confused because his eyes kept volleying between me and my cell phone. I wondered how he'd moved past the runes around my house. I didn't think he knew how to create portals. "His name is Mr. Cooper, and he's my best friend's father. He's been ill. Did you talk to Echo?"

"Not yet. His first priority was finding the person who tried to attack you. I know who it is now."

I wanted to know who it was, but Mr. Cooper was my first priority. I headed toward the mirror, engaging portal runes. The mirror responded.

"Where are we going? Did you hear what I said?" Dev asked.

"I did. Since you're not going anywhere, I need to find Raine." The portal opened into the mansion, but it was too quiet. A quick peek outside showed no cars. Raine's father followed me as though we were tethered.

"The old man is not too happy," Dev said. "He's not ready to go."

"How do you know that?"

"His energy is flickering, a sign of agitation."

"Of course he's freaked out. You threatened him."

"He came to you, a sign that he needs your help."

Last time Mr. Cooper flat-lined, he'd come straight to me. Then his soul had returned to his body. I texted Torin.

"Who is Torin? Why are you asking him to meet you?"

"Stop talking, Dev. I'm trying to focus." I texted Echo. The lights in the foyer flicked on just before I re-directed the portal to Raine's house.

"Cora, what in Hel's Mist is…?" Lavania called from the second floor balcony and raced downstairs at a hyper speed without finishing her question, runes blazing on her skin. "Tristan," she whispered, staring at Raine's father.

"I found him in my bedroom after Raine and the others left. I thought I'd check here first before going to her house."

"Come. His soul should stay by his body or he won't be reaped." Runes on the mirror responded to the ones on her body and she disappeared into Raine's living room.

"Who's the lady with the lovely voice?" Dev asked.

"Shh. I swear, if you don't stop talking, I'll kick you out of my phone," I whispered and followed Lavania with Raine's father trailing behind me. Femi was reading in the living room, saw us, and gasped.

Her eyes welled up. "I checked on him ten minutes ago, and he was still breathing. "

"He must have just died and went straight to Cora's house. Take him to his body. Pull yourself together, Femi, and find Raine. I'll get Svana." Lavania disappeared through the portal.

Tears continued to race down Femi's face. "I told Raine he was okay. She's going to be devastated."

"I already texted Torin and told him what's going on. He'll know what to do."

Femi wiped tears from her cheeks. "Okay, I'll stay with you and… and… Could you lead him back to his body?"

Who knew that Femi had grown attached to Raine's father? She came from ancient Egypt and was thousands of years old.

Inside the study, I watched as the soul stared down at his body. Then he looked at me. I knew that look only too well. I trusted Mr. Cooper, so I nodded and extended my hands toward him.

"Bond with me," I said. He moved closer.

"Don't bite my head again, but your medium runes are not on," Dev piped up from my cell phone.

"Excuse me?"

"Your medium runes should be blazing *before* you allow a soul to possess you."

I frowned. Was that what I'd been doing wrong? I raised my hand toward Mr. Cooper and he stopped. "Dev, you said souls see my medium runes from afar."

"Yes. You're like a beacon."

"Why then should I engage the runes if they're already there?"

He sighed, and when he spoke, he did it slowly. "So you tap into the runes and protect yourself. Some souls never want to leave because they can feel again when they're inside you. Oh, no wonder you get sick. You never engage your medium runes."

So that was what I'd been doing wrong all these months. You engage strength runes if you wanted to be strong, speed runes to move fast, invisibility runes to cloak… It made sense to use medium runes for possession.

I closed my eyes and willed the medium runes to appear on my skin. I rarely used them, so I wasn't sure what they looked like. I only recalled one bind rune. It appeared, inking my skin as though it was being etched in real time.

"I can feel their power," I whispered.

Something weird started to happen. More runes appeared even though I didn't will them. It was as though the first one was pulling the others to the surface. The same runes repeated themselves until my arms were covered with them.

I waited for them to glow like my other runes. They didn't. Majority of them continued to coil under my skin like tiny snakes. A surge of power shot through me, the effect stronger than anything I'd ever felt with other runes. Panic followed. Maybe I wasn't supposed to engage these runes.

"I can feel them, yet I'm inside your phone," Dev said. "I don't know if I can... if I can resist their pull." He sounded weird, breathless and weak.

"No, you stay in there," I yelled.

"But I feel their glow, their pull... I could feel again." His head slithered out of the power outlet on my phone.

"Go back inside, Dev, or I swear I'll tell Echo to reap you."

The door swung open, and Femi entered the room. "Cora? I heard a... What's going on? What have you done to yourself?"

Her questions registered, but I was busy trying to understand what Dev had said. What did he mean by their glow? The runes were like tats on my skin. The few that were glowing were pain and strength runes, which I must have automatically engaged without thinking. Maybe only souls could see the medium runes glow. They already did even when I didn't have them on the surface.

"They're medium runes," I said.

Femi had moved closer and was studying me as though I was an alien. Ignoring her, I extended my hands toward Raine's father, who was frowning.

"It's okay, Mr. Cooper. We can bond now."

I could see the concern on his face, but he couldn't resist the pull of the runes. I braced myself as he drew closer. A cold draft accompanied him, but it wasn't as chilly as before. The effect of bonding wasn't as nauseating. The need to push him out of me was still there, but it didn't overwhelm my senses.

I was aware of my surrounding, and my vision and my hearing weren't unimpaired. Raine burst through the doors. Her eyes darting around, tears racing down her face. She saw me and stopped, her eyes widening.

"It's okay," I reassured her, then my eyes met Echo's. He wore a bewildered expression. It turned furious fast.

"Who did this to you?" he asked, closing the gap between us.

"No one did." I stuck out my arms, the runes now covering every inch of my body. I was sure I looked like Lady Gaga's bestie, Zombie Boy. Not pretty. "These are the same medium runes Maliina etched on me. I just learned how to use them. Kinda," I added with a shrug.

"They don't glow," Echo said, studying my arms. "That can't be good."

"Where's my father?" Raine asked.

I opened my mouth to answer, but Dev said, "He's inside her."

Everyone's attention shifted to the phone clenched in my hand, and I sighed.

"Who's that?" Ingrid asked.

"Dev, the dark soul, who will be in trouble if he doesn't shut up!" I focused on Raine. She stood in Torin's arms, but she was no longer crying. I moved closer to her and expected her to cringe. The runes on my skin couldn't be pretty. She didn't cringe, a testament of our tightness.

"Your father bonded with me, Raine," I said. "He wants to talk to you, Torin, and your mother."

"Mother," Raine whispered. "I have to tell her."

"Lavania went to get her," Femi said. She looked at the others and indicated the door. They filed out, except Echo.

"You can talk when possessed?" Echo asked.

"Yeah. Weird, huh?" It was strange hearing my voice when I had a soul inside me. Usually I just listened to their thoughts while shivering and trying not to barf.

"We don't know anything about these medium runes," he said. "They could have side-effects. They don't even glow."

That was the second time he'd brought that up. "To us they don't, but to souls—"

"They're like a thousand stars," Dev said. "Don't let him stay for too long, Cora. You need to let him take over, finish his business, and kick him out. Even the most loving souls get addicted to possession."

This time, I couldn't tell Dev to shut up. "How do I let him take over?"

"Talk to him. Don't fight him when he wants control," Dev explained.

I gave Echo my cell phone. "Go. I'll be out as soon as we're done." His expression said he didn't want to leave. "I'll be fine," I reassured him. "The medium runes make a big difference. I'm in control. I'm talking in my normal voice. I'm not dizzy or nauseous. I can see and hear and feel, yet he's inside me."

He only scowled harder.

"Dev will explain. Please, go." I pushed my cell phone into his hand.

He nodded, still not looking happy. "Okay. If you need me, I'll be outside the door." I waited until the door closed behind him then turned and faced Raine and Torin. "Do you want to wait for your mom?"

Raine shook her head. Then she moved away from Torin and took my hands. "I want to talk to him first."

"Okay." I listened to her father's thoughts and smiled. "He doesn't want to wait either."

I didn't know how to give him control when he asked if he could speak. Part of me was scared of what I might feel. I focused on what I knew about him, that I trusted him and he would never hurt me. Then I took a leap of faith.

My mouth opened and words poured out, but it wasn't my voice I heard. It was Mr. Cooper's. He sounded weak. Tears filled my eyes as he talked to Raine. Raine was crying so hard, and I was an empathic crier. Or maybe it was his words.

He loved her and was proud of the woman she was becoming. He reminded her of little things they'd done together, and how she'd reacted. He wanted her to hold on to those memories and not worry about him.

His voice grew stronger. Raine cried harder. I cried even harder. Our arms were around each other. I knew she was really hugging her father, but I was in there, too, giving my best friend the comfort she needed.

Then I realized something. I was fading, growing weaker as Mr. Cooper's voice grew stronger. He was taking over my senses. His voice ebbed as he talked to Torin. One minute strong, the next so faint I strained to hear him.

I started to panic. He was in the middle of telling Torin what he expected from him as Raine's future husband and father to his grandchildren when my hearing disappeared.

I tried to tell Raine that I couldn't hear anything, but the words coming from my mouth were directed at Torin. Mr. Cooper was in control. I tried to push Raine away and signal help, but I couldn't control my arms. Medium runes weren't all they were cracked up to be was my last thought before I blacked out.

***

I opened my eyes slowly and the first face I saw was Echo's. Was I dead?

"No, you're not dead, but you're going to give me a heart attack, something I've never worried about."

I glanced around and frowned. Once again, I was on Raine's bed. "What happened?"

"Mr. Cooper finished talking to his wife, but as soon as he left your body, you dropped like a Raggedy Ann doll."

I narrowed my eyes. He sounded too dang pleased with himself. "I guess you plan to tell me 'I told you so.'"

He caressed my cheek. "No. I made it just in time to catch you."

"You did?"

"Yep. I told you I always know when you need me. Felt it right here." He pressed his hand to his left breast right where his heart was. "You were growing weaker the longer he stayed inside you. You're lucky Mr. Cooper was not interested in taking over your body. If he had been a different soul..."

I would be a suit. The thought that a soul could kick me out of the way and take over my body was scary.

"No more medium runes," I swore.

"Finally, we agree on something."

"Until I learn everything about them," I added.

He made a face. "Somehow I knew you'd add that. Why don't you ever listen to me? I'm older and wiser—"

I laughed. "Yeah, I've seen your wisest moves."

"That's insulting. I have wicked moves." He wiggled his eyebrows.

A knock and Raine stepped into the room with a bag of Twizzlers. I sat up and caught it when she threw it my way. Switching to supersonic speed, I ripped open the bag and pulled out several of the surgery treats. For a moment, all I thought about was replenishing my energy, everything else forgotten.

When I slowed down, Raine, Torin, and Echo were talking in low tones by the door while staring at me. She looked like crap now that I had a chance to study her. Her eyes were red from crying, and her hair was mussed.

I slipped to the edge of the bed and stood, but a wave of dizziness washed over me and I plopped back on the bed. Echo appeared by my side, his hands steadying me.

"Take it easy, doll-face. You've been out for nearly two hours."

"Two… I have to go home." I jumped up, or tried to, but Echo pinned me down. Raine had left the room before I could ask her about her father. "Did I help?"

He cupped my cheeks and peered at me. "You're not making sense, sweetheart. You must still be loopy from the possession."

I pouted. "I'm not."

"Those medium runes are a game changer. Next time you want to give a soul a voice, I'm staying. I don't care who the person is. About going home, your parents were fast asleep when I last checked on them. And no, don't lecture me about runing them. I had to. Your mother wanted to talk to you about your prom dresses." He rolled his eyes. "What's with women and prom?"

"It's a rite of passage." Prom wasn't even important anymore. "Is Torin taking Raine's father to Valhalla?"

Echo's expression changed. He stood and I thought I heard him swear, but I could have been mistaken. Now, he was worrying me.

"What is it?"

"Mr. Cooper's soul is not going to Valhalla."

"Why not?"

"Because he's bound for Hel."

I scoffed at the idea. "No, he's not."

"Yes, he is, doll-face. I've always been meant to reap him. It doesn't matter that I gave him a pass last year. He's going to Hel."

I shook my head as though the simple act would make him take back his words. "You can't take him. He has to go to Asgard. Raine and her mother are a big deal there."

"It doesn't matter. I've gone through this with Raine and her mother. They were blindsided, but rules are rules, and no one breaks them. When Odin's son didn't die in battle, where did he go? Hel's realm. Goddess Freya's husband? Hel. I could name a few more gods and goddesses who are there. Their parents and spouses couldn't stop the reapers. It's the one time we have power over the gods." He reached down and ran his knuckles down my cheek. "Sorry, doll-face, but Mr. Cooper's soul is mine."

I jumped up and paced, imagining Raine's reaction to this. She'd hate Echo. "What if you refused to reap him?"

"Then some other Grimnir will come for him."

"Tell them he's under our protection."

He grabbed my wrist and stopped me mid-stride. "What do you think will happen if I don't reap him? He'll hang around doing nothing and slowly fading like Torin's mother. Then he'll start longing for what he had with his wife and start possessing electronics just so he can talk to her. Next, he'll upgrade to animals so he can feel and feed. By then he'd lose whatever little humanity he still had left and go after Mortals. Before you know it, he'd become a dark mass of nothing we despise. Do you think Raine and her mother would like that?"

The fight left me, and I rested my forehead on his chest. A tear escaped. Then another. Poor Raine. She had to lose her father twice. Echo pulled me into his arms and tucked my head under his chin.

"Shh, don't. I can't stand it when you hurt."

"He was like a father to me. He'd challenge us to think deeper about things and current issues. Stupid rules! Someone as kind and smart as him deserves to go to Asgard."

"I know."

I clung to Echo until the tears stopped. "When do you leave?"

"Soon." He stroked my hair. "I gave her my word that I'd find him a comfortable, solitary room in case she wants to pay him a visit." He rubbed my back and pressed a kiss on my temple. "Hel is not a bad place. It is the perfect resting place for sick and weary souls."

"It's freezing," I countered.

"So are souls. The temperature is perfect for them. Most souls never want to leave once they settle into their rooms. They say most spend eternity reliving their happiest memories over and over."

I wasn't sure whether he was serious or not, but I knew Raine. If she wanted her father in Asgard, nothing was going to stop her from finding a way to make it happen. She was stubborn like that. Maybe she'd find a way around this stupid rule.

I saw the time on her dresser. It was almost ten. "Is everyone downstairs?"

"Yes. Mrs. Cooper wanted time alone with her husband, but we'll have to leave soon. I should be back by tomorrow sometime."

"Tomorrow? It takes that long to go to Hel and back?"

Echo chuckled. "No. Seconds, but I need to find him a resting place closer to the deities. I'll have to move through their wing and prepare one of the unused rooms undetected."

Finally, he was talking about Hel. "Unused rooms? Is Hel's Hall like a hotel with many rooms?"

"More like dorms with rows and columns of bunk beds. The gods and goddesses are pampered and have private rooms. Goddess Hel will never dream of looking for him there. The gods, especially dead ones, hate to be bothered from their resting places or they turn all nasty and vengeful." He shuddered. "Hateful bastards. You'd think it's everyone's fault they ended up in Hel and not Asgard. Yet when they're up, they want to be entertained. They're lucky Goddess Hel accommodates them."

"I don't get it. Why should the goddess care about Raine's father?"

"Eirik," Echo said. "She hasn't forgotten that the Norns placed Eirik close to Raine and her family so he'd be surrounded by love. Sure, it's the Norns' fault for bringing him here, but she has enough hatred to go around, and she's spreading it."

I frowned. "Does she know about me, too?"

Echo slanted me a glance, the corner of his lips lifting. "The girl her son loved so much he left Asgard to rescue her from me? Oh, yes."

I winced, and Echo chuckled. I punched his arm. He was such a jerk sometimes. "Quit playing. I'm serious."

He hugged me close. "No one touches what's mine, and you, *Cora mia*, are mine. According to her, you and Maliina are one and the same. Since she's dead, you're dead too. Since she's seen Maliina's soul, you ceased to matter. Come on." He snatched my hand, and we walked toward the mirror portal, which responded to his runes.

"Wait. Does Raine know how the goddess feels?" I whispered.

"Of course not. She's too impulsive and might decide to do something rash and anger the gods *and* the Norns. Only Torin knows."

And knowing him, he was keeping that secret from Raine. Probably best that way. I wouldn't want to know either. The portal to the living room opened, and I could see the others seated around the wet bar and the couch. The silence was spooky.

I tugged Echo's hand and stopped him. Once we joined the others, he'd be leaving to escort Raine's father to Hel. That in itself didn't bother me. His plans to find a special room under the goddess' very nose bothered me more. What if she found out what he was doing? What if her guards busted him? He could end up on Corpse Strand with the damned souls.

"Does Goddess Hel have lots of guards?"

"Three main ones, but I know their routine. Talking of guards, you need this." He fished my cell phone from his back pocket and pressed it in my hand.

Crap! I'd completely forgotten about Dev. "Did you talk to him?"

"Not really. Once he answered my question, I figured the rest could wait until I return."

"What question?"

"We'll talk when I come back," he whispered, gripped my hand, and pulled me through the portal. Most of the people in the room had a glass of something, except Raine and Torin. She was curled up beside him, her eyes glassy and red-rimmed. Torin's expression said he was hurting for her. She looked worse than before, possibly the result of accepting the fact that her father was heading for Hel's realm. If she knew about the goddess' hatred for her family, she'd probably go over the edge.

Femi's eyes were red, too. She always looked like nothing fazed her, but she was a softy inside. Blaine, Ingrid, and Andris stared into their drinks with gloomy expressions. Since they were at least several centuries old, I'd bet they were drinking alcohol.

Svana, Raine's mother, was missing. I wondered if she knew about the goddess' hatred. Knowing her, she probably did. Maybe she'd taken off with her husband's soul and stashed him some place in Asgard where Goddess Hel would never look. On the other hand, she'd just gotten re-instated as a Valkyrie and wouldn't jeopardize that.

Torin saw us first. "Ready?"

Echo nodded. "I just need to get my coat and gloves."

"And me. I'm going with you," Andris said, standing.

"No, you're not." Echo said. "Hel is my realm, and I decide who travels with me."

"Raine needs Torin," Andris said, speaking firmly and, for once, not baiting Echo. "Even you don't know how long you'll be gone."

I was surprised when Echo nodded grudgingly. If Raine heard their exchange, she didn't show it. She didn't even look up when the study door opened and her mother walked out with her father's soul trailing her. Mrs. Cooper looked as bad as Raine. Mr. Cooper looked calm. Since he was married to a Valkyrie, he must have been mentally prepared for all this. Most souls were often confused by the presence of Valkyries.

Raine's mother hugged me. "How are you doing?"

"Better." I stole a glance at the soul and read gratitude on his face. He smiled. "I'm sorry I blacked out."

"No, no, sweetheart. Don't ever apologize for that. What you did was very brave. Because of you," her chin trembled and tears filled her eyes, "I heard Tristan's voice once again. I don't want you to worry about these medium runes, because Lavania will find out what's going on and help you master their use." She kissed my cheeks then focused her attention on Echo. He stiffened.

"Find a good place for him," she whispered.

"I will, Mrs. Cooper," Echo said quickly, but he wasn't escaping Raine's mother that easily.

"Thank you." She kissed his cheeks and hugged him.

Echo gave me his rescue-me eyes, but I just shrugged. He'd better get used to it. Mothers smothered. Raine's mother and Lavania hugged. My mother cooked and plied you with food.

I only got a brief moment with Echo before they left. He cupped my face and rubbed my cheeks with his thumb.

"Dev stays with you at all times until I come back," he whispered.

I wasn't expecting that. "Um, okay. Why?"

"Because Torin and Raine won't be at school for the rest of the week, and even though I know Blaine and Ingrid are Immortals, they have no experience dealing with souls. Dev does."

He trusted his old buddy now. My job was done. "Okay."

His eyebrows flattened. "You're not going to argue with me?"

"Nope. What did he say to make you change your mind?"

"It's not what he said. He rescued you. I'll always be indebted to anyone who takes care of you." He planted a kiss on my lips and started to walk away, but I grabbed his shirt and pulled him back. I wasn't ready to let him go yet.

"Did he tell you who attacked me?"

"Yes. I'll take care of her when I come back," he vowed. "Can I go now?"

I reached up and kissed him. "Be careful."

He grinned. "Always."

He left to get his coat and gloves from the car. I stared after him and frowned. Something he'd said had bothered me, yet I couldn't put my finger on it. I went over our conversation, and my stomach dipped.

Her? He'd said he would deal with her—the dark soul that had attacked me—when he came back. That could only mean one woman, the only one who hated me enough to want to hurt me.

Maliina.

I shouldn't call her a woman. She was an evil Norn wannabe, a bitter, angry soul without a conscience, and she was back to steal my body. Again.

CHAPTER 16. THE TRUTH

My mind was still on Maliina as I watched Echo and Andris leave with Raine's father. The whole thing was kind of anti-climactic. I'd expected thunder and lightning *à la Thor*. Maybe the rainbow bridge Raine talked about.

Instead, Echo created a portal as usual, except it led to nothingness. An endless white wall of ice and floor of snow. A few flakes accompanied the frigid air that blew into the room. It was a different kind of cold. Biting. Piercing the skin to the bone. No wonder Echo often returned frozen. We all stood there with arms crossed and stared at them.

Mr. Cooper only wore his gray suit, but the cold didn't seem to bother him. I wondered if Svana had dressed his body in that suit or whether he could choose what to wear by just thinking it. When I'd gone into the study to see his body, only his face had been visible.

Echo turned, and our eyes met. My insides melted. I blew him a kiss and mouthed, "Love you. Be careful."

He spread his arms as though to say, "I'm in my realm. What could possible go wrong?"

Arrogant man. He didn't even button-up his duster while Andris was dressed like an Eskimo. I'd bet he was regretting going. Mr. Cooper turned and stared at us. Her mother pressed her hands to her heart. He imitated her gesture. Raine started to cry again.

Ooh, dang it. Tears rushed to my eyes.

No one spoke or seemed interested in leaving after the portal closed. They went back to their seats and drinks. I wanted to be here for Raine, who sobbed silently in Torin's arms, but I didn't really think she needed me. She had Torin, her mother, Femi, and Lavania. Actually, all the Immortals and Valkyries were here for her.

I wondered if they cared about the dead bodies or had funerals and viewings. From my experience at the nursing home, a funeral home picked up the body once the hospice nurse confirmed death. Femi was a hospice nurse. So far, no ambulance had come blazing into their cul-de-sac.

I rubbed Raine's arm and she gave me a weak smile. "Do you want me to stay?"

She nodded, pulled away from Torin, and hugged me. For a moment, we held on to each other and cried. When she went back to Torin's arms, she continued to grip my hand.

"No, sweetheart," her mother said. "Cora has school tomorrow and needs to go home."

Raine glared at her mother, and everyone held their breath. I was sure she was going to say something mean. But Torin whispered in her ear and she looked away.

"Fine, mother." The smile she gave me was weak, but her eyes still blazed.

Whoa. She was pissed. The silence that followed was uncomfortable.

"Before you leave, Cora, I wanted to thank your friend for the part he played tonight," Raine's mother said. "Maybe one day we'll get to meet him."

"I wish I could have done more, Mrs. Cooper," Dev said from my cell phone. His beautiful accent was back. "I'm sorry for your loss."

"What's your name?" Raine's mother asked.

"Dev, son of Graenen."

"Thank you, Dev," Raine's mother said.

"How long have you been around, Dev?" Lavania asked.

"A couple of millennia. I am a Druid. We don't lose our identity, even in death, because our souls live on."

He had everyone's attention. Even Raine stared at my cell phone. Maybe Dev's crazy sense of humor was what we needed to cheer people up.

"Did you know Echo before you died?" Blaine asked.

"We grew up together." I could hear the smile in his voice. "We—Echo, Rhys, Nara, and I—were inseparable."

"Rhys?" Ingrid asked.

"Great guy. A bit anal." He chuckled. "No, a lot anal."

"Why are Rhys and Nara after you now?" Torin asked.

"For the same reason Echo hasn't spoken to me since he killed me."

I winced. He made Echo sound so bad. "Dev," I said.

"I know. I deserved it. He did me a favor, the first of many. He let my soul go because he knew what was waiting for me on Corpse Strand. Over the years, our paths have crossed, and he always looked the other way." He chuckled. "That's one thing about the guy. He can be a real pain in the ass, but he's loyal to those he loves. He will not admit it, but he loves me. Like a brother. "

You didn't kill those you loved either. He'd piqued everyone's interest before. Now he had them hanging on his every word. Me included.

I placed my cell phone on the coffee table and everyone inched closer. Blaine and Ingrid even left their stools at the wet bar and came to sit by us. Even Raine stopped crying.

"When Echo defied Valkyrie laws and turned our people into Immortals, I was the first one he turned. I betrayed my people and many people died. I brought dishonor to my family and my friends. I would have been excommunicated by my people. To a Druid, that's a fate worse than death. I couldn't do that to my family. No one talked or associated with an impious criminal, but I knew my parents and sisters would not have believed the charges. They would've defied the laws and visited me, and they would've ended up sharing my fate. My death was the only option."

The silence that followed was deafening. I'd bet they were wondering why I was helping someone they probably believed should be on Corpse Strand. But they hadn't talked to Dev. They didn't know him like I did.

"But there's more to that story, right?" I said.

Silence. Gah, stubborn Druid. Now was not the time to play mute. The others shot me sympathetic glances. I didn't need their pity. Dev was not guilty. He wouldn't want to talk to Echo if he was.

"He didn't betray his people," I added, daring him to deny it.

"Then who did?" Raine's mother asked.

"I don't know. I just know he's innocent. Otherwise he wouldn't have come to me to help him reconnect with Echo. Echo is the one he wants to talk to, not us."

Dev sighed. "I'm so not liking you right now, Cora Jemison," he said, sounding so much like an American teenager.

"That's okay. I like you enough for both of us. I trust you, and I refuse to believe you are evil or that you betrayed your people. How can you be when you saved my life? A dark soul tried to possess me, but he fought her off," I added when the others looked at me curiously.

Dev sighed. "She's right. I meant to tell Echo everything first, but since she's making me feel like I walk on water... You're good, Cora."

I grinned. "Thanks."

"The woman I loved betrayed them."

Just one sentence and it packed quite a punch. I sighed with relief.

"I didn't know that at the time. Teléia was living with the sympathetic non-Druid Gaulish family I'd found for her. I paid her a visit whenever I could and shared information about what we were doing, where various groups were hiding, or where we were headed. Whenever I visited, she'd send me to a nearby Roman prison with a care package for the son of the family she was staying with. A lot of sons of non-Druids had joined the army. " He sighed. "The first time I delivered the baskets, one of our hiding places was attacked in the dead of the night." His voice changed as he continued, becoming raw with pain. "Innocent children, women, and the elderly were slaughtered. Not once but three times. We knew we had an informant and questioned everyone. No Druid could betray his or her people, we kept saying. We were wrong." His breathing was heavy, and if a soul could cry, he was. "Family comes first. Those we love come first. She was passing the information I'd shared with her to the Romans to secure the release of her two younger brothers from the dungeons."

Silence followed and I thought he was done talking.

"Unfortunately, the prisoners saw me give the guards the basket, saw them find and read the scrolls hidden under the food."

This time, the silence was longer, but no one spoke.

"I thought her brothers had died. With my people on the move and split into groups, it was hard to keep up with who was alive and who was dead. We thought the Romans didn't keep Druid prisoners. We'd heard them say over and over how it was a waste of good food. It was a lie. They were keeping Druid prisoners and using them to secure information from their relatives."

He stopped again. He would make a good narrator, especially for a tragic story.

"Although some of our people were being hidden by the non-Druids, the majority preferred to stay together as we journeyed to a safer place," Dev continued. "I noticed the patterns of the attack, the way they happened the nights after my visits," Dev continued. "I couldn't tell Echo or my fellow Immortals my suspicions. I didn't want to believe she could betray us, or that she'd used me, so I decided to confirm it. I gave her false information, which she passed on to the Romans. As usual, they rode to the forest, expecting to find defenseless Druids in hiding. But a group of us—Mortals and Immortal Druids—were waiting for them. None of the soldiers survived. Next, we mounted a rescue operation and got our people from the Roman dungeons. When we reached safety, they recounted what they'd seen—me passing the Romans a basket with hidden messages and betraying our people."

I didn't need to hear the rest to know how it had ended. Poor Dev. Of course, the betrayer was Teléia, the girl all the Druid boys seemed to have fallen in love with. Funny I'd been jealous of her and even felt sorry for her. Now, I wasn't sure what to think. She had betrayed her people to save her family. If my parents were being tortured by ruthless soldiers, I would do whatever I could to rescue them. The decision couldn't have been easy for her.

"I couldn't tell them what she'd done," Dev continued. "She would have been excommunicated, and I couldn't do that to her. Before I could confront her, the soldiers retaliated. They'd always known about the Druid sympathizers and looked the other way. Not this time. The raid was brutal. None of them survived, including Teléia and her host family. I keep telling myself I would have saved her. If only I hadn't been so angry with her and confronted her right away…"

Would she have confessed? From Dev's words, being excommunicated was a fate worse than death to a Druid. On the other hand, they might have understood her dilemma. Family should come before community or tribe.

"What a terrible tragedy," Lavania said, and I remembered she was Roman too, originally a Vestal Virgin. I'd been reading about Druids and knew she had already been an Immortal, possibly a Valkyrie, when the Romans slaughtered the Druids.

"Now I understand," Raine's mother said mysteriously. "I hope Echo reaped all those soldiers."

"He did, ma'am. He waited until the Valkyrie Council handed down their sentence, and he and his Druid brothers and sisters were banished to Hel."

"Banished?" Ingrid asked, and I wondered if she was thinking about Rhys.

"Echo and his group of Druid Valkyries turned so many of us into Immortals, even though they knew it was against the law. Once they were assigned to serve Goddess Hel, they went back for the souls of the soldiers. Even those bound for Asgard ended up in Hel."

"No wonder he has a reputation for stealing souls bound for Asgard," Torin said.

"He's made it his mission to reap souls of dictators or war-mongering leaders and their tin soldiers regardless of where they are from," I said. "Whenever innocent blood is spilled, the people responsible are his."

Raine studied me with narrowed eyes. I knew that look. She wasn't going to let me forget I'd kept Echo's past a secret. I'd figured that his past belonged in the past. Unfortunately, it was catching up with us.

"Did the brothers of the woman you loved make it to safety, Dev?" Raine asked.

"Yes. I personally escorted them to the Island of Mona in Wales where most Druids were headed. It was our remaining stronghold and a refuge. Not only for us, but also for British rebels fighting the Romans."

"Unfortunately, Governor Gaius Paulinus," Lavania said, speaking slowly, "the most hated Roman leader of our time, decided to level it." We all stared at her. "He built boats to cross the strait and destroyed every building and altar, every man, woman, and child. I was a Valkyrie by then, but I've never forgotten the sight. The Immortals fought back, but it wasn't enough."

No wonder Echo couldn't stand Andris, a Roman. He had told me how the Romans had massacred Druids on the Island of Anglesey as it was now called, and how the Immortals fought alongside the resistance led by a Celtic queen.

"So you've never told anyone your side of the story?" Raine's mother asked.

"No, ma'am. The Druid Grimnirs, all former Valkyries, are not interested in explanations. According to them, I belong with the damned souls in Hel. However, they'll have to catch me first. It's been two millennia and I'm still around."

There were chuckles. Lavania glanced at me. "Is this why you're helping him?"

I nodded. "If Echo listens to his story, the others will too."

Lavania nodded. "Well, I do hope they get to hear this. Dev's only guilty of being in love. He was not responsible for her actions."

"She died because of me," Dev insisted.

"The poor girl died because she tried to save her brothers and brought the wrath of the Roman army on her head," Lavania said in a hard voice. "You want to blame someone, blame the Norns for letting this happen. They're in charge of fate. Do you think you can stick around and talk to us about medium runes?"

"I'd love to, but it all depends on Echo and Cora."

Everyone looked at me. I had no answers. My job was already done. "After he talks to Echo, we'll see what to do next." I looked at my watch and saw the time. It was almost eleven. "I have to go home before my parents find me missing and call the police. I'll see you tomorrow," I added, looking at Raine. She nodded. I picked up my cell phone, said goodnight to everyone, and headed for the portal.

Once the portal closed behind me, I angled my head and listened for movements in the house. Nothing but silence.

"The girl you were talking about is Teléia, isn't it?" I asked.

"How do you know about her?" Dev asked.

"Echo told me. You were all in love with her at one time or another."

"But she chose me," Dev bragged.

"And she was your downfall," I wanted to say, but that would be cruel. I unlocked my door and peered down the hallway. I realized what I was doing—searching for dark souls in the shadows—and grimaced. Until this mess with the dark souls was over, I'd keep looking over my shoulder.

I could always lock my door, crawl in bed, and send Dev to patrol the farm, but my throat was dry and my mouth tasted funny. Served me right for almost finishing a bag of Twizzlers.

"I agree with Lavania, Dev."

"About?"

"Teléia." I headed toward the stairs. Dad's snoring greeted me before I reached the door to their bedroom. How the heck could Mom sleep through that ruckus?

"You shouldn't blame yourself for her death. She made her choice, tough as it was, and it had nothing to do with you."

"She doesn't feel that way," Dev muttered.

Doesn't? "What do you mean?"

"Nothing," Dev said quickly. Warning bells went off in my head, but I waited.

Downstairs, I turned on all the lights so I could see every corner of the room, got myself a cup of filtered water from the fridge, and hurried back upstairs. Dev hadn't spoken, but his presence in my phone was reassuring.

Who knew I'd feel that way about a dark soul?

Back in my room, I closed the door, chugged my drink, and then went to brush my teeth. "Do you know Echo said you'd watch over me while he's gone?" I asked, squeezing the paste onto my toothbrush.

"In his usual colorful language with dire warnings."

I could only imagine. "That's just his way of doing things. It's harmless."

"He should take lessons from you. You disarm with praise while he vows to unleash mayhem if he's not obeyed."

Yet his way was just as effective. Most of the time. "Echo is a product of what happened to your people. I'm not sweet when people lie to me either, so if you see a dark soul, tell me. Don't try to be a hero again. Tomorrow, I volunteer at the nursing home. If you feel I shouldn't go because a dark soul is lurking around, tell me. I'll listen."

"Yeah. Right."

"Really, I will."

"And if I say I can handle them?"

I chuckled. "I still would want to know. I have my iron rod and can help."

"Okay, doll-face."

"Don't call me that." I finished brushing my teeth and turned off the bathroom lights. I got my pjs, but hesitated. Just because he was in my phone didn't mean I could change in front of him. "Now that we have an understanding, can you tell me what you meant by "she doesn't feel that way"?"

"I was hoping you didn't catch that."

I grinned. "You'd be amazed by what I don't miss. The truth please."

"Teléia was never reaped. She was scared of ending up in Hel with the souls of the Roman soldiers, so she ran. Over the centuries, her guilt turned into bitterness. She hates what she's become, and she blames everyone, but herself."

"Typical. Well, after you tell Echo the truth, he'll probably reap her and throw her poor soul on Corpse Strand."

"Or you could make him understand why she did it and spare her the torture. He listens to you."

He did. "And he does have fond memories of her."

"Not anymore. He knows she's the one who tried to possess you."

I blinked. "What? Teléia is the one who attacked me?"

"*Tried* to possess you, not the same thing. Echo can forgive many things, but an attack on you in unacceptable, which reminds me, I need to walk through your house and the grounds."

I was still savoring the sweet rush of relief. Maliina hadn't tried to attack me. She was probably screaming on Corpse Strand. I could rest easy knowing she was out of the picture.

"Cora?"

"Hmm?"

"When I come back, I'll just stay in your room, so don't freak out if you see me."

"I'll get more blankets." I watched him slither out of my phone, waited until he disappeared through the wall, and then quickly changed into my sweatpants and shirt. My mind at rest, I had no problem falling asleep.

***

"Good morning, blondie. You have exactly thirty minutes to get to school. And you may want to wake up your parents."

For a moment, I wondered where the annoying radio announcer was coming from. Then I realized it was Dev, and what he'd said registered. One look at my clock and I sat up. Crap! I was going to be late.

I kicked the covers off and ran to the bathroom.

"You're welcome," Dev's voice followed me.

I splashed my face with water. "How was last night?"

"No unwanted visitors. Echo's runes scared them."

I left the bathroom frowning. "Does that mean some came close to the farm? And don't lie to me."

"Yes and no. FYI, your parents are still asleep."

My stomach dropped, and I stopped in the process of choosing a dress. I usually laid out an outfit the night before. I hadn't last night. "What do you mean?"

"Yes, some came close to the farm, and no, I'm not lying. Your parents are snoring loud enough to wake the damn state."

Icy fingers crawled up my spine. "Uh, okay. Can you make yourself useful and… wake them up?"

"Uh, I don't go 'boo,' missy. Hollywood gets everything wrong. And you wouldn't approve of the other things I could do to them."

Yeah, possession was not a fun trip. "Just float above their bed and let your cold front do the work."

He sighed. "You're trying to get rid of me. I've noticed you do that before you change. I cannot see you from this contraption unless you take a selfie. I've gone through your pictures and none show you naked or even half-naked. Echo's pictures? Too many. Made me want to gag. Don't you send him any naked pics, or do you delete them?"

For a second, I couldn't find my voice. "You bodiless perv."

"Perv? Really? I'm just stating the obvious. Most Mortals take naughty selfies, so I assumed—"

"Out!"

"You're a grouch in the morning. I was only trying to make conversation." He drifted from my phone, and I could swear he stuck out his tongue at me before drifting away.

A loud bump from down the hall had me racing to my door. I expected Mom to come out of her room yelling "A ghost!" Instead, her door swung open and she marched out still wearing her nightgown. Dad was right behind her.

"I don't understand how I overslept," Mom said, heading for the stairs. "In all my adult years, I've never…"

"Sweetheart, you did a lot of cooking last night for Cora's friends, and remember afterwards?"

I wasn't sure what "afterwards" meant, but I could only guess. Their voices grew faint and I went back into my room. Dev stood in the middle of the room. "Thank you."

He bowed and slithered back into my cell phone without speaking. I finished brushing my hair and applied makeup. Then I grabbed my backpack and phone and raced downstairs.

"Morning. Bye. I'm running late," I called out, heading for the door.

"See? She overslept, too," Dad said. "Must be something in the air. Morning, sweetheart. Have a nice day at school."

"Not so fast, young lady. You know how I feel about breakfast." She removed toast from the toaster and dropped them on a sheet of paper towel.

I detoured, took her offering, and pressed a kiss on her cheek. "Thanks, Mom. Love you, guys."

"I plan on calling your principal about the mystery meat. In fact, I'd planned to make you lunch this morning, but I overslept. Your father can drop it off later."

Eek. "No-ooo. I'm in high school, not junior high. Raine and I can eat..." Hel's Mist. Raine. I'd completely forgotten. "Mom, Dad, I, uh, got some bad news. Raine's father died last night."

"Oh, dear," Mom mumbled.

"How did you find out?" Dad asked.

"Torin texted me. I tried to tell you guys, but you'd gone to bed." The lies were beginning to slip out too easily.

Dad frowned, and for one insane moment, I thought he'd seen through my lie. But all he said was, "I thought he was getting better."

"That's what Svana told me, too," Mom said.

I knew I'd one day lose my parents, but right now, the thought of never seeing them was scary. I ran back and gave each of them a hug. "I'm happy you guys are okay." I started for the door, paused, and glanced at them. "But if one of you has cancer or some debilitating illness, don't hide it from me. I'd want to know from the moment you find out, okay?" From their expressions, I had blindsided them. "I'm not ready to lose either of you. Not yet. Not for a very long time." Tears rushed to my eyes. I turned before they could see them and ran to my car.

I was still in the I'd-hate-to-lose-my-parents mode and didn't pay attention to my surroundings until I was close to school. Then I remembered dark souls.

"Are you there, Dev?"

"Yep. I was letting you have your moment. You're an emotional woman."

"Shut up." I entered the road running in front of the school. "I'm an Immortal; they're not. I want them around for as long as I can have them."

"What about the part about wanting to know when they're sick? Do you really want to be burdened with every misdiagnosed ailment? If they have headaches or dizziness, you'd think brain tumor. Chest pains, you'd conclude heart disease. Stomach pains, kidney stones or cancer. And don't let me get started on senility and diseases. Everything stops working when Mortals get to a certain age. Prostate, bladder, liver—"

"Hel's Mist, you're a menace. Just keep your mouth shut." I didn't want to hear about my parents dying. I pulled into a parking spot. From the lack of students, the first bell had probably rung. I grabbed my backpack and hurried across the street. "If you must know, Raine's parents knew about her father's cancer and never told her. She only found out the truth later. I'd want to know if one of my parents was dying. Now, I'm officially putting you on mute until school is out."

"Then you won't like what's waiting for you inside," he said mysteriously.

"What?"

"I'm on mute. Remember?"

I rolled my eyes and tried to see through the big glass windows as I climbed up the stairs. "You just spoke, so out with it."

Silence.

"Please."

Nothing.

"I so hate you." I pushed open the door and entered the school building. The first people I saw in the foyer were Rhys, Nara, and two more Grimnirs—a mocha-skinned guy with dreadlocks and a redhead.

CHAPTER 17. TEACHERS

Since they were invisible, I couldn't talk to them without looking like a lunatic. I made eye contact with Rhys and cocked my eyebrows. He pressed a finger on his lips.

Yeah, like I was going to do something idiotic and talk to them.

I ignored him and hurried toward my English class. There was no time to drop off my backpack. Just before I entered the class, I glanced back and blinked. Rhys and Nara were behind me. When I stopped, they did too.

Nara rudely indicated I should keep walking. Bitch. I entered the class just as the second bell rang. I tried to focus, but my eyes kept darting around the room, searching for dark souls. Mrs. Bosnick was in the middle of discussing how a character's conflicts related to the theme of a book when Rhys walked through the door.

He didn't make eye contact. Instead, he walked toward me and planted himself behind me at the back corner of the class. Seriously? Was this about Dev? Were they so desperate to get their hands on him they were now hounding me? I'd bet they knew Echo was gone.

I ignored him during class, and when it ended, Kicker joined me before I could tell him to get lost.

"Are you excited?" she asked, beaming.

I stared at her, my mind processing at a slow pace. "About what?"

"The prom. Tomorrow night. It's Teachers' Work Day, so half-day. I heard they'll post the nominees to the court this afternoon."

I shook my head. "Oh, that."

Her brows furrowed, and the beaming dimmed. "What do you mean *oh that*?"

Rhys stood near the entrance, watching us. I took Kicker's arm and pulled her toward the main building. "Raine's father died last night."

Kicker's eyes widened. "Dang."

"I was planning on stopping by Doc's and letting him know. You know, he might want to inform the swim team."

Kicker nodded. "Are you going to her house after school?"

"Briefly, then to Moonbeam Terrace."

"Can I come with you to Raine's? I won't stay for long."

"Sure. Meet me by my car." I headed to my locker, put my backpack away, and collected the textbooks and folder I needed for my next classes. Rhys and Nara watched me from the other end of the hallway.

Ignoring them, I pulled out my cell phone and texted Torin, then Doc, our swim coach. Finally, I whispered into the phone, "Grimnirs are following me around, so don't try to leave my cell phone or say anything. You protected me last night. It's my turn to protect you now."

"Attagirl," Dev said.

"No talking."

"My bad," he said, and I could hear the laughter in his voice.

The Grimnirs continued to shadow me. After two classes, Rhys and Nara were replaced by Dreadlocks and Red. Glaring at them didn't make them go away. When Rhys and Nara reappeared just after I returned my books to my locker, I'd had it.

I marched to Rhys, grabbed his arm, and dragged him to the nearest broom closet, not caring about the stares from the other students. I was surprised he didn't fight me and that Nara didn't follow us.

He looked around and crossed his arms, his stance wide. "What are we—?"

"I'm the one asking the questions here, Rhys. Why are you stalking me?"

His eyebrows shot up. "Stalking?"

"Yes, stalking. I don't have Dev. If you're hoping to catch him by following me, you're wasting your time. He's too smart to come to me while you and your goons are around."

Rhys's expression didn't change, but his ridiculously gorgeous violet eyes narrowed. Why would nature give a man such beautiful eyes? So unfair.

"We know that Dev is hiding in your cell phone, Cora," he said.

I forgot about his eyes, my mouth opening and closing like a fish. How had they known? Of course, they'd sensed him. Grimnirs, like Valkyries, had soul radar encoded in their runes. I narrowed my eyes.

"Dev is under my protection. You want him, you'll have to go through me."

Rhys shifted, arms unlocking. Panic flashed through me, but I stood my ground and lifted my chin.

"You don't scare me, Grimnir," I said. "You'll have to pry my cell phone from my dead hands." His eyes narrowed. "Yeah, you heard me. But just be warned. If you touch me, Echo will chop you into little pieces so you die slowly, then escort you to the island while your body is still warm. And you know who will be waiting for you there?" My bravado ebbed when something flashed in his eyes. "The damned souls. They'll make you their bitch."

He laughed. "You're a feisty little thing, aren't you?"

"And you're an inked bully. Now, I'm going to walk out of here and you will tell your people to leave us alone."

"Poor, little Immortal," Nara said from behind me, and I whipped around. She was leaning against the door, studying her manicured nails, boredom on her face. "You really think we're scared of you and your threats? If we wanted Dev, we would have taken him last night when he was patrolling around your home."

They were outside my home? "What stopped you?"

Nara sneered. "Because we were there for you. Just like we're in this cesspool of teenage hormones and angst for you."

My stomach hollowed. "For me?"

"For your protection," Rhys cut in annoyance. "Echo told us what's going on, and we're here to help."

How convenient. Echo wasn't here to support their claim, and I knew he wouldn't accept help from them. "I don't need your protection."

Nara laughed. "Yes, you do. Your friend's father is dead. Echo and the pretty Valkyrie are trying to find him accommodation. The rest of the Valkyries and Immortals have rallied around Raine and forgotten about you. How am I doing?"

I hated her. "I have Dev."

"Can the two of you stop the dark souls circling your town like vultures on your own?"

"Yes."

"No, you can't. That's why he sent for us. There are twelve of us. Enough to reap a horde of dark souls without breaking a sweat. So play nice or I'll rune you faster than you can blink and lock you somewhere until Echo returns. And FYI, I'm not scared of him. Never have been and never will be."

Twelve? Wow. She didn't have to sound so annoyingly smug. "Yeah, whatever. Just keep your distance. Your presence is annoying."

I ignored their smirks, pushed open the door, and headed toward the stairs. Lunch was going to wait until after I spoke with Doc. Doc was really Matt "Doc" Fletcher, my geography teacher. Our meeting was brief, but he promised to contact the swim team.

"Text me with the funeral time."

I nodded. "Thanks, Doc."

Rhys and Nara were waiting when I left Doc's office. Nara smirked when I glared at them. They followed me to the nearest bathroom and stayed outside while I disappeared inside. I still didn't trust them. They could have easily made up that stuff to get their hands on Dev.

I searched under the stall doors to make sure they were empty, then pulled my artavus from the hidden sheath inside my boot and quickly etched runes on the mirror. I'd just engaged my invisibility runes when Nara walked in.

"Where are you going?" she asked.

"None of your business," I snapped.

She sighed. "Stop being childish, Cora. We are here because Echo asked us to be here. Do you know how big that is? He hasn't spoken to us in centuries, yet he swallowed his pride for you. He even promised to hand over Dev if we helped him."

"Echo would never throw Dev under the bus," I said. The old Echo would have. "He's honorable and loyal—"

"Except when it comes to you. For you he'd break rules, spit in Hel's eyes and not care about consequences." She shook her head and sighed. "There was a time when I thought I'd be the one to make him feel like that. Make him put my happiness and safety above his." She studied me, a weird expression settling on her face. I couldn't tell whether it was jealousy or regret. "I hope you realize how lucky you are."

Definitely jealousy. I felt a little sorry for her. "I know."

"Good. But just so you know, if you ever pull the crap Mortals do in the name of experiments and end up hurting him, I *will* make you regret it. I've seen enough of my Grimnir brothers and sisters go crazy over stupid things their Mortal and Immortal spouses do. We'd be better off staying with our own, but who can control love? So consider yourself warned."

I took a mental step back. I had no need to hate or doubt Nara after that revealing monologue. She might have loved Echo, but she didn't anymore. Besides, Echo would go ape if something bad happened to me.

"I'm going to Raine's house to check on her. She's the one who lost her father."

"I know who the young Norn is."

Of course she did. "I, uh, I'll be back after lunch. I'll use this bathroom."

Nara nodded. "We'll be here when you get back. As long as you stay in the house with the Valkyries, you'll be safe. The souls are circling, but they haven't come into town yet. The last one we reaped said they are waiting for orders from their leader."

Nara didn't sound bitchy anymore. In fact, she sounded downright nice. "I thought dark souls preferred to be solo."

"Not this lot. Their leader appears to know a lot about you."

I frowned. Could Teléia be their leader? "Uh, Nara, you should know that Dev didn't betray you or your people."

"He did," she countered, eyes narrowing.

"No, he didn't. Once you hear his side of the story, you'll understand. Someone else did, but he accepted the blame. It was very noble of him." I stepped into Raine's bedroom.

Nara did something and the portal stopped closing. "Your Valkyrie and Immortal friends didn't really desert you. I was being—"

"A bitch," I finished.

She chuckled as though I'd complimented her. "Yeah. St. James was at your place last night. Echo told him to expect us, so he came to make sure we were on duty. You and Echo are lucky to have such loyal friends." She waved and the portal closed.

***

Raine's bedroom was empty. Even her black cat was missing. I redirected the portal downstairs and heard laughter before I stepped into her living room. The three women, Raine's mother, Femi, and Lavania were in the kitchen. Lavania was cooking something at the stove.

Femi saw me first. "Cora, what a surprise."

"I don't want to intrude," I said slowly. "I just stopped by to check on Raine."

"Silly child. You can never intrude." Svana waved me over. "Torin took Raine away for a few hours. She's taking this harder than I thought." She gave me a hug and patted the empty seat beside her. "Sit."

"Have you eaten lunch?" Lavania asked from the stove.

"No. I was planning on it after I visited Raine."

"Then you can eat with us," Lavania said and reached for a large soup mug. She scooped a lumpy greenish-brown mixture into four more mugs. It didn't look appetizing.

"It's very nutritious," Raine's mother whispered, and I could tell she was trying not to laugh.

I frowned. "How did you...? You read my mind."

She looked at Femi and the two of them burst out laughing.

"We can't read minds, but you have an expressive face," Raine's mother said. "Raine reacted the same way the first time Lavania served it. Now she can't get enough of it."

"Because it's nutritious," I said, slowly. Nutritious usually didn't mean tasty.

"And very tasty," Femi added.

"Quit scaring the child," Lavania scolded them and carried the first two bowls to the table. She went back for two more and sat. They hummed as they ate their first scoops.

"What's in it?" I asked, removing my spoon from its cradle and eyeing the soup with misgivings.

"Eye of newt, lizard lips, and buzzard eggs," Femi said.

Lavania smacked her arm. "You are terrible, Femi." But she was trying hard not to laugh. "Chicken, green peas, and lentils."

Swallowing, I took a small scoop and tasted it. My mouth exploded with sensations. I took another scoop, then another, and another. I ignored their giggling and enjoyed every sip. They were like a bunch of teenagers. I half listened to their conversation, which seemed to center around Lavania finding teachers for her school.

"I expect you two to be part of my faculty," she said. "Svana can teach Portals. Solids, liquids, and gas."

"You can portal into water?" I asked.

"And out of water," Svana said.

"Femi can teach Disguise and... No, that's Ingrid. Femi?"

"Magic 101: Channeling your inner witch through objects," Femi said.

They laughed.

"Too mouthy," Lavania said.

"Magical Objects," I said, remembering how she'd shown Raine how to use amulets to see into the past and future.

"I like it. Have you asked Hawk?" Femi asked.

Hawk worked for Raine's parents at their store.

"I will," Lavania said. "And I have a few more lined up, which reminds me..." She looked at me. "I would really like to borrow your dark soul sometime, Cora. My knowledge of dark souls is limited, and he's an expert."

An idea popped in my head, and I went with it. "Or you could give him a job at your new school. He could teach about medium runes and dark souls, how to deal with them. I'm sure some of your students might be interested in becoming Mediums." She stared at me like I'd told her to mate with Dev. Heat flooded my cheeks. At least Svana and Femi nodded and smiled encouragingly as though they agreed with me. "It was just a thought. Thanks for the soup. It was really good and filling."

"Thank you." Lavania spoke slowly as though her mind was elsewhere.

I took my bowl to the sink and filled it with water. When I turned around, they were talking in whispers. "Um, Mrs. Cooper?"

Raine's mother looked at me. "Yes, dear."

"Is it okay if some of our swim friends stop by after school to see Raine? I, uh, kind of told them about Mr. Cooper. I hope you don't mind."

She dismissed my comment with a wave of her hand. "No, I don't mind. I like your swim team. They support each other. Besides, Raine could do with some cheering. When is the funeral, Femi?"

"Saturday morning," Femi said.

Going to the prom the day before would be weird. "I better head back to school. Miss Lavania, you can talk to Dev after he and Echo are done."

Lavania smiled. "I look forward to that."

She didn't say anything about my suggestion to add Dev to her teaching staff. Working with magical Mortals might earn him Brownie points and keep him off Corpse Strand, or give him access to bodies with medium runes to possess. What was I thinking? It was the worst idea ever. I waited until there was no one in the restroom before walking through the portal.

"You are unbelievable," Dev said.

227

I winced. "Sorry. I forgot you could hear me. I'm sure the last thing you want to do is teach a bunch of hormonal teenagers. I don't know what I was thinking."

"Shut up, Cora Jemison!" he snapped just as a girl walked into the bathroom. I brought the phone closer to my ear. She gave me a weird glance and disappeared in one of the stalls. "You're infuriating, opinionated—"

"You said I was sweet this morning," I protested.

"You are all the above, but you're also the most wonderful friend a soul could possibly have. You defended me, threatened Rhys with physical violence while shaking in your boots, overcame your jealousy and actually talked to Nara, and now you want to save me from eternal damnation."

"Stupid, huh?" I asked.

"No, brilliant."

"Are you saying you'd love to teach?"

"Duh. Of course I would. I know a lot about dark souls and their runes, and what they do and how they do it. You have no idea what this could mean. I could make up for all the people I possessed and whose heads I screwed with. I could get my soul back."

"Shh, keep it low," I whispered, my eyes on the stall with the girl.

"Are you kidding? I want to hug you and shout this from the tallest building. This is exciting. Huge."

The girl opened the door and shot me a weird look. I gave her a sheepish grin and indicated my phone. "Drama queen."

She smiled briefly and went to wash her hands, but kept an eye on me through the mirror above the sink.

"Cora?" Dev asked.

"Just a second." I waited until the girl left. "What do you mean you could get your soul back?"

"Long story. Just know that there's a reason why plants don't whither when I walk past them. I'll explain one day. Right now, Rhys and Nara are waiting for you, and you have class." He sighed. "Did I mention I think I'm crushing on you right now? I mean, seriously wishing I was a Mortal?"

I laughed. "You can't handle me, Dev."

"Don't you mean *Echo* can't handle the competition? He'll smash things. Snap my neck. Yank out my heart and win."

I was laughing hard by the time I left the bathroom.

***

Downstairs, I was surprised to see students filing into the auditorium. The principal must have called for an assembly during second lunch. Most students were already seated, and the thought of squeezing past pointy knees or brushing against people wasn't appealing.

I stood by the door and the next second wished I hadn't. Drew and his buddies walked in. I didn't like the way they looked at me and then him before planting themselves right by my side. I gave them a tiny smile. The other two guys smirked while Drew pretended I wasn't there.

Seriously? He needed to get a life.

Principal Johnson walked to the podium, and silence filled the hall. "We'll make this short. We received numerous calls this morning from parents concerned about the food we serve here at school."

Oh crap. Mom and Ingrid must have called. I cringed.

"We follow Health Department Food Safety Guidelines when we cook the meats, the vegetables are fresh, and our suppliers are up to code on food handling. If you have food poisoning from anything you've eaten at school, go to the nurse, and tell her what you ate."

Murmurs filled the auditorium.

"The second thing on the agenda is the prom," the principal continued. "We're still getting calls from parents concerned about the safety during prom. If your parents don't want you to attend the prom, respect their wishes. However, I want to reassure those attending that we have taken extra precautions to ensure everyone's safety. We will have twice the number of chaperones during both proms. Students must stay in the cafeteria at all times. If you..."

I tuned him out. Attending the prom was not on my agenda. Parents had a reason to worry. First was the swimming pool and then the football game. Luckily, they didn't know about the witches and the Immortals killing each other in the forest. That wasn't the reason I wasn't attending thought. With Echo gone, the whole prom thing had lost its appeal. Then there was the funeral on Saturday. I wanted to be there for Raine.

Assembly over, I waited for Drew to leave before racing to the exit. Nara and Rhys were by the windows. I made eye contact, smiled, and kept going.

I texted Raine between classes and checked on Dev. Raine didn't return my text, and Dev didn't want to talk.

"I'm napping," he growled.

I doubted souls napped. Talking to the Grimnirs were out of the question. I felt neglected. Lonely. I even texted Echo even though I knew the reception in Hel sucked.

Kicker, Sondra, and Naya were waiting by my car when I left the school building after school. Rhys and Nara kept their distance, but didn't miss a thing. I wasn't sure whether they had a ride or if they'd sprint alongside my car like The Flash.

The three girls crowded me when I reached my car.

"Poor, Raine," Kicker said. "She told me her father was getting better."

"When did he die?" Sondra asked.

"When is the funeral?" someone else asked.

I must have answered them. Then we piled into the two cars. I opened the back door and indicated for the Grimnirs to ride with us. Rhys shook his head.

Kicker rode with me while Sondra went with Naya. I didn't see the Grimnirs until I stopped at the red light and caught a glimpse of them from the corner of my eye. They ran parallel to the car, until I pulled into Raine's cul-de-sac and they disappeared. My mother's car was parked in Raine's driveway.

I was getting out of my car when I noticed two other cars behind Naya's. The three co-captains and several members of the team.

"Did you tell them?" I asked Kicker.

"We got an e-mail from Doc," Jared, a co-captain, said.

"Oh. Thanks for coming. I know Raine will appreciate it."
I led the way to their door, not too sure she would. She

opened the door looking a lot better than yesterday. Her smile was a bit wobbly as she welcomed us. Mom, Raine's mother, Lavania, and Femi were in the den. From what I could see through the open doorway, the bed was gone.

While Raine led the others to the living room to join Ingrid, Blaine, and Torin, who were watching basketball on TV, I went to give Mom a hug. She and the three women were eating pie, sipping wine, and giggling like a bunch of women on a girls' night out. The room was once again a den, no hint it was once a sick room. Even the large-screen TV was now in the living room.

"When are you heading to the nursing home? I brought an extra pie for your friends," Mom said.

I glanced at my watch. "I won't leave for another forty minutes."

"It's in a cooler in the car."

"Thanks, Mom." I gave the other women a brief smile and turned to leave.

"Not so fast, Cora," Lavania said. "We hear you and Echo are getting serious."

My cheeks grew warm. I was so going to kill my mother. I turned without making a comment, their laughter following me.

Torin and Blaine were passing out drinks. I helped Ingrid with the pies. Mom must have gone on a baking binge after I left. She'd even brought a tub of homemade whipped cream.

I didn't get a chance to talk to Raine. She didn't talk much and still looked like she hadn't slept in days. Torin and Ingrid basically played host and hostess. Not that it was difficult. They spent the entire time watching basketball.

"Are you going to be home this evening?" I asked Raine before I left at a quarter to four. She'd walked me to the car. The others were still inside.

"I'll probably be next door. Neighbors and Dad's friends keep calling. I can't stand it."

I could just imagine. Her father had been active at local sporting events and had belonged to a group of bikers. He'd been very sporty. Definitely Valhalla material.

"Have you, uh, contacted Eirik?" I asked.

Raine's chin trembled. "We went looking for him today, but he's disappeared again."

"Knowing him, he'll make a grand entrance."

"Or be a hero and then disappear again," Raine said and rolled her eyes.

"They're all drama queens."

We laughed and, across the street, Mrs. Rutledge's curtain moved. She was probably watching us with disapproval. She was such a nosy neighbor.

"Has the old hag stopped by yet?" I asked, sliding behind the wheel.

"Oh yeah. She brought lasagna. Mom's freezing the dishes for later. They'll become handy after Femi leaves."

I hadn't really thought about Femi leaving. Now that Raine's family didn't need her, she had no reason to stay. Probably go teach at Lavania's School of Magically Gifted Teens. From what Lavania had said, she wanted Raine and Ingrid to attend her special school. That meant Torin and Andris would leave, too. I was going to be left friendless.

At least, I'd still have Echo and his Druid Grimnirs now that they were back in his life. I remembered what I wanted to tell Raine, lowered the window, and called out, "Hey."

Raine turned.

"You want to hang out this evening? Maybe after dinner?"

"Sure. Or have dinner with us. We have plenty of food."

"Okay. See ya." I waved and took off. As soon as I pulled out of the cul-de-sac, I placed my cell phone on the front passenger seat. "You okay in there, Dev?"

"Hmm?" he sounded drowsy.

"Are you still napping?"

"Yeah," he said. "I haven't been able to do that in years."

I frowned. "Really?"

"Really. Souls, lost or dark, are always on the move, hiding from one place to another, always on the lookout for Grimnir Bounty Hunters."

"Who are Grimnir Bounty Hunters?" Echo hadn't wanted to discuss them.

"An army of specialized reapers who go after specific souls for the goddess. Echo was one of them until recently.

They know where we hide, how we hide, and can sense us as soon as they walk through a portal. Then there are Witches with the ability to find us. Teenagers who've watched too many sci-fi movies and think dispersing us with iron is cool."

I winced. "Sorry."

"No need to be. You never sliced me. Just threatened. However, because of you, I've found peace, even though it's only temporary."

I hoped it wasn't. "How did you survive all these years? And how come you don't suck life out of living things."

He chuckled. "Suck life... You have a mean way of putting it. I stopped using humans as vessels. It had become an obsession, and I didn't like how I felt when I wasn't inside someone."

"Did you always possess people?"

"No-oo. At first, I hid in empty caves and forests, shying away from people, but soon I wanted to be around them and upgraded to storage facilities, abandoned homes, and office buildings. Then I heard of possession. Lost souls don't move in groups, but our paths cross and you hear things. I started by possessing wild animals, then domesticated ones. Mortals love their pets. It felt nice to be loved, but animals make terrible vessels. Chasing my tail, humping some stranger's leg, or obsessing with scents is not my idea of fun."

I laughed. "I'm sure you were a wonderful dog."

"I sucked. Dogs don't have the will to fight possession, and I felt bad for them. I went back to wild animals, but after centuries, I caved. The lure of Mortals was too great, and I was too weak."

I pulled up into the parking lot of Moonbeam Terrace Nursing Home, but instead of the leaving the car, I waited for him to continue. I still had seven minutes to kill.

"I tried a Mortal, and it was the most amazing feeling. To eat real food, feel, love. I didn't care that the women thought their husbands or boyfriends had changed. I hopped from man to man. I was more attentive and loving. I tried to stay away from men with families..."

He became silent.

"It took a long time before I realized what I'd become," he added in a sad voice. "I was going through a Mortal a month. When not using a vessel, I affected things everywhere I went. People. Plants. Animals. I hated what I'd become. In fact, it was a wonder I rediscovered my humanity. Um, you're going to be late."

"Don't worry about that," I said. "How did you change?"

"Rhys and Nara are here. In fact, they've been following us since we left your friend's house."

I hadn't noticed. They stood by the entrance of the nursing home. I hated waiting for answers, but I didn't want to be late. I reached in the back seat for the pie. "Promise to finish that story, okay?"

"Aye, aye, Miss Jemison."

I grabbed my phone, cradled the pie in my arm, and bumped the door shut with my hip. The shrill sound of an ambulance pierced the air. Ambulances came to the nursing home all the time, so I didn't pay it any attention. Old people had so many ailments and most of them could become fatal fast. Occasionally, we lost a resident.

By the time I reached Rhys and Nara, the ambulance was screeching to a stop behind me. I stepped aside as the EMTs rushed into the building. I glanced at Nara then Rhys, but something in their expression set off warning bells. Before I could ask what was going on, the other two Grimnirs I'd seen with them at school appeared. My chest tightened with dread.

"What's going on, guys?" I asked, forgetting I was the only one who could see them.

CHAPTER 18. SHE IS BACK!

"Go inside, Cora," Rhys said.

I searched the parking lot, but there were no dark souls lurking around. "They're here?" I whispered.

"Just go," Rhys ordered.

"Oh for goddess' sake," Nara snapped. "Your friend is dying."

I gawked at her with round eyes. "What?"

"The old lady," Nara added impatiently. "She just had a heart attack."

Mrs. Jepson. Oh crap! I ran inside the building just as the EMTs rolled her into the foyer. She was so still and gray. I stood with the nurses and workers and watched helplessly as they wheeled her toward the main entrance.

The woman behind the desk called out to someone, "The daughter is not picking up her phone."

I pushed the boxed pie into the hands of the nearest nurse. "Give that to Captain G and Mr. Reeds." I shifted my attention to the two EMTs. "Can I go with her?"

"Are you a relative?"

"No, but I'm a close friend. Ask them," I waved toward the front desk. "She doesn't listen to anyone but me."

"Miss, that's no reason to—"

"I have Lauren's other number," I lied, my eyes locking eyes with Mrs. Hightower, the highest ranking administrator in the room. "She will take my call." Another lie. All I knew was her place of work and that her mother was proud of her. "I just want to be there for Mrs. J., so she doesn't wake up in a strange place and see unfamiliar faces." That part was true.

Mrs. Hightower nodded curtly and hurried outside after the EMTs. I followed and caught the tail end of her sentence.

"…she took to the girl. She might have a better chance at locating her daughter, too. We'll keep trying as well."

"Okay, Mrs. Hightower," one of the EMTs said, helping his partner push the stretcher with Mrs. J inside the ambulance. He inclined his head toward me and murmured, "Hop in," then hurried to the driver's seat.

My eyes met with Rhys'. "I'm going to the hospital with her."

The EMT with Mrs. J assumed I was talking to him and looked up from adjusting Mrs. J's straps.

"I heard," he said, eyeing me curiously. "Get inside and close the door."

When I boarded the ambulance, Rhys and Nara hopped in, too. It was a tight fit on the narrow bench. If the EMT wondered why I sat close to his seat at the head of the stretcher when I had the entire bench to myself, he didn't show it. Accommodating invisible people while acting natural was an art I hadn't mastered yet.

I gripped the handle bar mounted on the wall and braced myself as we took off. Rhys and Nara didn't seem bothered by the motion of the ambulance. The EMT also seemed to have mastered the art of fiddling around with the machines while the ambulance careened around corners and barreled downhill toward town. Poor Mrs. J looked like she was already dead. Her skin was gray, her lips bluish. An oxygen-reading thingamajigger was on her finger, an oxygen mask covered her nose and mouth, and a blood pressure band hugged her arm.

"She's not going to make it," Nara whispered to Rhys.

"She will," I shot back.

The EMT assumed I was talking to him again and cocked his eyebrows.

"She will make it, right?" I improvised.

His expression gave nothing away. "What's your name?"

"Cora," I said.

"Are you studying to be a nurse's aide?"

"No. I'm a high-school volunteer," I said.

He nodded. "It's obvious you care about Mrs. Jepson, Cora, but with someone with her condition and of such advanced age, anything is possible."

"He's right," Nara said. "She's—"

"Shut up!" The EMT stopped whatever he was doing and studied me with narrowed eyes. "Uh, sorry. That's me saying, 'no way'." That was so lame. "She needs to talk to her daughter before, uh, she gets too sick, or they'll both regret it." I glared at Nara.

She smirked. "Why will they regret it?"

I ignored her, my focus shifting to Mrs. J.

"Is she one of your cases?" Nara continued. "I didn't know you helped Mortals, too."

"Is she breathing?" I asked, continuing to ignore Nara. Didn't she get that I couldn't talk to her without confusing the EMT?

"Yes, she is. You see this?" The guy tapped the sensor on her finger. "It's called the oximeter. It monitors…"

He pointed out various instruments around the ambulance and answered my questions without acting irritated. He was in the middle of explaining symptoms of a heart attack and how to deal with it when Mrs. J jerked as though having an epileptic seizure. Then she went still.

"What happened?" I screeched.

"Her heart stopped!" the EMT snapped and reached for scissors. He ripped Mrs. J's gown and bared her wrinkly chest. I never knew the woman had breasts. She was always hunched over in her wheelchair. Then he reached for the defibrillator and warned me to stand back. But that wasn't the reason I started to panic. Mrs. J's soul was separating from her body. Slowly as though doing a sit-up.

"Told you her time was up," Nara said.

I wanted to tell her to shut up again. "She's going to be alright. She has to."

The EMT ignored me and charged the paddles of the defibrillator. He pressed them to her chest.

Mrs. J's body jerked as the electric charge zipped through her. Her soul continued to rise from her body. She was at ninety degrees, sitting up. Looking confused, she turned her head and zeroed in on Rhys and Nara.

They didn't seem bothered by her scrutiny. Immortality and centuries of watching people die had probably made them numb to death and souls. At least, they didn't reach for their scythes. My humanity made me celebrate life and hate death. The EMT was performing CPR on Mrs. J.

Her soul didn't move. She was still studying Nara and Rhys.

"No, no, no, Mrs. J," I muttered. "Not yet. Go back."

As though she'd heard me, her eyes turned to me and widened in recognition. I knew the moment she decided something was wrong. Fear flashed in her eyes, and she looked down at her body.

"I can help her," Dev's voice reached me as though from far.

I yanked my phone from my pocket. "What?"

"Remember the reason I don't suck life out of everything? This is why." I had no idea what he meant, but he slithered out of my phone without explaining. The EMT was busy recharging the paddles. A flash of light at the corner of my eye and I whipped around to see Rhys and Nara pull out their artavo.

"Don't!" I yelled.

The EMT was about to zap Mrs. J again and assumed I was talking to him. "One more word out of you and I *will* kick you out of the ambulance!" he snarled.

Dev grabbed Mrs. J's soul and pulled the two of them back into her body. What the...? What was he doing? A quick look at Nara and Rhys also showed their shock. At least they weren't pointing their mini scythes at Mrs. J. Then I saw something that gave me hope, or a reason to freak out. Her eyelids fluttered just as the EMT brought the pads toward her chest.

"No!" I pushed his arms away.

He cursed. "Are you crazy?"

"Look at her. She's okay. She's coming around."

He glanced down at Mrs. J. Her eyelids fluttered again.

"See? She's okay." I wasn't sure whether it was Dev making her eyes flutter or Mrs. J. The EMT put his defibrillator away and checked her pulse. I wanted to ask if she was going to be okay, but I didn't dare. I'd already pissed him off enough.

I reached out and touched Mrs. J's hand with the tips of my fingers. Her skin was dry and thin, but warm. Before I could lean back, she reached out and grabbed my wrist.

My heart leapt to my throat. She tugged, a little too strong for someone who'd just had a heart attack. Twice. It was probably Dev. "What is it, Mrs. J?"

Her eyes opened, and her mouth moved. I inched closer.

"I saw you," she whispered.

Okay, so it was her, not Dev, speaking. What was he doing inside her? "Yes, I'm here, Mrs. J. I'm not going anywhere."

"Angels," she whispered.

I didn't dare glance at Rhys and Nara. I gave Mrs. J a tiny smile. A quick glance at the EMT and I caught him frowning. Yeah, I was sure he'd never seen someone recover so fast after a heart attack.

We screeched to a halt in front of the hospital. It was nothing like on TV. No interns and doctors running out to grab the stretcher. Rhys and Nara created a portal on the wall of the ambulance and disappeared through it before the driver opened the back door. It was awkward getting down with Mrs. J clinging to my hand, but I managed.

"She's not going to leave," the EMT who'd driven the ambulance reassured her, but she wasn't having it. Her grip tightened, and once again, I wondered if Dev was the one doing all the physical work.

"I don't mind going inside with her," I said.

"I'll talk to the nurse," he said.

"You haven't called her daughter?" the EMT who'd ridden with us said.

"I will."

They wheeled her inside with me by her side. Unlike outside, inside had a bit more activity. Still not very *Grey's Anatomy*. A couple converged on Mrs. J's stretcher. One EMT passed papers from the nursing home to a nurse while the other explained what had happened. Mrs. J tugged at my hand. I braced myself as I leaned down, expecting her to say she'd seen me, or call me an angel.

"Get her daughter here." The voice that came out was Dev's. He sounded weird, like he was in pain. "I can't hold her down for too long or the urge to take over will be too tempting to resist." Then the voice changed into Mrs. J's raspy, shaky voice. "Who are you?"

"It's Cora, Mrs. J," I whispered past the fear clumping my throat. "I'm here to make sure you're okay and ready for Lauren. When she comes, the two of you can finally talk."

Tears filled her eyes. "An angel?"

Whatever calmed her, I decided. I touched my lips. "Shh. Go inside with the nice people. I'll be right there after I call Lauren."

I gently eased my hand from her grip, stepped back, and watched as they wheeled her inside. I glanced over my shoulder at Nara and Rhys, and grinned. Dev wasn't just possessing Mrs. J. He was holding her soul captive inside her body and buying her time. He and I did the same thing, except I helped the dead while he helped the living. How ironic was that? Maybe helping others was what he'd meant by getting his soul back?

"Come this way," a nurse said, waving me over.

"I need to call her daughter first." It was time Nara and Rhys did something useful, instead of shadowing me. They even ignored a few souls moving around the ER. One eyed them, then me and grinned and disappeared through a wall. I pulled out my phone, walked to where they stood, and faked talking on the phone.

"I need your help."

"Really? After *you* let Dev possess her," Nara retorted.

"Dev is detaining her soul until the daughter gets here, Nara. That's what he's been doing all these centuries to purify his soul. He's a good soul." I looked at Rhys.

"What do you want?"

"Lauren Michaels, Mrs. Jepson's daughter, works at Portland Art Museum. Find her and bring her here. She hates her mother, but—"

"Leave it to me," Rhys said.

"Rhys!" Nara snapped. "You can't enable her by doing her bidding."

He cut her a side-glance. "She said Dev didn't betray us."

"But he just possessed that dying woman's body. We can't allow—"

"He's not possessing her," I cut her off. A woman seated nearby with her son gave me a weird look. I pressed my cell phone closer to my ear and lowered my voice. "Give him a chance to explain about the past. He was protecting someone else, and right now, he's helping Mrs. J. He told me we need to hurry and get the daughter here because he can't hold her in there forever. Does that sound like an evil guy?"

Nara still looked undecided. Not Rhys.

"Okay, Cora," he said. "I'll get her daughter. No, Nara. We can discuss your doubts later. Stay here with her." I was surprised when Nara listened.

He created a portal in the air, and for a brief second, I saw a section of Portland Art Museum before the door closed. Mom had framed some of their artwork and I'd visited with her, so I knew the place well.

Nara still had a suspicious look, but I didn't try to convince her that Dev was innocent. I found the nurse who'd called me before and she led us—Nara followed me through the door by the registration station—down a short hallway to one of the sectioned exam rooms. She pushed back the corner of the heavy curtain and indicated I go in.

Two people were with Mrs. J. One was taking her blood while the other studied a machine attached to the tubes from her chest and asked her questions. Mrs. J seemed more interested in me than answering his questions. Nara stood near the head of the bed, where no one could bump into her, eyes narrowed on Mrs. J as though expecting Dev to appear. At least she wasn't holding her artavus.

I was trying to listen to what the doctor was saying when one of the Grimnirs from school appeared beside Nara. Up close, I realized his dark locks were actually braids. Above his right eyebrow was a jagged scar, which added something to a face that would have been merely handsome. He also wore diamond studs. If he noticed me studying him, he didn't show it. Nara didn't miss a thing.

"Syn with a Y," she said, pointing at him. Then she waved my way. "Echo's girl."

Rude much? I had a name, I wanted to remind her. But then Syn nodded and said, "Nice to finally meet you, Cora," and I forgave her. He had a deep, rumbling voice. I wondered about his background. Since he was black, I knew he couldn't be a Druid. Maybe an ancient Nubian high priest.

"You can't reap the old woman yet," Nara said.

"Says who?" Syn asked.

"Miss Goody Two Shoes over here." Nara jerked her head toward me. "She's playing guardian angel to the dying, too." She sighed and added in a bored tone, "The old woman needs to talk to her daughter, who hates her guts, so Rhys went to collect her, so they can talk. Blah… blah… blah."

Syn cursed. "I'm behind schedule."

Nara chuckled. "You're always behind schedule. Who's the woman?"

"None of your business. Why is she worrying about the dying when she has you-know-who to deal with?"

They must be discussing Teléia. Did all Grimnirs know about my business?

Nara shrugged. "Echo insists she shouldn't change her routine."

"I liked him better when he kept to himself," Syn murmured.

"He's back, bro. Deal with it. You two might be sharing the mic again."

My interest in their conversation shot up. Echo had mentioned a band made up of Grimnirs. Reapers. Not exactly original, but who cared? They were ravers. They blew off steam by wearing painted masks and playing at raves every few months. Echo had played with them, but stopped. I eavesdropped on their conversation, wishing I could ask them questions without appearing nosy. They were playing tomorrow at some secret location. I was dying to find out where when the nurse returned.

"It's Cora, right?" she asked, and I nodded. "We're taking Mrs. Jepson to get some X-rays. We should be done in twenty minutes."

"I can come with her if she wants me to," I said.

She glanced down and patted Mrs. J's hand. "No, she'll be okay. You're a brave lady, aren't you, Mrs. Jepson? A Mrs. Hightower from Moonbeam is here, too. Did you locate her daughter?"

Nara nodded.

"She's on her way," I said.

"Good." She unclasped things at the legs of the bed. Mrs. J gripped my hand briefly and attempted a smile.

"I'll be right here when you get back," I reassured her and stepped back. The nurse wheeled her out of the room. Nara and Syn were talking in whispers, but I heard them.

"Have you told Echo about you-know-who?"

"Not unless we have to." She glanced at me. "How long is this going to take?" Her attempt to redirect the conversation was pathetic.

"Who's you-know-who?" I asked.

They exchanged a glance and shrugged, faking ignorance.

"Teléia?" I asked.

Nara cocked her perfectly trimmed eyebrows. "You know about Teléia?"

"She attacked me a few nights ago. Dev rescued me."

"No wonder you're his champion," she murmured.

"Who's Dev?" Syn asked.

"A dark soul she's helping. Can we talk outside?" She didn't wait for an answer, just slanted me a look that said, "Stay here." Then she practically pushed him out the partitioned room and disappeared.

Deciding not to let her get to me, I pulled out my cell and called Mom. Dad picked it up. "Dad? How come you're answering Mom's phone?"

"Because she's my wife," he answered. He could be so lame sometimes. "Are you at the nursing home or on your way home?"

"I'm actually at the hospital. Mrs. J had a heart attack and I rode the ambulance with her. Where's Mom?"

He sighed. "Why is it you can't talk to me? I can deal with any crisis just as well as your mother."

I rolled my eyes. He was a selective listener and always tried to solve whatever problem I had instead of being a sympathetic listener like Mom. "I know, Dad. I really *need* to talk to Mom."

"Okay. I hope Mrs. Jackson is okay." Then I heard him say, "She's at the hospital and refuses to talk to me."

"You took Echo to the bar and your friends treated him like a felon," she teased, but then her voice became serious. "Sweetheart, what is this about the hospital, and who is Mrs. Jackson?"

Just hearing her voice brought all sort of crazy emotions to the surface. My throat tightened and tears rushed to my eyes. "It's Mrs. *Jepson*, not Jackson. She had a heart attack, Mom. The ambulance arrived to pick her up just as I got there."

"Oh dear. Is she going to be okay?"

"I don't think so. She looks bad. I promised to stay until her daughter gets here."

"Are you okay? Do you want me to come over and wait with you?"

This was why I'd wanted to talk to her. She always knew what to say to make me feel better. "No, I'll be fine, Mom. But I left my car at the nursing home."

"We can pick it up, and when you're ready to come home, I'll pick you up too."

"Thanks, Mom. I'll text you when I'm done here."

"Um, sweetheart? I don't want to sound pushy, but don't you think that you need a break from volunteering at the nursing home for a couple of weeks? Losing friends takes a toll on everyone. Between Raine's father and Mrs. J's condition, I think that's a lot to take on."

I was probably going to quit working at the nursing home anyway. Mrs. Jepson's soul had seen me and if she survived, she'd start asking questions I couldn't answer. And hiding every time a resident at the home died wouldn't work either because souls always found me.

"I think that's, uh..." The door opened and Rhys walked in with a short, curvy woman I recognized from the pictures Mrs. J kept by her bed. Her arm was wrapped around his like they'd known each other forever. How did they get here so fast? "That's a good idea, Mom. I'll text you." I hung up and stood.

"This is Cora Jemison," Rhys said and indicated me with a nod. "She's been taking good care of your mother." He lifted her hand to his lips and pressed a kiss on her knuckles. "Cora is family, so be nice to her."

She giggled, which was revolting coming from a middle-aged woman who looked twice his age. Her makeup was over the top even though she was in great shape and dressed well.

"Dinner later?" she asked breathlessly, staring at his face with cougar lust.

"Wouldn't miss it." He looked at me and winked, then left. The smile disappeared from Lauren's face as soon as the door closed behind him.

"Cora Jemison," she said, studying me with narrowed eyes, hands clasped in front of her. "I've heard so much about you from the nursing home staff and figured you were some lonely, middle-aged woman out to con Mom out of her life savings. How old are you?"

I tried not to be offended, but I'd disliked her before she arrived. "Eighteen."

"How are you related to Rhys?"

My annoyance shot up. It was sweet of Rhys to claim me, but I wasn't explaining Druid loyalty to this woman. She hadn't even asked about her mother. "They're running tests on your mother, but she should be back any minute now."

"Are you really related to him?"

"No." *Figure that out, you cow.* "Your mother is really proud of you. She always talks about your accomplishments, your loving family, and wonderful children. She said your oldest, Sierra, got a full ride to the University of Portland and your son is a gifted—"

Lauren laughed and not in a nice way. "I'm getting divorced, and Sierra just dropped out of college to drive around the country with her loser rock star wannabe boyfriend while Vaughn, my gifted son, is undergoing therapy because of an addiction to online gaming. He might not graduate from high school." She sat and waved me back to my chair. "Don't let that old woman fool you into thinking she's nice. She doesn't care about me or what's happening in my life. She started this vicious cycle by screwing up my life, and now I'm doing exactly the same to my children."

I blinked. Wow. She had to be in her forties or fifties and she still blamed her mother for all her problems. "Maybe she needs an occasional update—"

"And she'll get it today, so she knows exactly what her selfishness has done to my family."

Okay, the closure I had hoped for was so not going to happen. But that didn't mean I couldn't try. "She's changed."

"No, she hasn't. Is she ever nice to you? Has she ever thanked you for reading to her or bringing her homemade pies? Oh yeah, I do get updates from Moonbeam. She has a mean streak in her, and I have enough to deal with without putting up with her bullshit."

Mrs. J wasn't the thanking-people type, but her daughter was horrible. "Your mother is dying, Mrs. Michaels."

Lauren scoffed at the idea. "My mother is too mean to die. I'd bet she faked a heart attack to get me here. Well, here I am. Thanks to Rhys. The man is charming and persistent."

The door opened, and we both stood as they wheeled Mrs. J inside. She still looked frail and pale. I glanced at the daughter's face to see her reaction. She frowned as she stared down at her mother. I couldn't tell whether she still believed Mrs. J had faked a heart attack. I didn't know what caused the rift between them, but no one could look at a woman this ill and stayed unmoved.

When Lauren moved closer to the bed and whispered in a shaky voice, "Momma? It's Lauren. I came as soon as I heard," I became optimistic.

The nurses left the room, and I followed. I continued to the waiting room. Rhys and Nara were talking in low voices a few feet away, but I heard them as I got closer.

"We have to tell him the truth as soon as he gets back," Rhys said.

"Why?" Nara asked. "He'll turn into a raging lunatic and hunt down Kia and Fontaine. It wasn't their fault Maliina escaped. That evil bitch was never going to Corpse Strand willingly. And the last thing we need is fighting among Grimnirs before we face her and her dark soul followers."

My stomach had hurtled to my throat when Nara mentioned Maliina. Now, it raced and my stomach churned. I tried to speak, but all that came out was "goo-goo, ga-ga." The two Grimnirs looked up, realized I must have heard them, and cringed.

"Maliina escaped?" The words finally gurgled out of my throat.

CHAPTER 19. TRUST

"You were not supposed to hear that," Nara said. "Don't tell Echo."

Was she crazy? He'd want to know yesterday and haul ass from here to next week. "How did this happen?"

A nurse eyed me curiously a few feet away. I was sure I looked like a lunatic talking to myself. Lucky for me, I had my cell phone. I gave her a tiny smile and brought the phone closer to my mouth.

She shook her head and pointed at a sign that said, "No cell phones."

Even my lies were getting me into trouble. Face burning, I pocketed the phone. "Sorry." I looked up and down for the nearest restroom. The nurse was still eying me from the corner of her eye. "Is there a restroom I could use?"

"Two doors past the registration desk." She waved to my right.

"Thanks." I mouthed to Nara and Rhys, "Follow me."

I didn't look back to make sure they were behind me. As I passed the nurse, she added, "No phones in the restroom either."

"Got it." I could feel her eyes on me as I entered the bathroom. I flipped up the light switch and waited for the Grimnirs to enter. They didn't hesitate.

"Does Dev still possess the old woman?" Nara asked, dropping the lid of the can and sitting. Sheesh, didn't she know someone might see the stupid lid moving on its own? I closed the door and faced them. "If he stays too long we'll have to forcefully remove him," she added.

I'd never seen how Echo forced souls out of me, but I was sure it wasn't pretty. "We're not discussing Dev. What happened with Maliina?"

"She escaped," Nara said.

"I know that," I snapped. "How?"

"The Grimnirs escorted her to Hel's Hall, but unlike most souls, Maliina's been there before, knows her way around the place—where the portals are and how to get back to this realm. She escaped before they reached the main hall and was never seen again."

It hurt to breathe, and every vile insult I could think of danced at the tip of my tongue. "And no one bothered to tell Echo?" I asked, my voice rising.

"Damn right," Nara said. "He was already pissed about what she did to you. No one was going to tell him we lost her."

I wanted to gut her. Rhys was busy studying the writings and images on the wall explaining how women should get a urine sample. On a normal day, I would have been embarrassed. Now I just wanted his undivided attention.

"We? You weren't here the night she died, were you? Or I would have remembered."

"We were around," Rhys said. "After all, finding Maliina was a top priority. Most of us were searching for her."

"Yet she managed to give you the slip."

Nara gave me an evil look. "Your point is?"

"You suck," I wanted to tell her, but I had a Eureka moment. Their stalking and relentless attempts to get to Dev now made sense. "This is why you guys have been after Dev."

They glanced at each other and exchanged smiles.

"Told you she'd figure it out," Rhys said.

"Took her long enough," Nara said.

"Hey," I snapped. "Quit talking about me like I'm not here. You've been after Dev so he could lead you to Maliina."

Nara rolled her eyes. "Yes, and preferably before your boyfriend found out."

"What a bunch of… Do you know Dev thinks you're after him because of what happened with your people a millennia ago? Why couldn't you just tell Echo what happened? What could he possibly do that he hasn't already done? It's not like he could kill you guys."

Nara's eyes flashed with annoyance, but she didn't speak. At least Rhys had the decency to look uncomfortable.

"I thought you were really concerned about forgetting the past and working with Echo. He," I pointed at Rhys, "even offered to find the dark souls. You were just covering your asses."

"My offer was legit," Rhys said.

"Liar. You come anywhere near Dev and I'll tell Echo *everything*. He doesn't know you came to the nursing home to see me that first time or that *she*," I jabbed a finger at Nara, "almost killed me."

"If I wanted to kill you, you'd be—"

"Shut up, Nara," Rhys said. "She's right. We came here with an agenda and she now knows the truth. We apologize," he added, glancing at me. "We would still like to hear the truth from Dev."

"Ha! Like he owes you one now, you lying, sneaky Druids. Argh. Get out of my way." I yanked open the door to find three nurses outside the restroom. They all looked beyond me to see who I'd been talking to. I could either get thrown out for ignoring hospital rules or hauled to the nearest psyche ward for evaluation.

I pulled my phone from my pocket. "Sorry, I had to yell at some people."

"Call security," the nurse who'd warned me against using cell phones said.

"Can we give her a pass this once, Jess?" the second nurse asked. "My sister works at Moonbeam and told me about her. She's the high-school volunteer who came with the old woman from the nursing home. She takes homemade pies to the residents and the staff."

Nurse Jess didn't look like she was ready to play nice. Or maybe she was a pie-hater.

"I'm so sorry," I added. "I promise it won't happen again. I just wanted a friend to take care of my regular guys at the nursing home and he was being a total douche."

Jess' eyes narrowed. Yep, she saw through the lie.

I went for the kill. "A lot of my friends think working with sick or old people is uncool. I think it's noble. I plan to apply to nursing school next year."

I had them. "Okay," Nurse Jess said. "Consider this your final warning or I'll ask security to escort you out of the building."

"Thanks."

Ignoring Nara and Rhys, who were smirking at my lame fabrications, I hurried toward Mrs. J's room. I had reached my quota for caring what they thought. I pushed aside the curtain and peered inside. A tear-stained, raccoon-eyed Lauren looked up, her hand gripping her mother's. Mrs. J appeared to be sleeping or resting. Her color was better, but that could be due to Dev or having her daughter around.

"She's going to make it, right?" Lauren said.

Somehow I doubted it, but I nodded. "She's a tough lady."

"She said you've been very nice to her." When I didn't move from the doorway, she inclined her head. "Come inside."

I stepped inside the room and stayed by the foot of the bed. "My friend Dev and I need to go home now," I said out loud, but I doubted Lauren heard me. She was back staring at her mom and mumbling under her breath. I only caught a few phrases.

"...been here for you... so sorry... pointless fights... love you, Mama..."

Dev must have heard me because he slithered out through her nose and disappeared inside my phone. His movements were sluggish. Something must be wrong. Mrs. J's breathing seemed to have changed, and the pink tinge on her cheeks was starting to fade. Was she dying? I didn't want her soul to see me again.

"Uh, Lauren," I said softly. She looked up. With her makeup smudged, she looked older. "I have to leave now."

She reached out and shook my hand. "Thank you so much for being there for her. She said she always looked forward to your visits and your mother's pies."

Now that was new. "I'll make sure I bring her more." Mrs. J was ashen now. There was no way she was going to make it, which meant I needed to leave. Like now. "Let me know how she's doing. The nursing home has my number."

"I will. Mrs. Hightower was here a few minutes ago. I told her I'll be taking Mom to a nursing home in Portland as soon as she's well enough to travel." She stroked her Mom's hand again. "And, um, tell Rhys that I'll skip the dinner. It would never have worked between us anyway."

A raspy, gaggling sound came from the bed, and ours eyes flew to Mrs. J.

"What's happening?" Lauren asked in a panicky voice. "Call the nurse."

I ran out of the room screaming, "Nurse!"

Chaos followed as several nurses and a doctor raced toward the room. I barely managed to get out of the way. Rhys and Nara had been joined by Syn and Redhead. From their expressions, they all knew that I was aware of their agenda. I didn't slow down or even acknowledged them as I left, but I knew they were behind me. It was as though they released a pulse of energy I was tuned into.

Out in the waiting room, I found a chair and texted Mom. I brought my phone closer to my mouth and whispered, "You okay, Dev?"

"No," he sounded tired. "I hate trapping souls. It sucks so much of my energy. Do you mind if I rest now? Like for the next hour or two."

"Go ahead. You've earned it. Oh, and thank you for what you did back there. Without you, Mrs. J and her daughter would not have talked."

"It's what I do, doll-face. It's what I do." He sounded completely exhausted. Funny, I never thought how the souls felt after possessing me. I just knew I was drained afterwards. I always assumed they were the ones draining my energy. Fatigue must be the side effect of possession.

I didn't try to converse with him after that. When Mom walked into the waiting room half an hour later, my throat closed. I'd had it together until she appeared. Now, I wanted to bawl like a child and tell her everything: Maliina had escaped and she was after me. Again.

"Oh, sweetheart," Mom whispered, putting an arm around my shoulder. "It must have been one heck of a day," she added as she led me outside.

I managed to hold back the tears. "I just want to go home."

"Then home it is." She pressed a kiss on my temple. Once again, I didn't glance at the Grimnirs, but I was aware of them following us.

***

Mom fussed over me during dinner, studying me with worried eyes. Dad was more subtle, but I felt his concern too. Then my cell phone rang. My hand was a bit unsteady as I brought it to my ear. I listened to Mrs. Hightower's assistant. A mousy, petite woman who tended to blend in with the background. I could never remember her name.

"Thank you." I hung up and pocketed the phone. My parents stared at me with identical expressions. Funny I hadn't noticed how they tilted their heads in the same direction and scrunched up their faces in exactly the same way. Must be true what they said about people starting to look alike after living together for years. Would Echo and I make the same gestures after a couple of centuries together? Gah, I missed him so much.

"Mrs. Jepson is dead," I said in a tiny voice. "Her daughter was with her."

"Oh, sweetie." Mom reached out and rubbed my back.

"It's okay, Mom. I, uh, kind of saw it coming." *Once Dev left her body.* I stood. "I think I'll go to bed early. Goodnight."

They didn't complain, but I felt their eyes on me. Upstairs, I closed the door and fought tears as I dropped on my bed. I should be happy, not crying. I'd brought Mrs. J and her daughter together, and they'd found closure.

"Are you okay?" Dev asked. He still sounded like crap, his accent heavier.

"Yeah," I whispered in a shaky voice, fighting a losing battle with my tears. They pooled at the corners of my eyes and rolled down into my ears.

"Then why are you crying?"

I didn't try to deny it. "Did you know about Maliina?"

Silence. Then a soft, "Yes."

"Is that why you came looking for Echo?" I asked.

"Partly. I planned to warn him and gain his trust. I'd hoped that once he took care of Maliina, he'd be willing to listen to my story. Our paths have crossed so many times in the past, but he always looked the other way. Learning about Maliina and her plans to use your body as a vessel gave me a reason to approach him and maybe make him really look at me. I was thousands of years old, yet I had a form. I needed him to know I was making amends, that I hadn't betrayed him."

At least he had my interest as part of his agenda. "I wish you'd told me from the beginning, Dev."

"I'm sorry I've disappointed you, Cora. Even souls can be selfish."

That was an understatement. "I know."

Silence followed. "Besides, I didn't know you, Cora. You could have been working with Maliina for all I knew."

I rolled my eyes. "I'm not that sneaky, Dev."

"No, you're not. You are awesome." He chuckled. "And I'm proud to call you my friend."

I smiled. "Same here. What are we going to do now? Echo is gone, but Maliina is out there waiting to pounce."

"Nara and Rhys are on our side. I want to talk to them. It's time they knew the truth."

"You can't trust them. They're only after you so you can lead them to Maliina," I said.

"I figured as much, but you should trust them."

"Heck no."

"They're Druids, Cora. Rhys claimed you as family when he introduced you to Mrs. J's daughter. He meant it. Once a Druid accepts you as one of them, they stay loyal. Until you betray them, of course."

"Well, I don't want their loyalty."

Dev chuckled. "Can you give them your phone?"

"Do I have to? You must be tired after possessing Mrs. J for over an hour. Shouldn't you rest and get your strength back first? It takes me hours to recover."

"I still suck energy out of things around me. In this case, your cell phone. Haven't you noticed how often you've been recharging it? Please, let me talk to them. We helped Mrs. J find closure. Now help me find mine."

He didn't play fair. "Fine."

I went to the bathroom, splashed water on my face, and walked to the window where I counted four glowing Grimnirs spread out under the apple trees. How many more were on the other side of our farm? Nara had said there were twelve. They must've had my house surrounded.

Rhys saw me first and waved. Him I could take in small doses. Nara annoyed the crap out of me. I waved him over.

One minute he was near the orchard, the next in my bedroom. He looked around with interest. "Seen enough?" I asked.

His focus shifted to me. "You're still angry?"

"No, Rhys. This is my happy face. Dev wants to talk to you and Nara. For whatever reason, he trusts you. I don't." I slapped my cell phone in his palm. "Do not force him out of my cell. Bring him back when you're done. I'll be waiting."

He frowned. "You know why we want him."

"Bring him back, Rhys. If he agrees to help you, I want to hear it from his mouth, not yours. Yours spews lies."

He winced. "Okay. Thanks."

"Don't thank me yet. You still have to deal with Echo. I'm not going to tell him about Maliina. You will. As soon as he returns."

He nodded. "Don't worry about her. We'll get her. We might not have been honest about our reasons for getting close to you, but we all want the same thing—Maliina on Corpse Strand. I have Grimnirs stationed around town in case she appears, and we'll still be guarding you."

I nodded, waited until he left, and went to the bathroom to get ready for bed. Instead of wearing one of my usual pjs, I pulled on sweatpants and a T-shirt, and dropped on top of my bed.

They'd better bring back Dev or I swear…

Fighting the urge to check on them, I went over everything I knew about Maliina. She never did anything by the book. She might be evil and vile, but she was smart. When Andris had showed an interest in her sister, Ingrid, she'd asked him to turn her into an Immortal. When he'd showed interest in Raine, she'd marked me. I hated that I still didn't have the memory of that momentous occasion. Norns stole it from me. And when the Norns tried to use her, she'd turned around and betrayed them by making a deal with Goddess Hel. It took some serious guts to go against Norns.

I was still trying to figure out her next move when Nara appeared in my bedroom. I sat up and extended my hand toward her without speaking. It was going to take me a long time to like her. She placed the phone in my hand.

I sat cross-legged on my bed and glared at her as I brought the phone closer to my lips. "You there, Dev?"

"I'm here, doll-face."

He was getting a free pass on the nickname tonight. "Is everyone cool with the past?"

He chuckled. "We're cool."

"Are you going to help them find Maliina?"

"*After* Echo comes home. Right now, my priority is you. I gave him my word."

"That's our priority, too," Rhys said, appearing beside Nara.

I studied the two Grimnirs, not sure I should help them. On the other hand, we all wanted Maliina gone. "You can't predict Maliina's behavior. She's smart and ambitious. Everything she's done since I met her, and even before that, says she'll strike when you least expect it and in ways you haven't thought about."

"What do you mean?" Rhys asked.

I quickly explained what I knew about her. "If you want to learn more, talk to Ingrid." Interest sparked in Rhys' eyes. "Maliina might be her sister, but Ingrid is nothing like her. She's on our side."

"Can you arrange a meeting with her?" Nara asked.

I nodded. "I don't think they'll be at school tomorrow, but if they are, I'll do it. If not, I can arrange for you guys to talk to her somewhere."

Rhys looked like he wanted to ask more questions, but Nara spoke first. "In case you were wondering, Syn reaped

Mrs. J's soul. He found a nice place for her. Her soul is at peace."

I shifted to the edge of the bed, my stomach shifting. "He already went to Hel and came back?"

She nodded and looked away uneasily. The shift in my stomach became a churning vortex of dread. "Did he see Echo?"

Nara shook her head. "No."

The vortex became a tsunami. I tried to swallow, but my mouth tasted like sandpaper. "Is that normal? For you guys to take that long placing a soul?"

"No, but this is different," Nara said.

"How?"

"He's placing Mr. Cooper's soul in the gods' wing," Rhys said. "So many things go on in that wing."

"Like what?" Nara and Rhys looked at each other. Argh, I hated it when people did that. "Don't do that. Just tell me."

"The gods and goddess might like their privacy, but they get up a few times for Goddess Hel's parties." Rhys grimaced and rubbed his nape. "At times, she asks us to participate."

Their expression said it was something they didn't enjoy. I didn't want to speculate about the nature of the parties, but Eirik was born in Hel's Hall and his father was a soul. I wanted them to leave before I had a complete meltdown.

"Thanks for letting me know about Mrs. J. I'll, uh..." My voice shook to a stop and I had to clear it before continuing. "I'll see you guys tomorrow. I'll, uh, text Ingrid about Maliina."

I waited until they left before crawling back to the bed. I fought tears. What if the goddess had caught Echo and Andris? What was the worst thing she could do to them? Lock them with the damned on Corpse Strand?

Raine had said Eirik changed after staying with her. No one knew what she'd done to him. Andris and Echo weren't her children. Who was to stop her from doing something really terrible? I couldn't afford to lose Echo. Not now. Not ever. Tears filled my eyes.

"He'll be back," Dev said.

I wiped my cheeks, but the stupid tears kept flowing. Gah, I was such a girl.

"You mean everything to him, Cora."

"I know." I crawled under the covers and tried to control my stormy emotions. I knew the moment Dev left my phone. I watched him drift through the wall. A few moments later, he came back. Instead of entering the phone, he stayed by the window, keeping guard. His presence was reassuring.

**

I was calmer and more optimistic the next morning. I searched the back of my closet for my ugly pants—cargo pants. I shuddered. Cargo pants were the most unflattering pants ever invented for women.

I was a dresses-and-skirts girl. Jeggings, check. Leggings, oh yeah. Skinny jeans, bring them on. Regular jeans were for working around the farm, but Mom had bought the cargo pants online for herself—the first and last time she ever shopped online—and they'd turned out to be too small. To make her not feel bad, I'd offered to take them off her hands. I never had any intention of wearing them, until now.

I studied my reflection and cringed again. It was a good thing Echo wasn't around. I reached between my mattress and box spring, and retrieved the pouch with my artavo. I removed two more of the runic knives, wrapped them nicely with scarves, and hid them in the pockets of my pants.

Next was the fire poker, which didn't fit in my backpack. I put it at an angle for a better fit and wrapped the handle with a scarf. We might not have metal detectors at our school, but you never know. Rallying up the troops came last. Not wanting to bother Raine, I texted Torin.

He called back. "You okay?"

Now that I was packing. "Yeah."

"Stop by my place on your way to school."

Mom stared at my pants but made no comment. She probably thought I was going through post traumatic stuff because of all the deaths. Her hug was longer, and she stood by the window and watched me drive away.

Torin opened the door shirtless. At freaking seven in the morning. Raine was right about him. He was allergic to shirts. He cocked a questioning brow at my cargo pants. I doubted he'd ever seen me wear anything but girly clothes.

"Don't judge. I'm packing weapons of soul destruction. How's Raine doing?"

"Taking it hard." His voice said he didn't like to see her in pain. "She's still asleep and the longer the better. Come in."

He sauntered toward the kitchen, sweatpants riding low on his hips and threatening to lose the battle to gravity. That would be interesting. Raine might not find it amusing.

I focused on something else. The smell of bacon. My mouth approved. I loved bacon. It was one food item I could eat more of than Echo. My man might not cook, but he knew how to microwave. My heart ached. I missed him so much.

We entered the kitchen and I went on a bacon hunt. A pan of southern-style potatoes sat on the stovetop. Yum. Another pan had eggs. A plate of bacon on paper towel sat on the side counter beside a bouquet of roses. Vases of flowers were everywhere, probably sent by people who'd known Raine's father. I placed my backpack on the counter by the flowers and reached for a piece of bacon.

"Want some breakfast?" Torin threw over his shoulder.

I flashed a guilty smile. "I've actually eaten, but this looks good." Chewing, I watched him set the tray. Orange juice. Two plates of potatoes, eggs, and bacon. So domesticated.

Echo was right. We needed our own place. He could prepare breakfast for me in the morning, just like this. Burned or undercooked, I'd love anything he cooked and not complain. My eyes watered. I looked away and tried to control myself.

"You're worried about Echo," Torin said. From the way he was studying me, it wasn't the first time he'd spoken.

"Nah."

Torin's lips lifted in a smile, but it didn't reach his blue eyes. He saw through my lie. "One thing about Echo, Cora, is his resourcefulness. He'll be fine." Torin walked toward me, and for one crazy second, I thought he planned to hug me. I was too fragile for hugs. If he did, I'd started crying like a baby.

He didn't hug me. Instead, he reached for a rose, turned, and placed it on the tray. He stepped back, hands on his hips, and studied his handiwork. "What do you think?"

"Very romantic," I said with a tinge of envy.

He made a face. "I was going for cheerful. You know when I was on Hel duty, I learned a lot from watching Echo. He's driven and unstoppable, a real-pain-in-the-ass when he doesn't get his way, but I came to respect him. He will do what's right. Do you know why?"

"Because he promised Raine to place her father in the wing of the gods and he always keeps his word," I said.

Torin chuckled. "He does, but that's not it. He plans to come home to you, and nothing will stop him from doing that."

My eyes teared. I lifted my chin and blinked rapidly. "Now I know whose shoulder to cry on if he ever goes missing."

He smirked. "I have two of them, and I know Raine won't mind sharing. Do you want a hug?"

I made a face. "No."

"You sure? I don't want you going to school still worried about him, and my hugs, I've been told, are very comforting. I promise not to cop a feel," he added.

I laughed. From the grin on his face, that had been his intention. "No, I'm fine, but we have another problem."

Torin's eyebrows arched in question.

"Maliina is back."

His mood left relaxed, shot past shocked, and landed on furious in a fraction of a second. I expected him to curse, but that wasn't Torin's style. "I'm listening."

I told him everything, including Dev helping Mrs. J and what I learned from the Grimnirs.

"Wait here."

Yeah, like that was going to happen. I followed him. He marched to the mirror in his living room, runes flaring. The portal responded and opened into the mansion's foyer.

He stepped through and called out, "Lavania! We have a situation. Blaine! Ingrid! My place pronto."

"What's going on?" Lavania asked from somewhere on the second floor.

"Someone crawled from the underbelly of Hel, and we need to send her back," he practically snarled, turned, and came back to his place. Concern shimmered in the depth of his blue eyes. "You should skip school and stay here until we take care of this."

I was shaking my head before he finished talking. "No way. Remember your motto. 'Act normal. Let your enemies think you're unaware of them, and then surprise them when they attack.' Raine told me."

"Sometimes I talk too much," he mumbled, rubbing his forehead.

I hid a grin. "Besides, I have Grimnirs watching my back, thanks to Echo. And I'm packing artavo and a fire poker courtesy of Sam and Dean."

"Two fictional characters who've never met a real dark soul," he grumbled.

"Don't go disrespecting the Winchester boys," I rounded on him. "They kick ass."

"Grimnirs, huh?" Torin took off again. Runes still blazing, he opened the door and disappeared outside. Once again I followed, but I didn't make it to the door. Lavania chose that moment to float into the living room in a flowing lavender gown. As usual, it was impossible to ignore her.

"Cora! What's going on?"

"Uh, Ma…" Blaine and Ingrid walked in. "Let's wait for Torin."

Ingrid was going to take it hard. She looked relaxed in silk pajamas and a matching robe while Blaine had flannel pants and a tank top. From their clothing, they weren't planning on going to school. Today was a half-day and the junior prom was this evening.

"Where's Torin?" Lavania asked.

"He just left without explaining." We all headed to the kitchen. Blaine went straight for bacon and coffee. Ingrid grabbed the nearest chair. Lavania studied the tray Torin had arranged. I joined Ingrid. Soon, Lavania got busy serving herself breakfast while Blaine guzzled coffee like it was his lifeline. He handed Ingrid a cup. I told him I didn't want any.

My focus was on Ingrid. She wasn't going to like my news. "Thanks for calling the school about mystery meat," I whispered.

A naughty grin lifted Ingrid's lips. Then her eyes widened and her hand lifted to adjust the lapels of her robe. I turned to see what had caught her attention and groaned.

Torin was back. Rhys and Nara were with him.

CHAPTER 20. THE NORNS STRIKE AGAIN

Lavania studied the new arrivals and switched to being a gracious hostess. "I'm Lavania Celestina Ravilla. I never forget a face, and you two look familiar."

Torin picked up the tray and started out of the room.

"Where are you going?" Lavania called out. "You didn't introduce them."

"Cora can do the honors," Torin said, starting upstairs. "Be back in a few."

Silence followed his departure. Blaine recognized Rhys and gave him a manly nod. He didn't seem to be holding a grudge from their last meeting. Men were cool like that. Rhys didn't bother to hide his interest this time either. His eyes stayed on Ingrid, whose cheeks were rosy. I'd bet she wished she'd dressed up and brushed her hair. Not that she didn't look beautiful.

I made the necessary introductions. Rhys and Nara didn't give out their second names and the others didn't seem to care.

"Coffee?" Blaine asked.

"No, thanks," Nara said.

"I'll have some," Rhys said at the same time.

Lavania offered them breakfast, which they declined. "I know where I've seen you two before," she added, still studying them. "You were in Tyr's Court with Echo during the sentencing."

Nara wore an expression that said "so what?"

"It isn't often we have mass sentencing, and you all wore such defiant expressions." Lavania frowned. "If my memory serves me right, your sentences were completed a couple of centuries ago."

What? That was news to me. I studied Nara and Rhys, but they didn't speak. Even Blaine paused in the process of pouring Rhys' coffee and studied them.

When it became obvious they had no intention of explaining, Blaine offered Rhys the cup of coffee. "Cream? Sugar?"

"Black is good. May I?" Rhys indicated a chair near Ingrid, waited until she nodded, and sat. He was more interested in her than conversation about their service to Goddess Hel, but Lavania could not be stopped.

"Why are you still Grimnirs?" she asked, using her teacher voice.

"Why are you a Valkyrie?" Nara shot back. Guess she wasn't ready to be schooled.

Annoyance flashed across Lavania's face. Then it disappeared quickly. She chuckled. "I get it."

I didn't. "Get what?"

"They're Grimnirs because that's what they want to be," Lavania said. She sounded impressed. "Even though their sentence is over, they've chosen to stay."

That was the dumbest thing I'd ever heard. "Why? Hel's Hall is cold and dangerous. The goddess is unpredictable and a nutcase."

"What's a little cold and danger?" Rhys said, clearly showing off. It was paying off, too, because Ingrid stared at him with awe. "We're the judge, jury, and executioners of those who've wronged humanity, and that includes those not held accountable while alive. We're proud of who we are." He glanced at me, and his violet eyes grew frosty. "Don't ever call her that. Our goddess is many things, but crazy is not one of them."

"Don't talk to her like that," Blaine snapped.

"Stay out of this, Immortal," Rhys snapped. "She's Echo's girl, so her loyalty lies with him." The tension in the room shot up as the two men sized each other up. "Unless he's changed since he met her," Rhys added.

"He hasn't," I said, not liking his tone. I wanted to ask him what Goddess Hel had ever done to inspire such loyalty in her reapers, but the fight went out of me. These were Echo's friends. Technically my guards. Antagonizing them was pointless. My beef was with Echo. He'd never said anything nice about Goddess Hel, yet he was completely devoted to her.

"You know, we have a few presidents, prime ministers, and CEOs of major corporations on Corpse Strand. Quite a number of them were Echo's," Nara chipped in with glee. I wasn't sure whether she was trying to diffuse the situation or make it worse. Knowing her, worse.

Torin appeared through an air portal, and I sighed with relief. If he felt the tension in the room, he didn't show it, but he'd taken time to pull on a T-shirt. What surprised me even more was the fact that Raine hadn't followed him. She must have had quite a night.

"Cora has fifteen minutes before first period, so let's make this quick. You there, Dev?"

"Yes, sir," Dev's voice floated from the side of my backpack. I fished my cell phone out.

"Good. You continue staying with Cora." He glanced at Ingrid. "Maliina is back."

Ingrid sucked in a breath. "Wha...? How?"

"From what Cora told me, she managed to escape from Hel." He brought everyone up to speed on everything. I was surprised when Blaine moved closer to Ingrid and squeezed her shoulder. Rhys scowled, obviously not liking their closeness. There were no romantic vibes between Ingrid and Blaine, or Raine would have told me. Ingrid, Maliina, and Andris lived with Blaine's family when they first arrived in Kayville, so they must be pretty close.

"Cora, leave your car here and use a portal to and from school. Raine swears the north bathroom on the second floor is usually empty."

I nodded. "It is."

"Second, see if your parents can let you stay here over the weekend. Tell them Raine needs you. Having you here should make things easier for all of us. There are three empty bedrooms here, which brings us to Rhys and Nara. I'm sure you have your own places, but until Echo comes back, you stay here."

"All twelve of us?" Rhys asked.

"There are rooms at the mansion, too," Ingrid said, and I could hear fear in her voice. "Let's all stay there."

Torin nodded. "Okay, Ingrid. We'll find a way to accommodate everyone at the mansion."

The rest of the meeting went smoothly. Torin outlined what he expected from everyone and how to get in touch with each other.

"I'm not reaping until after the funeral, but I might be otherwise engaged. If you can't get a hold of me, find Blaine or Ingrid, and Lavania is always at the mansion. Raine and her mother are not to be disturbed with this unless absolutely necessary. I'll talk to Hawk and Femi." He made eye contact with Rhys and Nara. "You can meet them later."

"And you should all come to the mansion for lunch," Lavania said and smiled at Nara and Rhys. "All of you. I want to meet the remaining ten."

***

The upstairs bathroom was empty. As soon as the portal closed, Nara rounded on her cousin. "You and the Immortal will never work."

I stole a glance at Rhys. He didn't seem bothered by her dire prediction. In fact, he wore such a smug smile I doubted anything Nara said would stop him from pursuing Ingrid. Andris was going to hate it.

"See you guys, later," I threw over my shoulder and took off toward my locker. I ignored the stares. So I dressed differently for one day? Big freaking deal.

"Congrats, Cora," a girl from my P.E. class said when I got downstairs.

For what? Dressing like a slob? "Um, thanks."

"You have my vote," another added when I got downstairs.

Vote for what? Near my locker, Kicker's jaw dropped when she saw me.

"One word from you and I'll bitch-slap you into next week," I warned.

She pressed her lips tight and nodded, but she gave me a onceover. "You actually rock that look."

I shot her a mean look. Of course, I did. My top was gorgeous and compensated for the ugly pants.

"Okay, enough about your wardrobe change. Did you see the list for the Junior Prom Court?" she asked, eyes sparkling with excitement. "You made it! I'm already rallying the troops."

I smothered a groan. I had no intention of attending the junior prom and didn't want to discuss it either. "Don't bother. I'm not going."

"What? Why not? You're the most popular girl in school. Everyone reads your blog. You'll definitely be crowned Junior Prom Queen."

I highly doubted it. Students voted for the prom king and queen, and the most popular junior right now was Raine. I slammed my locker shut.

"I'll stop by the office and tell them I'm out, so they can select someone else. Oh, and the funeral is eleven o'clock tomorrow morning at Grandview Cemetery."

Kicker frowned. "Funeral? Whose?"

Seriously? Proms made people stupid. "Raine's father."

"Oh."

"Well, I thought you'd want to go." I brushed past her. "She should be crowned Junior Prom Queen."

"What?" Kicker asked like I'd lost my mind.

I wanted to say something scathing, but... this was Kicker. Clueless. Sweet. Sometimes annoying because she didn't know when to shut up.

"She lost her father, Kicker," I threw over my shoulder. "It might make her feel a little better."

"That's ridiculous," Kicker said, hurrying to keep up with me. "I mean, she doesn't go to school here anymore, so she *can't* be crowned. I didn't even know the two of you were still in touch."

What in Hel's Mist...? I stopped and whipped around, my stomach dropping somewhere near the arch of my feet. Kicker bumped into me and apologized. I raised my hand and cut her off. "What did you say about Raine?"

She blinked and took a step back. "Uh, she doesn't go to school here anymore and can't be Junior Prom Queen. I mean, she and Eirik moved away right after the accident at the swim meet."

No, no, no! This couldn't be happening. I shook my head. Kicker misunderstood. "What? You don't believe me?"

"Who's the QB?" I asked.

"Blaine Chapman. Cora, what's—?"

"The one who led us to the championship," I snapped. A few students walking by turned to stare at us. I glared back.

Kicker looked around uneasily then whispered, "Okay, Cora. You look totally wigged out. You're not forgetting stuff again, are you?"

I blinked at her like the village idiot. I'd used that as an excuse when I couldn't remember stuff Maliina did in my name *and* body while I was in the psyche ward. Finally, I found my voice. "No-ooo."

"Uh, you forgot stuff before after you were hurt at the game."

This wasn't time to explain my confusion. I needed distance from her and the questions in her eyes. I took a deep breath, then another. "Yeah, I did, but I'm okay now. Let's talk later."

I took off and pushed past people. A few yelled congratulations while others stared at me strangely. I was beyond caring what anyone thought. The Norns were erasing memories, which meant the Valkyries were about to disappear. Did that include Grimnirs?

I careened around the corner, almost bumping into students. My first destination was the football wall of fame. My heart squeezed when I saw the photograph of Blaine and the football team. His name and face had replaced Torin's. Obviously, Photoshop had nothing on the Norns.

"Cora," Kicker whispered from behind me.

I took a deep breath and turned to face her. "Don't ask. You mentioned Junior Prom Queen and I had déjà vu. Remember, Blaine and Casey were crowned Junior Prom King and Queen last year, and everyone said they'd probably take the senior crowns this year too?"

I must have convinced her I wasn't completely looney because she smiled. "He will. The teachers haven't selected the court for the seniors, but everyone knows he's the most popular guy at school. Too bad he's not really dating anyone right now." She gave me a pointed look I didn't understand.

I scowled as I fell in step with her, my mind racing. Why were the Norns doing this now?

"Aw, come on, Cora." Kicker turned and walked backwards, her expression annoying me. "You keep denying there's anything between the two of you, but I don't believe it. You two hang out a lot."

"I'm dating..." What if she didn't remember Echo?

"Who?"

My throat seized up. "No one."

Kicker rolled her eyes. "I know. You're still pining for Eirik," she said.

A crazed laugh escaped my lips. This was totally effed up. It was as though the last several months hadn't happened. Why now? Was it time for the Valkyries and Grimnirs to move on? Was that why the Norns had paired me with Blaine? He once told me Immortals stuck together. Maybe this was what he'd meant.

I didn't want to be paired with Blaine. I wanted Echo. My stomach heaved. I was so going to throw up right there in the hallway.

I pointed at the bathroom door. "I gotta go."

I didn't wait to see if she left or not. The first bell went off, but being late was the least of my problems. I pulled out my cell phone and called Torin. The phone kept ringing. Was he gone? I engaged my runes and reached for my artavus.

Please, let Raine and Lavania be at home. I wasn't ready to deal with dark souls and Immortal stuff without them or Echo.

"Cora?" Torin asked just before I started etching runes on the mirror, and relief washed over me.

"Thank goodness, you're still here," I said in a voice I didn't recognize.

He chuckled. "Of course I'm here. Didn't you get my—?"

269

"No one remembers you, your photographs are gone, and Raine…" My breathing grew raspy. "The Norns are wiping memories, Torin."

"I know," he said.

I blinked. "You know?"

"Yes. Don't worry about it. You won't be affected."

Was he crazy? "How can I not worry? Why are they doing this now?" What if this was about Echo? Did he anger the Norns by not reaping Raine's father months ago or escorting him to the luxurious wing of Hel's Hall? "Is this about Echo?"

"Whoa! Easy, Cora. This has nothing to do with Echo."

He answered way too quickly for my liking. "When did you find out, and why didn't you tell me?" I yelled.

"I barely found out," Torin said calmly. "*And* I did send you a text message. Blaine came to school as soon as we learned. If you need to cope, find him. He's had enough practice with this sort of thing. Don't talk to Mortals about us and try not to act differently."

Try not…? It was easy for him to say that. He'd been a Valkyrie for what now? A thousand years? People forgetting him must be as normal as breathing.

"Cora?"

"Are you and Raine going to leave? Is that why no one remembers you two?"

He groaned. "You already talked to people. Damn it." He mumbled something I didn't get. "You are one of us now, Cora. The Norns won't bother you, but you must learn to improvise. Don't talk to anyone about us. If it's too much for you to handle, come here." He hung up.

How am I supposed to focus with this over my head? A quick look at my text messages and I found the one from Torin.

"Don't panic if no one remembers us at school. Blaine will explain."

"A little too late for that, pal." I eyed the mirror and debated whether to just forget school and go to the mansion. I didn't want to deal with this alone, and I didn't trust Norns.

They'd deleted Torin's memories to punish Raine. What if they came after me?

"You okay?" Dev asked.

"No. You heard?"

"Yep. I've never had the pleasure of dealing with Norns, but I hear they're powerful."

"Raine is more powerful." They would not dare mess with me with Raine around. She'd kicked their wrinkly asses often enough to make me want to stay glued to her side, but I couldn't bother her now while she was in mourning.

Blowing out a breath, I left the bathroom. Nara and Rhys weren't around. They were probably consulting with their people.

From the lack of students in the hallway, the second bell must have rung. I wished I was confident engaging my runes. I'd shift to hyper-speed, cloak, and slip into the class undetected.

"I had to use the restroom," I said when I entered the class and Mrs. Bosnick looked up. She took one good look at me and grimaced. Maybe the pants did it, or maybe I looked like I felt, ready to barf.

"Do you need to see the nurse?" she asked.

"No." I avoided looking at Kicker even though I felt her eyes on me. Thankfully, I didn't get a tardy check.

Nara and Rhys sauntered into the classroom halfway through the class and stayed out of the students' way at the front of the room. I preferred them in the back, where I didn't have to see them. Worse, they stared at me and whispered the entire time. I'd bet they knew about the Norns and the deleted memories.

When the class ended, I took off before Kicker could catch up with me. She had the look in her eyes that said she was after information. She even called out my name, but I faked temporary deafness.

I disappeared in the throng of students hurrying to their next classes. Despite the crowded hallways, I felt alone, miserable, and sick to my stomach. Last time I felt like this I'd just seen my first Valkyries escorting the dead. I imagined my life without Raine. She'd been my friend since forever and we often discussed the supernatural world.

Just before I entered my next class, I bumped into Blaine with a bunch of guys. I'd never been so happy to see him. I elbowed the guys around him and hugged him tight.

"That bad?" he whispered.

"You have no idea. How do you do it?" I whispered back.

"You adjust slowly. It gets easier with time." He leaned back, looked into my eyes, and said, "You'll be okay."

"Do I get a hug, too?" Drew said from behind me, and I glanced over my shoulder. The cocky jock was back. Even his smile appeared genuine and relaxed. "I like your new style," he added, giving me a onceover. The other two guys with them smirked.

"Um, thanks." I gave him a wobbly smile. The Norns had deleted his memories too, which meant he didn't remember my Doppelganger messing with his head or being ditched in the middle of his party for Echo. Hugging him was not the way to go, though.

"It has its perks," Blaine added and squeezed my shoulder. "See you after school."

"What has perks?" Drew asked as the four continued down the hallway. I understood what Blaine meant. The Norns had just taken care of my problems with Drew.

The Grimnirs trailed me the entire morning, but kept their distance as per Torin's instruction. Juniors were excited about the prom and girls in my classes yapped about outfits and prom dates. Apparently, junior prom court had been posted yesterday afternoon and some of the nominees were doing their best to sway voters.

I walked past Sabrina 'Bree' Hinckley and her friends passing out Reese's Peanut Butter Cups and bags of Skittles with Vote for Bree stickers. Bree was an assistant head of the cheer squad. Caryn Jennings, the girl I'd locked out of the bathroom, turned out to be the captain of the basketball team and a nominee. She elbowed her friends and they gave me the evil eye as I walked by. They were handing out homemade cookies and complimentary tickets to Walkersville Girls

Basketball Team games. She didn't stand a chance against Bree or me.

Funny how I'd looked forward to attending the prom and now I couldn't be bothered. Raine and I would have rocked the All That Jazz theme with our outfits. Her mother had picked her a gorgeous dress.

I couldn't wait to leave. I was collecting my backpack from the locker when Kicker stood right smack in front of me and blocked me, demanding my attention.

"What?" I asked.

"Do you want to have lunch with us?" she asked. Sondra and Naya flanked her, and I didn't care for their this-is-an-intervention expressions.

"Can't. I'm having lunch with Blaine." I wedged my hands between Kicker and Sondra, pushed them aside, and walked past them. They turned and flanked me.

"Why can't you admit you two are dating?" Kicker asked.

"Why are you interested? You want him?" I cocked my eyebrow, wishing they'd just disappear.

Kicker giggled. "Doesn't every girl? He's so hot, the most popular guy at school, *and* he hasn't dated anyone since Casey."

"And he's staring at you right now," Sondra added.

Sure enough, Blaine and the invisible Grimnirs were at the end of the hallway waiting for me. "Blaine and I are just friends, Kicker."

"Is it true they finally found Raine's father's body?" Sondra asked.

"Are they burying him here?" Kicker asked.

My first instinct was to say, "Yes." But then I remembered Torin and his lecture. I had to tread carefully. "What?"

"Sorry. I didn't mean to tell them, but it kind of slipped out," Kicker whispered and twirled a lock of her hair. I couldn't get mad at her when she just gave me the opportunity to fix this mess.

"That's okay. I misunderstood her text."

"Is it a memorial service then?" Sondra asked. "The plane crash was last year in April. Or was it May?"

"April," Kicker said.

"May," Sondra insisted. "First the crash, then the accident at the pool. No wonder her family moved."

Twilight Zone anyone? These girls were at Raine's yesterday, and now they couldn't remember anything about it. Totally weird.

"I gotta go, guys." I took off.

"We'll swing by your place at four," Kicker called out.

I glanced at her. "I told you I'm not going."

"Uh, makeup and hair. You promised," she said, and Sondra nodded.

"I'm coming, too," Naya added.

I so didn't need this. I could tell them to come to Raine's or Torin's but they'd just get confused. Maybe the mansion? It was closer and bigger, and they believed I still had a crush on Eirik. Lavania could continue to pretend she was Eirik's aunt. It might work, except Kicker was nosy and everyone might be there, including Raine.

"I'll come to your place, Kicker. Between four and five. The prom starts at six, right?"

They nodded, eyes sparkling with excitement. To be that carefree again would be amazing. Or not. I couldn't trade Echo for prom.

Blaine was talking to Jen, or should I say she was attempting to wrap herself around him. Weird, the Norns hadn't erased her obsession with him. I wondered why. Rhys and Nara seemed to have disappeared.

"Ready to go?" Blaine asked when I reached them.

"Nope." I ignored the venomous look Jen threw my way. "I need to talk to my counselor."

"Is Dev on duty?"

"Always." I patted the side pocket of my pants. Jen frowned.

"Who's Dev?" she asked as I walked away.

"A friend," he responded. "So, about the prom..."

They followed me and stayed by the entrance of the hallway leading to the counselors' offices. I was beginning to notice a pattern with Blaine. When talking to me, he often spoke like the others weren't there. How did he explain things to his Mortal friends? First, he'd mentioned perks of being an Immortal in Drew's hearing, and now Dev in front of Jen. I might have to learn how to survive as an Immortal from him.

The waiting area in the counselors' offices was packed with students. The seats and the wall between them were taken. Mrs. Fennier, the dragon lady guarding the counselors' offices saw me and smiled. Her husband was a farmer and often sold goods at the Farmer's Market with my parents.

"Hey, Cora. What's going on?" she asked.

I ignored the students. "I want my name removed from the junior prom court. I won't be going."

"Oh, that's too bad. Why?"

"A dark soul is after me and my best friend's father is being buried tomorrow morning and no one remembers anything that's happened the last year." No, I didn't say that. I should have just to see people's reaction, but I wasn't that girl anymore. "Outrageous just for crap and giggles" was the former me.

"I'm coming down with something, and I'd rather not spread it." The students nearest the door shifted away as though not to breathe the same air as me. "In fact, I really shouldn't be near people right now."

She smiled. "That's considerate of you. I'll let your counselor know."

"You can be crowned even if you're not there," a girl seated near her desk said. I recognized her from my math class. I gripped the straps of my backpack and shrugged.

"Thanks, Mrs. Fennier." I turned, took two steps, and a hand cupped my elbow. I stared over my shoulder in confusion. "Drew?"

He indicated the door behind him with a conspiratorial nod.

I frowned. "What's going on?"

His grip tightened as he pushed the door. "We need to talk."

My jaw dropped. His voice. I tried to jerk my arm free, but he pulled me inside the room and closed the door. Adrenaline surging through me, I reached into my pockets and pulled out two artavo.

"Is that any way to greet an old friend, Cora?"

I pointed at him with the magical weapons and, at the same time, engaged my pain and strength runes. "You and I were never friends, Maliina."

CHAPTER 21. MALIINA

"What do you want?" I snarled.

Drew crossed his arms and leaned against the door. "Your body." He smirked. I had to remind myself that this wasn't Drew talking. Maliina had taken him over. Just like she'd taken over his head before and screwed with it. Every word from his mouth was hers.

"Let him go, Maliina."

"Why? He's perfect. You know how to pick them, don't you? First Eirik, whom I played like a banjo. Now this knucklehead. At least Eirik got over you fast. This idiot will always be crazy about you. Even the Norns scrambling his memories didn't take away his feelings. All I did was plant an idea in his feeble Mortal brain and he did my bidding."

Her voice grated on my nerves. I opened my mouth to tell her exactly what I thought about her, but she, he, or whatever you called a possessed person chuckled.

"Get her alone, Drew, and ask her to go with you to the senior prom," she said in a sweet voice and rolled her eyes. "Blaine already told him there was nothing going on between the two of you, paving the way for lover boy." He pushed against the door and moved toward me. "Guess he doesn't know about Echo."

I stepped back, almost tripping on a chair. We were inside someone's office. It was empty, but not for long. Today was Teachers' Work Day, so teachers were going to be around most of the afternoon.

"I'm not playing your stupid game if you don't let Drew go, Maliina."

"Oh, but you will, Cora. That body," she pointed at me, "belongs to me, and I've come to collect."

I tried to swallow, but my mouth had gone dry. "You're crazy if you think I'm going to let you possess me."

She chuckled. "Then you choose. Drew or you."

My jaw dropped. "I'm not going to let you blackmail me. Get out of him, now." My grip tightened on the weapons.

She laughed. "Or what? You think I'm scared of what you might do with those blades? Please." She opened a drawer and rummaged through it. "Be a nice little Immortal and engage the right runes for me."

"No." My phone beeped.

"Don't touch that." She must have found what she was searching for because I caught a glimpse of something metallic before she palmed it. "I guess I have to give you a reason to do the right thing."

I shook my head. "What happened to you? How could you have turned so evil when your sister is sweet and nice—?"

"Ingrid is *sweet* and *nice* because of me," Maliina hissed. "*I* protected her from ugliness and pain. *I* made sure she wasn't a punching bag for our drunken father. *I* stopped vile men from abusing her. Why do you think I studied hard to be the best witch our town ever had? I made sure…" A gleam entered his eyes, and I saw the thing in his palm. It was a letter opener. "Why am I explaining myself to you? You're nothing but a means to an end. I'm going to count to three, then this is going here." He pointed at his gut.

"No."

"Yes." He ripped his shirt, buttons flying everywhere. "I can absorb the pain. He can't. He'll have the wounds and the scars without understanding how he got them. That is if he survives." She dug the sharp tip into his skin.

"Please, don't hurt him." I wanted to fight back, but the situation was hopeless. My hands flexed uselessly on my weapons. I couldn't attack her because I'd only hurt Drew. My phone beeped again.

"Stop wasting my time, Cora." Blood pooled at the tip of the letter opener. "Put the artavo away and engage the medium runes."

"Okay. Just let him go." I dropped the weapons in my pockets. As I straightened, a familiar cold invaded my body. My skin grew taut as though it was being sucked into my core. My breath stalled in my chest and my eyes stung.

Maliina. This possession was worse than anything I'd ever experienced.

Let her get out of him; then I'll take over.

Dev?

Sorry I dived in. I'm leaving soon. When I say go, race for the door. I'll jump out and take her down.

"The wound is growing bigger, Cora," Maliina warned in a sing-song voice. The cut was about an inch now, the blood starting to roll down his stomach.

My body was still adjusting to the effects of possession. My chest hurt with each breath. I shivered, my fingers turning into icicles.

"I'll do it," I said, but my voice sounded distorted. I needed to engage the medium runes. "Just give me a minute."

"Drew doesn't have a minute," Maliina snapped.

Taking a deep breath, I let the need for possession fill me, and the medium runes appeared, coiling under my skin like a tapestry coming to life. With them came an energy surge, which lessened the effect of Dev's possession.

"I knew you'd see things my way," Maliina whispered with glee, eyes gleaming. "With these runes, we can share the same body. I like that you have a sense of style, just like me. In fact, that was the reason I chose you. You also do a decent job with your hair." She gave me a onceover and shuddered. "But those pants are fashion *faux pas*. We cannot be seen wearing anything like that. Ever."

We. She was completely insane, and the thought of sharing my body with her made me want to throw up.

"Your hair." He reached out as though to touch my hair. I moved back. Way, way back until there was a huge space between us. Smirking, he eyed me like a cat sizing up a rat before pouncing. What was she waiting for? Drew placed a foot on the chair and got comfortable on the table, eyes on the runes. "We'll experiment with colors and styles later. We have different tastes in men, so keeping our love lives apart should be easy."

She was Echo's ex-girlfriend. Anger coursed through me, and my hands clenched. She saw that and chuckled.

"No offense, sweetie, but Echo was a means to an end. He's too damaged for my liking. You can keep him as long as I have Andris." A smile creased his face, and his eyes became gentle. "I was a fool to let him go. He's the only person who's ever understood me."

"So this is about Andris?"

The dopey look disappeared from his face. "No, this is about living again," he snapped. "Feeling and loving again. I want all of it. With Andris. Ah, you're ready."

So that was what she'd been waiting for. For the runes to cover my entire body. She separated from Drew the same way I'd seen Mrs. J leave her body, head and chest first. Drew fell backwards, the back of his head connecting with the wooden desk. I winced, imagining the size of the bump and headache he'd get.

Maliina stepped away from Drew's limp body, and I swallowed.

She looked exactly the way she used to look, trendy white dress and a pink blazer. How could she look normal? There was no way the crazy bitch had spent the last several months floating around without possessing people.

I wanted to reach for my artavo, but she was too close to Drew and could easily slip back inside him.

Go!

I heard Dev's voice, but I couldn't move. Maybe I was too cold. Maybe I was too petrified. I just stood there like a statue and waited. Totally lame. Even worse, I did the dumbest, most stupid thing ever. I raised my hands and protected my head as though expecting a blow.

But something weird happened. Maliina's soul bounced off me as though we were made of rubber. But the full frontal body slam pushed me backwards. I would have hit the wall if it weren't for my backpack. I straightened, my eyes not leaving her. Her expression changed from eagerness to shock. Her mouth opened and closed, her face distorted as rage took over. What had stopped her from possessing me?

Not what. Who. Dev's presence inside me. I guess I had one too many souls.

She reached the same conclusion and turned to look at Drew. Crap! She was going back into his body. Adrenaline kicked in, and my paralysis disappeared. I reached for my artavo and threw them at her.

She ducked, both blades missing her. They hit the metal cabinet on the other end of the room with a clang and fell to the floor. She smirked, sending rage through me.

Leave, Dev screamed inside my head, but I was on an adrenaline rush. Mixed with an energy surge from the runes, I felt invincible. I remembered the fire poker sticking out of my backpack like a sword, reached over my shoulder, and pulled it out. Gripping it with two hands, I swung it across Maliina's soul just before she reached Drew.

She stopped and looked down in shock as her stomach became hazy and wispy. The effect spread. She looked weird, the bottom and top part of her body whole while the middle section disappeared. She looked at me with so much hatred I stepped back.

Good job, Dev said and separated from me. Maliina saw him, various expressions chasing across her face. The cold seeped out of me slower than it had pierced my core. Air rushed into my starved lungs. But with air came nausea. I pressed my stomach hard as though to stop the gag reflex and staggered forward.

Dev gestured for me to leave. I reached for the doorknob and yanked. I shot a glance over my shoulder to see something strange. Maliina's soul extended her hands toward Dev as though asking for a hug or begging him to do something. Then he did something that didn't make sense either. He floated forward and merged with her two halves.

Hands grabbed me, and I smothered a scream.

"It's me," Blaine said.

For a second, I clung to him, my heart pounding.

"What happened? A student said you were inside with a counselor," Blaine said somewhere above my head.

What was I doing clinging to him like some damsel in distress? Drew was out cold and Dev was… What had Dev done?

I peered inside the office, but it was empty, except for Drew's legs dangling over the edge of the table. My stomach heaved, my gag reflex gone to crap in a hand basket.

I pushed Blaine's arms away, but they only tightened. "Let go, Blaine. Maliina tried to possess me. Dev took her away, but she used Drew. He's in there. We need to help him before someone finds him."

Blaine transformed from the über rich, preppy boy into the take-no-prisoners, centuries-old Immortal I knew him to be. He anchored me against the wall and pushed my backpack into my arms. "Stay here. Don't move."

Then he was gone.

I exhaled, my knees finally giving away. I slid down until my butt touched the floor. Deep breaths and slow exhales didn't seem to help my stomach. Possession by a dark soul was a bitch.

"Are you okay?"

I glanced up at a girl. She must have just left the counselors' offices.

"Yeah. No. I think I'm going to barf." She took a step back and yelled something. The next second, someone thrust a garbage bag under my nose. I buried my face inside it and threw up, my body spasming as though to squeeze out every essence of Dev's energy.

A hand landed on my shoulder and I jumped, but it was only one of the janitorial staff. He took the garbage can, pointed to a door at the end of the hallway, and mumbled something. All I heard was restroom, which I desperately needed to hide in and never come out of. Ever. Barfing at school was something one did behind closed doors, sickness or not.

I struggled to my feet and several unwanted hands came to help. I didn't verify their owners. Otherwise, I'd never look them in the eye again.

"Thanks," I mumbled and staggered away.

"Mystery meat strikes again," someone said.

Great. Blame the school food. I felt sorry for the principal, but better the food than rumors that I was pregnant or bulimic. I pushed the door and disappeared inside. One glance at the mirror and I cringed.

Shit warmed over couldn't begin to describe me. My entire body felt raw as though I'd tangoed with a meat grinder and lost. I rinsed my mouth and splashed water on my face.

"Hey," Blaine said from the doorway. I turned and gave him a wobbly smile. He had my backpack and my poker. Before I asked, he showed me my artavo and dropped them in the side zippered pocket of my backpack.

"Thanks. Is Drew okay?"

He scowled. "He'll live."

"Where did you put him?"

"In bed. I took him home. Luckily, his parents are at work and the housekeeper didn't question me when she saw me. I runed him, so he'll forget the possession, but there's nothing I can do about its effect. I'll check on him later."

Blaine had lived with Drew until a few months ago, so their housekeeper knew him. "How will you explain what happened?"

"Members of the football team were helping the student council prepare the gym for the prom. He slipped and banged his head. He has a bruise to prove it. The housekeeper will tell him I dropped him off. With all the trucks and farm equipment at their vineyard, anyone could easily have missed my car."

"Uh, excuse me?"

We both turned to stare at Mrs. Fennier. How much had she heard?

"Are you okay, Cora?"

I nodded.

"I, uh, called your mother and told her you're sick," she said, smiling. "She's on her way."

"I'm not sick," I wanted to scream, but I couldn't. I'd used it as an excuse to skip prom. Every freakin' time I lied, it came back and bit me in the butt.

"Thank you," I said through gritted teeth and waited until she was gone.

"Looks like no lunch at the mansion," Blaine mumbled.

"I'll call Mom and tell her I'm going to Raine's." I reached for my phone.

"Not a good idea," Blaine said.

I scowled at him, wishing I had Twizzlers. My mouth tasted like puke. "Why not?"

"Chances are their memories were…" He imitated wiped with his hand.

The Norns. Crap! How do I go about asking Mom? I speed dialed her number and brought the phone to my ear, taking Blaine's arm. I still felt weak and my legs felt rubbery. He didn't seem to mind supporting my weight.

Mom picked up after one ring. "Mom?"

"We're just leaving, hun. Stay inside until we get there."

"You don't have to pick me up. B—"

"I don't want you driving when you're sick, Cora. I shouldn't have let you go to school this morning."

"Blaine is driving me home, Mom." Students in the counselors' waiting area watched us like we were a freak show as we walked by. I was sure pictures of me barfing had already gone viral.

"Blaine?" Mom asked.

"Remember Blaine Chapman? The quarterback?" *Please say you remember him.*

"Of course, I remember Blaine. But he *was* the quarterback before Raine's boyfriend."

I laughed with relief. Memories intact, yes! "Yes, he was the QB before Torin." I exchanged a grin with Blaine. "We're already on our way." Mom reluctantly gave in. The grin disappeared from Blaine's face. "You don't have to drive me home if you have other plans."

"That's strange," he said slowly as though talking to himself.

"Driving me home or having other plans?"

"No, your mother. Everyone at school had their memories erased, but she remembers Torin."

"I guess I'm getting a pass," I said as we left the building. Blaine made a face, but he didn't respond. Something about my parents being spared by the Norns bothered him. Not me. Being best friends with Raine had its perks.

Rhys and Nara appeared by Blaine's car as we crossed the street. Even though Blaine's insanely expensive sports car was the epitome of luxury, I missed my car and my stash of Twizzlers.

"What happened to you guys?" I asked when we reached the two Grimnirs.

"Several dark souls managed to get inside your school," Rhys said. "Maliina must have been testing our responses."

"We showed her," Nara bragged.

"No, she *showed* you," Blaine said, chuckling. He unlocked his car and threw my backpack in the passenger seat. "While her dark souls were distracting you, she was attacking Cora."

The two Grimnirs stared at me with horror. I was sure they were imagining Echo's reaction. "I'm okay, guys. Since no one was hurt, except Drew, no one needs to know what happened."

They got it—Echo didn't need to know. The smirk on Blaine's face said he did, too.

"How did you escape?" Nara asked.

I pulled the fire poker from my backpack, kissed it, and brandished it. "Never fails me. One swing and it cut through her. She started to disperse. You should have seen the look on her face. Dev did something weird. He absorbed her."

The smiles disappeared from the faces of the Grimnirs.

"What?" I asked.

"We need to find him," Rhys said. The next second, they were gone.

"Oh. That was weird. Do you know what's going on? Why a soul would absorb another soul," I asked, replacing my backpack in the passenger seat and hugging it.

Blaine shook his head. "I know very little about souls, and I'm not interested in knowing either."

"Chicken."

He laughed. "Immortals focus on the living, not the dead. You are the only pure Immortal medium I've heard of. Witches can be Mediums too, but they are Mortal."

Yeah, I was so lucky. I hoped Dev was okay. When I looked up, Blaine was studying me with a weird expression. "What?"

"You're really not going to tell Echo?"

I rolled my eyes. "Let's go."

"Really?" he asked again as he started the engine and backed out of the parking lot.

"Blaine, I don't report everything that happens to me to Echo. It's been years since he trusted these guys, and I'd hate for this incident with Maliina to divide them again. They're the only family he has. You have no idea how lucky we are to have our parents and friends."

He made a face, sadness darkening his eyes. "For most Immortals, their family either believes they're dead or the Norns delete their parents' and friends' memories, and relocate them as far away from them as humanly possible."

That sounded too personal. "Unless your parents are Immortals, like yours."

His grip tightened on the steering wheel. "The Chapmans are not my parents."

***

I was half asleep by the time he pulled up outside my home. Mom ran out of the house, eyes frantic. Stumbling when I stepped away from the car only made things worse.

"Remember, I have to stay until the Grimnirs return," Blaine whispered.

"I know. I'm fine, Mom," I added louder when she converged on us, but that didn't stop her fussing. Dad was just as bad when we reached him.

"Was it something you ate at school?" he asked.

"I didn't eat anything. It's probably the stomach flu. In fact, I'm starving."

Mom asked Blaine if he'd eaten then took off to get us food. I got chicken broth. Boring, tasteless chicken broth when all I wanted was to go upstairs, pig out on Twizzlers, and crash. Blaine got sandwiches with all the condiments, apple cider, and a large slice of cherry pie, which he ate with such relish. I hated him.

"Can I stay at Raine's over the weekend, Mom? The funeral is tomorrow morning, but she could use some company. I promise to be home Sunday evening."

She shook her head. "Not when you're not well. We'll go to the funeral tomorrow as a family, and if you're feeling better, you can spend some time with her. I have to keep an eye on you in case you throw up again. If you can't hold anything down, I'm taking you to the doctor."

Whining ensued, but she didn't back down. Worse, Dad supported her. When they presented a unified front, I always lost.

"I'll go lie down. Blaine, come with me." I indicated the stairs with my head. Unease flashed on his face, but he followed me.

Mom followed us and stopped at the bottom of the stairs. "Are you still planning on going to the prom tonight?"

"No, Mom. It wouldn't feel right without Raine."

"What about Moonbeam?"

I sighed. "I'll call Mrs. Hightower and tell her I'm quitting." Or tell her in person. I planned to swing by and say goodbye to Captain G and Mr. Reeds.

"Blaine, Cora needs her rest, so don't stay up there too long."

"Yes, ma'am."

Mom gave me a strange look. I wondered whether she thought I was messing around with Blaine behind Echo's back. "He'll leave as soon as Echo gets here, Mom. And the door will stay open."

"What's with the door?" Blaine asked as soon as we were out of Mom's hearing range.

"Her way of making sure no monkey business is going on in my room." I entered my bedroom and went straight for the Twizzlers.

"So you and Echo have never—"

"None of your business, Blaine." I attacked the licorice sweets, eating several at a time. Blaine eyed me with a frown. "Want some?"

He shook his head.

"Feel free to use my laptop." I kicked off my boots and crawled under the blankets, cargo pants and all. "Wake me up around four. I have a date with three girls." He didn't question me, but I told him anyway. "I'm doing Kicker, Sondra, and Naya's makeup and hair for the prom."

CHAPTER 22. A VERY SPECIAL PROM

"Time to wake up," a voice whispered.

I forced my eyelids to lift. It was dark, but I recognized the outline of the man looming over me. I laughed and attacked him.

There was no other way to explain the way I grabbed Echo, pulled him down, and wrapped myself around him, cover and all. Squeezed the crap out of him. Kissed whichever parts of his face I could reach.

He laughed. "I can't breathe, doll-face."

Air was overrated. "I'm never letting you out of my sight or—"

Then I remembered the things that had happened earlier. Dev. Maliina.

I half pushed him away, half wiggled out of his arms and touched the lamp. Light flooded my room and bathed his beautiful face. He was dressed in his reaper clothes and his coat was buttoned up—a first. I wanted to fly back into his arms, but darn it, he shouldn't worry me like he had.

"What took you so long? I was scared the Goddess decided to lock you up or something. Did you place Raine's father? Dev is gone and—"

He kissed me, effectively shutting me up. When he lifted his head, his lips twitched and his eyes gleamed. He enjoyed messing with my head. "I'll explain everything, but first, you need to get dressed."

I shook my head.

"Yes, doll-face. I'm not answering questions until you are dressed. The dark souls are about to attack, and we need you as bait."

My stomach hollowed out. Did I hear him right? "Bait?"

"Yes, bait. I know I wanted you to stop helping souls, but I was wrong and selfish. Now I'm putting my selfish ways aside to help your Mortal friends. They need you. *I* need you.

Souls can only see reapers when we are in the same room with them. You, they see from miles away. We want them to find you."

Okay, someone had replaced my usually overprotective boyfriend with a Doppelganger. Echo would never use me as bait. "Who are you, and what have you done with my Echo?"

He chuckled and stood. I noticed my prom dress, neatly draped over the chair complete with satin gloves and head gear. "What's that doing out?"

He saw the direction of my gaze. "Raine chose it when she was here earlier. We are going to the prom, *Cora mia.*"

Except he was wearing reaper clothes. "No, I'm not."

He crossed his arms and arched his eyebrows. "You don't have to, but I thought you might want to stop the dark souls from attacking the students at the prom tonight. After all, you took up this challenge when you joined forces with Dev."

My stomach had dropped at the part about dark souls attacking students. Now, it churned. I scooted to the edge of my bed and started unbuttoning my top. "Start talking. Who said they were attacking? When did you talk to Dev? Is he okay? When I last saw him, he was blending with that evil soul..." Maybe he didn't need to know that.

Echo chuckled as though he'd read my mind. "He talked, and I listened. I know about Teléia and Maliina attacking you. We're cool now."

"Is he okay?" I threw the top on my bed and started on my cargo pants. "He absorbed her soul."

"*Trapped,* not absorbed," Echo corrected. "He delivered her to Rhys and Nara, who escorted her to Hel and personally placed her on the boat to Corpse Strand. No one escapes that boat. I got the entire story from Rhys and Nara, along with how they'd stalked you, and I didn't touch a hair on their heads." He smirked as though proud of himself. I know I was. "Bottom line is Maliina knew about the prom and told the dark souls that this town is full of Immortals with artavo—the blades souls need to etch medium runes on their Mortal vessels. She told them that you and the other Immortals would be at the prom tonight. All they have to do is follow your beacon. You were hers. They are free to take over the Mortals. According to Dev, the attack is in," he glanced at his cell phone clock, "fifteen… no fourteen minutes and twenty seconds."

"Why didn't you wake me up earlier?"

"You were sleeping so peacefully I couldn't bring myself to do it. Besides, we needed to take care of a few things."

"What things?" Now only in my bra and panties, I shimmied into the gold and black flapper prom dress. Echo watched my every move with utter enjoyment as though I was undressing instead of dressing. "What if they'd attacked earlier and come to my house?"

"There are Grimnirs stationed outside, and Dev is on top of things. What are you doing?"

I was on my knees, searching under my bed. "Looking for my stupid boots?"

"Oh, I put them away. You need these."

I turned and found him holding black heeled shoes. "I can't hide my artavo inside those. My boots have special pouches."

"You don't need your artavo tonight. Give me your foot."

I glared. "Echo," I warned.

"I'll carry one artavus for you," he said. "Just one."

"Then I'll carry my poker. It disperses them better."

"Not tonight. We plan to reap them all." He took my foot, propped it on his thighs, and proceeded to put on my shoe for me. I slapped his hands when they crept along my leg. He moved to the next one and pulled me up straight into his arms. I knew what he was up to.

I tried to wiggle out of his arms, but they tightened. "I need to do my hair." As soon as the words left my mouth I realized something else. Blaine had forgotten to wake me up. "Oh crap!"

"What?"

"Kicker, Sondra, and Naya are never going to talk to me again. I was supposed to do their hair and makeup for tonight, and I slept through it." I wiggled out of his arms and marched to my dresser. With Raine and the Valkyries moving on, Kicker and the others were the only friends I had left. "It's Blaine's fault."

"No, it's not. Your friends' hair and makeup were done," Echo said. "I told you, I took care of things while you rested."

I paused in the process of making a loose bun and studied him through the mirror. "Who did their hair?"

"Ingrid's people. Blaine said he had to wake you up to do it, and I told him to piss off. Ingrid overheard us and offered to help. She knew people who made house calls. I think she mentioned facials, hair, makeup, nails, and then she gave them directions."

I blinked. Had the whole gang decided to hang out in my bedroom while I slept? "She did that for me?"

"Yes, but I paid for the whole thing." He was cute when he bragged.

"You're the best."

"I know." He stood behind me and played with the hair on my nape. My eyes went to the clock. We didn't have time for anything else.

I moved my head, forcing him to step away. While I finished pinning up my hair, Echo walk to the window and signaled the Grimnirs. I left a few locks to frame my face, put on the hairband, and quickly applied lipstick. The twenties hairstyles were shorter and more chic. I had planned to curl my hair and try to achieve the look without chopping half my mane off, but a loose bun was the best I could do now.

I was pulling on the satin gloves when Echo turned around. He stared at me in awe without saying a thing. That was good.

What was I forgetting? "My parents. We can't leave them here unprotected. What if Maliina told the dark souls where I live?"

"We're leaving two Grimnirs to keep an eye on them. They think you're asleep. In fact, your mother checked on you just before I woke you up. She was doing it every hour when we were all here earlier, so we have about an hour before she does it again."

He closed the gap between us and lifted my chin. He studied my face as though memorizing it. "You take my breath away, *Cora mia*. You'll always do." He touched the corner of my lips, and I was sure he was going to kiss me, but all he said was, "engage your invisibility runes." His voice had gone husky.

I did and allowed him to lead me through the portal. We appeared in a bathroom, but the silence was spooky. Where was the music? The voices of students?

"Where are we?" I asked.

"The Sports Complex." He pushed open the door and we started down a hallway, the runes on our skin lighting the way.

The Sports Complex housed the gyms, the pool, and the exercise room. It was separated from the school's main building by a large patio and a parking lot.

"The prom is supposed to be in this building, in the gym," I said.

"It is."

"Why is it deserted?" I'd attended three Homecoming and Valentine dances at school, and the hallways were always packed with couples making out or talking. I threw a glance at Echo. "And I can't hear the music. You don't think they've already attacked, do you?"

"Nope." He didn't seem worried. "I'm sorry you didn't get the prom you wanted," he said.

Was he seriously discussing *that* now? "I don't care. Something is not right, Echo."

We turned a corner, and I saw flashing lights from the gym falling in the hallway, yet the music wasn't playing. There was also a sudden chill in the air. Had they forgotten to adjust the thermostat again?

"It's freezing." And the silence was ominous.

As we approached the entrance to the gym, I swallowed, imagining students unconscious on the floor. I glanced at Echo one last time, but he was smiling. Not sure what that meant, I peered inside.

My jaw dropped. No wonder he hadn't seemed worried. Instead of juniors from my school, the place was packed with souls wearing twenties outfits and dancing the foxtrot, yet there was no music.

"This is why it's cold," Echo whispered in my ear. "Not exactly the prom you wanted, but we improvised." He nudged me forward, and I crossed the threshold.

Jazz music blasted my senses, the shift from silence to noise jarring. I looked down and saw the runes running along the floor and the door frame. They were creating a dampening effect and preventing the music from escaping the room. In fact, the entire room was covered with runes—the floor, parts of the walls that I could see, the bleachers, and the ceiling.

"Are all the runes for dampening the sounds?" I asked.

"Some," he said. "The rest can let the dark souls in, but not out. They're opposite those I put around your house."

My eyes returned to the dancers. The women were dressed like me in flapper outfits—sparkling, drop-waist dresses with fringes, fancy hairbands with or without feathers, and satin gloves. Some even carried fake long cigarette holders. The guys looked sophisticated in tuxedoes or three-piece suits.

Echo pressed a kiss on my temple. "What do you think?"

"Still processing. Are dark souls really coming tonight?" I asked.

"Oh yes. We spread the word that they were after you and regular souls came out in support. Unfortunately, most of them need closure and will probably want to meet you ASAP."

I grinned. "I don't mind. Where is the real prom?"

"Hey, this is real. Supernatural, yes, but absolutely real."

I rolled my eyes. "Where are the other students?"

"In the cafeteria. There's food, drinks, and live music, and we runed the walls so no one can leave. If Maliina hadn't told the dark souls about the prom, we would have gone elsewhere to trap them. Blaine came up with this."

"It's brilliant." The cafeteria was in the school's main building, and with no sounds coming from the Sports Complex, no one would suspect there was another prom, or a trap.

The gym was decorated with All That Jazz paraphernalia—black and silver tulle with gold, red, and silver stars, and a city skyline draped the walls. A bandstand mural gave the illusion of a live band. Standees of a jazz guy, flapper girls, and twenties cars added to the mood. Around the floor were lamp posts covered with black gossamer and silver.

Immortals, Valkyries, and Grimnirs were easy to spot. They glowed with invisibility runes, adding to the effect. They were also dressed for the prom, even though they didn't dance. I spotted Raine and Torin. I would have thought she'd be too grief-stricken to come. Maybe this was what she needed.

She saw me and waved. Then she left Torin and cut across the floor. She looked amazing in a moss-green outfit. I remember when she'd complained that her mother would dress her up like a character from *The Great Gatsby*. Book or movie, not sure which one. She totally channeled the era down to her frilled head piece. It sparkled as though it had real jewels.

"You made it," she said, giving me a hug.

"Couldn't miss this. Prom and reaping is an unbeatable combo. Everyone's here."

She glanced back at Torin, who couldn't take his eyes off her. He wore a white suit with a moss-green vest matching her dress. He lifted his hat and bowed.

"Yep. Torin has some amazing memories of this era. Mom too. I've heard nothing else for weeks." Her mother, Femi, and Lavania must have raided some boutique because they sparkled in high-fashion flapper outfits, including necklaces and cigarette holders.

"I assume the rest are Grimnirs," I said, counting at least fifteen of them. Most stayed together in groups, although they did dress the part. Andris must have decided less was more. He wore black skinny pants, a white shirt with a sweater, and a bow tie. He appeared to be listening to Hawk—the guy who ran Raine's family's store—but his eyes were on Ingrid, who stood with Rhys, Blaine, and a group of Grimnirs. Ingrid looked ethereal in white.

"Where are Nara and Syn?" I turned toward Echo, and my eyes widened. He'd removed his duster to reveal a black tux, white shirt, and waistcoat. Typical him, he'd not worn a bow tie. It was my turn to be speechless.

Raine chuckled. "Pick up your tongue from the floor," she teased.

My eyes followed Echo as he closed and locked the door, wishing he would turn around. He etched more runes on the door. "I wish this was a real prom."

"It *is* a real prom," Raine insisted. She took my arm and dragged me from my super dreamy man. "We just happen to have a few more dead than live attendees. Did Echo take you to see the cafeteria?"

"No. We just arrived." I glanced over my shoulder at him. He dropped his duster on a bench. I wanted to dance with him. I could just imagine him in the era, smiling at some girl. I wanted to be that girl.

"Blaine had to pull some serious strings to make the student council and the teachers switch venues, but your man placed the cherry on top."

I dragged my eyes from Echo. "What did he do?"

"He found a live band. Reapers. Never heard of them, but the reaction in the cafeteria was worth it. I heard they were supposed to be playing elsewhere tonight, but since our town is the destination for everything supernatural, they didn't mind. I sneaked off to watch earlier. They're good."

Nara and Syn must be performing. "They're Grimnirs."

"I knew it." She punched my arm. "Another thing you kept from me."

I winced. "They kicked Echo out, so they weren't exactly my favorite subject. Can we go see?"

"Sorry." She pulled me forward. "You need to be here until this is over. Maliina's followers might end up there and we wouldn't like that."

I searched the dancers, but there were no dark souls among them. "Have you seen Dev?"

"Didn't Echo tell you? He's the one leading the dark souls, or pretending to lead them. Engage your special runes."

As the runes appeared, the souls nearest us stopped dancing and turned. It was as though they'd felt me. The ones next to them followed until a wave swept through the dance floor. Within seconds, we were surrounded by souls.

"Thank you for coming," I said, pressing my hands together. "I promise I will be available starting tomorrow afternoon." I often used the mansion as the meeting place before my lessons. Lavania had insisted on it. Now that she was a back and I was no longer volunteering at the nursing home, I'd have more time for them.

"I remember you from the hospital." I doubted he heard me, but he smiled and nodded. "And you were at The Hub. You two," I pointed at two to my left, "are always by the vineyard. When you're ready, come find me." I didn't chase down souls. I usually waited for them to come to me. Some reached out as though to touch me. Funny how I wasn't feeling cold now that I'd engaged the medium runes.

The music was so loud I didn't hear the first warning. Then, someone turned off the music and Echo's voice filled the gym.

"They're here."

I looked toward the door, but I couldn't see anything. The souls were in the way, and they seemed to press around me. To avoid contact, I shuffled sideways. They shuffled along with me, deliberately shielding me and pushing me out of the way.

When some of them lifted off the floor, I realized the dark souls were floating in through the roof and walls.

"Move," I yelled.

Either they suddenly became deaf or they were ignoring me. I couldn't push them aside without going through their energy, yet I had to see what was going on.

I closed my eyes and plunged through them. The usual iciness was barely there. The medium runes helped, but they didn't protect me from their thoughts, which seemed to be the same.

Must protect the medium. Must protect Cora… the medium… Cora…

The moment propelled me to the edge of the group and the next second, I was staring at a giant portal on the floor, sucking souls to the frozen land that was Hel. Sounds of Hel's hound howling and snarling and screams escaped the portal, filling the gym. Weird how the souls attained physical form and an ability to make sounds once they crossed over.

An arm wrapped around my waist, pulling me back from the edge of the portal and against a hard chest.

"What are you doing?" Echo snarled in my ear. "Protect her," he yelled over his shoulder.

I stepped back, feeling useless. Bait. Yep, that was me.

The dark souls zipped around the room in a frenzy, trying to escape the portal and the deadly rays from the scythes and artavo, but the runes trapped them inside the gym. Who knew the same lights used to etch runes could also immobilize souls?

I couldn't tell how many souls were left. Their energies blended together until I couldn't see the ceiling. The immobilized ones left the mass and tumbled down the hole, but the swirling dark mass didn't seem to lessen. The huge scythes packed more punch than the smaller blades. Not surprising since Grimnirs chased souls bound, while Valkyries didn't. I mean, who wouldn't want to go to Asgard. Hel on the other hand...

More screams and howls came through the portal, and I jumped.

I needed to help instead of standing uselessly on the sideline. Echo had planted himself in front of me and the regular souls to make sure we were okay. Everyone was fighting. Even Raine had her witch staff out and was busy zapping. Her staff was even more powerful than the scythes. I reached out and tugged Echo's coat.

"What?" he threw over his shoulder.

"Give me my artavus. I want to help."

"You don't have the right runes."

Dang it! I had to do something to help. Where was Dev? I couldn't see him.

"Dev!" I screamed and immediately wished I hadn't. The mass from the ceiling seemed to find a new escape route. Me. The mass changed directions and gunned for me.

Echo cursed, his scythe elongating to giant proportions. He zapped them at hyper speed, but they kept coming. Others noticed, too.

Me and my big mouth. I was sure I was a goner.

Two things happened simultaneously—Dev managed to escape the dark mass and reached me first. Before he could enter me, something big leaped out of the portal and landed on all fours over it. I wasn't sure whether it was a dragon or a werewolf or some weird mythical creature. It was huge and black. Something slapped the floor somewhere to my right, probably its tail, and hot breath fogged the air to my left. The souls changed course and headed back to the ceiling.

Garm. Hel's hound.

Too petrified to move, I tilted my head back and stared at it with round eyes. Echo moved back as though to protect me, and then he did something strange. He covered my ears. Still, I heard the growl, felt its journey as it rumbled up the hound's throat and became a howl. The entire gym vibrated.

The mass of dark souls must have decided the portal was the better escape route. They poured through it, their screams echoing in the barren, icy land. One left the doomed souls and darted around the room, trying to escape the bursts of light from the magical blades.

"Teléia," Echo yelled and drew its attention. Her attention.

The hound turned its massive head toward us, fangs dripping, four red eyes unblinking, and a scratching sound filling the air. I was sure those were his nails scraping the gym floor. It tilted its head as though undecided whether we all belonged down there in Hel. Dev was now hiding behind me, ready to enter me if need be. I didn't blame him. Echo was focused on the souls.

I was too busy watching the hound and missed what Echo did next, until a lone dark soul floated to the hound's head and slid down the side of its face. Teléia? Possibly. The hound's tongue, wet and long, snaked out and swept her into its mouth, then spat her into the portal.

No one made a sound. Even the Grimnirs, whom I was sure saw it several times a day, didn't move. Then a shrill whistle came through the portal, and the hound's ears lifted. Its tongue lolled to the side as it wagged its tail. The next second, it hopped through the portal and was gone.

The relief in the air was tangible. Still, no one moved.

"Here, boy!" a familiar voice called out from the other side of the portal. "Catch!"

As though prodded, we all converged around the portal and stared down at Eirik. Dressed like a reaper, he threw something, probably his magical flail, and the ground shook as the hound chased it.

He looked up and waved. "Is anyone hurt?"

"Damn show off," Echo grumbled.

"We're okay," Raine yelled, waving.

"Hey, Raine. Sorry I've been MIA. See you soon. I promise. You okay, Cora?" Eirik asked.

I laughed. He was truly the master of grand entrances. "I'm fine, Eirik."

"What? He thinks I can't protect you?" Echo snarled.

"Quit whining, Echo. I can hear you. Enjoy the rest of the prom, guys. We'll round up these guys and take them to the boat." He waved his hand and the portal closed.

Everyone started talking at once. Raine and I exchanged a smile. Somehow, we'd known he would show up. Someone started the music again. As though the dark souls hadn't attacked and Eirik hadn't saved our asses again by sending Hel's hound, we all started dancing.

Foxtrot. Charleston. Waltz. Echo even taught me a few moves. Surprisingly, the Grimnirs didn't leave. They danced, socialized with Lavania and Raine's mother, and totally ignored the regular souls. It was an unusual prom, yet I wouldn't trade it for any other.

"Time for you to head home before your mother finds your room empty," Echo whispered as we waltzed to a smooth jazz tune.

"But I wanted to stop by the cafeteria and check out your old band," I said, pouting and burrowing in his chest.

"You'll see plenty of them from now on."

I leaned back and studied his face. "Are you back with the band now?"

"Absolutely. How else am I going to get girls to fantasize about me?"

I laughed and hugged him. I didn't care if girls fantasized about him as long as he came home to me.

EPILOGUE

I tucked my head under Echo's chin and closed my eyes. For a moment, I listened to his heart. He'd brought me home, then left to talk to his Grimnir buddies. Not only had he made up with his Druid brothers and sisters, he'd bridged a gap between him and the rest of the Grimnirs. So what they had lost Maliina months ago? She was finally gone. Taken up permanent residency on Hel's little island of the damned. Good riddance.

"What are we going to do about Dev?" I asked.

"Don't care."

I lifted my head. "You didn't reap him, did you?"

"No." I thought he was done talking, but then he added, "He's decided to join the Valkyrie."

He was being vague. Not a good sign. "We know several Valkyries, Echo. Which one?"

"Your teacher." He lifted my chin and claimed my lips in an attempt to silence me, or maybe he was just bored with the topic.

I let him distract me, but not for long. I needed answers. I turned my head and broke the kiss. "Did she explain why?" My voice was breathless, which earned me a smug grin from Echo. "Did she?"

"We didn't talk."

I heard a 'but' in his voice. "Yes?"

"He always lands on his feet, the conniving bastard," Echo growled.

"Dev is not conniving. He's charming. What happened?"

"Torin said your teacher is starting a school for witches, or future Valkyries and Grimnirs, and Dev has somehow been invited to join her staff. I don't know how he does it, but he can sell sand to desert people."

I laughed. "Yes! I knew I had her. And stop being so hard on Dev. He's going to be an awesome teacher. Probably make all the witches fall in love with him."

"What do you mean you had her?"

"I suggested it while you were away sulking. Dev knows everything about dark souls—their strengths and weaknesses, how to fight them off or contain them. I mean, he's a dark soul who strayed and found his way back. Did he tell you how he helps those dying—?"

Echo cut off my question with a kiss. "I don't care," he whispered against my lips. "He's no longer my problem. But you, my lovely mate and future wife, are mine. One I carry willingly." He kissed me and the subject of Dev was forgotten.

THE END

THE RUNES SERIES READING ORDER

Thank you for reading The RUNES Series. If you enjoyed it, please consider writing a review. Reviews can make a difference in the ranking of a book. The links are available here:

Runes Series: http://bit.ly/RunesSeries-ByEdnahWalters

Check out the other books in The Runes series (See below) and what book is next in the series. I've also included a bonus chapter for GODS as a thank you for pre-ordering HEROES, Eirik Book 2.

I still have one more Echo/Cora book and Torin/Raine book to release in 2016. To be updated on more Runes exclusives, the next book in Eirik's story, giveaways, teasers, and deleted scenes, join my newsletter.

http://bit.ly/EdnahWNewsletter

For the discussion about the series, join my private page on FB:

http://bit.ly/EdnahsEliteValkyries

READING ORDER

Runes: http://bit.ly/RunesbyEdnahWalters
Immortals: http://bit.ly/ImmortalsbyEdnahWalters
Grimnirs: http://bit.ly/GrimnirsbyEdnahWalters
Seeress: http://bit.ly/SeeressbyEdnahWalters
Souls: http://bit.ly/SoulsbyEdnahWalters
Witches: http://bit.ly/WitchesbyEdnahWalters
Demons: http://bit.ly/DemonsbyEdnahwalters
Heroes: http://bit.ly/HeroesbyEdnahWalters
Gods: http://bit.ly/GodsByEdnahWalters

ORDER THE NEXT IN THE SERIES

Witches, A Runes Novel. Book 6
Witches: http://bit.ly/WitchesbyEdnahWalters

NOTES FROM THE AUTHOR

In Runes, readers are introduced to three best friends, Raine, Cora, and Eirik. Runes, Immortals, Seeress, and Witches chronicles Raine's story and her journey to fulfill her destiny and find true love with Torin St. James, a Valkyrie (there's one more story left). Grimnirs and Souls chronicles Cora's journey to fulfill her destiny and find love with Echo, a Grimnir. There's one more story left in their story.

Eirik's story ends with Gods and I promise you, you won't be disappointed, so buy your copy NOW. It is only fair that Eirik gets the same love as Cora and Raine, and I'm sure by now you have fallen in love with him and Celestia, so don't waste another moment and pre-order Gods coming June 2016. Why did I write Eirik's stories before finishing Raine/Torin and Cora/Echo? Torin and Raine are going to need him and his connections in Hel to kick some serious Norn booties.

ABOUT THE AUTHOR

Ednah Walters holds a PhD in Chemistry and is a stay-at-home mother of five. She is also a USA Today bestselling author. She writes about flawed heroes and the women who love them.

Her award-winning YA Paranormal Romance—Runes Series— started with Runes and has a total of 7 books to date. The next one, Heroes, will be released in March 2016. Her last book, Witches, was a Readers' Favorite Awards winner.

She writes YA Urban Fantasy series—The Guardian Legacy Series, which focuses on the Nephilim, children of the fallen angels. GL Series started with Awakened and has a total of 4 books. The latest book in the series, Forgotten, was released in June 2015. The GL series is published by Spencer Hill Press (Beaufort Books)

Ednah also writes Contemporary Romance as E.B. Walters. Her contemporary works started with The Fitzgerald Family series, which has six books, to her USA Today bestselling series, Infinitus Billionaires.

Whether she's writing about Valkyries, Norns, and Grimnirs, or Guardians, Demons, and Archangels, or even contemporary Irish family in the west coast, love, family, and friendship play crucial roles in all her books.

To stay up to date with her work, exclusives, giveaways, teasers, and deleted scenes, join my newsletter.

EDNAH WALTERS' LINKS:

YA/Ednah Walters': http://bit.ly/EdnahWNewsletter
For the discussion about her series, join her private pages on FB:
RUNES and GL: http://bit.ly/EdnahsEliteValkyries
Ednah Walters' Website: http://www.ednahwalters.com
Ednah Walters in Facebook: http://bit.ly/EdnahWFans
Ednah Walters on Twitter: http://bit.ly/EdnahTwitter
Facebook Fanpage:
https://www.facebook.com/AuthorEdnahwalters
Instagram: http://bit.ly/EdnahW-Instagram
Tumblr: http://bit.ly/EdnahWaltersTumblr
Blog: http://ednahwalters.blogspot.com

E.B. WALTERS' LINKS:

E.B.'s mailing list.
http://bit.ly/EdnahsNewsletter
Discussion group about her billionaires, join her private page:
http://bit.ly/LetsTalkBillionaires
E. B. Walters' Website: www.author-ebwalters.com
Facebook Fanpage:
https://www.facebook.com/AuthorEBWalters
Twitter: https://twitter.com/eb_walters
Blog: http://enwalters.blogspot.com

The College of Saint Rose Library

3 3554 00553 7722

89950268R00185

Made in the USA
Lexington, KY
05 June 2018